Also by Ana Huang

KINGS OF SIN SERIES

A series of interconnected standalones

King of Wrath

King of Pride

King of Greed

King of Sloth

TWISTED SERIES

A series of interconnected standalones

Twisted Love

Twisted Games

Twisted Hate

Twisted Lies

IF LOVE SERIES

If We Ever Meet Again (Duet Book 1)

If the Sun Never Sets (Duet Book 2)

If Love Had a Price (Standalone)

If We Were Perfect (Standalone)

KING OF SLOTH

ANA HUANG

Bloom books

Cover design by Cat at TRC Designs
Internal images © Elalalala.yandex.ru/Depositphotos, ARTSTOK/Depositphotos

Published by Bloom Books, an imprint of Sourcebooks
P.O. Box 4410, Naperville, Illinois 60567-4410
(630) 961-3900
sourcebooks.com

Cataloging-in-Publication data is on file with the Library of Congress.

Printed and bound in the United States of America.
LSC 10 9 8 7 6 5 4 3 2 1

To every woman who's ever been told to "smile more."
Fuck that. Do what you want.

Playlist

"Midnight Rain"—Taylor Swift

"Sex, Drugs, Etc."—Beach Weather

"Top of the World"—Pussycat Dolls

"The Lazy Song"—Bruno Mars

"Flawless"—Beyonce

"Most Girls"—P!nk

"Talking Body—Tove Lo

"Rude Boy"—Rihanna

"I Wanna Be Yours"—Arctic Monkeys

"Te Amo"—Rihanna

CHAPTER 1

Sloane

BREAKING INTO A TEN-THOUSAND-DOLLAR-A-NIGHT Greek villa hadn't been in my plans for the day, but plans changed and people adapted, especially when they had clients who insisted on making their life as difficult as possible.

My knees scraped against concrete as I hauled myself onto the terrace ledge and over the railing. If I ruined my brand-new Stella Alonso dress over this, I'd kill him, bring him back to clean up the mess, then kill him again.

Luckily for him, I landed on the terrace without incident and slipped back into the heels I'd tossed over earlier. The heavy drum of my heartbeats followed me to the sliding glass door, where I tapped the master key I'd "borrowed" from one of the maids against the card reader.

I would've gone through the front door, but it was too exposed. The back terrace was the only way.

The card reader whirred, and for a single terrifying second, I thought it wouldn't open. Then the reader flashed green, and I allowed myself a breath of relief before I set my jaw again.

Breaking in was the easy part. Getting *him* to another country by sunset was another.

I made a quick detour to the kitchen, then crossed the living room to the primary suite. I winced when I saw the empty beer bottles littering the kitchen counter, and it took every ounce of willpower not to toss them in the recycling bin, sterilize the marble, and spray the room with air freshener.

Stay focused. My professional *and* personal reputations were on the line.

The villa was cool and quiet despite the early-afternoon sun splashing through the windows, and the bedroom was cooler and quieter still.

Perhaps that was why, when I walked to the bed and unceremoniously dumped a large bowl of ice-cold water over its slumbering occupant, the speed of his response startled a rare gasp out of me.

A strong hand shot out and grasped my wrist. The empty bowl clattered to the ground, and the room tilted as he yanked me down, rolled over, and pinned me against the bed before the gasp fully left my mouth.

Xavier Castillo stared down at me, his handsome face etched with a scowl.

The only son of Colombia's wealthiest man and my least cooperative client was usually laid-back to a fault, but there was nothing laid-back about the way his forearm pressed against my throat or the one hundred eighty pounds of solid muscle trapping me beneath him.

His scowl relaxed as anger gave way to recognition and a touch of horror. "Sloane?"

"That *is* my name." I lifted my chin, trying not to focus on how warm he was compared to the damp mattress against my back. "Now, if you could release me immediately, it would be appreciated. I'm ruining a seven-hundred-dollar dress."

"Mierda." He spit out the curse and relaxed his hold on my neck so I could get up. "What the *hell* are you doing here?"

"My job." I pushed him off me and stood. Was it just me, or was it exponentially colder now than it'd been five minutes ago? "It's the twelfth. You know where you're supposed to be, and it's not here." I glared at him, daring him to argue.

"I thought you were an intruder. I could've hurt you." Now that we'd established I wasn't here to rob or kidnap him, a familiar grin replaced his frown. Xavier retook his spot on the bed, the picture of insouciance. "Technically, you *are* an intruder, but a very beautiful one. If you wanted to join me in bed, you only had to say so. No need to go to all this trouble." He arched an eyebrow at the bowl on the floor. "How'd you get in anyway?"

"I stole a master key, and don't try to distract me." After three years of working with Xavier, I was used to his tricks. "It's one in the afternoon. Your jet is waiting for us at the airport. If we leave in the next half hour, we'll make it to London in time to get ready before tonight's gala."

"Great plan." Xavier stretched his arms over his head and yawned. "Except for one problem—I'm not going."

My nails dug into my palms before I caught myself. *Breathe. Remember, murdering a client is considered unprofessional.*

"You *will* get out of bed," I said, my voice chilly enough to freeze the droplets of water lingering on his skin. "You will board that jet, attend the gala with a smile, and stay for the entirety of the event like a good representative of the Castillo family because if you don't, I will make it my personal mission to ensure you never have another second of peace. I will crash every party you attend, warn off any woman stupid enough to fall into your orbit, and blacklist any of your friends who enable your worst impulses from my events. I can make your life a living hell, so *don't* make an enemy out of me."

Xavier yawned again.

This had been our dynamic since Xavier's father hired me

three years ago, right before Xavier moved from Los Angeles to New York, but I was done going easy on him.

"So, you're my new publicist." Xavier kicked back in his chair and propped his feet on my desk. White teeth flashed against tanned skin, and his eyes sparkled with a slyness that made me bristle.

Ten seconds after meeting my most lucrative client, and I already hated him.

"Remove your feet from my desk and sit like a proper adult." I didn't care that Alberto Castillo was paying me triple my usual fee to look after his son. No one disrespected me in my own office. "Otherwise, you can leave and explain to your father why you got dropped by your publicist on the very first day. I imagine that'll have a negative impact on your cash flow."

"Ah, you're one of those.*" He acquiesced, but his smile hardened at the mention of his father. "Uptight rule follower. Got it. You should've introduced yourself that way instead of with your name."*

My favorite pen cracked from the force of my grip.

I wasn't a superstitious person, but even I could tell that didn't bode well for the future of our relationship.

I'd been right.

I let him slide when it came to certain things because the Castillos were my biggest contract, but my job was to keep his family's reputation pristine, not kiss the heir's ass.

Xavier was a grown man. It was time he acted like it.

"That's quite a threat," he drawled. "*Every* party and woman? You must really like me."

He slunk out of bed with the lazy grace of a panther awakening from slumber. A pair of gray sweatpants rode low on his hips, revealing golden-brown skin and a V cut one wouldn't expect from someone who spent the majority of his days partying and sleeping. Inky tattoos swirled up his bare chest and shoulders and down his arms in intricate patterns.

If it were anyone else, I would've admired the raw masculine beauty on display, but this was Xavier Castillo. The day I admired anything except his commitment to non-commitment was the day I could somehow physically cry again.

"Don't worry, Luna," he said, catching my scrutiny with a small grin. "I won't tell your other clients I'm your favorite."

Sometimes he called me by my actual name. Other times he called me Luna. It wasn't my nickname, middle name, or any name close to Sloane, but he refused to tell me why and I'd given up on getting him to stop or explain long ago.

"Be serious for once," I said. "The event is honoring *your* father."

"Even more reason not to go. It's not like my old man will be there to accept the award." Xavier's smile didn't budge, but his eyes flickered with a spark of danger. "He's dying, remember?"

The words crashed between us and sucked all the oxygen out of the room as we stared at each other, his unflappable calm a rock against my mounting frustration.

The Castillos' father-son relationship was notoriously thorny, but Alberto Castillo hired me to manage their reputation, not their personal issues—that was, until what happened behind closed doors spilled into the public eye.

"People already think you're a good-for-nothing trust fund brat for shirking your responsibilities after your father was diagnosed." I didn't mince words. "If you miss an event honoring him as Philanthropist of the Year, the media will eat you alive."

"They already do, and *honor*?" Xavier raised his eyebrows. "The man writes a check for a couple million every year, and he not only gets a tax write-off but also fawning praise for being a philanthropist. You and I both know the award doesn't mean shit. Anyone with deep enough pockets can get it. Besides..." He leaned against the wall and crossed his arms. "Mykonos is way more fun than another stuffy gala. You should stay. The ocean air will be good for you."

Dammit, I recognized that tone. It was his "you can put a gun to my head and I still won't cave because it'll piss you off" tone. I'd heard it more times than I cared to count.

I did a quick mental calculation.

I hadn't gotten to where I was in my career by fighting losing battles. I *needed* to be in London tonight, and our window for a timely departure was rapidly shrinking. Missing my rendezvous was not an option, but if Xavier stayed in Greece, my job required me to stay as well and look after him.

Since I didn't have the time to guilt, threaten, or persuade him into doing what I wanted like I usually did, I was left with one last resort.

A bargain.

I crossed my arms, mirroring his stance. "Let's hear it."

His brows arched higher.

"Your condition," I said. "The one thing you want in exchange for attending the awards ceremony. Anything involving sex, drugs, or illegal activities is off the table. Other than that, I'm willing to bargain."

His eyes narrowed. He hadn't expected me to give in so easily, and if I didn't need to be in London by eight p.m., I wouldn't have. But I couldn't miss my date, so a deal with the devil it was.

"Fine." Xavier's cheeks dimpled with his signature smile, though a shadow of suspicion remained on his face. "Since you're so forthcoming, I will be too. I want a vacation."

"You're already on vacation."

"Not me. You." He pushed off the wall, his steps languid yet deliberate as he crossed the room and stopped mere inches from me. "I'll attend the gala if you promise to join me on vacation after. Three weeks in Spain. No work, just play."

The request soared from so far out of left field I gave myself whiplash trying to follow it. "You want me to take *three weeks* off work?"

"Yes."

"You're out of your mind."

I'd taken a total of two vacation days since I started Kensington PR, my boutique public relations firm, six years ago. The first was for my grandmother's funeral. The second was when I was hospitalized with pneumonia (chasing paparazzi in the dead of winter would do that to you). Even then, I'd kept up with emails on my phone.

I was work. Work was me. The thought of abandoning it for even a minute made my stomach cramp.

"That's the deal." Xavier shrugged. "Take it or leave it."

"Forget it. It's not happening."

"Fine." He turned toward the bed again. "In that case, I'm going back to sleep. Feel free to stay or fly home. It doesn't matter to me."

My teeth clenched.

That bastard. He *knew* I wouldn't fly home and leave him here to sow chaos in my absence. With my luck, he'd throw a public orgy on the beach tonight just to set tongues wagging and drive home the fact he wasn't at the gala when he should be.

I glanced at the clock on the wall. We needed to leave in the next fifteen minutes if we were to make it to the gala in time.

If it weren't for my eight o'clock date in London, I might have called Xavier's bluff, but…

Dammit.

"I can do two days," I said, relenting. One weekend wouldn't kill me, right?

"Two weeks."

"*One* week."

"Deal." His dimples blinded me again, and I realized I'd been tricked. He'd deliberately started with a higher offer to barter me down to his original plan.

Unfortunately, it was too late for regrets, and when he held out his hand, I had no choice but to shake on the time frame I'd proposed.

That was the worst part about Xavier. He was smart, but he applied it to all the wrong things.

"Don't look at me like I killed your pet fish," he drawled. "I'm taking you on vacation. It'll be fun. Trust me."

His smile widened at my icy stare.

One week in Spain with one of my least favorite people on the planet. What could possibly go wrong?

CHAPTER 2

NOTHING BRIGHTENED MY DAY MORE THAN RILING Sloane up. She was so predictable in her responses and so spectacular in her anger, and I loved seeing her ice-queen facade melt long enough to reveal a glimpse of the real person underneath.

It didn't happen often, but when it did, I added it to the mental drawer where I collected all things Sloane.

"Ah, you're one of those.*" I flicked a gaze over my new publicist's tight bun and tailored dress. "Uptight rule follower. Got it. You should've introduced yourself that way instead of with your name."*

The glare she bestowed on me could've leveled an entire city block.

Objectively, Sloane was one of the most beautiful women I'd ever met. Blue eyes, long legs, symmetrical face…Michelangelo himself couldn't have sculpted a better female form.

Too bad none of that came with a sense of humor.

She said something sharp in response, but I'd already tuned her out.

Fuck my father for forcing me into this stupid arrangement. If it weren't for my inheritance, I'd tell him to piss off.

Publicists were glorified babysitters, and I didn't want or need a babysitter. Besides, as pleasing to the eye as she was, I could already tell Sloane was going to be a major buzzkill.

That'd been our first meeting. My initial animosity toward her had run out of oxygen since then, leaving...hell, I didn't know. Curiosity. Attraction. Frustration.

Much more complicated emotions than hostility, unfortunately.

I didn't know when the switch flipped, but I wished I could go back and *un*flip it. I'd much rather hate her than be intrigued by her.

"Stand up straight," Sloane said without taking her eyes off the man beelining toward us. "You're at a black-tie event, not the beach. Try to *pretend* you want to be here."

"There's alcohol, food, and a gorgeous woman by my side. Of course I want to be here," I drawled, telling the truth in the first part and lying my ass off in the second.

My gaze skimmed over her quickly enough to escape her notice yet long enough to imprint the image in my mind. On anyone else, her simple black gown would've been boring, but Sloane could wear a grocery bag and still blow everyone else out of the water.

The silk skimmed her lean frame, highlighting her flawless skin and smooth, bare shoulders. She'd swept her hair into a fancier version of its usual bun, and other than a pair of small diamond-drop earrings, she wore no accessories and barely any makeup. She'd obviously dressed with the intention of blending in, but she could no more blend into a crowd than a jewel could blend into mud.

I'll be honest—I hadn't expected her to accept my deal. I'd hoped she would, but she was married to her job and the gala wasn't *that* important. It was a run-of-the-mill event honoring my father, not the Legacy Ball or a royal wedding.

The fact she would give up a week of precious work time in

exchange for my attendance here? It reeked of fishiness, but I wasn't going to look a gift horse in the mouth.

I'd been dying to get Sloane away from the office for a while. She was wound so tight she was bound to explode, and I didn't want to be there when it happened. She needed a release. Plus, the trip was the perfect opportunity to corrupt her—get her to let her hair down (literally and figuratively), loosen up, have some fun. I would *pay* to see her lounging on the beach like a normal person instead of making people cry on the phone.

Sloane Kensington needed a vacation more than anyone else I knew, and I needed—

"Xavier!" Eduardo finally reached us. My father's best friend and interim CEO of the Castillo Group clapped a hand on my shoulder, interrupting my thoughts before they strayed down a dangerous path. "I didn't expect to see you here, *mijo*."

"Me neither," I said dryly. "Good to see you, *tío*."

He wasn't my biological uncle, but he might as well have been. He and my father had been friends since childhood, and he'd been one of his most trusted advisors before my father fell ill. Eduardo was currently running the ship until the board made a final decision on whether to wait for my father to get better or find a new permanent CEO.

Eduardo turned to Sloane and gave her a customary Colombian cheek kiss. "Sloane, you look lovely," he said. "I assume I have you to thank for this one showing up. I know how hard it is to wrangle him, eh? When he was a kid, we called him *pequeño toro*. Stubborn as a little bull."

Her earlier ire melted into a professional smile. "It's my job. I'm happy to do it."

She was as good a liar as I was.

The three of us chatted for a bit until another guest pulled Eduardo away. He was accepting the Philanthropist of the Year award on behalf of my father since I'd refused to do it, but everyone seemed eager to talk business instead of charity with him.

Typical.

I caught Sloane checking her watch again as we wound our way toward our table. "That's the dozenth time you've looked at your watch since we've arrived," I said. "If you're that eager to leave, we can skip the boring ceremony and get hammered at the bar."

"I don't get *hammered*, and if you must know, I'm meeting someone in an hour. I trust you can behave yourself after I leave." Despite her cool tone, visible tension lined her jaw and shoulders.

"Meeting someone this late in London?" We settled in our seats just as the emcee took the stage and applause filled the room. "Don't tell me you have a hot date."

"Whether I do or don't is none of your business." She picked up the calligraphed menu card and scanned it for walnuts, no doubt. Sloane had a strange vendetta against them (and it wasn't an allergy; I'd checked).

"I'm surprised you find time to date." The emcee began his welcome speech. Reason told me to drop the issue, but I couldn't. There was something about Sloane that always made reason fly out the window. "Who's the lucky guy?"

"Xavier." She dropped the menu and looked at me. "Now's not the time. We don't want a repeat of the Cannes fiasco."

I rolled my eyes. Get caught dozing off *once* during a major awards speech and I was suddenly the bad guy. If these types of events weren't so damn boring, maybe I'd have an easier time staying awake.

People didn't know entertainment these days. Who wanted stuffy elevator music and the same boring drinks they served at every gala? No one. If I cared enough, I'd give the organizers a few pointers, but I didn't.

The servers brought out the food, which I ignored in favor of more champagne as the ceremony trudged on.

I tuned it out and ruminated on what type of guy Sloane might be seeing. In all our years working together, I'd never seen her with or heard her mention a date, but obviously, she had to have been with someone.

She was prickly as hell, but she was also beautiful, smart, and accomplished. Even now, there were multiple men sneaking peeks at her from surrounding tables.

I downed my drink and glared at one of them until he looked away, his face red. Sloane was my date in name only, but it was bad form for other people to ogle her when she'd come with me. Did no one observe proper etiquette anymore?

The room erupted into its loudest round of applause. Eduardo stood, and I realized the emcee had just announced my father as the organization's Philanthropist of the Year.

"Clap," Sloane said without looking at me. A tight smile affixed her face. "The cameras are watching."

"When *aren't* they watching?" I clapped half-heartedly for Eduardo and Eduardo only.

"It's my honor to accept this award on Alberto's behalf tonight," he said. "As you know, he's been my friend and business partner for more years than I can count..."

Sloane glanced at her watch and gathered her belongings when Eduardo wrapped up his thankfully short speech.

I straightened. "You're leaving already?" It'd only been fifty minutes, not an hour.

"In case there's traffic. I trust you'll behave in my absence." She emphasized her last sentence with a warning stare.

"The minute you leave, I'm throwing my drink in another guest's face and hijacking the music system," I said. "Sure you don't want to stay?"

She didn't look amused.

"Do that, and our deal is off," she said flatly. "I'll check in at the end of the night."

She slipped discreetly out of her chair and toward the exit. I was so focused on watching her leave, I didn't notice Eduardo's approach until he placed a hand on my shoulder.

"Do you have time to talk? There's something we need to discuss."

"Sure." With Sloane gone, I'd do anything to get out of sitting here with the most boring tablemates in existence.

I followed Eduardo into the hall. Now that the ceremony was over, the guests had resumed their drinking and mingling, and no one paid us much mind.

"I was going to call and tell you, but in person is better." Free from the watchful eyes of photographers, Eduardo's mouth settled into a grim line that had my pulse quickening. "Xavier..."

"Let me guess. It's my father."

"No. Yes. Well..." Eduardo wiped a hand over his face, uncharacteristically hesitant. "His condition is stable. There's been no change."

A twist of either relief or disappointment loosened the knot in my chest. How fucked up was it that I had mixed feelings over what should've been good news?

"That means he's not getting worse, but he's also not getting better," Eduardo said. "You haven't visited him in months. You should see him. It might help. The doctors say having loved ones around—"

"The key phrase is *loved ones*. Since my mom isn't around, I guess he's fucked."

The only person my father had ever truly cared about was my mother.

"He's your father." My honorary uncle's mouth thinned.

"Deja de ser tan terco. Haz las paces antes de que sea demasiado tarde." Stop being so stubborn. Make amends before it's too late.

"I'm not the one who needs to make amends," I said. There were only so many times a guy could try before he gave up, and I'd reached my limit years ago. "Anyway, good talk, but I have somewhere else to be."

"Xavi—"

"Safe travels home." I turned. "Say hi to everyone else for me."

"It's your family's company," Eduardo called after me. He sounded resigned. He'd only taken the interim CEO position because I'd turned it down, and I knew he clung to the hope that I'd magically "come to my senses" about continuing the family legacy one day. "You can't run from it forever."

I didn't break my stride.

With the ceremony done, the gala was basically over, which meant I wouldn't be breaking my deal with Sloane if I left.

The reminder of her and where she was right now—probably on some date with some asshole—darkened my already-thunderous mood.

I usually tried to look on the bright side, but fuck it, sometimes a guy had to wallow.

I grabbed my jacket from coat check and climbed into one of the black cabs waiting outside the event space.

"Neon," I said, naming the city's hottest new nightclub. "I'll tip you a hundred pounds if you can get me there in under fifteen minutes."

The cab pulled away from the curb. I stared out the window at the passing lights of London, eager for the moment I could drink away any thoughts of Eduardo, my father, and a certain publicist who occupied my waking moments far more than she should.

CHAPTER 3

Sloane

THE RED "DON'T WALK" SIGN STARED ME DOWN. I ignored it and power walked across the street, tuning out the blaring car horn of an oncoming truck.

I was already late, and if I didn't take off my shoes soon, my bloodied feet would kill me faster than getting hit by a car. Four-inch stilettos *looked* great, but they weren't made for ten blocks of city walking.

Unfortunately, London traffic was a shitshow, so I'd ditched my cab after being stuck on the same street for twenty minutes.

By the time I reached the hotel, my dress stuck to my body with sweat and I could barely feel my feet, but I made it to the penthouse without incident (unless I counted the other guests' horrified stares).

Please don't be asleep.

I knocked on the door, my heart in my throat.

Please don't be asleep. Please don't be—

My breath exhaled in a puff of relief when a familiar round face answered the door.

"There you are." Rhea ushered me in, her eyes darting toward the entrance like George and Caroline would walk in at any minute. She put her job in jeopardy every time she texted me, but we both took our risks for the same reason. "I was afraid you couldn't make it."

"I got held up by traffic, but I wouldn't miss it for the world." I took off my shoes and sighed. *Much better.*

With Rhea's help, I quickly cleaned my bloody feet before walking into the suite's living room. My heart clenched when I saw her sitting on the floor, watching a kids' cartoon about ballerinas. She always gravitated toward shows about dance or sports.

Her back faced me, but she must have had a sixth sense because she turned the instant I entered the room.

"Sloane!" Penny scrambled to her feet and ran toward me. "You came."

"Of course I came." I bent down to hug her. God, she'd grown so much since the last time I saw her.

She buried her face in my stomach, and if I could cry, I would've at how tightly she clung to me. Besides Rhea, I was probably her first hug of the day.

Her nanny left the room, giving us time alone, and I eventually, reluctantly released her so I could fish her gift out of my bag. "Happy birthday, Pen. This is for you."

My half sister's eyes lit up. She took the gift and unwrapped it, taking great care not to rip the silver-striped paper.

She was Penelope to her parents and Penny to everyone else, but she'd always be Pen to me. The sister I never knew I needed, the only one who'd cried when I left, and the only Kensington I still considered family after my grandmother died.

She finished unwrapping the gift, and her delighted gasp brought a smile to my face.

"The new American Sports doll!" She clutched the precious item to her chest. "How did you get this?"

"I know people. Your older sister is pretty cool, you know," I teased.

The limited-edition doll was one of the most sought-after toys in the world. There were only two dozen in existence, but my friend Vivian's husband pulled some strings and got me one in time for Pen's birthday.

She couldn't play with it openly, but one of the upsides to her parents' neglect was that they wouldn't notice or question how she'd gotten the toy.

"So, how does nine feel?" I sat next to her on the floor. "You're almost in the double digits."

"Gross. Soon I'll be old like you—ah!" Pen erupted into hysterical giggles when I tickled her side. "Stop! I'm sorry! I'm sorry!" She gasped. "You're not *that* old."

"That's what you get for insulting me," I quipped, but I stopped tickling her, mindful not to overexert her. I always trod a line between treating her like a normal kid while knowing she wasn't, at least not in terms of physical stamina.

Two years ago, Pen was diagnosed with chronic fatigue syndrome, or CFS, after an unusually lengthy bout of mono. Characterized by extreme fatigue, sleep issues, and joint and muscle pain, among other things, CFS had no cure or approved treatment. It was difficult to determine the cause, though her doctors suspected it was triggered by a change in the way her immune system responded to illness, and the best we could do was manage the symptoms.

Despite having no FDA-approved treatments, CFS had spawned a thousand and one snake oil salesmen who promised a "cure" via special vitamins, antiretrovirals, and other "miracle" medications. Pen's parents had flushed a ton of money down the drain trying to find something that worked. Nothing ever did, so eventually, they gave up and simply shoved her at home where they didn't have to think about her.

Luckily, Pen had mild CFS, so she could carry out everyday activities better than those with more severe cases, but she couldn't play sports like she wanted or attend school like her peers. On bad days, it was difficult for her to walk. She was currently homeschooled, and Rhea stayed with her pretty much twenty-four seven in case she crashed.

"I made something for you." Pen sounded out of breath, but my concern ebbed when she walked to the coffee table and returned without missing a beat. A knot formed in my throat. It was a good day; she deserved a good day on her birthday. "It's a friendship bracelet." She placed the jewelry carefully in my palm. "I have a matching one. See?"

The beaded bracelet simply had five hearts. Hers were pink; mine were blue.

The pressure from the knot wound its way up behind my nose and ears. "It's beautiful. Thank you, Pen." I slid the bracelet onto my wrist. "But you should receive gifts on your birthday, not give them." Especially not when making the jewelry probably cost her hours' worth of energy.

"I don't get to see you on your birthday," she said in a small voice.

I hated that she was right. We only saw each other a few times a year when Rhea could sneak me in. My family was spiteful enough that they'd lock her in a vault before they'd willingly let me visit, and I was proud enough never to apologize for something I wasn't at fault for. I'd thought about it, but I couldn't do it. Not even for Pen.

"Well, we're together now," I said, pushing thoughts of the past aside. "What do you want to do? We can watch a movie, play with your new doll..."

"I want to watch the Blackcastle versus Holchester game." Pen looked at me with big doe eyes. "Please?"

I wasn't a sports person, but she loved soccer, so I acquiesced to a taped replay. The game made headlines earlier this year because it'd been the first time Asher Donovan, the darling of the Premier League and the newest transfer to Blackcastle, had played against his old team.

Besides Xavier, Asher was my most difficult client, but he was also Pen's hero. She'd nearly ruptured my eardrum when he signed with my firm a few years ago.

Speaking of Xavier...

While Pen curled against my side and watched the match with rapt attention, I quickly checked my phone for any new gossip items. I ignored a text from an old hookup asking to meet up again—the man could *not* take a hint—and scanned the news.

I had alerts for all my clients, but there were only two names that made my blood pressure rise whenever they popped up onscreen. One of their initials: XC.

Nothing. *Good.* He was behaving. I swore Rhea had an easier time taking care of Pen than I did keeping Xavier in line.

Pen and I didn't talk throughout the game, but we didn't need to. Even though we didn't see each other often, the best part of our reunions was being comfortable together. Sometimes that meant talking nonstop; other times it meant watching a movie in content silence.

She shifted half an hour in, and when I looked down, my pulse spiked with worry. Pale face, glazed eyes—she was about to crash.

"I'm okay," she said when I called for Rhea. The older woman rushed into the room, her face wreathed with concern. "Stay." Pen clutched my sleeve with her little hand. "I never get to see you."

Despite her words, her voice faded into a whisper toward the end. The night had taken its toll, and it was a testament to her fatigue that she didn't argue again when I kissed her goodbye on the forehead.

"We'll see each other again soon," I said fiercely. "I promise."

I wished we had more time together, but Pen's health came before anything else.

Rhea and I took her into the bedroom, where she instantly crashed. I hoped she slept through the night. Otherwise, tomorrow would be rough.

I smoothed back her hair, my throat clogged with emotion. Another visit finished too soon. Our time together never lasted as long as I would've liked, but at least I saw her. It was the best I could've asked for given our circumstances.

"It's good she got to see you for a bit tonight," Rhea said after we returned to the living room. "Mr. and Mrs. Kensington didn't spend a lot of time with her before they went out."

Of course they hadn't. My father and stepmother considered Pen's condition an embarrassment and kept her away from the public as much as possible.

"Thank you for letting me know about tonight," I said. Rhea had called last week and told me they would be in London. George and Caroline had dinner and show reservations tonight, which gave me a large enough window to see Pen. "I appreciate—"

"...absolutely *terrible.*" A familiar voice outside the door stopped us in our tracks and made my stomach plunge. "Honestly, George, I've never had a more abysmal lobster."

Rhea and I stared at each other, her huge eyes mirroring mine.

"They're not supposed to be back for another two hours." Her mouth trembled. "If they see you..."

We'd be done for. Rhea loved Pen like a mother. If she were fired, they would both be devastated, and if I couldn't see Pen anymore...

Do something. CEOs and celebrities paid me exorbitant amounts of money to guide them through rough patches, but a strange disassociation rooted my feet to the floor. It was like I was watching an actor play me in the hotel room while the real me spiraled down a tunnel of unwanted memories.

Dating you is like dating a block of ice...I don't know if you even like me...

Can you blame him for what he did?

If you actually cared that much, you'd cry or show some *emotion.*

Don't embarrass us, Sloane.

If you walk out that door, there's no coming back.

Pressure pushed against the backs of my eyes, desperate for a way out. As always, it found none.

A key whirred against the suite's card reader.

Move! a voice inside my head screamed. *Are you stupid? You're going to get caught.*

The soft click of the door unlocking finally snapped me out of my trance and into crisis-management mode.

I didn't think. I simply grabbed my bloodied heels from the entryway, scanned the living room for any traces I might've left behind and, satisfied there were none, ducked behind the floor-to-ceiling drapes.

The door opened, revealing a glimpse of gray hair before I fully ensconced myself behind thick red velvet. My palms curled, slick with sweat.

I hadn't planned on running into my family today. I wasn't mentally prepared for that, and though I wasn't a particularly religious person, I prayed with everything I had that they were too tired to do anything except go straight to sleep.

"We should've stuck with our regular spot." Caroline's clipped tone echoed in rhythm with her heels. "This is what happens when you give so-called rising stars a chance, George. They're rarely up to par."

"You're right." My father's deep, familiar voice rumbled through me like thunder on a Friday night when I was tucked in bed with a book and flashlight. Equal parts comforting and ominous, it chipped at the wall I'd erected long ago until a sliver of nostalgia escaped.

It'd been years since I heard his voice in person.

"Next time, we'll go to the club," he said. "Rhea, order room service for us. We barely ate anything at the restaurant."

"Yes, sir."

"And *why* are the drapes open?" Caroline's voice grew louder. "You know they must be closed immediately at sunset. Lord knows who could be looking in right now."

No one because you're on the twelfth floor and not facing any other buildings.

My snarky mental reply didn't prevent the taste of copper from filling my mouth when my stepmother's footsteps stopped in front of me. I stood frozen, staring at the swath of velvet that was the only thing separating me from disaster.

Don't look behind the drapes. Don't look behind—

She grasped the curtains with one hand. I pressed my back against the window, but she was centimeters from my face and I had nowhere else to go.

Thud.

Thud.

THUD.

The ominous drum of my heartbeat intensified with each passing second. I was already devising multiple plans and backup plans for what I would say, what I would do, and who I would hire to help if Caroline found me and shipped Pen off to some remote location where I couldn't see her.

Caroline's hand tightened around the drapes. For a heart-stopping moment, I thought the jig was up.

Then she dragged the curtains closed, hiding me completely, and resumed her complaints about that night's dinner.

"Honestly, I don't know how *Vogue* could've named him one of the best new chefs of the year..." The sound of her heels faded along with my father's murmured response and the click of a door closing.

Neither one asked about Pen or acknowledged Rhea again.

My body sagged, light with relief, but when Rhea pulled back the drapes, I didn't waste time loitering. George and Caroline could come back out any minute.

I squeezed Rhea's hand in a silent goodbye and escaped out the front door. She smiled, her eyes worried, and I didn't breathe properly until I hit the sidewalk outside the hotel.

The shock of unexpectedly being in the same room as my father again disoriented me for a few minutes, but the cool October air poured over me like an ice shower, and by the time I reached the corner, the buzz had vanished from my ears and the streetlights no longer blurred into an orange stream.

I'm fine. This is fine. I hadn't been caught, I'd spent time with Pen on her birthday, and now I could—

My phone buzzed with a news alert.

I glanced at it, my stomach plummeting the minute I saw Perry Wilson's distinctive blog logo.

I clicked into the article, and a crimson haze wiped away any lingering unease over my narrow escape from the hotel.

You've got *to be kidding me.*

Two hours. I left him alone for *two* hours and he still couldn't follow simple instructions.

I shoved my phone into my bag and hailed a passing cab. "Neon." I slammed the door shut, causing the driver to wince. "I'll give you your biggest tip of the month if you get me there in ten minutes."

Every second counted when I had a client to strangle.

CHAPTER 4

Sloane

THE SOCIETY PAPERS CALLED THEM THE MODERN JET Set. The trashier gossip columns derided them as Heirs and Spares—the children of the rich who squandered their days drinking and partying instead of doing anything useful with their lives. I simply called them Xavier and Friends (derogatory).

Eight minutes after I left Pen's hotel, I strong-armed my way into Neon, where Xavier and Friends had taken over the VIP room. The scene was almost a replica of the photos splashed across Perry Wilson's latest blog post.

One of Xavier's friends was snorting cocaine off a bottle girl's stomach, another was giving someone a lap dance, and a half dressed couple was basically having sex in the corner.

Lounging amidst the hedonism like a king surveying his court was Xavier, one arm tossed over the back of a velvet banquette while the other held a bottle of tequila.

Xavier, who was supposed to be at the awards gala happening this very second.

Xavier, who desperately needed more of an image cleanup than usual after Perry Wilson's hit piece about his birthday party gone wild in Miami a few months ago.

Xavier, who'd promised me he wouldn't step foot in a nightclub until we fixed said image.

I barely felt the pain in my feet as I stalked toward the banquette and stopped directly in front of him, blocking his view of the crowd. The women fluttering around him must've picked up on my intent to kill because they scattered faster than falling leaves on a gusty day.

Xavier took a long swig of tequila before addressing me. "First Mykonos, now this." A slow smile spread across his face. "You stalking me, Luna?"

"If I were, you make it easy." I held up my phone, which displayed a lurid photo of Xavier tossing back a shot while a pretty blond straddled his lap. *Castillo heir ditches gala honoring his dying father!* "No clubs until we fix your image, and you were supposed to stay for the entirety of the gala. That was our deal."

"No, our deal was that I stay for the entire *ceremony*, which I did. The ceremony and the gala are not the same. As for the club thing..." A casual shrug. "Maybe you should've put it in writing."

I grabbed the bottle from his hand. What I *really* wanted was to grab him and shake him, but I was mindful of the cameras "secretly" trained on us. People were less discreet than they thought they were.

"Get up," I said through gritted teeth. "We're going back to the hotel." *Where I can knock some sense into you in peace.*

"How was your date?" Xavier ignored my order and flicked his gaze over my face, down my dress, and to my feet. A tiny pinch formed between his brows.

"Fantastic." I didn't dispel his assumption of why I'd left the gala early. "Less fantastic was getting another Perry Wilson notification about you."

A strange glow of satisfaction settled in his eyes. "Did it interrupt your evening?" he asked silkily. "My bad."

I kept my expression neutral as I shifted my stance and carefully stepped on his foot with a razor-sharp stiletto. The table hid what I was doing from prying eyes, so from a distance, it looked like nothing was wrong.

Xavier's cockiness instantly disappeared beneath a grimace.

"You have thirty seconds to get up, or you'll lose not only a toe but a much more important part of your anatomy." I cocked my head and tapped a finger against the tequila bottle. "Did you know there are online tutorials for everything? Including how to castrate a home invader with common household items."

To his credit, he didn't flinch at the word *castrate*. "Let me guess. You've watched all of them, overachiever." He slunk deeper in his seat and stared up at me with hooded nonchalance. "Relax, Luna. It's Friday night. Take the stick out of your ass and have a little fun."

A muscle twitched beneath my eye. *Do not take the bait.* "I'm not here to have fun." It came out as a near growl.

"Obviously." Xavier gave me another once-over. "It's too bad you're wasting a perfectly nice dress on such a boring end to the night. Speaking of which, how did your date feel about you leaving early?"

"They felt it was in their best interest to do as I say." I stepped harder on his foot, a smile flashing at his renewed grimace. "Since I'm having such a *boring* night, I'm tempted to spice things up. Of course, I can't guarantee my idea of a fun time matches yours—especially when you're surrounded by your friends, and the chances of embarrassment are high." My smile disappeared. "Rest assured, I *will* drag you out of here like you're an insolent child throwing a temper tantrum, and no, I do *not* care if I'm the one who has to clean up the mess afterward. It would be worth it for the shit you'll get from your friends for the rest of your days. So unless you want that to happen, get the hell up."

Xavier listened to my tirade without a hint of concern. After I finished, he yawned, stretched his other arm over the back of the banquette, and cast a pointed glance at the heel impaling his five-thousand-dollar shoe. "Can't get up unless you let me go, sweetheart."

I didn't take my eyes off him as I released him, suspicious of his sudden obeisance.

He unfolded himself from the banquette and stared down at me, a glint of amusement reentering his eyes. Even when I wore my Jimmy Choos, he towered over me by a good three inches.

I hated it.

"In my defense, I did fulfill my end of our deal," he said. "Like I said, the ceremony and gala are two different things. The ceremony ended when Eduardo finished his speech, which also happened to be when *you* left. So don't try to use it as an excuse to back out of our vacation."

"That's semantics."

"Maybe," he drawled. "But it's also the truth."

"And what about your promise not to go clubbing until we fixed your image?"

"My image *was* fixed. There hasn't been a single bad story about me for weeks." Xavier's eyes gleamed with laughter. "You never specified your definition of a 'fixed image,' Luna. It's not my fault if we have different ideas of what that means."

God, he was insufferable. Even more annoying was the fact he was right, but I would rather throw myself off Big Ben than admit it.

"Just shut up and follow me," I snapped, wishing I had a wittier reply.

"Yes, ma'am." His cheeks dimpled. "I love a woman in charge."

I ignored the sexual innuendo and turned on my heel. He followed me to the exit without saying goodbye to his friends.

I didn't know if he'd tired of arguing with me or if I'd genuinely scared him with the threat of embarrassment—I doubted it—but the reasons for his about-face didn't matter. The only things that mattered were if he listened to me and stayed out of trouble.

"What's the story behind the bracelet?" he asked on our way down the elevator.

"Excuse me?"

"The bracelet." Xavier tipped his chin toward the friendship bracelet on my wrist. "You weren't wearing that at the gala."

My muscles coiled. Only my best friends knew about my visits to Pen, and there was no way I was adding him to that trusted circle.

"It was a gift." I didn't elaborate.

"Hmm." A shadow of knowing passed over his face. For someone who'd been drinking all night, he was shockingly observant.

Luckily, he didn't press the issue, and we walked the remaining distance to the main exit in silence.

However, I should've known the peace wouldn't last.

"New terms," he said when we climbed into the back seat of a cab. "You can't be such a buzzkill when we're on vacation."

"Then don't take me with you." I answered a work email about a potential new client without looking up. It was still business hours in New York.

"Nice try. For someone who's stalking me, you don't seem to like my company much." He placed a hand on his chest with a mock-wounded look. "It hurts my soul. Truly."

"What would hurt more is getting cut off."

Xavier was set to inherit billions of dollars if and when his father died. However, his current income came from an extravagant annual allowance that would immediately cease if he violated one of the two terms: 1) He must retain me as his publicist, and 2) He couldn't do anything that damaged the family reputation.

There was a three strikes policy for the second condition, and somehow, I was in charge of determining whether Xavier was in compliance. He'd raised holy hell when he first found out about it, but he'd settled into grudging acceptance since.

I didn't abuse my power. However, I was *this* close to adding a second strike to his record (the first had been his twenty-ninth birthday in Miami).

"Maybe," Xavier said, sounding unconcerned. "Regardless, you can't do that on vacation." He nodded at my phone.

"What, check my emails?"

"Exactly. A vacation isn't a vacation if you're working the entire time."

I scoffed. "If you think I'm spending an entire week without checking my emails, you're more delusional than I thought. I run a business, Xavier, and if you want me in Spain, then you'll agree to my terms."

"I see." He cocked an eyebrow. "I never took you for a liar, Sloane. Our trip hasn't even started, and you're already going back on your word."

He might as well have slapped me in the face. "*Excuse me*?"

I'd been called many things in my life, but I'd never once been called a liar. Sure, I might've bent the truth at times—which publicist worth their salt didn't?—but when it came to promises, I kept mine. Always.

That was one of the reasons I'd agreed to this stupid bargain with Xavier in the first place. I'd promised Pen I'd see her tonight, and the only way I could do that was by giving in to his demands.

"No work, just play," he said. "I distinctly remember that being one of the terms when you agreed to them. Checking emails is considered work, which means you'd be reneging on your promise."

Dammit, he was right. *Again.* I'd somehow blocked out that condition of our deal, if only because it was so absurd. I couldn't ignore my messages for a week, but I couldn't go back on my word, either.

"I propose an amendment," I said tightly. "I can check my *personal* emails at any time, and I can check my work ones if all I do is delegate them to my team."

Xavier's eyes narrowed. Several beats passed before his face relaxed into a smile again. "Amendment accepted. Now—"

"*Ahem.*" The driver cut him off before he could finish his sentence. Apparently, he'd tired of our conversation "Where to?" he asked pointedly.

Xavier and I answered at the same time.

"Claridge's."

"Stansted Airport."

"You promised me a vacation," Xavier said when I stared at him. "Time to put your money where your mouth is."

"We literally arrived in London hours ago, and we don't leave for Spain until tomorrow."

That much travel in one day made me want to die.

"Check your watch. It's five past midnight."

It was, indeed, five past midnight. I just kept taking losses tonight.

Note to self: in the future, specify a departure time and not just a departure day.

"My luggage is at my hotel. I need to get it," I said, trying to stall.

"Already taken care of." He held up his phone. "I just messaged my hotel butler. Our luggage will be waiting for us on the jet when we arrive."

"It's too late." I grasped for another excuse to delay the trip. "It's dangerous to fly at this time."

Xavier didn't deign to acknowledge my ridiculous statement. Red-eye flights took off after midnight all the time.

The cab driver twisted around to glare at us. "Claridge's or Stansted?" he demanded. "I don't have all night."

"Stansted. Sorry, my man." Xavier shoved a handful of bills toward the front seat. "Appreciate it."

Mollified, the other man grabbed the cash and sped off.

I guess I wasn't the only one who bribed drivers when the occasion called for it.

"Relax, Luna." Xavier laughed as we wound through the near-empty streets at a breakneck pace. "You're officially off the clock for the next week. Enjoy it."

I pressed my lips together.

All I have to do is get through the week without slipping up. I wasn't sure what "slipping up" would look like, but foreboding inched beneath my skin the closer we got to the airport.

I didn't know what would happen when I didn't have the buffer of work to shield me, but if Xavier thought he could trick me into letting down my guard in Spain, he had another thing coming.

Vacation or not, I was still me. I didn't let people see past what I wanted them to see, and nothing would change that—not even a forced week off with my client nemesis.

CHAPTER 5

Xavier

SLOANE AND I FLEW TO MALLORCA IN SILENCE. I COULD tell she was plotting my demise the entire time, but luckily, all sharp objects remained blood-free when we landed.

By then, we were so tired she didn't argue over sharing a villa with me, and I didn't protest when she took the primary suite. I was simply happy to fall into bed and pass out.

Despite my exhaustion, it was a fitful sleep plagued by replays of the same dream. I was crossing a bridge with Hershey, my pet chocolate Lab from childhood, but every time I made it halfway, the gaps between the planks widened. No matter how hard I tried to jump the distance or cling to the railing, we fell through the gap. I plunged into quicksand and watched helplessly as the surrounding river swept my beloved dog away.

Hershey died years ago from old age, but that didn't matter to Dream Me. The crushing anchor of failure weighed me down more than the quicksand.

The fall happened over and over and over until I woke up, heart pounding and body drenched in sweat.

Variations of the dream had haunted me for years.

Sometimes, I was with Hershey. Other times, I was with my mother, an old friend, or an ex-girlfriend. Whoever it was, the result remained the same.

I was stuck watching them die.

"Fuck this." My harsh voice chased some of the ghosts away as I tossed my covers off.

It was only eight. I usually didn't get up until past ten, but I couldn't stay in that bed any longer.

I turned the shower as cold as it would go and washed away the remnants of the night.

It was just a stupid dream. I wasn't going to let it ruin my trip, and I sure as hell wasn't going to dig deeper into what it meant. Ignorance was bliss.

I scrubbed harder with the soap.

By the time I toweled off and threw on a shirt and pants, I'd corralled my unease to the back corners of my mind where it belonged.

I headed to the kitchen but stopped halfway when a flash of movement caught my eye.

I came to a dead halt.

Sloane was exercising on the back deck, wearing a tank top and yoga pants. *Yoga pants*.

It might seem normal to see someone wearing workout clothes to work out, but this was Sloane. I'd known her for three years and I had never, not once, seen her in anything other than an evening dress or business wear. I was convinced she slept in those knife-sharp suits she favored so much.

I walked closer, fascinated by the unnatural sight.

Sloane switched from one impossible-looking yoga pose to another. Sunlight gilded her lithe form and turned her golden hair into a halo. She hadn't noticed me yet, which meant her expression didn't hold disdain, frustration, or general annoyance.

It was...nice, but also a little alarming, like seeing a lioness stripped of her claws.

Her phone pinged with a new notification. My mouth twitched when she balanced herself so she could type out a reply with one hand before she resettled into her original position and closed her eyes.

"Impressive." I couldn't resist commenting. I leaned against the doorframe and pushed a hand into the pocket of my sweatpants. "But you know the point of yoga is to relax, right?"

Sloane's eyes popped open again. Her head swiveled so she could glare at me."How long have you been standing there?" she demanded.

Ah, there's that comforting irritation. Let's see if we can notch it higher, shall we?

"Long enough to see you answer your phone." I tsked with disappointment. "It's the first day, and you're already breaking the rules. I expected more from you."

My smile inched wider when she unfolded herself, stood, and came to a stop inches from me. This close, I could see flecks of gray in her blue eyes and smell a trace of her perfume. It was clean and light, like fresh linen with a hint of jasmine.

They were things I shouldn't notice about a woman who tolerated me at best and despised me at worst. But I did, and once I noticed them, I couldn't stop thinking about them.

"They weren't rules," Sloane said. "They were mutually agreed conditions. "Plus, it wasn't a work text. It was personal."

"Let me guess. It was your date from the other night."

"You're strangely obsessed with that date."

So it *had* been a date. I was unprepared for the little kick in my stomach, which I masked with a shrug. "Nothing strange about it. You're notorious for turning down men."

"Lucky me. Maybe they'll get the hint and leave me alone."

Sloane abandoned her yoga session and brushed past me into the living room.

I trailed after her. "So, your first vacation in years. What are your plans for the day?"

I'd made a wild guess about the last time she took off work, but she didn't correct me, which was damn sad. People could scold me for "not living up to my potential," but at least I wasn't chained to my inbox and the whims of others.

"I haven't decided yet. Perhaps I'll finish my book." Her eyes flicked around at our luxurious surroundings. The three-bedroom villa boasted an infinity pool, a Jacuzzi, and access to a private beach, but she seemed unimpressed by all of it.

"The book you were reading on the plane?" I asked in disbelief. "*25 Principles of Crisis Communications? That* book?"

Pink colored her cheeks and the bridge of her nose. "It's the latest edition."

"Jesus." The CIA couldn't torture me into reading that book, and she was doing it for fun.

I'd assumed that once she arrived in Mallorca, the island would work its magic and she'd automatically loosen up. Obviously, that wasn't the case.

If I wanted to see a different side of her, I had to coax it out of her; otherwise, she'd spend the week buried in some boring nonfiction book and the entire trip would go to waste.

The chances of me convincing Sloane to take off work again in the future were slim to none, which meant this was my *one* opportunity to drag her out of her comfort zone.

I chose not to examine why doing that was so important to me. Sometimes, it was better not to ask questions I wouldn't like the answers to.

"Fuck that. You're at the best resort in Mallorca. You need to take advantage of it." An idea popped up in my head. "I have just the thing. Let's go."

Sloane didn't budge. "I'm not day drinking with you."

"Not everything I do involves partying." My grin made a wicked return. "You'll love this. I promise."

"I do not love this." The heat of Sloane's glare rivaled the one-hundred-fifty-degree air billowing around us. "I do not love this at all."

"See, that's exactly the type of frustration we're working on today." I leaned back and laced my hands behind my head. "It'll be tough, but we *will* pull that stick out of your ass."

Sloane's eyes narrowed, and I almost patted her down to ensure she hadn't smuggled in a hair pin that she could fashion into a weapon. Since that would be rude, and I valued my life, I kept my hands to myself.

After I convinced her to leave her ridiculous nonfiction book in the villa, I dragged her to the resort's restaurant for breakfast followed by a trip to the spa. If anyone needed a good massage, it was her.

Fortunately, the spa had one package available at the last minute. Unfortunately, it was a couples' package, which was how Sloane and I ended up in a private igloo dry sauna together, kickstarting the first of many stops on our Signature Honeymoon Ritual.

Sloane had put up a hell of a fight, but between my irresistible charm and the spa concierge's firm but gentle insistence, she'd reluctantly caved.

"Is this all you do with your days?" She glanced around the cedar-paneled room.

"No. I also eat, sleep, and fuck." My lips curved when she stiffened at the word *fuck*. "If you tried it some time, you might be less uptight. Newsflash, Luna, your headaches aren't from your hair." Even now, her blond locks were slicked back in a bun tight enough to cut off circulation. "It's from pent-up tension."

"Wrong. My headaches are from dealing with *you.*" She shifted, and I tried not to notice the way her towel slipped the tiniest bit—not enough to reveal anything scandalous, but enough to make my imagination run wild. "Besides, I'm plenty happy with my sex life, which is more than your bedmates can say, I'm sure."

Something dark and unidentifiable stirred behind my ribcage. *Fucking breakfast.* I should've known better than to eat the last piece of sausage at the buffet.

I better not have food poisoning, or I was suing the resort.

"They've never had complaints, but is that any way to speak to a client?" I drawled.

"You're not my client. Your family is. You're merely the trade-off for one of my most lucrative contracts."

"Ouch. Treat a girl to a luxury spa and get verbally attacked in return. Decorum doesn't exist anymore."

Sloane rolled her eyes. "I'm sure there are plenty of women here who'd be happy to stroke your ego. Our server at breakfast, for example. I was afraid she'd fly away from how fast she was batting her eyes at you."

A smile stole across my face, erasing the surprise sting from her *trade-off* comment. "I didn't realize you paid that much attention to who flirted with me."

"I'm your publicist. It's my job to pay attention to everything about you."

My smile melted into something slower, more languid. "*Everything*, huh?"

I'd meant it as a joke, but when her gaze touched mine, oxygen thinned in a way that had nothing to do with the heat.

Sloane was beautiful. Fact.

I'd been physically attracted to her since the moment we met. Also fact.

But it'd been a low-simmering attraction, the type I could brush off by focusing on something else. Recently, however, it'd ramped up to the point where there *was* nothing else.

I didn't know the reason for the change, but I knew that right now, as we sat in the sauna I'd stupidly insisted on going into, I looked at her and couldn't breathe.

Sloane swallowed. Beads of sweat trickled down her throat and disappeared into the shadow of her towel.

She didn't respond to my innuendo, and the silence hummed beneath my skin like tiny bolts of electricity.

If I stood, it would take five steps to reach her.

If I lifted my hand, it would take two seconds to touch her.

If—

"You never answered my question yesterday." My abrupt statement severed the spell, but my pulse continued to pound and my hands instinctively curled around the edge of my seat.

Fuck, this wasn't what I'd had in mind when I'd dragged Sloane to Spain with me. I enjoyed flirting with her, but there was a difference between flirting and…whatever the hell happened in the past two minutes.

She blinked, seemingly thrown off by the sudden change in atmosphere. "About what?"

"Your bracelet." She wore the same friendship bracelet from last night. Sloane was a Cartier girl; friendship bracelets weren't exactly her vibe. "You left the gala without it and showed up at Neon with it. If it's a gift from your mystery lover, you might have to upgrade. Find someone who can buy you real jewelry."

"It's the thought that counts, not the carats."

"The only people who say that are people who can't afford carats." But even the stupidest guy wouldn't gift someone like

Sloane a piece of kid's jewelry. Unless... "Who did you really go see?" I asked softly.

Sloane's face darkened.

I didn't get a reply, nor had I expected one, but I could guess. There was only one topic that made her shut down: her family.

Everyone knew about the Kensingtons' estrangement. They were New York society staples, and barrels of ink had been spilled over the rift between investment tycoon George Kensington III and his eldest daughter. The cause of said rift had been a topic of speculation for years.

Had she visited her family after the gala? If so, who'd gifted her that bracelet and why? Obviously, it had to be someone she cared about or she wouldn't wear it, but from what I understood, her separation from her family had been ugly. She hadn't talked to another Kensington in years.

Sloane's eyes stayed on mine, her emotions inscrutable beneath their wintry blue depths. It was as if she were physically restraining herself from looking away lest I mistook the move for weakness.

Little did she know, there was *nothing* she could do that I'd mistake for weakness. She was one of the strongest people I knew, and only a fool would think otherwise.

The minutes ticked by. The longer the silence stretched, the more I wanted to dig beneath her stoic façade until I reached the real her—the one with flaws and insecurities like everyone else, not the perfect CEO she projected to the world.

Come on, Luna. Give me something.

A shadow crossed her face, and just when I thought she'd provide some sort of answer, the heater shut off, indicating our time in the sauna was up.

I blinked, ending our unwitting stare down.

Sloane's expression hardened again before she stood and walked to the exit.

"Okay, good talk," I said, following her. My voice sounded abnormally loud after the silence. "I learned a lot about you. Thanks."

"You're the one who said this trip is supposed to be relaxing." She twisted the door handle. "Being interrogated isn't relaxing."

"*Interrogated* is a strong word," I muttered. But fair enough.

Honestly, I didn't know why I cared so much about a stupid bracelet. So what if it had to do with her family? My own family dynamics were shitty enough without me worrying about someone else's.

"You can open the door anytime now," I said when Sloane didn't move. "I don't want to miss a second of my massage."

She turned, and my stomach dropped at her tight expression.

"I can't," she said. "The door is jammed. We're stuck."

Sloane

ON MY LIST OF WORST WAYS TO DIE, OVERHEATING half naked in a sauna with Xavier Castillo ranked somewhere between medieval torture and getting eaten alive by piranhas, which was why it was *not* going to happen.

I tried the handle again. Still jammed. *Dammit.*

"If we had our phones, we could call the front desk, but we don't," I muttered. That was why I brought my phone everywhere. I didn't care about screen addiction; at least it could save my life if and when the occasion arose.

"Sloane."

"There's nothing heavy enough to break the door unless I push you through it." *Tempting.*

He sighed. "Sloane, there's—"

"We *could* hope someone finds us when the next appointment shows up, but who knows when that'll be? The spa is fully booked, but that doesn't mean—"

"Sloane!" Xavier grabbed my shoulders and turned me around. "There's an emergency button for these situations."

I followed his gaze to the wall. Sure enough, the button was right there, mounted on a piece of wood. How the hell had I missed that?

Embarrassment scorched my cheeks.

I blamed the sauna. That much heat in a confined space couldn't be healthy.

I managed to retain a shred of dignity as I pressed the button, mostly by ignoring Xavier's shit-eating grin.

The staff came quickly after that, averting our potential demise. However, even though we weren't in danger anymore, the possibility of dying next to Xavier—no matter how fleeting—did not bode well for the rest of the trip.

"I think it's a great start to the week," he said as we walked to our couples massage. The spa concierge had been so apologetic about the sauna lock-in that she'd added an extra half hour to our treatment. "We survived death. It can only go uphill from here."

I pushed him into a nearby bush.

It was pure pettiness on my part, but it felt good. If it weren't for him, I would be sitting happily in my office in New York, putting out fires instead of "relaxing."

To my disgruntlement, Xavier didn't fall; he merely stumbled into the hedge, and his laugh followed us into our massage room, where I made a point not to look at him as we disrobed. I'd already seen him half naked in the sauna, but it was hard to ignore the glimpses of tanned skin and sculpted muscle out of the corner of my eye.

The fact he was built like a Greek god when he did nothing except lounge around and party proved there was no justice in the universe.

We settled on our respective tables in silence. I couldn't see him, but I could *feel* him two feet away. His presence filled the room, unearthing memories from our short-lived but unnerving sauna adventure.

There'd been a moment, just one, when I looked at Xavier and my heart skipped a beat.

Who did you really go see?

There'd also been a moment, just one, when I almost answered truthfully. Maybe it was the lack of judgment in his face...or maybe the heat had melted my brain. That was far more likely.

My lids drifted closed as our massage therapists reentered the room and worked out our knots, but I couldn't shut off my brain.

How many emails had piled up in my inbox in the past hour? I'd never gone this long without checking my phone. What if my office was on fire? That was the thing about working in a skyscraper. You were subject to the idiocy of other tenants, many of whom didn't understand the basic tenets of fire safety.

Speaking of idiocy, what if Asher Donovan crashed another car? Did Jillian remember to send Ayana our terms of engagement? Was Isabella feeding The Fish properly?

Isabella wasn't an idiot, but I had specific instructions for taking care of my pet goldfish, and she tended to get lost in her own world when she was in the middle of writing a book.

Anxiety spurred my heart rate into an agitated gallop.

"You're very stressed," my therapist said softly. Her hands worked magic on my back and shoulders, but the poor woman would need a full week to loosen all my knots.

"I'm from New York," I said as an explanation. Everyone was stressed. The only people who weren't were the lazy—

"That's not an excuse." Xavier's interjection destroyed my cocoon of attempted bliss. "I'm from New York, and I don't walk around with headaches every day."

I lifted my head to glare at him, but my therapist's warning *tsk* forced me back down. "First of all, you're not from New York. You're from Bogotá. Second of all, you know nothing about my health. Third of all—"

"Turn over, please," my therapist said.

I obeyed with more force than necessary. "*Third of all*, you're not stressed because you don't do anything. You just sit there and spend your family's money and look pretty."

It was harsh, but a trust fund kid lecturing me was my last straw. Yes, I'd also grown up with money and all the privileges that came with it, but I gave that up when I left my family. Everything I had now, I'd earned.

Xavier never had to work for a single thing in his life. He had no right criticizing my choices, stress levels, or anything about me.

"So," he said, "you think I'm pretty."

"You—"

"Breathe." My massage therapist pressed down on my shoulders. "That's it. Release the tension from your shoulders..."

Her gentle tone slowly smoothed the edges of my irritation. I inhaled a deep breath and swallowed an acerbic reply.

I prided myself on maintaining my composure at all times, but Xavier was the only person who could make me lose my cool.

"Seriously, you have enough money to step back and let your staff take the reins," he said. "Why kill yourself at your job?"

Don't take the bait.

"I like my job." For the most part. But between Xavier and Asher, who had a penchant for fast cars and reckless driving, I was pushing my friends' therapy skills to the limit.

I used to have a professional (non-massage) therapist, but she retired and I've hated every new one I tried after her. Maybe I should resume my search. God knew I needed one.

"What do you like about it?" Xavier must've missed the memo that massages were meant to be *silent*.

"Everything."

"Bullshit. You don't like me."

His response was so frank and unexpected, I almost smiled. Almost.

"Fine. I like fixing things. Solving problems no one else can solve." Crisis management was only part of my job, but it gave me the biggest thrill. Writing press releases and managing media relations was fine, but I could do those things in my sleep.

"So you like to be needed."

I turned my head before my therapist could stop me. Xavier met my gaze with a knowing one of his own, and…there it was again. A little skip in my chest, followed by the unnerving sense that he could see right past the shields I'd painstakingly built over the years.

Then I blinked, and the moment was gone.

I faced forward again and waited for my heartbeat to normalize before I spoke. "Don't you get bored of doing nothing?"

I didn't touch on the keenness of his observation or the truth behind it.

I expected Xavier to brush off my question with his usual flippancy, but he answered with surprising honesty.

"Sometimes," he said, sounding uncharacteristically subdued. "But I'm good at doing nothing, so I stick to it. It's better than fucking things up."

I closed my eyes, listening to the faint crash of waves outside the window and the deep, steady breaths of the man next to me.

We didn't talk again after that.

Three hours, one facial, one lunch, and one extremely awkward aromatherapy soak for two later, I emerged from the spa marginally less stressed than when I walked in.

I hated to admit it, but the day had helped. I even stopped worrying about my neglected inbox halfway through ignoring Xavier while we floated in a lavender-scented tub together.

Neither of us brought up anything substantial after our massage talk, but I kept thinking about what he'd said.

I'm good at doing nothing, so I stick to it. It's better than fucking things up.

Xavier was unmotivated, but he wasn't dumb. If he tried, he could probably run circles around the people sitting in the Castillo Group's boardroom. Plus, he had an ample cushion of money and connections.

Why would he be so afraid of screwing up that he *didn't* try?

I cast a sideways glance at him. He didn't make any quips on our walk back to the villa, but my concern over his silence gave way to horror when we reached our home for the week.

"What...?" My mouth parted as I stared at the sprawling building.

When we left that morning, it'd been a peaceful oasis of pale stone and floor-to-ceiling windows. Now, it resembled a frat house. Spanish music blasted from deep within the interior, and the scent of booze overpowered the wildflowers surrounding the entrance.

A pretty brunette in a bikini raced through the half-open door and shrieked as a Chris Hemsworth lookalike doused her in champagne. Squeals and laughter echoed from deeper in the villa, followed by the splash of someone jumping into the pool.

"Xavi! There you are!" the Hemsworth lookalike called out. "Hope you don't mind that we started the party without you."

I wheeled around and glared at Xavier.

"I forgot to mention my friends are joining us." He had the grace to look embarrassed. "One of them just broke up with his girlfriend. We're trying to make him feel better."

Was he freaking *kidding* me?

"He can feel better in his own villa. This is a shared space." I pointed at the building and tried to breathe through the bubbling anger in my chest. "I didn't consent to having a bunch of strangers overrun my hotel room for the week. Shut. It. Down."

"I would, but my friends are, uh, *difficult* to dislodge once they've settled into a party." Xavier shrugged. "It'd be a waste of energy. Trust me."

The knots my massage therapist spent ninety minutes kneading out returned with a vengeance.

"Since they're *your* friends, that sounds like a *you* problem." A headache hammered at the sides of my skull. "I swear to God, Xavier, if they're not out of here in the next fifteen minutes, I'm calling the police and having them arrested for trespassing."

"Don't think that'll fly. One of them is the president's niece." Xavier paused. "President of Spain," he clarified.

"Then the *president* can come here and bail her out." I jabbed a finger at his chest, so pissed I could barely see straight. "This wasn't what I agreed to when we made our deal. Figure out a way to fix this, or I'm leaving on the next flight out."

His insouciance fell away, replaced by what looked like true regret. "Shit, I'm sorry, Luna. I honestly forgot that..." He glanced at the villa. "Look, I'll make you a new deal."

"No."

Xavier pressed on, undeterred. "Let them stay today. I wasn't kidding when I said it's impossible to move them after they get the party going. I already see two people passed out in the hall." A quick peek confirmed his statement. "In return, I promise not to throw another party for the next month unless you've approved it."

"That's not a good deal," I said flatly. He must take me for a naïve newborn.

"Two months."

"No."

"*Three* months. Come on," he coaxed. "Think of how much

easier your job would be if you didn't have to worry about me setting a bar on fire or getting shut down by the cops."

I pursed my lips. Xavier's parties tended to spiral out of control. All the bad press he'd gotten in the past was linked to one of his infamous soirées; if I could prevent him from hosting them in the first place, that'd be a load off my plate.

"No unapproved parties for six months," I said, making up my mind. Giving up one afternoon was worth months of potential peace and quiet down the road—hopefully. "We're putting it in writing, and your friends have to be out by midnight tonight."

"Six months? Are you fucking kid—" Xavier's mouth snapped shut when I narrowed my eyes. "Fine," he muttered. "You have a deal."

"Good." I spun back around toward the villa and prayed I hadn't just made a huge mistake. "I can't believe you invited me on a heartbreak trip with your friends."

"Hey, a trip can serve multiple purposes. The more the merrier!" he called after me as I stormed inside.

Prickles crawled over my skin at the cushions littering the floor and the half-empty alcohol bottles crowding every available surface. The knickknacks I'd reorganized to geometric perfection that morning had been knocked askew, and scantily clad men and women were...

Oh God. I did *not* need to see that.

I averted my eyes from the couple on the couch and zeroed in on a familiar face. "Luca?"

Luca Russo blinked at me from the corner, his surprise mirroring my own. "*Sloane?* What are you doing here?"

"I could ask you the same question."

Luca was my best friend Vivian's brother-in-law. The second son of the massive Russo luxury goods fortune, he'd been a mainstay in Xavier's circle until he cleaned up his act a few years ago, stopped partying, and started working for his family's company. Apparently, he'd fallen off the wagon again.

"I'm here to mend my broken heart." He slumped dramatically in his armchair. "Leaf and I broke up. She moved to a goat farm in Tennessee."

"Isn't she vegan?"

"She's there to save the goats."

"Oh." I didn't know Luca or Leaf well enough to muster more than an inkling of sympathy. Besides, I'd never liked his ex-girlfriend's holier-than-thou, New Age hippie vibes. "How tragic."

Now the poor goats had to put up with her savior complex.

"S'okay. That's why I'm here. To feel better." He took a swig of beer. "Oh, hey, Xavi."

Xavier came up beside me. "I forgot you know each other." There was a strange note in his voice, but when I glanced at him, he turned away.

"Here." He handed me an unopened bottle from a nearby table. "I have a feeling you're going to need this."

I couldn't do it anymore.

After I rejected Xavier's beer, made him a hastily drawn-up contract for our latest deal, locked myself in my room, read about the sixth principle of crisis communications, and confirmed with the resort and every other resort within a five-mile radius that there were no available rooms for the night, I gave up trying to pretend Xavier and Friends didn't exist.

I wanted to stay in my room, but I couldn't stop thinking about what Xavier said during our massage.

So you like to be needed.

Who didn't like to be needed? Being needed meant we were

good at and good *for* something. People didn't leave those they needed. It wasn't the same as being loved, but it was better than nothing.

There was a lot to unpack there, but since I had no desire to do that, I finally wandered outside and joined the party, if only so I didn't have to be alone with my thoughts.

The festivities had migrated from our living room to the private beach after sunset, and the bonfire made it easy for me to locate the heart of the party. Xavier's eyebrows shot up when he saw me, but he didn't stop me from downing my first, second, *or* third glass of sangria.

If I were to survive the night around him and his friends, I needed to be (very) drunk.

However, despite my presence, I held off on actually participating in the revelry until Luca spotted me and attempted to drag me from my seat by the bonfire.

"You have to dance," he insisted. "It's one of the island's rules."

I didn't budge. "Rules are meant to be broken."

"I didn't expect a cliché from you, of all people." His cheeks were flushed from alcohol, and a sparkle brightened his eyes.

Realization dawned. He was flirting with me.

With his dark hair and olive skin, Luca was certainly good-looking enough, but I searched for any flicker of attraction and found none. Even if I *were* attracted to him, I had no interest in being a rebound hookup.

"I like to surprise people every once in a while." I glanced across the bonfire and caught Xavier's eye.

He was sandwiched between the brunette from earlier and her twin. He appeared uninterested in what they were saying, but when he saw me looking, his gaze flicked to Luca before he turned to face one of the twins.

He'd left me alone since we arrived at the beach, which I was obviously grateful for. It wasn't like I needed his company.

"Still, you can't sit on the sidelines for this song." Luca's voice brought my attention back to him. "It's practically illegal."

The twins burst into laughter at something Xavier said. His dimples flashed, and one of them placed her hand on his arm.

I suppressed an eye roll. I doubted anything he said was *that* funny.

I tried to tune out the party around me and focus on the sound of the waves, but Luca continued pestering me until my headache reached new heights and I'd do anything, even freaking dance, to get him to stop.

I should've stayed in my room.

"Stop talking." I held up a hand, cutting him off mid-sentence. "If I dance for *one* song, will you go away?"

Maybe that was a bit rude, but I was grumpy, annoyed, and not nearly drunk enough. I wasn't in the mood to coddle anyone's feelings.

Luca appeared unfazed by my sharp response. "Sure."

"Fine." I stood, my irritation escalating when the twins laughed again at something else Xavier said. You'd think he was a one-man *Saturday Night Live* show by the way they were carrying on. "But I need another drink first."

Luca and I swung by the beach bar for the resort's signature cocktail, which was thankfully stronger than the sangria. However, my renewed buzz wasn't enough to erase my self-consciousness when we hit the makeshift dance floor.

I'd never been a great dancer. I took the requisite ballet lessons as a kid and stopped when Madame Olga dismissed me as one of her "most difficult" pupils. I tried ballroom dancing when I was older and didn't fare much better.

When I went out with my friends, I could lose myself in our group and not worry about how stupid I looked, but I didn't have Vivian, Isabella, or Alessandra to shield me here. It was just me, the music, and a dozen pair of eyes that were inexplicably trained on me.

"Whoa." Luca half laughed, half winced when I accidentally stepped on his foot. He steadied me with a hand on my hip. "Maybe we shouldn't have gotten that drink earlier."

My cheeks heated. The song hadn't finished, and I already regretted my decision.

"It's okay." Despite his drunkenness, Luca picked up on my embarrassment. "Here." He placed his other hand on my hip. "Let's try—"

"Don't bother."

My spine stiffened at the familiar voice behind me.

"You're so drunk, you'll be lucky if you don't take both of you down." An edge ran beneath Xavier's otherwise affable tone. "Why don't you sober up and come back?"

Luca glanced at his friend, then at me. He dropped his hands and stepped back. "Good idea."

I crossed my arms and didn't move while Xavier came around to face me. "Here I thought you were perfect at everything." The edge was gone, replaced by a teasing lilt. "I need to give you dance lessons. Can't have you making me look bad in front of my friends."

He'd changed out of his earlier outfit into a white linen shirt and casual pants. Here, in the glow of the firelight, with his hair tousled by the wind and his muscles loose from drink and relaxation, he was disturbingly, devastatingly attractive.

Freed from the weight of sobriety, I could even admit that my dislike of him partly stemmed from envy. What was it like to live life so carefree every day? To not worry about being perceived by others or being good enough, successful enough, *impactful* enough to justify my existence?

My throat dried before I shook off the unwanted thoughts.

"Look bad?" I covered up the momentary lapse in my defenses with a defiant chin tilt. "I'm the one who apparently can't dance, not you."

"We can change that. I've been told I'm an excellent instructor."

"Doubtful."

"You always underestimate me."

"And you always provoke me."

He gave a casual shrug. "I like it when you get mad. Proves you're not an ice queen after all."

My buzz disappeared fast enough for me to feel the punch of his words.

If you weren't such an ice queen all the time, maybe I wouldn't have gone looking elsewhere.

She's hot, but I bet she's frigid in bed...

For God's sake, Sloane, smile. Why can't you look happy for once?

The pressure returned. A lump crawled into my throat, but as always, my eyes remained dry.

No wonder people called me an ice queen. I couldn't even show emotion properly.

Xavier must've noticed the sudden shift in my mood because his smile vanished. "Hey, I wasn't—"

"I have to go." I pushed past him, my chest tight.

His hand touched my shoulder. "Sloane—"

"Don't touch me, and do *not* follow me." I injected my trademark coldness into my words. "Enjoy the rest of the party."

I shrugged him off and didn't stop walking until I'd locked myself in my bathroom and turned the shower on at full blast.

I didn't care that I'd already showered a few hours ago. I needed something to drown out the noise in my head.

I pressed my forehead against the tile and closed my eyes.

I stayed there until the lump in my throat dissolved, and as droplets of water cascaded down my face, I pretended they were tears.

CHAPTER 7

I DIDN'T SLEEP WELL FOR THE SECOND NIGHT IN A ROW.

Instead of the bridge dream, I was haunted by images of Sloane's face before she left last night.

What the hell had I said wrong? She usually took my comments in stride, and she never left a conversation when I had the upper hand.

She couldn't be that upset about a stupid bad-dancer joke, right?

My foul mood worsened when I woke to an empty villa. Her luggage was still in her room, but she was a ghost from morning to early evening.

I tried to put Sloane out of my mind and focus on Luca. He'd been pretty bummed since he and Leaf broke up, though my sympathy for him had dwindled when I saw him flirting with my fucking publicist at the beach.

She wasn't even his type.

I brooded over my drink while my friends engaged in their usual shenanigans at the resort's private beach club.

I should be having the time of my life, but ennui had grabbed hold of me and refused to let go. I'd seen it all and done it all. After the initial rush of a good time, these parties were all the same.

I could've given the club owner some tips on how to improve. The sound system wasn't picking up the music's underlying bass, and the girl-to-guy ratio was off. The decor, the entertainment, the food...they were good, not great, but how people ran their business wasn't my business, so I kept my mouth shut.

Don't you get bored of doing nothing? Sloane's question echoed in my head.

I pushed it aside, downed my drink and faced Luca, who lounged next to me by the pool, nursing a hangover and a beer. The sun had set, but the beach club was just getting into the swing of things. "Dante know you're hanging out with us again?"

Luca's brother and CEO of the Russo Group, the multibillion-dollar luxury goods conglomerate, wasn't a fan of anyone in our circle.

Honestly, I didn't blame him. If I'd had a younger brother, I wouldn't want him hanging out with me either.

"He's not my warden." Nevertheless, Luca glanced around like the intimidating older Russo was going to pop out from behind a potted plant. "I get vacation days like everyone else, and I can spend them however I like."

"Hmm."

"Speaking of which, where's Sloane?"

An unpleasant burn ignited in my chest. "Probably reading a boring nonfiction book somewhere. Why?"

Luca shrugged. "She's hot. She's single. I could use a distraction from the Leaf situation."

The burn exploded into a wildfire and set my teeth on my edge. "She's not the rebound type."

"How do you know?"

"I just do." I slammed my empty drink on the side table. "Go for the Daugherty twins. They're looking for a good time."

"Can't. Their family is in textiles, which reminds me of goats, which reminds of Leaf."

For fuck's sake. "What about Evelyn? She just broke up with her boyfriend. You can rebound together."

"Nah. I hooked up with her years ago." Luca stared up at the sky with a drunk, dreamy expression. "I think Sloane works best. She's so...*shit*!" He bolted upright when I knocked over a champagne ice bucket and its contents spilled across his chest. "What the fuck, man?"

"Sorry. Must've had more to drink than I thought." I stood. I didn't know why the idea of him and Sloane bothered me so much, but I knew I needed to get out of here before I did something more unforgivable than dousing my friend in ice. "I'm calling it a night."

"Wait! What about..."

The crowd drowned out the rest of Luca's words as I stormed out of the beach club and toward the villa.

I'd convinced Sloane to come to Spain, hoping it would break her from her comfort zone, but I was turning out to be the one in over my head.

Sloane

By the time I woke up, I'd already brushed off my moment of weakness from last night, but I wasn't in the mood to face Xavier or his friends—who were thankfully staying at their own villa instead of ours—so I actively avoided them all day.

I woke up at the crack of dawn for a hike, holed myself up in a conference room for lunch, and waited until Xavier left for the beach club before I snuck back to the villa.

It was early evening, so I had a few hours to myself before he returned. I was tempted to work, but I'd promised him I wouldn't, and a pesky sense of honor prevented me from going back on my word.

Instead, I curled up beneath a blanket in the living room and watched the Spanish rom-com onscreen with increasing disgust.

"*Te amo*," the actor whispered in Spanish. English subtitles translated what he said. "*Nunca te dejaré.*" *I'll never leave you.*

"Ugh." I scribbled furiously in my review notebook. "Film an after-the-movie special and see if that's *really* true."

Romantic comedy was the most unrealistic genre in Hollywood. Falling off a seventh-floor balcony and getting up a minute later to chase after the bad guy was more believable than workplace rivals who suddenly "discover" they have feelings for each other and live happily ever after.

The concept of happily ever after was the biggest scam since the advent of the overpriced college textbook industry.

"It's not *The Bachelor*, Luna. The after-the-movie special would just be the actors leaving set."

My head snapped up.

Xavier leaned against the entryway, wearing a pair of linen pants, an amused expression, and nothing else.

"It's rude to sneak up on someone," I said, my pulse pounding from his unexpected interruption. *Give me a heart attack, why don't you?* "And for God's sake, put on a shirt. You're not Matthew McConaughey."

His laugh did nothing to ease my annoyance.

Two minutes later, he dropped onto the seat next to mine, fully clothed. "Happy? Now you won't be distracted by my incredible physique."

"No, I'll just suffocate beneath the weight of your inflated ego."

"There are worse ways to go."

I sighed, my prospects of a quiet, peaceful evening going up in smoke. "Isn't there a party at the beach club? Why are you here?"

Our deal prevented him from hosting parties without my approval, but they didn't stop him from attending them. That was another oversight on my part. *I'm losing my touch*. Something about Spain muddled my usually sharp instincts, and it put me on edge.

"I was at the club all day, and I wanted a change of scenery." Xavier glanced at my notebook. "What have you been up to?"

"Relaxing," I said pointedly.

"Touché." He rubbed a hand over his mouth, his expression conflicted. "Listen, about last night...I'm sorry if I hurt your feelings. You aren't *that* bad of a dancer."

I would've laughed at the idea that I was upset over my dancing skills if I hadn't been so thrown off by his apology. So few people apologized and meant it that a simple *I'm sorry* stripped away my knee-jerk defensiveness.

"Thank you," I said stiffly. I didn't correct his assumption about the source of my upset.

"You're welcome." His eyes crinkled at the corners when I didn't tack on a snarky reply. "Wait, are we having a bonding moment? Is this the start of a new Xavier and Sloane era?"

"Don't push it." I tapped my pen against my notebook. "By the way, how's Luca doing?" I'd texted Vivian earlier about seeing him in Spain, and she'd mentioned how concerned she and Dante were about him. I'd promised to update her on his well-being if and when I could.

Xavier's dimples disappeared. "Fine." He shifted, his leg brushing mine. I was so startled by the contact, I almost yanked my knee away before I caught myself. "I didn't realize you two were so close."

"We're not. I was just curious." A burn spread from my knee up to my stomach. *Huh*. I knew I should've worn more sunscreen while hiking. This was not normal.

"Hmm." A shadow crossed Xavier's face. He opened his mouth, then gave a small shake of his head like he'd changed his mind about whatever he was going to say. "So what's the movie about?"

"Office rivals who fall in love. Your basic rom-com." A whiff of his cologne floated into my lungs, and I wished it didn't smell as good as it did. People like Xavier should *only* smell like day-old pizza and beer. It would be a more accurate representation of his lifestyle than this clean, woodsy thing he had going on.

"I didn't peg you as a rom-com lover." His leg brushed mine again, and I glared at it for a second before answering.

Note to self: Buy more sunscreen ASAP. The continued burn on my skin wasn't normal.

"I'm not. I *hate*-watch them." My drawer of handwritten movie reviews at home attested to that.

"Right. And how many have you *hate*-watched so far?"

Hundreds, but he didn't need to know that.

"Shut up and watch the movie."

However, as I rewound the parts I'd missed when he showed up, a teeny-tiny part of me was grateful for his company, unwanted leg grazes and all.

It was a little sad to watch rom-coms alone while on vacation in Spain, even for me.

I never had movie nights with anyone other than my friends, but Xavier was a surprisingly fun companion. He was mostly quiet, but every once in a while, he'd toss out a blithe remark about the plot or acting that made me smirk.

As a client, he was difficult, but as a person, he was decent.

I'd never heard him raise his voice once in our time working together. When he found out about his father's cancer diagnosis, he hadn't cried, and when an ex leaked lurid photos of them to the press, he hadn't sought vengeance the way I would've. He was unflappable no matter what life threw his way.

Then again, maybe his preternatural calm wasn't a good thing. Maybe it was a different manifestation of the same issues that kept me guarded from anyone outside my inner circle.

Ugh. The only thing sadder than watching a rom-com alone on vacation was psychoanalyzing Xavier while watching said rom-com.

"What do you keep writing in your notebook?" he asked during the movie's obligatory post-breakup montage of the couple's relationship.

A needle of self-consciousness pricked my skin. I debated lying but eventually opted for the truth. "I write reviews of all the rom-coms I watch."

It was nothing to be ashamed of. If Roger Ebert could do it, so could I, but nerves rattled in my veins when Xavier leaned over to read my notes.

"The film strives for charm but falls flat in its attempt," he read aloud. "Although fiction generally requires some suspension of disbelief, the utter ridiculousness of the balcony scene gives me so much secondhand embarrassment I want to bleach my memory so I never have to think about it again. I have more chemistry with my bedroom lamp than the lead actors have with each other, and the dialogue sounds like that of a parody rather than an actual romantic comedy. If AI wrote and performed a movie, it would look like this." He was quiet for a second before looking at me. "What the hell have you been doing with your bedroom lamp?"

Laughter rustled my throat, so quick and unexpected it took me a second to realize the sound came from me.

Shock flashed across Xavier's face, followed by a slow bloom of pleasure. An answering warmth pooled in my stomach.

"Turning it on," I said in response to his question. I cringed before the words fully left my mouth. "Oh God. That was terrible." His howl of laughter drowned out my next words. "Do not *ever* tell anyone I said that. I—*stop laughing*."

"Don't worry." His shoulders convulsed as he wiped tears from his eyes. "It'll be our little secret."

"It wasn't that funny," I grumbled. I tried to maintain my sternness, but his amusement was contagious, and soon another smile cracked my face.

If someone had told me two days ago that I'd have a movie night with Xavier Castillo and *enjoy* it, I would've asked what drugs they were on, but Friday's gala and visit with Penny seemed like a lifetime ago.

Perhaps that was why I rarely went on vacation. It lulled us into a false sense of security only to thrust us back into our regular lives, where we were confronted with a world that kept spinning without us and the realization that our presence didn't matter at all in the grand scheme of things.

My mood sobered.

"You know rom-coms aren't supposed to be realistic." Xavier wasn't over my review. "They're supposed to be entertaining."

"They would be more entertaining if they were realistic." I pointed at the end credits rolling across the screen. "What are the chances longtime rivals would fall in love just because they're thrown together on a work project?"

"Less than a hundred and more than zero."

"Your optimism is nauseating."

"I think that might be the gallon of ice cream you ate." He cocked an eyebrow at the half-empty carton of French vanilla melting on the coffee table.

Embarrassment crawled over my face, hot and itchy. "You drink your beer, I eat my ice cream. Now, since the movie is over, it's time for us to part ways and go to sleep."

Xavier stared at me like I'd asked him to fly to the moon. "Are you joking? It's only nine." He tapped his phone. "The night's barely started."

I hated how he always made me feel like a buzzkill, but a girl had to draw the line somewhere. "I have no desire to get wasted."

"Who said anything about getting wasted?" He stood and extended a hand to me. "Come on. It's time for your dance lessons."

I crossed my arms. "Absolutely not." That was even worse than getting wasted.

"So you enjoy looking like a malfunctioning robot every time you dance?"

"I don't..." *Breathe.* I counted to three and tried again. "I rarely dance. Therefore, I don't need lessons."

"You go out with your friends all the time, so that's not true... unless you're afraid of failing." Xavier dropped his hand and shrugged. "I understand. No one succeeds at everything."

That fucker. He was good.

He was also clearly baiting me, but the competitiveness that'd fueled my rise in the cutthroat PR world bristled at his taunt. Once it was triggered, there was no going back.

"Don't think I don't know what you're doing." I stood, ignoring memories of Madame Olga's pinched disapproval and Xavier's present-day shit-eating grin. "But I'll allow it just so I can wipe that smug look off your face. Let's go."

Who was to say I hadn't developed a talent for movement overnight?

Xavier was laughing now, but I was going to make him eat his words.

CHAPTER 8

Sloane

"I TAKE BACK WHAT I SAID ABOUT THE MALFUNCTIONing robot," Xavier said. "I don't want to insult robots."

I dropped my arms and glared at him. "If I had a better teacher, I'd be *doing* better."

We were on the villa's terrace, where heated lamps warded off the late-night chill and portable speakers played a medley of local and international music. Xavier had insisted the outdoors would help me "relax," but so far, I was embarrassed, frustrated, and no closer to improving my dance skills than when we started my lessons an hour earlier.

"You have to loosen up." Xavier brushed off my indictment of his teaching abilities. "Dancing is about movement. You can't move properly if you're imitating a petrified piece of wood."

"I'm loosened up." A defensive note crept into my voice. "Also, might I remind you I could be sleeping right now instead of enduring your insults?"

I should walk away because there was nothing worse than trying my best and failing, but the competitor in me refused to give up.

I was Sloane Kensington. I didn't fail, and I didn't quit. (The only reason I'd stopped my childhood ballet lessons was because I outgrew my age group. Also, I was pretty sure I'd given Madame Olga an ulcer when she retired).

"Yet you're here." Xavier placed his hands on my hips.

I stiffened, every muscle turning rigid at the warmth seeping through my dress.

"See what I mean about petrified wood?" He shook his head. "Pretend you're back at the spa. You're getting a massage, your muscles are loose...now move your hips like this. No, the other way." His touch seared my skin and distracted me from his instructions. He probably had a fever from walking around shirtless all the time. He should really get that checked out. "Move them in a circle, Luna, not a square."

"It *is* a circle."

"No offense, but you might need to brush up on your geometry." Xavier's grip tightened, stilling my movements. "What are you thinking about?"

"Moving my hips in a circle."

"That's your problem," he said. "You shouldn't be thinking about that."

"You just said—"

"You have to *feel* the movement. The more you think, the less natural it looks."

My teeth ground together in frustration."I'm sorry, but I like thinking. It's something I try to do on a daily basis."

"That explains a lot." Xavier released me and stepped back.

A cool wave of relief coasted through my chest, followed by an alarming pinch of...disappointment? No, that couldn't be right.

I waited for him to continue the lesson, but he simply studied me with that deep, dark gaze.

Tousled black hair fell carelessly over one eye, shielding his thoughts as the silence stretched into uncomfortable territory. There was a pensiveness to him that I rarely saw, and it molded his features into a devastating portrait Michelangelo himself would've been proud of.

The dramatic slant of his cheekbones, the thick dark brows, the sculpted mouth that seemed infinitely more inviting when it wasn't wearing a provocative smile...his face dared me to look away, and I couldn't.

Electric awareness dripped into the air and snuffed out the oxygen.

Xavier and I had been alone many times before, but this was the first time I recognized the danger in him. Beneath the layers of indolent self-possession, there was a man who could set my world aflame if he wanted.

God, what is wrong with me? I'd gone years without reacting to his presence in any discernible way (unless irritation counted), but ever since we arrived in Spain, my shields had slipped. Maybe it was the brief glimpses into a realer, more vulnerable side of Xavier—the side that wasn't all about drinking and sleeping—or maybe our spa day had rewired my brain.

Whatever it was, I didn't like it.

Self-preservation punctured my awareness right as he spoke again. "Let's get a drink."

He turned and walked toward the bar cart nestled in the corner.

The remaining static fizzled into nothing as I tried to keep up with the whiplash. "What about the lessons?"

"We'll resume after the break." Xavier grabbed two glasses and started mixing drinks right there in the middle of the terrace.

My eyebrows skyrocketed. I'd never seen him make cocktails before, but he moved with the fluid grace of a seasoned bartender.

"So much for not getting wasted," I groused when he handed me an admittedly delicious-looking pale orange drink.

"It's one drink. You won't get wasted unless you have the tolerance of a five-year-old." Xavier's mouth tilted at the corner. "*Salud.*"

I kept my eyes on his as I took a small sip. Fuck, that was good. "Did you make this up on the spot?"

I didn't recognize the taste, and yesterday's party had cleared out half the bar, leaving only a handful of ingredients for him to work with.

"You make do with what you have." A roll of his shoulders, followed by a teasing smile. "I'm naming it the Sloane. Bitter at first but with a sweet aftertaste. Just like someone I know."

"You don't know how I taste."

His smile took on a decidedly more wicked slant. "Not yet."

My body reacted, instantly and viscerally, like he'd flipped the *on* switch in a long-untouched room.

My breasts tightened as heat flickered between my thighs, turning my body warm and languid. Less-than-innocent images flashed through my mind before I wrestled them into a box and slammed the lid shut.

No. Absolutely not.

I could not be having this reaction to Xavier, of all people. This was what I got for ending my sex-only situationship with Mark. If I'd slept with him before I left, I wouldn't be so wound up.

"How's delusion treating you?" I asked, striving for indifference even as I strangled my glass.

"Quite well." Xavier's eyes gleamed like he could reach inside me and pick out every filthy, inappropriate thought. He leaned against the wall, seemingly unaware of the havoc he'd just wreaked. "Since we're still on break, let's try something else. Truth or dare. You choose."

"Truth or dare? What are we, twelve?"

"It's a timeless game." He arched one brow. "Unless you're scared."

Fuck it. Playing the stupid game was better than humiliating myself dancing again. "Truth."

"If you could be anything other than a publicist, what would you be?"

I blinked. It wasn't a question I'd expected, nor was it one I'd given much thought to before. "Nothing. I love my job."

And I did. Despite the frustrations, the breakneck pace, and the clients who made me want to tear my hair out sometimes, I thrived under pressure. There was no downtime for reflection. There were only problems I could solve and solutions I could implement.

People could call me a bitch or an ice queen, but there was one unshakeable, undeniable truth—I was the best at what I did. Hands down. That was why CEOs, celebrities, and socialites paid me the big bucks. They didn't all like me personally, but they respected me and they needed me.

So you like to be needed.

Xavier's observation floated to the surface before I brushed it aside. So what? *Everyone* liked to be needed. Those who said they didn't were lying.

"Nothing? There's not a single career you would consider outside PR?" He looked unconvinced. "I call bullshit."

"Maybe I'd be a surgeon," I allowed. It was another high-pressure, fast-paced career. I had steady hands and I wasn't squeamish about blood. Commanding an operating room and saving lives could be exciting.

Xavier's mouth quirked. "Unsurprising."

"I'll take that as a compliment." I finished my drink. "Your turn. Truth or dare."

"Truth."

Interesting. I would've pegged him as a dare guy.

"Similar question," I said. "If you had to choose an *actual* career, what would you choose?" I was genuinely curious. Xavier had never expressed an ambition for any type of job. What made someone like him tick?

He languished in the shadow of the villa, untouched by the moon or terrace lights, but his eyes sparked at my question.

"One I'm good at," he said.

"Like?"

A cloud passed over his expression before his smile reappeared. "Like teaching you how to dance. I think we've taken a long enough break." He pushed off the wall and poured two shots of whiskey. "One more for courage. *Salud.*"

His hand brushed mine as he handed me my shot, and a tiny jolt zipped down my spine.

The whiskey burned smooth enough to dampen any concerns over my body's strange reactions tonight. "You didn't answer my question truthfully," I said.

Warmth buzzed over my skin and pooled in my veins. I held my liquor pretty well, but the drinks were *strong*, and I didn't resist the intoxication as fiercely as I normally did.

It felt good to let my control slip. Just a little bit.

"I wasn't lying when I said I would choose a career I'd be good at." A smile still played at the corners of his mouth, but his eyes contained a soft warning. "I even gave you an example."

"Semantics. You don't play fair."

"I never do." He came around behind me. His hands found my hips, and my breaths slowed beneath the weight of renewed static. "Let's try this again."

The music changed to something sultrier, easier to follow.

Maybe it was the new rhythm. Maybe it was the alcohol. Or

maybe it was my attempt to focus on anything *except* Xavier that loosened my inhibitions.

Whatever it was, it worked. I didn't hyperfocus on moving exactly the way I should, and the ironic result was that my movements flowed so much more easily.

I wouldn't win competitions anytime soon, but I no longer resembled a malfunctioning robot, as someone had so rudely pointed out earlier.

"Much better." Xavier's murmur grazed the nape of my neck, eliciting an involuntary shiver of pleasure. "There might be hope for you yet."

The seeds of a witty reply died on my tongue when he lowered his head so his face came next to mine. A delicious earthy scent seeped into my senses, heightening taste, smell, and touch until my mouth watered and I could feel every beat of his heart against my back.

I turned my head a fraction of an inch, just enough to meet his eyes.

I wished I hadn't.

Xavier's gaze smoldered like a lit match in the dark, scorching every inch of skin and any semblance of distance between us.

Beads of sweat dripped between my breasts. It was an inferno out here, but he was so close, and my head was so light, that if I just...

My lips parted.

His eyes darkened, and—

"*Luca!*" A girlish squeal from the neighboring villa tore between us. "That's my favorite bag!"

There was an indecipherable reply, followed by a riot of laughter and then...silence. But it was too late.

The interruption snapped me out of whatever trance Xavier's drinks/unholy magic/suspiciously glorious cologne put me under.

I jerked away from him, the loss of body warmth as sobering as the bowl of ice water I'd thrown on him mere days ago.

What was I *doing*?

He was my client, and I'd almost…he'd almost…

Xavier stared at me, his expression unreadable. If it weren't for the heavy rise and fall of his chest, I would've thought him unmoved by what just happened—or didn't happen.

My heart crashed against my ribcage, but I lifted my chin, broke eye contact, and forced myself to walk calmly into the villa without another word.

He didn't stop me, and as I closed my bedroom door behind me and slumped to the floor, I hated how a tiny part of me wished he had.

CHAPTER 9

Xavier

FUCK.

Fuck, fuck, triple fuck.

It wasn't the most mature response, but it was the only one that accurately summed up my situation.

It'd been thirty-six hours since my movie night with Sloane.

Thirty-six hours since our dance lessons.

Thirty-six hours since I'd discovered how perfectly her curves fit beneath my palms and how much more intoxicating her scent was compared to even the finest whiskey.

It was knowledge I could've done without because now that I'd experienced it, I couldn't imagine not reliving it.

Unfortunately, the chances of that were slim, considering how badly I'd fucked up.

If my friends hadn't interrupted us, I would've kissed her Sunday night, and I was certain, *positive*, that she would've let me. Otherwise, she wouldn't be avoiding me like I was the devil out to corrupt her.

I glanced down the beach to where Sloane sat by herself, reading that damn communications book of hers.

With my friends' help, I'd convinced her to join our boat excursion for the day, but she'd kept to herself the entire time.

Snorkeling in the crystal clear waters? No.

Taking advantage of the gourmet tapas and open bar? No.

Saying a single word to me after we boarded the yacht? Absolutely not.

"Where are you going?" Evelyn asked when I stood. Despite what Luca said about not hooking up with her again, the two of them had been all over each other all day.

I made a vague excuse and left my friends to their devices.

Other than Luca, I wasn't particularly close to anyone in the group. We partied together often, but I wouldn't spill my deepest, darkest secrets to them or anything. In fact, I was starting to resent their presence because they took time away from Sloane.

"It's a shame to waste a beautiful day like this," I said when I came within earshot of her. We'd stopped at one of Mallorca's hidden coves for lunch, and while we weren't the only ones on the beach, the early-October crowd was sparse enough to give us relative privacy.

"I have sun, sea, food, and a good book," she said without looking up. "I'm not wasting anything."

I sat beside her. "We have different definitions of *good*," I drawled.

She didn't respond.

When I was a kid, my friends and I used to argue over which superpower we'd rather have. I'd fluctuated between flight and invisibility, but right now, I'd sell my Ferrari for a glimpse into Sloane's thoughts.

Fuck it. There was only one way to get her attention.

"We should talk about our kiss."

Her movements stilled. Then slowly, deliberately, she slid a bookmark between the pages, closed her book, and looked up. It was seventy-eight degrees, but goosebumps coated my skin like I'd walked into a meat freezer.

"We never kissed." She enunciated each word with terrifying precision.

"Technically, no, but we almost did. So let's talk about it."

Sloane's knuckles whitened. "There's nothing to talk about. It was late, and we had too much to drink. Period."

"So it doesn't affect our relationship in any way."

"Of course not."

"Then you have no reason to avoid me."

Recognition of my trap flared in her eyes. "I'm not avoiding you."

"I didn't say you were," I replied easily. "I said you had no *reason* to."

Sloane inhaled an audible breath. I could practically see her counting to ten in her head. "Is there a point to this conversation?"

"I just wanted to clear the air about Sunday night."

"Consider it cleared."

"Good."

"Good."

We sat in silence for a second.

"Is there anything else?" Sloane asked pointedly.

"Sure. If you could have any superpower, what would it be?"

She closed her eyes and rubbed her temple. "Xavier..."

"Indulge me. This is what people do. Talk." I gestured between us. "We've worked together for years, and I don't even know your favorite food."

That was a lie.

I knew she loved sushi because it was neat and easy to eat on the go. I knew she preferred double cheeseburgers when she was on her period and steak, medium rare, at client dinners unless her client was vegetarian, in which case she ordered soup and salad.

She liked her wine white, her coffee black, and her gin with a splash of tonic.

I knew all of these things because despite her assumption that I paid attention to no one except myself, I couldn't *stop* noticing her if my life depended on it. Every detail, every moment, all filed and categorized in the Sloane cabinet of my mind.

I would never tell her any of that, though, because if there was one thing sure to send Sloane Kensington running, it was the possibility of intimacy.

"Fine," she said, bringing me back to the present. "I'd choose time travel so I could go back and fix any mistakes I make."

"But then your life wouldn't be what it is now."

She glanced away. "That's not necessarily a bad thing."

The crash of waves filled the silence.

From the outside, Sloane appeared to have the perfect life. She was beautiful, smart, and successful, and she counted some of the most powerful people in the world as either her friends or her clients.

But I, of all people, knew appearances were deceiving, and the shiniest surfaces often hid the ugliest secrets.

"If you had the chance, wouldn't you go back and change things in your past?" she asked.

My hand involuntarily fisted the towel. Regret swelled and collided with memories I thought I'd locked away long ago.

"Xavier!" The panic in my mom's voice bled through the roar of the flames. "¿Dónde estás mi hijo?"

He's just a kid. It was an accident...

If he'd been more responsible...

It should've been you.

The reek of smoke and charred wood filled my lungs. The beach cove closed around me, the steep cliffs forming prison walls and the glare of sun against sand whitening my vision.

Then I blinked and the nightmare receded, replaced by my friends' laughter in the background and the touch of concern on Sloane's face.

I loosened my grip on the towel and forced a smile. "Everyone would change something if they could." I still tasted ash on my tongue. I wanted to spit it out and drown it with beer, but I couldn't do that without raising suspicion. "Do you still talk to anyone from your family?"

It was the only topic I could think of that would divert Sloane's attention. She was sharp enough to pick up on the shift in my mood, but I didn't want to discuss the reason with her or anyone else. Ever.

As expected, her face shut down. "When I have to. Have you talked to your father recently?"

Touché.

She wasn't the only one who considered family relations a taboo subject.

"No. He's not exactly in the right state for friendly phone calls." Even before he'd fallen sick, he hadn't been a great communicator. With his business partners and friends, yes. With his only son? Not so much.

Sloane tilted her head, obviously trying to gauge my true feelings regarding my father's illness.

Good luck, considering even I didn't know how I felt.

He was the only direct family I had left, so I *should* have felt strongly about his potential death. Instead, I only felt numb, like I was watching an actor who looked like my father wither away on a movie screen.

My father and I had never been close, partly because he blamed me for my mother's death and partly because I blamed myself too.

Every time he looked at me, he saw the person who'd taken the love of his life away—and he couldn't do a damn thing about it because I was the only piece of her he had left.

Every time I looked at him, I saw disappointment, frustration, and resentment. I saw the parent who'd taken out his anger on me when I'd been too young to understand the complexities of grief, who'd given up on me and made me give up on myself before I even started.

"He'll pull through," Sloane said.

She didn't try to comfort me often, so I didn't ruin the moment by wondering if, maybe, things would be simpler if he didn't.

It was a terrible, ugly thought, the kind only monsters harbored, so I never uttered it out aloud. But it was always there, festering beneath the surface, waiting for the right moment to strike.

Sloane's phone lit up with a notification. I glimpsed a telltale email icon before she snatched her cell off the ground and the moment collapsed around us like a sand castle at high tide.

"No work," I reminded her.

"It's not work, it's..." Her skin took on the hue of bleached bone.

I straightened, concern washing away the remnants of unwanted memories. "What's wrong?"

"Nothing." She stood, her expression frozen. "I'll...I'll be right back."

Did she just stutter? Sloane *never* stuttered.

She walked away, leaving me to stare after her and wonder what kind of message was possibly bad enough to throw Sloane Kensington off her game.

CHAPTER 10

Sloane

YOUR SISTER IS PREGNANT.

Four words shouldn't have the power to nauseate me, but they did.

I reread the email for the dozenth time. Soon after I received it that afternoon, Xavier's friends decided they'd had enough of the cove. They'd wanted to sail to another beach, but I'd convinced Xavier to drop me off at the resort first. Thankfully, he'd done so without comment.

Now here I was hours later, sitting in my bed and staring at the first piece of direct correspondence I'd had from my father since the day I walked out of his office and out of my family.

Of *course* he would break his years-long silence for Georgia. She was my full sister, but we'd never clicked the way I did with Pen.

And now, she was pregnant.

I'd known it would happen eventually, but I hadn't expected it so soon.

The smoothie I'd forced down for dinner sloshed in my stomach as I read the rest of his message again.

In true George Kensington form (and yes, my sister was named after him), the message was stiffer than a freshly starched tuxedo at the Legacy Ball.

Sloane,

I'm writing to inform you that your sister is pregnant. Given the circumstances, it's time you make amends and release your childish grudge against an incident that occurred years ago. Pettiness is not an attractive trait.

Regards,
George Kensington III

I thought my indignation would've run out of fumes long ago, but it intensified with every reread.

It's time you make amends and give up your childish grudge.

Childish grudge? *Childish grudge?*

The phone creaked from the force of my grip. Trust my father to *still* pin the blame on me instead of his favorite.

Part of me recognized the clichéd irony of my situation. Poor little rich girl wasn't as loved as the golden child, the one who could smile and dance and charm anyone in the room. Georgia could cry like a normal human and act like the perfect socialite. She was the daughter my father had always wanted, and I was the disgrace.

If I were watching a movie starring me, I would scoff at myself, but this wasn't a movie. It was my life, and as much as I pretended it didn't bother me, my broken relationship with my family would always be a sore spot.

I tossed my phone on the bed and stood.

If I thought too hard about Georgia's present life, I'd start thinking about the past, and if I thought about the past...

No. I wasn't going there.

Determination hardened my nausea into steely resolve.

Fuck Georgia, fuck the past, and fuck my father's attempts to guilt me into apologizing for things *they'd* done wrong. It would be a cold day in hell before I crawled back to them.

I was doing just fine without them, thank you very much.

Pressure built behind my eyes, but I set my jaw and ignored it as I rifled through the closet for something to wear.

Most evenings, I preferred a quiet night in with a book, wine, and movies.

Not tonight.

Tonight, I wanted company.

Xavier

After I dropped Sloane off at our villa, my friends and I stayed out on the water until sunset. We grabbed room service at Luca's place before hitting up the resort's famous nightclub.

Objectively, the club had great music, great service, and great drinks. I would change a few things—the retro lighting design didn't fit with the futuristic vibes, and the layout of the VIP lounge didn't flow as well as it could've—but overall, it met my criteria for a memorable night out.

So why wasn't I enjoying myself?

"This is fun," Luca said. He and Evelyn had gotten into a fight earlier, so their whirlwind hookup was dead before it fully revived. "Right?"

"Yep." My enthusiasm rivaled that of a prisoner on his way to death row.

What was Sloane doing at the villa? Was she eviscerating some poor rom-com again? Her reviews were vicious, but I found the passion with which she wrote them oddly charming. She was so reserved all the time that it was nice to see an area in her life where she fully let herself go.

Luca said something else, but I barely heard him.

What the hell was in that email she'd gotten? She'd said it wasn't a work thing. Was it her family? Her friends? Her unconfirmed mystery lover? If only she were here so—

A flash of blond caught my eye.

I stilled, my gaze honing in on the newcomer turning heads.

Platinum hair. Ice-blue eyes. Legs that went on for miles. She looked exactly like Sloane, but it couldn't be her because... holy hell.

Heat crawled beneath my skin as she strode through the room, either unaware or unimpressed by the eyes following her.

Rich cobalt silk poured over her frame, baring her shoulders and stopping high enough on her thigh to tease the imagination without revealing too much. Silver heels added four inches to her height, and her skin glowed like pearls kissed by moonlight.

I grimaced. *Pearls kissed by moonlight?* Where the hell had that come from? I wasn't a poetic person in the least, but she looked good enough to inspire Shakespeare himself.

It wasn't her clothes or her body.

It was the way she moved, looser and more fluid than normal.

It was the way she carried herself, confident with a hint of vulnerability.

And it was the way she *commanded* attention without trying, like she was a fucking goddess among mortals.

I'd never seen anything like it.

She stopped in front of me and Luca, and my blood burned just a little hotter in her presence.

"Sloane Kensington entering a nightclub for fun." I hid my body's visceral reaction behind a lazy smile. "Someone check the temperature in hell. It must be freezing down there."

"Very original." Now that she was closer, I spotted a telltale flush on her cheeks. Was she already *drunk*?

It was so out of character, I could only stare, astonished, as she took a fresh drink from Luca's hand and downed it in one smooth pull.

I cast a warning glare at my friend. Now that Evelyn was out of the picture again, I didn't want him getting any more ideas about using Sloane as a rebound. She was a mutual acquaintance. Any relationship between them would be too complicated, obviously.

So would any relationship between us, which was why I switched to water and made a pointed effort to stay away from Sloane for the next hour as she circulated the room.

Unfortunately, the VIP lounge was a confined space. No matter what I did or who I talked to, she was always there, occupying my thoughts and drawing my attention until whatever conversation I was holding drifted into silence.

"Dude, just ask her to dance." Luca hadn't left my side on the banquette, though he'd suddenly become fascinated with something on his phone in the past twenty minutes.

Across the room, Sloane said something to the DJ, who nodded and smiled at her in a way I didn't appreciate.

"I don't know what you're talking about." I tipped my head back and closed my eyes, trying to erase her image from my mind.

Were DJs allowed to flirt with club goers? Wasn't that a professional liability or something?

"Sloane." Luca's voice was barely audible over the music. "You haven't looked away from her once since she showed up."

"Because I don't want her surprising me. She's like a predator in the wild. You have to keep an eye on her at all times."

"Right." I could hear the smirk in my friend's voice. "So you don't mind if *I* dance with her then?"

My eyes popped open, and I lifted my head to glare at him. "Actually, I do fucking mind, and not for the reason you're thinking of. That shit will get messy."

"Why? She's your publicist, not mine. I barely know her."

"She's your sister-in-law's best friend."

"So?"

"So?" I sputtered. "So that's *messy*."

"Says the guy who hooked up with his roommate's ex."

"That was in boarding school, and that was different." My roommate had been an asshole. "Vivian will kill you if you touch Sloane."

"No, she won't. And all I said was I wanted to dance with her, not sleep with her." Luca shrugged. "But hey, you never know. We're on vacation. I could get lucky."

I wasn't a violent person, but in that moment, I'd never wanted to punch someone more than one of my oldest friends.

"If you—"

An eruption of cheers interrupted me midsentence. My gaze swung toward the DJ booth, where Sloane was dancing barefoot on a neighboring tabletop.

Sloane. Dancing. *On a tabletop*.

Hell must be an ice playground by now.

Every pair of eyes in the room was glued to her as she swayed to the music, which had transitioned from a dance mix to a sultry rendition of the latest R&B hit.

Either I was the world's best dance teacher, or she wasn't merely drunk—she was wasted.

On the bright side, I'd been right. Her stiffness came from

overthinking, and when she wasn't so focused on making every move perfect, she danced...well, she danced in a way that ignited every cell in my body.

I rubbed a hand over my mouth, torn between watching and stepping in. Sober Sloane was going to *hate* this in the morning.

My lips curved at the thought of her reaction, but my amusement died a quick death when one of the other club goers climbed onto the table, grabbed her by the waist, and started grinding against her.

My reaction was so swift, so visceral, that I couldn't have explained what happened next if someone put a gun to my head.

One second, I was sitting.

The next, I was up and across the floor, my vision tinting with scarlet as I bulldozed through the startled crowd.

Sober Sloane would've kneed the guy in the balls for touching her. Drunk Sloane had no such qualms.

She turned to face the guy whose hands crept perilously close to her ass. If she moved another inch, the throng of people crowded around the table would get a perfect view up her skirt. Several already had their phones out, but they quickly dropped them when I approached.

Whatever they saw in my expression made them scramble out of the way as I climbed onto the table and yanked the guy off her.

I towered over him by several inches, but even if I hadn't, the fury churning in my gut would've given me an unfair advantage.

He made a noise of dissatisfaction. "What—"

"You have three seconds to leave," I said, my voice deadly calm. "Three."

I didn't make it to two before he gulped and disappeared into the depths of the club. Fucking coward.

Part of me was disappointed I didn't get the chance to slam my fist into his nose, but there were more pressing matters at hand.

I faced Sloane again. She hadn't noticed her dance partner's absence or my arrival; she was too busy taking shots with one of the clubbers on the ground and, consequently, giving everyone an eyeful of her cleavage.

I grabbed the double shot of tequila before it reached her lips and tossed it to the side.

"Hey! I was—" Her protest cut off in a yelp when I swept her off her feet and tossed her over my shoulder. I didn't trust her to walk straight in those heels after God knew how many drinks.

"Let me go, you Neanderthal!" She pounded on my back as I carried her off the table and out the door.

The club sat on several hundred feet of prime oceanfront real estate, and it didn't take long before the sound of the waves overpowered the music leaking into the night air.

"Be careful what you ask for." I dropped Sloane on a thick patch of white sand. I was tempted to dunk her in the ocean to sober her up, but even I wasn't stupid or assholish enough to do that.

Yet.

"You *asshole.*" She pushed herself to her feet with surprising grace given her inebriation. "What the hell do you think you're doing?"

"What the hell do I think *I'm* doing? I think I'm making sure you don't wake up to photos of your bare ass splashed all over the fucking internet!"

Her glare skewered me to the spot.

As always, Sloane was glorious in her wrath. On any other night, I would've sat back and watched that cool mask of hers explode in the most spectacular way, but she wasn't the only one seething tonight.

"Don't be ridiculous," she said. "I'm not you. People don't care what I do in my free time."

"That's not true." *I care*. The thought rose, unbidden, before I banished it. "You're a Kensington and a high-profile publicist, and the cameras are *always* watching. You're the one who taught me that."

"I'm a Kensington in name only." A tiny flicker of vulnerability crossed Sloane's face and stabbed at my chest before her expression iced again. "You're always telling me to 'loosen up.' Now that I am, you have a problem with it?"

"I have a problem with some random guy groping you in public," I snapped.

"Why?"

Because the thought of anyone else touching you fucking kills me.

"Because." Irrational anger blanketed my words with heat. "*It's not you.*"

"Stop acting like you know me." Her voice rose to the level of a shout. "We are not friends. We are not dating. *You* are simply a client, and *you* are the one who forced me to come here. You have no right to act like my boyfriend or handler."

"I'm trying to help!"

"I don't need your help!"

Every piece of vitriol dragged us closer until we stood inches apart, our chests heaving and our bodies shaking from the force of our convictions. Animosity blazed between us, fanned by years of pent-up frustration and a spark of something far more dangerous.

I didn't know why I cared so much because she was right. I had no claim on her beyond work, and I was always telling her to loosen up.

But not like this. Not when it came from a place of pain rather than freedom.

"You're right. I don't know you," I said. "But I know Sloane, and Sloane would never put herself in a situation like the one you were in. *Sloane* would've kicked that guy's ass, and she would've pulled you out the same way I did."

Part of my intervention had been selfish, but another part had stemmed from true concern. Who knew what photos and videos people grabbed before I got her down?

Perhaps I was overstepping, but screw it. It was better to be safe than sorry. Sloane's professional reputation meant everything to her, and she would never forgive herself if one drunken night jeopardized what it'd taken her years to build.

"Well, maybe Sloane doesn't always want to be Sloane." Her heels wobbled in the soft sand, and she let out a curse before yanking her shoes off. "Also, I *hate* when people talk about themselves in the third person."

My phone vibrated with an incoming call, but I ignored it. "Stop deflecting. What happened this afternoon? Why did you leave?"

I'd bet my entire inheritance the mysterious email was directly related to her desire to drink herself into oblivion.

My phone vibrated again. I ended the call without looking at it.

Sloane swallowed. She was more fragile beneath the moonlight, her hair a gilded silver instead of ice-blond, her eyes shining with a wary truth that only the depths of night could lay bare.

More than anything, I wanted that truth and, by extension, the trust that came with it.

Let me in, Luna.

She opened her mouth, but a familiar ringtone cut her off. Her eyes shuttered, and fragility hardened into cool professionalism as she turned to take the call. "This is Sloane."

Fuck. I rubbed a hand over my face, frustration chafing beneath my skin.

I'd never hated the invention of the cell phone more than tonight.

"Yes, we are…I see." Her tone changed, and an ominous foreboding prickled my scalp. "Of course. I'll handle it."

Sloane hung up and faced me again.

A heavy sensation dropped like a lead weight in my stomach. I knew what she was going to say before she said it, but that didn't soften the impact of her words.

"It's your father," she said, her eyes sober for the first time since she showed up at the club. "He's taken a turn for the worse. They don't know if he'll make it through the night."

CHAPTER 11

Sloane

THERE WAS NOTHING LIKE A DEATH SCARE TO SHOCK someone sober.

After I broke the news to Xavier, we returned to the villa and started packing. We didn't say a word to each other on our walk back or the subsequent ride to the airport.

It was late, but I'd successfully roused his pilot, who got us in the air hours after Eduardo's call. I also checked out early from our resort, left a brief note for Xavier's friends, and tied up other loose ends while the younger Castillo retreated within himself.

I glanced across the aisle at Xavier. He was sleeping or pretending to sleep, but even if he were awake, it would be impossible to gauge his true thoughts regarding his father's health. That was the one topic where he completely shut down.

I rubbed my temple and tried to hold down my meager breakfast. I'd grabbed a few hours of sleep right after we boarded, but a vicious hangover kept me from true rest.

On the bright side, I had plenty of work to distract me from everything that happened yesterday, including my father's email and my argument with Xavier.

Now that I was sober, I was grateful he'd stopped me before I humiliated myself further at the club, but I still didn't appreciate how he'd hauled me out of there like a caveman.

I didn't dwell on the small flutter I'd experienced on the beach, which had clearly been the result of too much alcohol and nothing else.

As I was halfway through crafting a press strategy for if and when Alberto Castillo died, my phone went wild with incoming texts. Considering it was the crack of dawn in New York, that couldn't be good, and a quick scroll through my texts confirmed it.

Vivian: Just wanted to check in on you. Call me when you get a chance.
Alessandra: Have fun! Drink some sangria for me <3
Isa: You look so hot! And so does Xavier ;) Go, girl

My breakfast rose in my throat again when I clicked on the link Isabella sent and saw the photos splashed across the front page of Perry Wilson's blog along with a blaring red headline.

Girl Gone Wild! Celebrity Publicist Gets Down and Dirty in Spain with Client!

In one photo, I was talking to Xavier while he was sitting and staring up at me with an amused smile. The second photo showed him carrying me over his shoulder and out of the club.

The article itself was a mishmash of speculation and outright lies.

The PR queen has allegedly been hooking up with her most infamous client for weeks, which may explain why the notoriously unflappable Castillo heir went all caveman when he saw her dancing with someone else at Mallorca's most exclusive nightclub...

Sources also say Castillo's friends crashed their secret romantic getaway, which led to an "explosive" argument between the couple and a plan to make Castillo jealous. Did the plan work? See for yourself...

There were more photos interspersed within the text, including a grainy shot of us on the beach, another of me dancing with some random guy, and a close-up of Xavier facing down said guy on the fucking tabletop.

Rising anger burned my initial shock to ash.

Perry fucking Wilson. That little toad was probably enacting revenge for the time I'd gotten him booted from *Mode de Vie*'s Fashion Week party, which everyone knew was *the* party to attend for those who wanted to see, be seen, and gather society intel.

I didn't care that he was the most influential gossip blogger in Manhattan; I was going to peel the skin from his sorry body and use it as a canvas for his obituary.

I replied to my friends with a brief message telling them I was okay and that I'd explain later (plus another ask for Isabella to please keep feeding The Fish while I was in Colombia). I was about to email Perry and chew him out when Xavier woke up.

"I know that look," he said, his first words in hours colored with exhaustion. "Who pissed you off?"

I handed him my phone with the article open.

He scanned it with a disinterested expression. "Ah."

I was still too riled up to pay much attention to his unusual subduedness. "That's all you have to say?"

"What else do you want me to say? It's Perry. This is what he does." Xavier shrugged and handed the phone back to me. "Besides, he's the least of my worries right now."

My anger collapsed like a house of cards caught in a sudden gust of wind.

I was so used to butting heads with Xavier that it was hard to turn off the default mode in our relationship, but now that I was no longer steaming over the blog post, I noticed the shadows in his eyes and the seemingly unconscious clench and unclench of his fists. It was a different Xavier from the one pictured on Perry's blog, and it made a weird little pinch slide in between my ribs.

"No news is good news," I said, my voice gentling. "You'll get a chance to talk to your father."

"Maybe." Xavier's mouth tilted up for a second before sobering again. "We used to be close, you know, when I was younger. I was his only child, his heir. I was supposed to continue his legacy, and he spent all his free time preparing me for the task. Office visits, tutors, enrollment at the best international schools where I could network with the people I would do business with one day."

Emotions flitted across his face in a rare display of vulnerability.

I kept my eyes on his, afraid to breathe yet unable to look away, and worried the smallest movement on my part would spook him into silence. Xavier never talked about his relationship with his father, and the glimpse into their past both fascinated and saddened me.

"But it wasn't all business," he said. "We had normal father-son days. He took me to *fútbol* games—or soccer, as you know it. We had family dinners and vacations abroad. It was nice. Then..."

I suppressed an involuntary flinch.

I knew what happened next. Everyone did.

"My mom died," Xavier said, his handsome face devoid of emotion. "And everything changed."

A heavy ache slipped past my defenses and burrowed deep inside my heart.

He'd been eleven when his mom died. The fire that took

Patricia Castillo's life made international news given her marriage to Colombia's richest man, the sheer destruction left in the fire's wake, and a viral image of a preteen Xavier being carried out by firefighters.

That image anchored every article and TV segment about the fire. The authorities ruled out arson, but details about how the blaze started remained murky.

"Do you miss her?" Xavier asked quietly. "Your mom."

My mom had died in a freak horseback riding accident when I was fourteen. My parents' marriage had been a socially expedient but loveless one, and unlike Xavier's father, who never stopped grieving his wife's death, mine had remarried less than two years after burying his first wife.

A new, different kind of ache blossomed. "All the time."

My admission bled between us, forming a strange, tenuous bond that sent tingles over every inch of my body.

Xavier's shoulders relaxed, as if my words had somehow lifted a weight off them.

We were different in so many ways, but sometimes, all people needed was one point of commonality. One infinitesimal thing that made them feel less alone.

I swallowed past the hitch in my throat.

We were the only people in the main cabin. Our private flight attendants were in the kitchen, preparing lunch, but the distant clink of plates and silverware soon faded beneath the thuds of my heartbeat.

Xavier and I stared at each other, both recognizing the lazy swirl of tension in the air, but neither acknowledging it.

I wanted to look away. I *should* look away, but his gaze held mine captive, its tumultuous depths sparking with an emotion I couldn't identify.

I swallowed again, and something else flared in those hot,

dark eyes before they made a slow descent over my face, tracing the slope of my nose, the curve of my mouth, and the point of my chin before gliding down my neck. They settled at the base of my throat, where my pulse fluttered with wild abandon.

The same pesky butterflies that'd snuck into my stomach during our dance lessons broke free again. Only this time, I couldn't blame it on the alcohol.

I was stone-cold sober, and I—

"Mr. Castillo, Ms. Kensington, would you like something to drink before we serve lunch?" Our attendant's smooth voice tossed a bucket of ice water over the moment.

The tension fizzled with an inaudible *pop* as Xavier and I yanked our gazes apart.

"Water." His smile looked forced. "Thank you, Petra."

"Same." I cleared my throat of its hoarseness. "Thank you."

We ate our lunch in silence. However, even though we didn't discuss our pasts again, a sense of connection lingered.

Xavier and I weren't the first or last people to miss a parent. But the way we responded to our losses, and the masks we presented to the world...perhaps we were more similar than we realized.

CHAPTER 12

THANKS TO THE TIME DIFFERENCE, WE ARRIVED IN Bogotá before noon.

My father's driver was already waiting when we landed, and he whisked us through the city's winding roads and densely packed neighborhoods with enviable skill.

I was born in Colombia but educated abroad my entire life. I spent more time in the halls of boarding schools than I did at home, and I'd only visited my birthplace twice since my father was diagnosed with cancer last year.

The first had been after the diagnosis. The second had been right before my Miami birthday trip, when he'd summoned and berated me for failing to "uphold the family legacy" while he was dying.

If there was one person who'd use their illness to manipulate other people into doing what they wanted, it was Alberto Castillo.

"Xavier." Sloane's voice sliced through my thoughts. "We're here."

I blinked, the pastel haze from the streets morphing into twin guardhouses and fully armed security personnel. Behind the black iron gates, a familiar white mansion rose three stories high, crowned by red tiles and latticed windows.

"Home sweet home." Sarcasm threaded my words, but a sick feeling stirred in my stomach as we walked inside.

Decades-old smoke clung to the walls, making me nauseous.

My mother had died here. She'd burned alive right on this plot of land, and instead of moving, my father had rebuilt the house right over her deathplace.

People said he wanted to stay close to her in his own morbid way, but I knew the truth. It was his way of punishing me and making sure I never forgot who the real villain was in this house.

"You don't have to stay here," I told Sloane. Her clean, crisp scent drifted over me, masking echoes of the smoke. "I'll be happy to book you a suite at the Four Seasons."

Sloane had visited the Bogotá house before for work, but beneath the shine and luxury, heaviness shrouded the mansion's foundation. I couldn't be the only one who felt it.

"Trying to kick me out already? That's record timing."

"You'll be more comfortable at a hotel." We passed by a giant oil portrait of my father. He glared down at us, his face stern and disapproving. "That's all I meant."

"Maybe. But I'd rather be here." Sloane stared straight ahead, her stride purposeful, but warmth flickered in my chest all the same.

She was prickly, uptight, and as cuddly as a cactus. Yet somehow, she had a way of making even the worst situations more tolerable.

However, the warmth hardened into ice when we entered my father's room. His staff had transformed it into a private hospital suite complete with the latest medical technology, a twenty-four-hour rotation of nurses and attendants (all of whom signed ironclad NDAs), and the best care money could buy.

But that was the thing about death—it came for everyone. Young and old, rich and poor, good and evil. It was life's greatest equalizer.

And it was clear that, despite Alberto Castillo's billions, he was standing at death's door.

Conversation vanished when the room's occupants noticed me.

My father was the second youngest of two sisters and one brother. They were all gathered here along with my cousins, the family doctor, the family lawyer, and various attendants.

Eduardo was the only one who stepped toward me, but he halted when I approached my father's bedside.

The carpet was so thick it muffled even the slightest noise from my footsteps. I might as well have been a ghost, gliding soundlessly to where my father lay with his eyes closed, his frail frame hooked up to a mass of tubes and monitors.

In perfect health, he was a titan both in reputation and appearance. He dominated any room he walked into and was equal parts feared and revered, even by his competitors. But over the past year, he'd withered into a husk of himself. He'd lost so much weight he was almost unrecognizable, and his olive skin resembled ashen wax beneath the sheets.

A rope snaked through my chest, winding tighter and tighter—

"He made it through the night." Dr. Cruz came up beside me, his voice pitched low so only I could hear him. "That's a positive sign."

I didn't take my eyes off the motionless form before me. "But?"

Dr. Cruz had been with my family since I was born. Tall and reedy, he resembled a swarthy beanstalk with silver hair and a prominent nose, but he was the best doctor in the country.

However, there were some things even the best doctor couldn't hide, and I knew him well enough to pick up on the hesitation rolling off him.

"His situation remains critical. Of course, we'll take care of him the best we can, but…I'm glad you arrived when you did."

Meaning my father's passing was inevitable, and soon.

The rope pulled tauter. I wanted to reach inside and tear it out. I wanted to run away from this fucking house and never come back. I wanted *peace*, once and for all.

But I didn't say any of that to Dr. Cruz when I mumbled a generic reply, or to Eduardo when he came up to embrace me, or to my aunts and uncles and cousins, half of whom were here solely for their cut of my father's fortune.

The only person who didn't smother me with pity or concern was Sloane. She stood by the door, respectful of the family's privacy but staying close enough in case anyone needed anything.

When my father passed, she would be the one crafting the press statement and media strategy. Knowing her, she'd already started both.

Regular families buried the dead and grieved. Families like mine had to issue *press statements*.

Here lies Alberto Castillo, shitty father and guilt tripper extraordinaire. He was emotionally abusive and wished his only son had died, but man, he was a hell of a businessman.

The absurdity of it all punched a hole in my composure, and I couldn't stop laughter from leaking out in the middle of Tía Lupe's platitudes. The more I tried, the harder my shoulders shook until my aunt stopped and stared at me in horror.

Some of my cousins had drifted off to take advantage of the mansion's pool or arcade, but the remaining family observed me like I'd murdered their favorite pet.

"What's so funny?" Tía Lupe demanded in Spanish. "Your father is on his *deathbed*, and you're laughing? That is beyond disrespectful!"

"It's funny you should say that, *tía*, considering you only come around when you want *my father* to pay your bills. How's the house in Cartagena? Still under the million-peso renovation you so *desperately* needed?" Steel flickered beneath my amusement.

"You should talk. You're a spoiled little brat who wastes my brother's money without ever—"

"Lupe. Enough." My uncle placed a hand on her arm and firmly steered her away from me. "Now's not the time." He cast an apologetic glance at me, and I summoned a wan smile in response.

Unlike Tía Lupe, Tío Martin was quiet, even-tempered, and cautious. He lived in the same half dozen outfits year-round and didn't give a crap about the lifestyles of the rich. I had no idea how he'd ended up with someone like my aunt, but I supposed opposites did attract.

"No, Lupe is right," Tío Esteban, my father's eldest sibling, said. "What's so funny, Xavier? You haven't been home in months. You refused to take over the company, so poor Eduardo here is stuck doing your job. You are constantly pictured in the gossip rags, partying and wasting God knows how much money. I told Alberto to cut you off a long time ago, but no, he refuses." He shook his head. "I don't know what he was thinking."

I did. Money was another form of control for my father, and the threat of cutting me off was more powerful than the act. If he actually cut me off, that would be it. I would be free.

I could've cut myself off, but I'll be honest—I was a hypocrite. I railed against Lupe for using my father as an ATM machine when I did the same. The difference was I admitted it.

The money was a prison, but it was all I had. Without it, Xavier Castillo as the world knew him would cease to exist, and the possibility of losing the only value I had was more terrifying than living the rest of my life in a gilded cage.

"Oh, you know Alberto." Tía Lupe scoffed. "Always holding on to the romantic notion that my dear nephew will someday stop being a disappointment. Honestly, Xavier, if your mother were alive, she would hate—" The rest of her sentence cut off with a shriek when I grabbed her by the front of her shirt and yanked her toward me.

"Do not *ever* talk about my mother," I said, my voice deceptively soft. "You may be family, but sometimes, that's not enough. Do you understand?"

My aunt's pupils were the size of dimes, and when she spoke, her words shook. "How dare you. Let go of me this instant, or—"

"Do. You. Understand?"

The feather in her ridiculous hat quivered with increasing intensity. It was a testament to her unlikability that no one, not even her husband, stepped forth to intervene.

"Yes," she spit out.

I released her, and she scrambled back to Tío Martin's side.

"Excuse us." Sloane's cool touch soothed some of the flames raging in my gut. "Xavier and I need to discuss some media matters in private."

I followed her out of the room, passing my aunt's vengeful gaze, Dr. Cruz's frown, and a host of other silent judgment.

I wished I cared.

I was glad I didn't.

Sloane led me to my father's office down the hall. She closed the door behind us and faced me, her expression not betraying an ounce of emotion. "Are you done?"

"She had it coming."

"That wasn't my question." Four strides brought her close. "Are. You. Done?" She punctuated each word with precision.

My jaw tensed. "Yes."

Was what I'd done smart? Probably not. But it'd felt damn good.

Of everyone in my family, Tía Lupe was the *last* person who should talk about how my mom would feel. The two had never gotten along. Tía Lupe had seen my mother as competition for my father's time and money—which was disturbing on so many levels—and my mother had disliked her sister-in-law's shameless self-aggrandizement.

"Good, because if you're done, it's my turn to speak." Sloane tapped the globe on my father's desk. Red pins highlighted every country where the Castillo Group's beer had the biggest market share.

Half the globe was red.

"This is your inheritance," she said. "A global empire. Thousands of employees. *Billions* of dollars. You are the only direct heir to the Castillo Group, and even if you refuse a corporate position, your name means something. It means there will always be people looking to take you down, to take from you, to get what they feel like they deserve. Some of those people are right down the hall. *Your* job"—she jabbed a finger at my chest—"is to be smart. This is a critical time not only for your father's health but for your future. If he dies, it'll be a feeding frenzy, no matter what his will says. So unless you're willing to give up your inheritance and work for once in your life, keep your hands to yourself and your temper under control."

Unlike earlier, her touch burned.

Indignation shriveled beneath her steady stare. She wasn't being malicious or unsympathetic; she was being practical, and in typical Sloane fashion, she was right.

"Tough love, Luna," I drawled. "You're good at that."

I stepped away from her and toward the globe. I spun it idly, watching the Americas roll by, followed by Europe and Africa, then Asia, then Australia.

I stopped it when South America came into view again and plucked the pin out of Colombia. It pricked my thumb, but I hardly felt it.

"Have you ever wished someone would die?" I asked softly. "I don't mean figuratively or in a moment of anger. I mean, have you ever lain awake at night, dreaming of how life would be better if a specific person didn't exist?"

It was the closest I'd ever come to shining a light on my darkest thoughts, and the somber *ticks* and *tocks* that followed sounded like hammers striking at my walls.

The English grandfather clock in the corner was one of my father's prized possessions. Rosewood case carved with an intricate inlay design, face crafted of chased silver, hallmarked numerals by a famous London silversmith. He'd paid over one hundred thousand dollars for it at an auction, and its imposing sentry felt like an avatar for his reproach.

A breeze brushed my skin as Sloane reached for the pin.

"Yes." Her fingers grazed my palm for a single, lingering second before she pushed the pin back into the globe. "It doesn't make us bad people, nor is it an excuse. We can't always control our thoughts, but we can control what we do about them."

Her gaze coasted from the antique surface of the globe to my eyes.

"The question then," she said, "is what are you going to do next?"

CHAPTER 13

Sloane

GLOOM SHROUDED THE CASTILLO ESTATE FOR THE next twenty-four hours as the patriarch hovered on the precipice between life and death. The staff worked more slowly, the family talked more quietly, and the sunshine streaming through the windows dulled the second they hit the mansion's dread-laced air.

I stayed out of everyone's way except for Xavier's.

I didn't deal well with broody billionaires, nor was I particularly good at comforting people. However, I couldn't bring myself to let him wallow alone, which was how I ended up searching the mansion for him with reinforcements in hand.

I had some free time—I'd finished the press statement last night, and no major outlets had picked up Perry's piece about my misadventures in Spain. I wasn't a celebrity, but the lack of response was suspicious. Nevertheless, I took it as a gift from the universe; I had enough real problems without creating hypothetical ones.

I finally found Xavier camped out in the den with an ESPN documentary about the world's top athletes. One of his arms draped across the back of the couch while the other held a bottle of the Castillo Group's signature drink.

Tousled hair, cashmere sweats, three-hundred-dollar T-shirt.

That was the Xavier I knew and didn't quite love.

Something akin to relief stirred in my chest. At least he wasn't acting *totally* out of character.

"Sorry, Luna, you'll have to find another TV for your rom-coms," Xavier said without looking away from the screen. "This one is occupied."

"I know. I didn't come to watch a movie." I sat beside him and unloaded my armful of goods on the coffee table. "I came to see you."

His gaze flicked to me with apparent surprise before it cooled again. "Why?"

"You need to eat." I eyed the empty beer bottles scattered around us. "And drink something *without* alcohol."

"You came to feed and hydrate me?" A thread of amusement ran beneath Xavier's otherwise dubious tone.

"Like you're a pesky pet I got stuck with. Here." I shoved a bottle of water in his hand and a plate of homemade empanadas in his lap.

He hissed and quickly lifted the plate off his legs, only to drop it back just as fast. "Jesus, that's *hot*."

"Then you should eat them before they burn your favorite appendage," I said innocently.

A hint of laughter pulled on his mouth, and he wiped at it with his hand before he picked up an empanada. "Doris's specialty and my favorite. How did you know?"

"I didn't. I saw you weren't eating, so I asked if she'd make some food for you, and she produced those."

With my admission came the tiniest tremor—a frisson of electricity that hummed between us and swallowed the lightheartedness in the air.

Xavier's hint of laughter disappeared. Warmth rushed to

the pit of my stomach, and I unconsciously shifted beneath his burning gaze.

"Thank you," he said, a strange note in his voice. "That was... very thoughtful of you."

I replied with a stiff smile, hoping he didn't see the blood rising to the surface of my skin. It occurred to me that I might've been the only person who'd checked on Xavier's well-being since he arrived—everyone else was too busy or didn't care—and the realization sent a conflicting rush of emotions through me.

He was an adult. He didn't need someone looking after him, but I felt gratified when he ate the empanadas and drank the water without complaint anyway.

"How many do you represent?" Xavier tilted his chin toward the screen, where a gallery of superstar athletes flashed in between clips. They represented the best and brightest of every major professional sports league in the Western Hemisphere: NFL. NBA. MLB. Premier League. La Liga. So on and so forth.

I crossed my legs, still a touch unnerved by my reaction to him earlier. *That's what happens when I don't get enough sleep.* "One."

A deep baritone recounted the meteoric rise of Asher Donovan over footage of his teen and early club years, culminating with the legendary halfway line goal against Liverpool that'd catapulted him into a household name.

I glanced at Xavier as the screen flipped to headlines about Asher's record-setting transfer to Blackcastle.

"But you knew that already," I said.

His mouth quirked into a crooked smile. "Sure. As long as I'm still your favorite."

Despite his disheveled appearance, he smelled like soap and fresh laundry. He reached for a napkin, his leg grazing mine, and heat traveled from my thigh to my stomach.

"Try one." Xavier used the napkin to pick up an empanada and handed it to me. "You haven't lived until you've had one of Doris's empanadas."

I took a tentative bite. Flaky, tender butteriness melted in my mouth, followed by a rich explosion of flavor. Ground beef, tomatoes, onions, garlic. Perfectly seasoned and perfectly balanced against the dough.

"*Wow*," I said, slightly stunned. It'd been a while since I'd eaten something so simple yet so good. "You weren't kidding."

"Told you." Xavier's dimples made a surprise appearance. "Have another one. She loves making them. Says it's soothing."

"I'm not hungry."

"Did you eat lunch or breakfast?"

No. "I brought the food for you."

"Yes, and I'm sharing it with you." He nudged the plate toward me. "I insist."

Xavier wouldn't ease up until I agreed, so I reached for another piece and settled deeper in the couch. Sharing food was a simple, platonic act that people did every day, so why did my stomach feel like a breeding ground for a fresh swarm of butterflies?

I kept my gaze planted on the television until I finished eating and brushed the crumbs from my hands. "What?" I asked when he continued staring at me instead of the TV.

"Still wearing this, I see." His fingers brushed Pen's friendship bracelet, and my muscles instinctively tensed. The bracelet wasn't the most professional accessory, but I could easily hide it with long sleeves. "You ever going to tell me about the mystery gifter?"

"I'll tell you the day you get a job."

His low laugh sent the butterflies soaring. "Touché."

Xavier dropped his hand, and oxygen flowed a little more freely. "When I was a kid, I thought I would be the next Diego

Maradona," he said. "Unfortunately, I was more interested in hanging out with my friends than training."

"Really? I never would've guessed." The sad part was, I bet he *could've* gone pro if he'd put the time and effort in.

That was what galled me about him and why I was harder on him than anyone else. Xavier wasn't my rudest or most entitled client, but he had the greatest wasted potential.

"At least I'm consistent." His smile didn't reach his eyes. "You can always count on me for a good time."

Maybe. But beneath the champagne showers and yacht parties, how good a time was he actually having?

"So, spill it," he said when the documentary segued from Asher to LeBron James. "What sport did you play growing up?"

"What makes you so sure I played one?"

"Sloane." Xavier side-eyed me with a look that made my mouth curve despite myself. "You are too competitive not to have captained a team or three."

True.

"Tennis, volleyball, and golf," I admitted. "I tried soccer, but it wasn't for me. My sister loves it though."

The last part slipped out without thought, and Xavier perked up like a predator sensing prey.

"Your sister?" A speculative gleam entered his eyes. "Georgia, right?"

Shit. I never brought up my family, so I didn't blame him for being curious, but the sound of her name on his lips brought those empanadas back up.

"No." The thought of Georgia playing soccer, of all things, was laughable. "My other sister, Penelope."

Xavier's brows scrunched. "I didn't know you had another sister."

"Most people don't."

Pen was too young to have made her official society debut yet, and George and Caroline paid a fortune to keep her and her condition out of the press.

"She's my half-sister" I clarified. "Same father, different mother. I'm pretty sure she's watched every soccer game that's ever been recorded. I got her an autographed Donovan jersey for her seventh birthday a few years ago, and you should've seen her smile."

My heart pinched at the memory. Her birthday had been weeks before her CFS diagnosis. I took her to a local game while George was at work and Caroline was at a charity luncheon. I hadn't seen her so happy since.

"How old is she now?" Xavier asked.

"Nine."

"Two years ago." His gaze burned a hole in my cheek, and I realized my mistake.

My estrangement happened five years ago. I'd basically admitted I was breaking the terms of my family split.

Vivian, Isabella, Alessandra, and now Xavier. Besides Rhea and Pen herself, I could count the number of people who knew I was in touch with my sister on one hand.

The thought should've terrified me, but something about Xavier muted my usual worries. My gut told me he could keep a secret, and while I didn't trust my gut one hundred percent when it came to him, he'd shared enough vulnerability of his own that I was willing to give him this piece of myself without much resistance.

Nevertheless, I lifted my chin and met his eyes, daring him to follow through with his train of thought. "Yes."

Xavier didn't flinch beneath the force of my stare. "She's almost in the double digits," he said. "Big milestone."

So, how does nine feel? You're almost in the double digits.

Pressure expanded in my throat. I hadn't discussed Pen with

anyone other than Rhea in so long that a conversation about something as simple as her age was tearing through my composure.

My secret had bubbled inside me for years. It needed a release valve, and somehow, in the most unexpected of ways, I'd found it in Xavier Castillo.

He didn't ask for details about Pen or how long I'd been in touch with her. He didn't ask if I was talking to anyone else in the family. He didn't ask anything at all.

He simply watched me with those dark, fathomless eyes, and the unseen force that'd brought me here reared its head again, urging me to confide in him and let someone in fully for once.

My self-preservation fought back like hell.

Moments of connection were one thing. Opening up to someone was something else entirely.

Luckily, I was saved from making a decision when a familiar shadow spilled across the floor.

I straightened, snapping into work mode while Xavier visibly tensed.

"It's your father." Eduardo cut straight to the chase. "He's awake."

Xavier

They left me alone with him.

My father wasn't up for seeing a crowd, so Dr. Cruz forced everyone else to stay in the hall while I…well, I didn't know what I was supposed to do.

I'd run out of things to say to him a long time ago.

Nevertheless, I came up to his bedside, my heart thumping to an anxious beat when dark eyes latched onto mine.

"Xavier."

His paper-thin whisper sent a chill down my spine. The last time I saw him, he could speak normally and I could pretend the status quo was still intact. Even if the status quo sucked, there was comfort in familiarity.

But this? I didn't know what to make of this man or situation.

Should I forgive and forget because he was terminally ill? Did the last moments of his life erase the moments of mine that he'd made a living hell? What did a son say to the parent he was supposed to love but hated?

"Father." I forced a smile. It presented as a grimace.

His rheumy gaze traveled from the top of my sleep-mussed hair to the toes of my sneakers. It ascended to rest on my sweat-pants. "*Esos pantalones otra vez.*" *Those pants again.*

My jaw clenched. Of course our first interaction in months revolved around his disapproval of my choices. *The status quo lives and breathes.*

"You know me." I pushed a hand into my pocket and tossed out a careless smile. "I aim to displease."

"You're the Castillo heir," he snapped in Spanish. "Act like it, especially..." A fit of coughs rattled his lungs. When they finally died down, he inhaled a wheezing breath before continuing. "Especially when I'll be gone within the week."

The hand in my pocket fisted. It was the first time my father had ever acknowledged his mortality, and it took every ounce of willpower not to flinch.

"We've had this conversation multiple times," I said. "I'm not taking over the company."

"Then what are you going to do? Live off my money forever? Raise another..." He coughed again. "Raise another crop of degenerates who'll turn the family fortune into nothing?"

The monitors beeped with his increased heart rate.

"Grow up, Xavier," he said harshly. "It's time for you..." This time, a hacking cough took him out of commission for a full minute. "It's time for you to be useful for once."

"You want me, someone who doesn't want the job and will *never* want the job, to be CEO? You're supposed to have good business sense, Father, but even I can tell you that's not a sound strategy."

His cough morphed into a phlegmy laugh. "You? CEO of the Castillo Group as you are now? No. I would be better off putting Lupe's dog in charge." My father's eyes slid to the closed door. "Eduardo will train you. This is your legacy."

My hand ached from the force of my grip. "No, it's not. It's *yours*."

Perhaps it was crass to argue with a dying man, but this was what our relationship was like to the very end: him trying to force me into a mold I didn't fit into; me resisting.

There'd been a time when I tried. Before my mom died, I soaked up all my time with him, whether that was at a *fútbol* game or in his office. I lived for the dreams, the pats on the head, the bonding over a shared future. I was going to carry on the family legacy, and we were going to rule the world.

That was before we became the villains in each other's stories.

"Yours or mine, it's all the same." My father's mouth twisted, the thought as appealing to him as it was to me.

I stared out the window at the gardens. Beyond them lay the rest of Bogotá, and Colombia, and the world.

In our household, tradition formed a prison in which no change entered and no member escaped. I'd come the closest, but a yoke of fear tethered me to the grounds the way a curse tethered spirits to the mortal plane.

I'd been here for one day, and I was already suffocating.

I needed a breath of fresh air. *Just one.*

"Your mother left you a letter."

Six words. One sentence.

That was all it took to obliterate my defenses.

My attention snapped back to the bed, where satisfaction filled my father's smile. Physically weak though he may be, he was back in control, and he knew it.

"She wrote it when you were born," he said, each word tumbling through me like boulders in an avalanche. "She wanted to give it to you on your twenty-first birthday."

Static crackled in my ears until the implications of what he was saying crashed down around me and detonated. Mushroom clouds billowed into the air, robbing me of breath.

Everything of hers had been destroyed in the fire—photos, clothing, mementos. Anything that could've reminded me of her, gone.

But if she wrote me a letter...my father wouldn't have mentioned it unless it was intact. And if it was intact, it meant a piece of her lived on.

I swallowed the emotion burning in my throat. "It's far past my twenty-first birthday."

"I didn't remember it. It was so long ago." His voice was fading. We didn't have long before he went under again, but I *needed* to know about the letter. How had it not burned alongside the rest of her things? Where was it? Most importantly, what was in it?

"She kept it in one of our safes." Another wheezing breath. "Santos found it when he was tidying up my affairs."

Santos was our family lawyer.

The safe explained why the letter was intact, but it gave rise to another host of questions.

"When did he find it?" I asked quietly.

How long had my father been keeping it from me, and why was he choosing to tell me now?

He averted his gaze. "Top drawer of my desk," he rasped. His eyes drooped closed, and his breathing steadied into a slower rhythm.

Foreboding sank its teeth into me as I stared at his prone form. He was skin and bones, so frail I could snap him in half with one hand, but in true Alberto Castillo form, he exerted undue control over me even from his deathbed.

The room was eerily quiet despite the monitors, and a cold sensation trailed after me when I finally turned and walked out.

My family had dispersed from the hall, tired of waiting. Only Dr. Cruz and Sloane remained outside the door.

"I'll check on your father," the doctor said, astute enough to pick up on my volatile mood. He slipped into the room, and the door closed behind him with a soft *click*.

Concern shadowed Sloane's face. She opened her mouth, but I brushed past her before she could get a word out.

A strange underwater silence bloomed in the hall, muffling every noise except the thud of my footsteps.

Thud.

Thud.

Thud.

The hall split into opposite directions at the end. The left led to my bedroom; the right led to my father's study.

I should retreat to my room. I wasn't in the right headspace for reading the letter, and a part of me worried there *was* no letter. I wouldn't put it past my father to play some sick game where he got my hopes up only to crush them.

I swung left and made it two steps before morbid curiosity pressed replay on my father's confession.

Your mother left you a letter.

Top drawer of my desk.

I came to a halt and squeezed my eyes shut. *Dammit.*

If I were smart, I wouldn't give him the satisfaction of taking the bait. But this was my chance to potentially hold a piece of my mother again, and even if he was lying, I had to know.

I backtracked to the other end of the hall and into his office. The top drawer was unlocked, and a sticky mess of dread, anticipation, and anxiety roiled my stomach as I slid it open.

The first thing I saw was a gold pocket watch. Beneath it, a yellowing envelope sat tucked against the dark wood.

I unsealed it with a shaky hand, smoothed out the letter inside...and there it was. A page filled with my mother's flowing script.

My throat constricted.

Emotion swept through me, quick and violent as a summer storm, but relief didn't get a chance to settle before I started reading.

It was only then that I understood exactly why my father had told me about the letter.

CHAPTER 14

Sloane

AFTER HIS BRIEF SPELL OF LUCIDITY ON THURSDAY, Alberto's condition took a turn for the worse. He slipped into a coma the day after, and this time, the doctor appeared less optimistic about his chances of surviving the next forty-eight hours.

Both the family and I started preparing for the worst. While I monitored the media excessively for leaks, a priest arrived to be on hand for last rites, and Xavier's family ambushed the lawyer every time he stepped foot inside the house. Sometimes, at night, I swore I heard the ghostly wail of someone crying.

Since I wasn't a superstitious person, I attributed it to the wind. I also didn't mind the busywork. It kept my mind off my father's email, which I'd deleted without reply.

Xavier himself didn't return to his father's side. I didn't know what they'd talked about when Alberto was awake, but he'd barely left his room since then. Even an offer to watch a rom-com and drink every time the quirky female lead did something klutzy didn't rouse him from his seclusion.

By Saturday, I'd had enough. It was time to take matters into my own hands.

I strode down the hall and stopped in front of Xavier's room. I'd convinced the head housekeeper to lend me her master key, but a pinch of apprehension needled me when I knocked and didn't get a reply.

I hadn't expected one, but that didn't stop my mind from conjuring the worst images of what lay beyond the door.

Piles of empty bottles and filth. Drugs. Xavier overdosed and dead.

I'd never known him to dabble in drugs, but there was a first time for everything.

The apprehension swelled as I inserted the key into the knob. One twist and the door opened, revealing…

What the hell?

My mouth parted at the scene before me. It wasn't the crisp, perfectly made bed or the curtains thrown wide over the windows that shocked me. It wasn't even the lack of visible food and alcohol.

It was the sight of Xavier…drawing?

He sat by the window, his focus unwavering despite my entrance. The easel in front of him held a large sheet of paper covered with what looked like a sketch of a living room. Beside him, a small mountain of crumpled paper balls littered the ground.

He looked remarkably put together for someone I'd been convinced was in the throes of self-destruction minutes ago. His hair gleamed thick and glossy in the sunlight; a stray lock fell over his eye, brushing his cheekbone and softening the bold lines of his face. He wore a plain gray T-shirt and jeans that molded to his body like they were made for him, and his biceps flexed with every swoop and curve of his pencil.

A tingle of sudden awareness cascaded down my spine.

I had no idea why I was noticing these things about Xavier, but from a purely physical point of view, he was—

Stop. Get a grip. I caught myself before my thoughts wandered further down inappropriate paths. Clearly, I'd been cooped up in the mansion for too long if I was drawn in by his *arms,* of all things.

I was here to check on him, *not* ogle him.

"You have a habit of breaking into my bedroom, Luna," he said without taking his eyes off the canvas. "Let's hear it."

I forced my mind off the light hum of electricity in my veins and walked toward him. My heels echoed against the polished wooden floors, the sound a welcome reprieve from…other distractions.

"I don't know what you mean." I came up beside him as he sketched a set of stools around a curved counter. It wasn't Picasso, but it was better than anything I could've done. Plus, based on the notes he'd scribbled in the top left corner, he wasn't aiming for artistic expression so much as brainstorming.

CONSIDERATIONS: BAR DEPTH / HEIGHT, BACKBAR SPACE
FLEX SPACE FOR SUMMER / WINTER
MARK HIGH-TRAFFIC AREAS

My heart stuttered beneath twin blows of realization and surprise.

It wasn't a living room sketch. It was a blueprint for a bar.

"I mean the scolding." Xavier shaded in one of the stools, his voice flat and absent of its usual irreverence. "Tell me how I'm supposed to be spending time with my father and making amends instead of shirking my duties. Or how I should be preparing to take over the household after he passes and how I'm heartless for not caring whether he lives or dies." He moved on to the backbar space of the sketch. "You wouldn't be the first or last to say those things."

I should've. In any other situation, I *would've*, but something held me back.

It wasn't my job to police how other people processed their grief—or lack of it—and Xavier's moodiness bothered me more than I cared to admit.

I hadn't realized how accustomed I was to his annoying but familiar sunshine optimism until its warmth was gone.

"You never told me you were a designer," I said, deliberately bypassing the topics he'd mentioned.

His hand paused for the briefest moment before he resumed drawing. "I'm not. This is just something I do to pass the time."

I picked up a discarded paper ball from the ground and unfolded it. It was a variation of the current sketch. So was the next one I picked up and the one after that. "Interesting. Because to me, it looks like you're trying to perfect a design."

Xavier's jaw tightened. "Is there a reason you broke into my room again, or are you really that bored?"

"I wanted to see how you're doing." The answer slipped out without thought, but it was true.

Despite his faults, Xavier was human. An infuriating one, yes, but he wasn't malicious or mean-spirited, and there was more to him than the carefree image he portrayed to the world.

Besides, I of all people understood the complexities of a fraught paternal relationship. I could only imagine his struggle with reconciling his personal feelings toward his father and the prospect of losing the only parent he had left.

Xavier finally glanced at me. "Are my ears deceiving me? Is Sloane Kensington checking in on me *of her own free will*?" A hint of teasing slipped into his tone and restored a sense of normalcy.

Relief pushed the weight off my shoulders. I could deal with an uncooperative Xavier. I didn't know how to deal with a brooding one.

"Don't push it." My voice cooled, but it lacked bite. "I merely want to ensure you don't do anything stupid. It's my job."

Xavier's eyes lingered on mine for a moment, making my stomach twist in the strangest way, before he returned to the canvas. "I thought your job was dealing with the vultures."

The vultures, aka the media.

News of Alberto's failing health had leaked after someone spotted the priest entering the compound, and there were currently a dozen reporters camped out in front of the gates as we spoke.

So far, I'd held them at bay, but if Alberto died, it would be a feeding frenzy, especially since he had no clear heir. Eduardo was an interim CEO, and Xavier had washed his hands of company obligations. That left the fate of the country's largest private corporation up in the air. It would dominate headlines for weeks if not months.

Luckily, I'd been planning for that day since Alberto received his cancer diagnosis, so I wasn't too worried.

"They're handled," I said. "Which brings me back to this." I inclined my head toward the easel. "How are you doing?"

"Fine." Xavier added details to a banquette. "I've come to terms with the fact we won't mend our relationship before he passes. Not everyone gets closure. Sometimes, the wounds run too deep, and the end of the road looks just as shitty as the miles that came before it."

He placed his pencil on the easel and faced me again. Resignation and anger sculpted his mouth into a humorless smile. "Does that answer your question?" he asked.

"It does." I was still holding the sketches I'd picked up earlier. I crumpled them and dropped them back on the ground. "But I have a more important question for you."

His brows formed questioning arches.

"Why a bar?" I purposely changed the topic. Xavier was okay. Otherwise, he would've ignored me or deflected instead of giving a straightforward answer.

We'd discussed our families at length the past few days. We didn't need to rehash it now that I knew he wasn't going to spiral into an Alberto-induced depression.

We had shitty fathers whom we'd never forgive. End of story.

"The sketch," I clarified, nodding at the easel. How had I not known about his hobby when we'd worked together for so long? Granted, most of our communication had been over text and email until recently, but still. There was a whole other side to him that I found infuriatingly fascinating. "I know it's your natural habitat, but most people start with a house. Maybe a nice landscape."

"Landscapes are boring, and I don't care much for home design." Xavier shrugged. "I go to enough bars that I can easily spot the flaws in each one. I thought it'd be fun to try and design the perfect one."

I wrinkled my nose. "And you say I'm boring."

His smile peeked out like a tiny ray of sunshine through gray storm clouds. "Hey, if it's good enough for Prince Rhys, it's good enough for me. He likes sketching in his free time too."

"Now you're just making stuff up." I couldn't imagine the gorgeous but broody crown prince of Eldorra enjoying something as soft as drawing. He looked like he wrestled bears for fun.

"I swear. I read about it in an interview last year. Besides..." Xavier's dimples deepened. "I said your hobbies are boring, not you. I don't find a single thing about you boring."

My heartbeat stumbled.

God, I wished he were an asshole. It would make things so much easier.

"Yes, well..." I cleared my throat and nudged a paper ball out of the way with the toe of my pump. "That doesn't change the fact you need to leave your room sometime. I thought you'd—" I cut myself off before the word *died*. "I thought you'd passed out in here," I finished, inwardly wincing at the lame substitution.

"I like my room." Xavier's smile took on a devilish slant. "You're welcome to join me. There's plenty of space."

Ah, there was the shameless flirt. I knew he was still lurking under there somewhere.

I marshaled my expression into some semblance of professional disapproval, but I didn't get a chance to respond before a knock sounded on the door.

Its owner didn't wait for a response; the door opened, revealing Eduardo's dark suit and somber face.

My sarcastic reply withered, and Xavier's smile dissolved into grim understanding. He turned to the easel and ripped his near-complete sketch off the canvas. It soon joined the rest of the drawings on the floor.

Acid ate at my stomach. We'd been getting somewhere, and now…

"Xavier. Sloane." Eduardo's voice was heavy. "It's time."

We didn't need elaboration, and neither of us spoke as we followed him into the hall. I could practically hear the camera flashes outside; the vultures were circling, and it was only a matter of time before they landed.

We made it halfway before a light touch on my shoulder forced me to halt.

"Before we go in there…" Xavier swallowed, his eyes clouded with turmoil. "Thank you for checking on me."

The words landed like arrows, each in its vulnerable target.

It hadn't occurred to me before, but in a house filled with his family, I was the first person to check and see if he was okay.

"You're welcome," I said quietly.

There was nothing else I could say in that moment.

The only thing I could do was step aside, let him say his goodbyes, and prepare him for the storm to come.

CHAPTER 15

IT SHOULD COME AS NO SURPRISE THAT A MAN WHO'D barely been there for me in life was equally absent in death.

Alberto Castillo, Colombia's richest man, former CEO of the Castillo Group, and father of one, died at home at five minutes past three on Saturday afternoon.

I made it to his room just in time to witness his last heartbeat.

He never woke from his coma before he passed, and we never exchanged a proper goodbye.

If this were a movie, we'd have some dramatic heart-to-heart or big confrontation before he died. I would unload my grievances on him; he would confess his regrets to me. We would have a cathartic fight or make up. Either way, we'd have closure.

But this wasn't a movie. It was real life, and sometimes, that meant loose ends didn't get tied up.

In the wake of his death, I felt a strange mix of nothing and everything all at once. I was relieved that we no longer hung on tenterhooks, waiting for a final health verdict, but I couldn't fully process that he was gone and never coming back. I despised the last-minute manipulation he'd pulled with my mother's letter, but the overwhelming *closeness* I'd felt to her when I read her words was worth it.

Yet constraining that sea of complicated emotions was a layer of numbness I couldn't shake no matter how hard I tried.

Top drawer of my desk.

Those were the last words my father had uttered to me, and I supposed it was fitting that our chapter ended with ties to my mother. Dead or alive, she was the bedrock of our relationship.

The pocket watch I found in his desk drawer burned a hole against my thigh.

"Do you think I'm a monster for not crying?" I stared at the scotch in my hand. It was midnight and I was in the kitchen, drinking my worries away because what else would one do the night after their father died?

"No," Sloane said simply. "People grieve in different ways." She poured a glass of water and slid it toward me.

She'd stayed with me through the immediate aftermath of my father's death, forcing me to eat and turning away my family members when they tried to accost me with questions about my inheritance.

Thankfully, she didn't smother me with pity. I could always count on Sloane to be Sloane. Whenever I was drowning, she was my anchor in the storm.

Part of me was embarrassed to show her this side of me—raw and exposed, tangled in the pieces of the mask I usually wore for the world. It was easy being Xavier Castillo, the billionaire heir and party boy; it was torturous being Xavier Castillo, the man and disappointment. The one with a fucked-up past and uncertain future, who had plenty of friends yet no one to lean on.

Sloane was the closest thing I had to a support system, and she didn't even like me. But she was here, I *wanted* her here, and that was more than I could say for anyone else in my life.

She examined me, her face softer than usual. "But I might be the wrong person to ask about grief. I can't..." A beat of hesitation. "I can't cry."

That surprised me enough to shake off some of my self-loathing. "Figuratively?"

"Literally." She rubbed her thumb across the beads of her friendship bracelet as if debating whether to elaborate.

"I can cry if I'm in pain," she finally said. "But I've never cried out of sadness. I've been that way since I was young. I didn't cry when our family cat died or when my favorite grandmother passed. I didn't shed a single tear when my fiancé—" She stopped abruptly, her face darkening for a split second before her composure slid back into place with a near-audible *clank*. "Anyway, you're not the only one who's felt like a monster for not crying when you should."

She grabbed the bottle of scotch from the counter and poured some into a crystal tumbler. It was her third of the evening.

Fiancé. There were rumors she'd been engaged years ago, but no one could confirm it—until now. Sloane was notoriously private about her personal life, and it helped that she'd been living in London at the time, away from the vicious Manhattan gossip machine.

I watched in silence as she sipped her drink.

Perfect hair. Perfect clothes. Perfect skin. She was the picture of flawlessness, but I was starting to see the cracks beneath her polished facade.

Instead of detracting from her beauty, they added to it.

They made her more real, like she wasn't an elusive dream that would slip through my fingers if I tried to touch her.

"We seem to have more and more in common," I drawled.

Shitty fathers. Commitment issues. Major need of therapy. Who said adults couldn't bond over trauma?

Sloane must've expected me to pry about her fiancé because her shoulders visibly relaxed when I lifted my glass instead.

"To monsters."

A soft gleam brightened her eyes, and she raised her glass in turn. "To monsters."

We drank in silence. The house was dark, the clock ticked toward one, and an army of reporters gathered outside the gates, waiting to turn my father's death into a media circus.

But that was a problem for the morning. For now, I basked in the warmth of my drink and Sloane's presence.

She wasn't a friend or family, and on a bad day, she made the *Titanic* iceberg look like tropical paradise. And yet, despite all that, there was no one else I would rather spend tonight with.

Saturday marked my last gasp of breath before the tsunami of press and paperwork descended.

The next few days blew by in a whirlwind of funeral arrangements (extravagant), media requests (incessant but unanswered save for the press statement Sloane had crafted), and legalese (complicated and headache-inducing).

My father had left meticulous directions for his funeral, so all we had to do was execute them.

His will was an entirely different matter.

The Tuesday after his passing, I gathered in the library along with my family, Eduardo, Sloane, and Santos, our estate lawyer.

The reading of the will started off as expected.

Tía Lupe received the vacation house in Uruguay, Tío Esteban received my father's rare car collection, so on and so forth.

Then it got to me, and apparently, my father had made a last-minute change to the terms of my inheritance.

Murmurs rippled through the room at the news, and I straightened when Santos started reading the conditions.

"To my son Xavier, I bequeath all remaining fixed and liquid assets, totaling seven point nine billion dollars, provided he assumes the chief executive officer position before the day of his thirtieth birthday and serves the role for a minimum of five consecutive years thereafter. The company must turn a profit in each of those five years, and he must fulfill the chief executive officer position to the best of his abilities as determined by a preselected committee every six months, starting from his official first day as CEO. Should he not meet the above terms, all remaining fixed and liquid assets shall be distributed to charity according to the terms below."

The room erupted before Santos read the next paragraph.

"*All* assets to charity?" Tía Lupe screeched. "I'm his sister, and I get a measly vacation home while *charity* gets eight billion dollars?"

"You must've read that wrong. There's *no way* Alberto would do that..."

"Xavier as CEO? Does he want to run the company into the ground?"

"This is outrageous! I'm calling my own lawyers..."

Spanish shouts and curses ricocheted off the walls like bullets as my family devolved into chaos.

Throughout it all, Eduardo, Sloane, and I were the only ones who didn't utter a word. They sat on either side of me, Eduardo's face pensive, Sloane's impassive. Across the room, Santos maintained a neutral expression as he waited for the indignation to die down.

The first line of my inheritance clause rang in my head.

I bequeath all remaining fixed and liquid assets, totaling seven point nine billion dollars, provided he assumes the chief executive officer position...before the day of his thirtieth birthday.

My thirtieth birthday was in six months. Of course, my father knew that; trust the bastard to force my hand even in death.

The shouting matches around me retreated before an onslaught of memories.

My last conversation with him. The pocket watch. The letter.

The drum of my heartbeats chased away the silence as I stared at my mother's familiar handwriting. She'd loved calligraphy and insisted I learn cursive, even though no one used it much anymore.

I used to sit next to her as she hand wrote thank-you cards and birthday greetings and get-well-soon wishes, tracing the loops and swirls on my own piece of paper.

Some people found her handwriting difficult to read, but I parsed it easily.

Dear Xavier,

I met you for the first time yesterday.

I'd imagined the moment many times, but no amount of imagination could've prepared me for holding you in my arms. For seeing you stare up at me, then falling asleep together because we're both exhausted, and hearing you laugh as you grabbed my fingers on our way out of the hospital.

You're only two days old at the time of this writing, so tiny I can almost fit you into the palm of my hand. But a parent's best gift is watching their child grow up, and I can't wait for the journey ahead.

I can't wait to see you off to your first day of school. I'll probably (definitely) cry, but they'll be happy tears because you'll be starting a new chapter of your life.

I can't wait to teach you how to swim and ride a bike, to give you advice about girls, and to see you fall in love for the first time.

I can't wait to watch you discover your passions, whether it's music, sports, business, or anything else you want to do. (Don't tell your father, but I'm rooting for art.)

However, I'll be happy with anything you choose, and I mean that from the bottom of my heart. The world is big enough for all of our dreams.

There's potential in each and every one of us, and I hope you fulfill yours to the point of happiness.

Your father says I'm getting ahead of myself because you're so young, but by the time you read this, you'll have turned twenty-one. Old enough to attend college, drive a car, and travel on your own. My heart hurts just thinking about it, not because I'm sad, but because I'm so excited for you to experience my favorite parts of the world and to find your own. (And if you can't decide where to go, choose a spot close to the beach. Trust me. The water heals us in ways we can't comprehend.)

I can't say for certain what the future will hold, but at the risk of sounding like a cheesy motivational poster, know this: life ebbs and flows, and there's always room for change. Humans have the capacity for growth until they leave this earth, so never feel like it's too late for you to take another road if you're unhappy with the one you're traveling.

No matter which road you take, I'm proud of you. I hope you are too.

Be proud of the person you've become and the person you'll grow into. Even though you've just arrived in the world, I know you'll make it a better place.

You're my greatest joy, and you always will be.

Love always,
Mom

P.S. I left you a special gift. The pocket watch has been handed down through generations in my family, and it's time I passed it on to you. I hope you cherish it as much as I did.

Something dripped onto the paper, smudging the words.

Tears. The first I'd shed since I arrived.

I retrieved the pocket watch from the drawer with a trembling hand and opened it. It was so old the numbers had faded, but the message engraved inside remained legible.

THE GREATEST GIFT WE HAVE IS TIME. USE IT WISELY.

"Xavier? Xavier!"

The present rushed back in a tidal wave of noise.

I blinked away the memories fogging my brain as Tía Lupe's face came into focus. Not the first person I wanted to see under any circumstance.

"Well?" she demanded. "What do you have to say about this will? It's utterly—"

"Tía? Shut the hell up."

I thought I saw Sloane smirk out of the corner of my eye as Tía Lupe gasped. Eduardo made a strange noise that fell somewhere between a laugh and a cough.

I tuned out my aunt's splutters and focused on Santos.

The echoes of my mother's letter lived in my heart like a blade lodged between my ribs, but I couldn't afford to dwell on the past right now.

The greatest gift we have is time. Use it wisely.

"Can you repeat the condition of the will in plain terms?" I asked calmly. I understood what it meant, but I wanted to be sure.

The room quieted as everyone waited for Santos's response.

He met my gaze with an unflinching one of his own. "It means if you don't assume the CEO position by your next birthday, you will lose every cent of your inheritance."

A collective shudder swept through the library.

My family didn't want me inheriting the billions because I didn't "deserve it" (fair enough, though that was like the pot calling the kettle black), but they would rather die than see all that money flow *outside* the family.

"That's what I thought." My hand curled around the arm of my chair. "Who are the preselected committee members my father mentioned?"

"Ah, yes." Santos adjusted his glasses and read from the will again. "The committee will consist of the following five members: Eduardo Aguilar..." *Expected.* "Martin Herrera..." Tía Lupe's husband. Less expected, but he was the fairest and most level-headed person in my family. "Mariana Acevedo..." Chairwoman of the Castillo Group's board. "Dante Russo..." *Wait. What the fuck?* "And Sloane Kensington."

Pin-drop silence followed his proclamation.

Then, as one, every head in the room swiveled toward Sloane. She sat ramrod straight, her face pale. For the first time since I'd met her, she resembled a deer caught in headlights.

Five people were in charge of my family fortune's fate, and my publicist was one of them.

Once again: *What the fuck?*

CHAPTER 16

Sloane

CERTAIN THINGS IN LIFE MADE SENSE. FOR EXAMPLE, the concept of cause and effect, the heat of the sun, and female praying mantises killing their partners after sex. No muss, no fuss—they got their pleasure, and they were done.

Some things made less sense, like the encroachment of Christmas songs in October and my being the judge of whether Xavier should continue receiving his annual allowance prior to his father's death. It wasn't ideal, but since the terms of his allowance revolved around media exposure, I understood it.

Then there were things that made *no* sense at all, such as being placed on a committee that would determine the fate of seven point nine billion dollars.

I wasn't family, I wasn't a corporate executive, and I wasn't sure what the hell I was doing on that list.

"I didn't know," I said. "Your father never mentioned it to me."

It was the day after the reading of the will, and Xavier and I sat by the pool while two of his preteen cousins argued over the latest *New York Times* crossword a few chairs down.

I woke up early that morning for yoga and found him here on

my way back from the mansion's attached gym. I needed a break from the constant glares and whispers, and I wasn't entirely confident Lupe wouldn't try to stab me in my sleep.

The Castillos were not happy about my involvement in their family's financial affairs, to put it mildly.

"I believe you." Xavier scrubbed a hand over his face and shook his head. He was unusually subdued for someone who'd just found out his entire inheritance hinged on one job and the judgment of one committee. "This whole thing is classic Alberto Castillo."

I sensed there was more to his words than he let on, but it wasn't the time to pry.

Other than the occasional consulting call and press release, my dealings with his father had been limited. Alberto hired me to handle PR for his family three years ago, right before Xavier moved to New York. Since his direct family consisted of two people, and Alberto rarely used my services for himself, that meant I was basically Xavier's personal publicist.

I had no idea why Alberto trusted me so much with his money as it pertained to Xavier, but his will also stipulated I was to remain the family's publicist unless I quit, so it was my job to see things through.

"I can see the wheels spinning in your head, but there's an easy fix for this," I said. "You're smart. You have a degree in business and plenty of advisors who can guide you. Take the CEO position."

Normally, I wouldn't advocate for nepotism, but I truly believed Xavier was intelligent enough to do the role justice.

A muscle worked in his jaw. "No."

I stared at him. "This is your *entire* inheritance. You have billions of dollars riding on this decision."

"I'm aware." Xavier glanced at his cousins, who were too

young and too engrossed in their crossword to care about our conversation. "That clause was just another attempt by my father to make me do his bidding. It's manipulation, plain and simple, and I won't give into it."

For God's sake. I understood why his family had called him *pequeño toro* when he was a kid. He truly was stubborn as a bull, and that stubbornness had followed him all the way to adulthood.

"Manipulation or not, the consequences are real." I shouldn't care that much about whether Xavier received the money or not because, honestly, it wasn't like he'd worked for it. But the prospect of him being penniless because he was too hardheaded to take on something he could be great at didn't sit right with me. "Don't be impulsive. Think about what saying no means. What will you do for money?"

"Get a job." Xavier's mouth twisted. "Who knows? Maybe I'll finally be a productive member of society."

"The CEO position *is* a job."

"But it's *not* the job for me!"

I reared back, stunned by the ferocity of his reply. His cousins lapsed into silence and gaped at us.

Xavier's knuckles turned white around the edge of his chair before he relaxed them. He took a deep breath and said, in a quieter, more strained voice, "Tell me, Sloane. Who do you think would do the company more justice? Someone qualified who actually wants to be there, or me, the reluctant heir who was placed there by default?"

Someone qualified. The tone of his voice, the shadows in his eyes...

And there it was.

Beneath the jokes and stubbornness lurked the root of his refusal: fear. Fear of failure. Fear of not living up to expectations. Fear of running and ruining an empire built on his last name.

I'd never noticed it before, but now that I saw it, I couldn't unsee it. It was a bright silver thread that wove through every word and underpinned every decision. It was stamped all over his face, closed off as it was, and something inside me cracked open just wide enough for it to dart in and steal a fistful of rationality.

"I think we need to go out and clear our heads." I made up a plan on the spot. "We've been cooped up here for too long."

The mansion was huge, but even a palace would feel oppressive if one couldn't leave.

Xavier's eyes sparked with wary intrigue. "I thought we were supposed to stay inside and avoid the press."

"Since when do you do what you're supposed to do?"

A smile snuck across his mouth, as slow and smooth as honey. "Good point. I assume you have a plan?"

"I always do."

All the reporters were camped out in front, which made it easy for us to slip out the back through the gardener's entrance. We wore basic hat-and-glasses disguises, but they worked, and they blended well into the crowd.

After we exited the grounds, we hightailed it to the nearest busy street, where we grabbed a cab and drove straight to La Candelaria, home to some of Bogotá's most popular attractions. It was cold, but not so cold that it deterred us from going.

Once we arrived, it was easy to get lost in the throngs of tourists heading to one of the nearby museums or oohing and aahing over the street murals.

I had a feeling Xavier was like me. In times of crisis, I didn't want to be alone with my thoughts; I wanted to lose myself in noise and activity and let the world drown out my worries.

Over the next four hours, that was exactly what we did.

Bogotá was a vibrant city, its rainbow-hued colonial architecture a striking contrast against the surrounding green mountains. Musicians filled the air with reggaeton and *vallenato* beats, and the mouthwatering smell of onion, garlic, and spices spilled from restaurants and street carts. There was no shortage of distractions.

Xavier and I wandered through the Botero Museum before we joined a free graffiti walking tour and admired the intricate design of Teatro Colón. When we got hungry, we ducked into a nearby restaurant for *ajiaco santafereño*, a local specialty stew of chicken, potatoes, capers, and corn, and indulged in *oblea* wafers for dessert.

We didn't talk about work, family, or money. We simply enjoyed our first taste of freedom since we'd landed in Colombia, but as with all good things, it had to come to an end.

Alberto's funeral was tomorrow, and we were supposed to fly home the day after that. Colombian funerals usually took place within twenty-four hours of death, but Alberto's elaborate wishes and stature dictated a slower turnaround. International CEOs and heads of state required more planning than your standard funeral guests.

"Since it's just the two of us, be honest," I said as we wandered past a row of colorful houses toward Bolivar Square. "Are you really willing to give up everything to spite your father?" I kept my voice gentle.

Xavier's emotions were running understandably high, but he had to understand the gravity of his situation.

He'd grown up a billionaire's son. He had no concept of what it was like to live without a massive cushion of money.

He was quiet for a long moment. "What did your parents want you to be when you were little?"

I startled at the abrupt question and answered frankly. "They wanted me to be the perfect socialite. Attend an Ivy League college to get a husband instead of a job, marry someone from a respectable family, and spend the rest of my life decorating and hosting charity galas."

There was nothing wrong with any of those things. They just weren't for me.

"And now you're a hotshot publicist." We turned the corner, and the square came into view. "Let's say you and your father are still talking. What would you do if he said he'll cut you off unless you quit your job and marry some polo-playing douche named Gideon?"

Touché.

"I'd tell him to fuck off." Which I basically had. "Though ironically, I dated a polo player named Gideon in high school and yes, he was a douche."

That earned me a soft laugh.

"Your turn to be honest," he said. "People's reputations and livelihoods depend on you. Are you ever scared you'll fuck it up?"

"Sometimes." I was confident in my skills, but like everyone, I had my moments of doubt. Was I giving my client bad advice? Did I use the wrong turn of phrase? Should I have pushed them to do an interview with this outlet or that one? The second-guessing was enough to drive me out of my mind, but at the end of the day, I had to trust my gut. "But that's the thing about reputations and livelihoods. They can be rebuilt."

"Careful, Luna. You sound almost optimistic."

I rolled my eyes, but a smile threatened to escape as we wound toward the Palace of Justice anchoring one side of the plaza.

"You make it sound like I'm doom and gloom all the time. I'm a fun person."

"Hmm."

I frowned. "Just because I don't go clubbing every night or party on yachts every weekend doesn't mean I'm not fun."

"Mm-hmm."

"Stop doing that!"

"Doing what?" Xavier asked innocently.

"Making that noise. I can *hear* your skepticism."

It was stupid to take offense, considering my job wasn't to be *fun*, but I knew how to have a good time. My friends and I met for weekly happy hours in New York, and I'd (reluctantly) agreed to a lap dance during Isabella's bachelorette party. I'd danced on a tabletop in Spain, for Christ's sake! Granted, I'd been wasted at the time, but it was the action that counted.

"I didn't say a single word. What you infer from my noises is on you," Xavier quipped.

"If manipulating semantics were a job, you'd be the CEO," I muttered. "You—" *Wait a minute.*

I came to such a sudden halt, the tourists behind us almost crashed into me.

"No." My heart picked up speed until it thrummed like a trapped hummingbird. "It can't be that simple."

"What?" Xavier demanded. He glanced around us in case of trouble.

I replayed the reading of the will in my head. I was almost certain…no, I was *positive* I was right.

"I have it," I said breathlessly.

"Have what? You gotta give me more than that, Luna."

"I have a solution to your problem." I grabbed his arm, too excited to contain myself. "Your father's will says you have to assume the CEO position. It didn't specify what you have to be the CEO *of*."

Xavier stared at me.

Tourists streamed around us, muttering their annoyances in various languages, but I could practically hear the gears cranking behind those dark eyes.

Then slowly, so slowly it dawned like the sun over the horizon, a smile blossomed across his mouth.

"Sloane Kensington, I like the way you think."

CHAPTER 17

Xavier

MY FATHER'S FUNERAL CAME AND WENT IN A BLUR OF solemn faces and whispered condolences. I gave a brief eulogy at Sloane's and Eduardo's insistence and spent the rest of the memorial floating between numbness and hyperactivity.

My brain hadn't stopped churning since Sloane and I returned from La Candelaria. We made it back to the house without being ambushed by reporters and confirmed with Santos about the will's wording.

She was right. My father hadn't specified *what* I should be the CEO of, which was a glaring omission for a man with a famed sharklike business sense, but that was a question for another day.

After Santos's confirmation, things moved quickly. We gathered the rest of the inheritance committee, as I called them, and explained the situation.

It boiled down to this: My first CEO evaluation was in six months, which coincided with my thirtieth birthday. That meant I had half a year to figure out how to fulfill the will's terms. Meanwhile, Eduardo would remain interim CEO of the Castillo Group while the company searched for a permanent leader.

Six months to become CEO of a company that didn't exist and that had to pass muster with the committee at the first evaluation. Easier said than done.

The greatest gift we have is time.

My mother's pocket watch weighed heavy in my pocket as I entered the Valhalla Club's bar.

It was a week after my father's funeral and my return to New York. I'd spent the past six days brooding over my situation, but it was time to get off my ass and do something.

I ordered the club's signature drink and glanced around the dark-paneled room. Valhalla was an ultraexclusive club for the world's wealthiest and most powerful. It had chapters all over the globe, and I was a member thanks to my mother, a descendant of one of the founding families. My father had made his fortune, but my mother had been born into money.

Despite my coveted membership, I rarely hung out at Valhalla. It was too stuffy for me, but it was the only place I could think of where I wouldn't run into my New York circle of friends. They were fine for a good time, but they weren't who I wanted to see in my current state of mind.

The bar was quiet this early in the afternoon. I was one of two people sitting at the counter; several stools down, a perfectly put-together Asian man with glasses and a bespoke Delamonte suit observed me with polite curiosity.

"No comment," I said before he opened his mouth.

I slid the bartender a fifty-dollar tip when he brought my drink and drain half the glass in one swallow.

Kai Young lifted an amused brow. The CEO of the world's most powerful media conglomerate wasn't the type to ambush someone with questions about a family member's death, but you couldn't be too careful.

"I heard you were back in New York," he said, tactfully

ignoring my rudeness. His polished British accent fit seamlessly into our elegant surroundings, whereas I felt as out of place as a penguin in the Sahara. "How are you doing?"

"I'm drinking at one in the afternoon," I said. "I've been better."

If Sloane were here, she'd say my day drinking was par for the course. Luckily, she was too busy catching up on work to be on my ass about the CEO thing, though I wished she were here anyway.

After having her around twenty-four-seven for over a week, I missed her.

"If it makes you feel better, you're not the only one." Kai tipped his head toward his glass. "I had a meeting earlier with a techpreneur who's convinced he's the next Steve Jobs, hence the scotch. I have to drown out an hour's worth of misguided god complex."

I snorted out a laugh. "Sounds like Silicon Valley." Misguided god complex. If only I had one. It would make things easier.

I had a degree in business, which was a precondition for accessing my trust fund when I graduated, but I'd never *started* a business. I didn't have the luxury of flying under the radar. If I failed, I failed in front of the entire world.

If I *didn't* try, I would lose my inheritance. And yes, I recognized the irony of trying to grasp something I resented—aka my father's money—but when I looked past my knee-jerk reaction, I recognized the truth in Sloane's words. I had no idea what it was like to live without that financial cushion, and to be honest, the thought terrified me.

The only thing that made me feel less like a hypocrite was the fact I wouldn't keep all the money, but that was a secret I kept to myself for now.

I glanced at Kai. Our social circles overlapped in the way most of Manhattan society's did, but I didn't know him well. He had a dry sense of humor I appreciated the hell out of though, and more importantly, he was best friends with Dante Russo, who'd somehow landed on my inheritance committee.

Dante hadn't reached out save for a polite condolence note. Did he even know he was in my father's will?

Most likely, which made his silence all the more suspicious.

"Have you talked to Dante recently?" I asked, abandoning subtlety in favor of directness.

A knowing smile tugged at the corner of Kai's mouth. If Dante made it his job to know everything, Kai's job *was* to know everything. I wouldn't be surprised if he'd gotten his hands on the will before I touched down in New York.

"We spoke yesterday," he said, his tone mild. "Why?"

"No reason." I drummed my fingers on the counter, mentally running through the committee members.

Sloane was on my side, but she wouldn't lie if my business turned out to be crap in six months. Eduardo and Tío Martin would give me as much grace as they could. Mariana hated my fucking guts. Dante...well, he was the wild card.

Luca's brother wasn't my biggest fan, but could I trust him to be fair regardless of his feelings toward me?

"Xavier, I'm not a journalist after a story. What we discuss is strictly private." Kai paused, then added, "I speak with Sloane often. I understand how to keep confidentiality."

It suddenly clicked. *That* was why Kai was suddenly so interested in my affairs. Since Sloane was the one who'd discovered the loophole in the will, she'd taken it upon herself to act as my unofficial business consultant. My inheritance clause wasn't a secret, though the committee members were; she must've said something to either Vivian, Dante, Kai, or all of the above.

The wheels started spinning. If I was serious about starting a new company, I needed allies, and the CEO of the Young Corporation was one of the most powerful allies I could get.

"As a matter of fact," I said, piecing together a plan on the spot. "There *is* something I want to discuss with you..."

Two hours and several drinks later, Kai left for another meeting while I headed upstairs to the library.

It was the heart of the club, and it buzzed with activity as people forged deals, cemented alliances, and shared intel. However, no one paid me any mind as I took a seat at the grand center table, directly beneath the founding families' panels, where my mother's bear family crest was carved in between the Russos' dragon and the Youngs' lion.

I retrieved the watch from my pocket and rubbed a thumb over the smooth gold case, my mind churning from my conversation with Kai and the events of the past week.

Fact #1: There was no way my father could've overlooked something as basic as naming the company in his will. Granted, he'd been deathly ill when he changed it, which wasn't an inconsiderable factor, but if he *had* been aware of the omission, what was his endgame? To make me do *something* even if it wasn't what he wanted?

No. My father would never be that compromising. Last option dismissed.

Fact #2: On paper, I had six months to figure my shit out. In reality, I should've figured it out yesterday. Starting a solid business in New York, in that short amount of time, was near impossible.

Fact #3: If I didn't at least try, I would regret it forever. Out of all life's questions, *what if* was one of the worst.

There's potential in each and every one of us, and I hope you fulfill yours to the point of happiness.

My chest clenched. Would my mother think I'd fulfilled my potential? Probably not, but fuck, I missed her. I always did, but it used to be a dull, steady ache that hummed in the background. Ever since I read her letter, it'd been a knife that lanced through me, frequently and often.

I'd never stopped blaming myself for what happened to her. It didn't matter what my childhood therapists or grief counselors said; guilt wasn't bound by reason or technicalities.

That being said, I couldn't change the past. I could, however, dictate my future.

Be proud of the person you've become and the person you'll grow into.

I pulled out the sheet of paper Kai had handed me before he left. Like me, he'd been born into wealth, but his position hadn't been handed to him. He'd worked his way up from the mailroom to the head position at the Young Corporation, and his circle was a who's who of the corporate world.

My contacts could get anyone an invite to any party and access to any club, but his contacts could help build an empire.

I stared at the list of names he'd scribbled down.

In order to be a CEO, I needed a team. To hire a team, I needed a plan. To execute that plan, I required funding and legitimacy.

My reputation as a partier worked against me, which meant I needed a partner people respected. Someone reliable, established, trustworthy, and relevant to the business I had in mind.

There was only one man in Manhattan who fit that description.

I dialed the first number on the list. It was his private line, and he picked up on the first ring.

"This is Xavier Castillo," I said, hoping to God I wouldn't regret this down the road. "Are you free next week? I'd like to talk."

CHAPTER 18

Sloane

"I'M SORRY. BACK THE FUCK UP." ISABELLA HELD UP one hand. "You can't *not* elaborate on Spain. What happened with Xavier after he carried you out like an extremely hot caveman?"

I sighed, regretting my decision to fill my friends in on the past two weeks. I'd flown to Spain at the beginning of the month, but it felt like a lifetime ago. "That's your takeaway? Did you miss the part about Alberto Castillo's death?"

"Yes, it's very sad," Isabella said. "Now, about the beach. What did he say?"

"Was he jealous?" Vivian added.

"Did you two kiss?" Alessandra asked.

I glared at them, wishing past me had had the foresight to befriend less nosy people.

"I'm not telling you what he said, he has no reason to be jealous, and *absolutely not*," I said, appalled. "He's a client."

The four of us were enjoying "happy hour" with homemade cocktails, takeout, and a new rom-com at my apartment. Normally, we'd go out, but I was too tired after work and my recent travels.

Looking back, I would've canceled our plans had I known I would be subjected to an interrogation.

"Technically, his family is your client. It's not the same thing, and you should totally kiss him. He's so cute." Isabella stretched her arms over her head and glanced fondly at my goldfish, whom she'd taken care of during my time abroad.

He was a temporary pet I'd adopted after the previous tenant left him behind five years ago, hence why I'd simply named him The Fish. There was no use attaching sentimentality to something that wouldn't last.

"Regardless, I wouldn't kiss Xavier Castillo if he were the last man on earth," I said coolly. "He is not my type."

He's also gorgeous, and kind, and smarter than people give him credit for, a voice sang in my head.

I pressed the tip of my pen against my notepad with more force than necessary. *Shut up.*

Sure, Xavier and I had reached a tentative understanding after Colombia. And yes, I was helping him fulfill the inheritance clause, which *might* be ethically murky since I was on the committee, but the will never stated members couldn't assist.

Besides, from a PR perspective, the story of a prodigal party son turned responsible business owner was *gold*, so I was technically just doing my job.

Sure. The same annoying voice tittered. *That's why you're helping him. Because of your* job.

I said shut. UP.

I was so distracted by the shit stirrer in my head that I almost missed Alessandra's next words.

"Maybe he's not your type, but never say never." Her blue eyes twinkled with mischief. "I think he has a thing for you. I've seen him staring at you at *multiple* events over the years. He can't look away."

"Not you too." I gave up writing my review and exchanged my pen for wine. "We're not in middle school. He doesn't have a 'thing' for me, and he stares at me because...well, who knows why he does the things he does?"

The twinkle grew brighter. "If you say so."

She sounded suspiciously like my internal voice.

Isabella, Vivian, and I had been a trio for years before we brought Alessandra into the fold, but she fit into the group seamlessly. I liked her as much as I could like any human (most of whom were deeply unlikable), but I did not appreciate being ganged up on.

"Perry Wilson never elaborated on that beach picture he posted," Isabella mused. "God, we never see the good stuff."

"Don't talk to me about Perry Wilson." I was still devising a plan to dethrone that sniveling, slandering toad. "Mark my words. By this time next year, his blog will be dead. I'll make sure of it."

No friend ever served me, and no enemy ever wronged me, whom I have not repaid in full. Lucius Cornelius Sulla's self-written epitaph.

There was a reason it was one of my favorite quotes.

"Anyway, on to cheerier topics," I said. "How's Josephine?"

Josephine, or Josie, was Vivian and Dante's daughter. She was less than two months old, and she already had her parents wrapped around her tiny finger.

"She's great. I mean, she cries all the time, and I haven't had a proper night's sleep in a month, but..." A smile touched Vivian's lips. "It's worth it."

I suppressed a grimace. Josie was adorable, but if I didn't love her and her mother so much, the mushiness would make me gag.

"It's hard being away from her, but she's in good hands. Greta fusses over her like she's her own daughter," Vivian added. Greta was her housekeeper and Dante's de facto mother since his parents were too busy gallivanting around the world to be, well, parents.

"And Dante?" Isabella's eyes sparkled. "How's he doing?"

"He thinks Josie or I will break if he looks away for more than five minutes." Vivian rolled her eyes, but her voice was filled with affection. "Did I tell you he tried to hire bodyguards to stand outside her room twenty-four seven? I swear..."

My phone pinged with a new text while my friends teased her about Dante's legendary overprotectiveness. He terrified pretty much everyone around him, but when it came to his wife and daughter, he was a teddy bear.

Xavier: Can you meet me at Valhalla in an hour? I have some important updates
Xavier: P.S. I talked to Kai

My heart skipped a beat.

I wasn't sure if I'd overstepped by asking Kai for help, but I trusted him, and Xavier needed assistance beyond what I could give.

Important updates. Did that mean he'd committed to a plan? I'd held off on pushing him about it because 1) I had a ton of work to catch up on at the office, and 2) I didn't want to spook him.

But the clock was ticking, and he needed to get moving if he wanted to meet the May deadline.

"Sloane? Everything okay?" Alessandra asked.

"Yes." I tore my eyes from my phone. "Everything's fine."

As curious as I was about Xavier's updates, it was girls' night. He could wait.

An hour and a half later, I arrived at Valhalla.

By a stroke of coincidence, Vivian had to leave our movie night early because Josie couldn't go to sleep without her. Then a very drunk Isabella had tried to take The Fish out of his aquarium and pet him, which was when Alessandra took her firmly by the hand and escorted her home.

"You know how to keep a guy waiting," Xavier drawled as I approached. I wasn't a club member, so he had to meet me at the entrance and bring me inside.

He leaned against a marble column, the picture of casual devastation in a white cashmere sweater and jeans. Despite the fall chill, he was coatless, and his sweater contrasted sharply with the richness of his tan.

As I approached, Xavier's eyes swept over my black coat dress, tights, and boots and back up again, where they lingered on my face just long enough to make my cheeks heat.

"I told you I would be late," I said as a passing breeze ruffled in his hair in the most distracting manner. "Though I don't understand why you insisted on updating me in person when texts, phone calls, and emails exist."

I fell into step beside him and deliberately focused on the impressive foyer instead of the man beside me.

I'd visited Valhalla as a guest a few times, but its splendor never failed to amaze. Gourmet restaurants, a Regency-worthy ballroom, a world-class spa, a helipad in case a member was arriving by air, and an exclusive slip at Chelsea Piers in case they were arriving by water—no detail went unchecked.

"True, but then I wouldn't get to see you." Xavier's dimples made a dazzling appearance.

The heat spread from my cheeks to my neck. I'd never had a problem thinking clearly when he was around, but a dangerous haze permeated the brain as we ascended the staircase to the second floor.

I blamed my friends. They'd put the stupid idea of a kiss in my head, and now I couldn't stop picturing the press of his lush, sensual mouth against mine and the—

No, stop it. *This is deeply inappropriate behavior.*

"Stop flirting and get to the point," I snapped for my benefit as much as his. I deliberately kept a foot of distance between us, but my nerve endings sparked and sizzled like live wires in the rain. "What are the quote unquote 'important updates'?"

God, I shouldn't have worn this stupid dress. I was roasting in cashmere.

"I've decided what I want to do." We stopped in front of carved-oak double doors. Xavier turned the knobs, the lean muscles of his arms flexing at the movement. *Stop noticing his arms.* "I'm opening a nightclub."

The doors swung open noiselessly, revealing a gorgeous library that put the one from *Beauty and the Beast* to shame. Normally, it'd be heaven, but my feet remained rooted to the hall.

A line etched between Xavier's brows. "Sloane?"

"A nightclub," I repeated. My heart beat double time. "That's brilliant."

If there was one thing he knew and knew well, it was parties. Entertainment. And his bar-design sketches…the answer had been obvious all along.

"Yeah? You think so?" Vulnerability touched his face for a moment before retreating behind a smile. "It's actually a mixed concept. Kind of like Legends except less sports oriented."

Legends was a well-known nightspot owned by former college football star and Heisman winner Blake Ryan, and it was the preferred watering hole for many top athletes.

"I love that," I said honestly. As an unapologetic multitasker, I appreciated anything that served multiple functions.

"Come on. I want to show you something." Xavier led me

deeper into the library, which was nearly empty this late at night. On any other day, I would've been enraptured by the forest of leather-bound books and rare stained-glass windows, but I was too intrigued by Xavier's plan.

We stopped at a massive table anchoring the center of the room. A spill of papers scattered across the mahogany surface, and I recognized Xavier's distinctive scrawl from several feet away.

"I've been here since the afternoon," he said. "I ran into Kai at the bar, and our conversation got me thinking..." He handed me a printout of the top ten clubs in the world. "What do these have in common?"

"Music and alcohol?"

Xavier fixed me with a wry stare. "Besides that."

"I have no idea." I knew enough to do my job, but I wasn't a nightlife aficionado.

"Interesting locations. Signature features. A tightly targeted clientele. And yes, great music and drinks." Xavier tapped the printout, his eyes brightening the more he talked. "This is Manhattan. Nightspots come and go every week. To stand out, you need something that makes people talk. Something they haven't seen before that they'll automatically associate with you."

His voice lowered. "Picture it, Luna. A club that's tucked away, hidden behind an unassuming door—the type you walk past every day without a second thought. But when you walk in... it's a different world. You don't just hear the thump of the bass; you *feel* it in your bones. The music, the rhythm, the laughter. The lights are low, and you can practically smell the pheromones in the air." His words took on a hypnotic cadence, transforming the stately library around us into a den of hedonism—of sensual touches, insistent beats, and beautiful bodies grinding against each other amidst a backdrop of velvet and liquor.

My breath shortened. Blood rushed to the surface of my skin, warming it to an uncomfortable degree. I was suddenly hyperaware of Xavier's proximity, and when he spoke again, the velvety timbre sent a shot of pure dopamine through my system.

"Everyone around you is lost in the intoxication of the moment," he said softly. "There are no worries, only wants. Every corner is an opportunity for clandestine meetings; every drink is another step away from the real world. That's the true secret to a memorable nightclub. The minute you step inside, you're not in a club; you're in a place where anything can happen with anyone." His voice lowered even further. "Whatever your greatest desire, you have a chance to realize it. All you have to do is let go."

All you have to do is let go.

Call me delusional, but I could've sworn he wasn't talking about the club anymore.

His gaze rained embers on my face, dark and hot and knowing. My head swam like I'd downed half a dozen of the drinks he'd mentioned, and though we were still at Valhalla, surrounded by serious-looking men and women in suits, my senses ignited like we were somewhere else. Somewhere secluded, where we—

The library doors opened to a loud peal of laughter. Glares swung toward the entrance, where the newcomers quickly quieted, still grinning, but the interruption was enough to restore my rationality. It washed over me like a cold shower, wiping away the haze Xavier's words had induced.

He was my client, and we were discussing business. That was all.

I took a tiny step back and forced a cool smile. "Spoken like a business graduate." I examined the list again, hoping he hadn't noticed my temporary loss of control. "Do you have a location idea and business plan in the works?"

Xavier's eyes gleamed with amused knowledge, but he didn't call me out. "Yes. The location will be tough to get, but Kai gave me some useful contacts." He retrieved another paper from the table.

My heart skipped a beat when I saw the list.

There were only eight names, but they were the only eight that mattered for his purposes.

"This is...impressive," I said, for lack of a better word. "Have you spoken to any of them yet?"

"Only the first one. We have a meeting scheduled in two weeks."

The first and arguably most intimidating one. God. Every entrepreneur in the country would *kill* for a team like this. I knew Kai would pull through.

He'd been skeptical about Xavier, but I'd finally convinced him after pointing out what a great profile it would make for *Mode de Vie*'s annual Movers and Shakers issue.

"Also, thank you for talking to Kai for me." Xavier's face softened. "You didn't have to do that."

Just like that, a soft hum buzzed to life in my veins again.

"You don't have to thank me." I deliberately avoided his eyes as I set the papers down on the table. "That was the easy part. Opening a club in six months in Manhattan? That's the hard part."

"Don't I know it," he said with a rueful laugh. "But I have a plan, which is more than I had a week ago."

"I'm glad." My smile formed of its own accord. His father had forced his hand, but Xavier appeared genuinely excited about the project. Okay, maybe *excited* was pushing it, but he was committed.

"Anyway, I wanted to show you since this was your idea." Xavier gestured at the remaining documents, which contained notes, scribbles, and ideas for the club. "If it weren't for you..." His face softened further. "I don't know where I'd be."

The hum in my blood intensified.

I attempted a witty reply, but a strange haze permeated the air and robbed me of speech. It was different from the one earlier, when he'd been talking about the club. It was thicker, more potent, and I was suddenly, painfully aware of how empty the library had gotten.

Of how close Xavier stood.

Of how his body heat sank into my skin, urging me to step closer, just a little bit, so my chest pressed against his and I could discover for myself whether his hair felt as soft as it looked between my fingers.

It's the alcohol. Never mind the fact I'd had my last drink two hours ago or that it'd become my default excuse. It was the only plausible explanation for why I was feeling these...*things* around Xavier Castillo, of all people.

"Sloane." His quiet voice made my name sound like a caress.

"Yes?" The breathlessness that escaped sounded nothing like me. It belonged to a stranger, the type who would succumb to dimples and broad shoulders and eyes the color of rich melting chocolate.

"You should leave." A rough edge turned his words into a warning.

He was right. I should. It was late, and I had to finish writing my movie review, and...and...My mind blanked.

"Why?"

Another shiver ran down my neck when the distance between us shortened by another inch.

"Because it's late," Xavier said softly. "And because..." He trailed off when I licked my lips in a brief, involuntary movement.

His gaze latched on to my mouth, and my parched throat dried even more.

The world narrowed to this very moment, beneath the dim lights of the library, listening to our escalating breaths sync with each other.

And when he let out a tortured "fuck" and dipped his head, molding his mouth to mine, it didn't even occur to me to pull away.

This was the world, and I never wanted to leave.

Logic and reasoning fell to tatters in the scorching tangle of lips and teeth. One hand grabbed my nape and pulled me closer; the other splayed across my back, burning through cashmere and skin to turn me boneless.

My mouth parted in a moan, and his tongue pushed inside, caressing mine in strokes so lazy and sensual, I couldn't tell where one ended and the other began. He tasted like an addictive combination of heat and spices, and the warmth of his touch curled through my stomach, between my thighs, and traveled all the way down to my toes.

I didn't know how long we stayed there, but it was enough for me to slide my fingers through his hair and confirm that yes, it really was that soft, and yes, he really did taste that good, and no, I'd never, ever come this close to unraveling.

I would've happily drowned in the embrace, but reality intervened as it always did, and we broke apart with a gasp for breath.

We stared at each other, our chests heaving. My lips tingled in the aftermath, and the air felt like ice water after the heat of our kiss.

A hint of red glazed Xavier's cheekbones. I noticed with some embarrassment that his lips were swollen, and...

Fuck. I did that. *We* did that.

I...We'd...I'd let him...

This time, reality wasn't so much a gentle slip as it was a slap in the face.

Every muscle locked as the implications of what just happened crashed over me.

I'd just kissed a client. Not only a client, but someone whose inheritance I was one-fifths in charge of thanks to some stupid fucking will I'd never asked to participate in.

Dread curdled in my gut.

Xavier must've picked up on my mood shift because his shoulders tensed to match mine. "Sloane—"

"I have to go." I grabbed my purse, which had fallen to the ground sometime during our kiss. "We'll discuss your business plan later."

I spun around and scrambled out of the library before he had a chance to respond.

The thunder of my pulse followed me all the way downstairs, out the door, and across the grounds to Valhalla's gated entrance.

I'd just told my friends Xavier wasn't my type, and then I'd gone and done *that. What the hell was I thinking?*

I hadn't been thinking. That was the problem. I'd let my hormones take the wheel, and they'd driven me straight to Stupidville.

"It's the dry spell," I said aloud. Either that, or Isabella had acquired a magical ability to manifest anything she said into reality. Normally, I'd be terrified—she read way too much dinosaur erotica to safely possess such a power—but I would rather deal with that than consider the remaining explanation.

I, Sloane Kensington, was attracted to Xavier Castillo.

No, not just attracted to, but *liked*. Enough to forget my strict rules about not getting involved with clients. Enough to let him kiss me and to kiss him *back*.

I groaned and pressed the heels of my hands against my eyes.

I'm so fucked.

CHAPTER 19

Xavier

KISSING SLOANE HAD BEEN A MISTAKE. NOT BECAUSE I regretted doing it, but because once I did it, I couldn't imagine *not* doing it again.

It'd been a week since the library, and I still couldn't get her out of my mind. The warmth of her skin, the softness of her lips, the way her curves fit against my body like they were made for me. She'd smelled like fresh snow and lavender and tasted like heaven, and I couldn't even pass by a damn bakery without remembering how sweet her mouth had been against mine.

I had a ton of important business meetings lined up over the next two weeks, but our kiss had taken my focus hostage.

The physical attraction had been there since we met, but besides lighthearted flirting, I never made a move before Valhalla. I told myself I didn't want to complicate our relationship or fuck up the terms of my allowance, when in reality, a part of me suspected that giving in to that attraction would spell the end for me.

Then we'd started working together and I'd discovered the layers beneath her rigid exterior. The intelligence. The conviction. The fierce loyalty to those she cared about. And I no longer suspected but *knew*, especially after that kiss, that Sloane Kensington was it. Just like that.

The only problem was I doubted she felt the same way, and even if she *did* feel the same way, her defenses were so locked down she'd never admit it.

"Are you listening to me?" She dragged my thoughts away from their brooding and back to the task at hand.

"Of course." I flashed an easy smile that was more muscle memory than emotion.

We were at her office in Midtown. It was our first time meeting in person since the library, and Sloane had jumped right into business like our kiss never happened.

I'd expected it, but it prickled nonetheless.

"What did I just say?" She crossed her arms.

"I need to get the ball rolling on licenses, location and staffing. I should meet with Dante. I have a preliminary phone interview with *Mode de Vie* about this new venture, and as a courtesy, the chairwoman of Castillo Group's board has sent me a shortlist of CEO candidates." A genuine grin peeked out at her frown. "Do I get a gold medal?"

"For doing the bare minimum? No." She tapped her tablet. "Okay, let's go over the PR strategy for the grand opening. I realize this may be putting the cart before the horse, but if everything goes smoothly, the event is in six months. People's calendars are probably already booked, but I'll make it work. We want a curated group of influencers and tastemakers in attendance, and if you insist on bringing your friends, you *need* to get them under control. I don't want to see Tilly Denman stealing gift bags again."

"Is it really a party if Tilly isn't her usual kleptomaniac self?" I yawned, already bored. I would rather bury myself in logistics than publicity. "We've been at this for hours. Let's have lunch."

"It's eleven a.m."

"Then let's have brunch."

Sloane's frown deepened. "Be serious. I'm trying to help you."

"I *am* serious. Jillian!" I called out.

Her assistant poked her head into the room. "Yes?"

"Has Sloane eaten yet?"

"She had a banana and black coffee for breakfast," Jillian said. "That was right when I came into the office, so around seven forty-five."

"Thank you, darling."

"Anytime." She beamed at me, ignoring her boss's death glare before a ringing phone drew her back to her desk.

I faced Sloane again. "A banana and coffee doesn't last three hours. We need fuel." I pulled out my phone, already ordering an Uber. "Come to brunch with me, and I'm all yours afterward. I'll even go through that list of invitees one by one."

"I have other work commitments besides you."

"Sure, but not today. Jillian mentioned she cleared your calendar this afternoon so you can catch up on emails, and you can do that anywhere."

Sloane's lips seamed together, but she eventually relented.

Twenty minutes later, the hostess seated us at Cafe Amelie, one of the many restaurants in the Laurents' dining empire. I'd attended boarding school with Sebastian Laurent, and I had a guaranteed seat at any of their establishments.

We placed our orders. I added bottomless mimosas, much to Sloane's disapproval, but hey, brunch wasn't brunch without champagne, and Cafe Amelie was one of those blessed places that served a bottomless supply.

Outside the office, fortified by the drinks and protected by the chatter of other diners, I finally broached the elephant in the room.

We had to talk about it eventually. I would rather talk about it now than wait for it to blow up in the future.

"About what happened the other day..."

Sloane stiffened. "Don't. This isn't the appropriate place or time to discuss it."

"We're drinking mimosas in public on a beautiful Thursday afternoon. I can't think of a better place or time *to* discuss it."

Our server brought our food. Sloane waited for her to leave before she replied.

"Fine. Here's how I see it." She cut into her pancakes with controlled precision. "Emotions were running high, and a client kissed me in the heat of the moment. I didn't shut it down immediately, and that was on me. But now, it's over and done with. Time to move on with our lives and focus on what's important—work. Namely, my capacity as your *publicist*..." She emphasized the last word. "And your inheritance clause."

Despite her cool response, a faint wash of color edged her cheeks and the bridge of her nose.

"Hmm. I've never heard you so verbose." I tore off a piece of bread and tossed it in my mouth. I chewed and swallowed before musing, "Trying to bury your feelings with more words, Luna?"

"I promise, there are better places to live than in delusion."

"Better? Maybe. More fun? I doubt it." I leaned forward, my face sobering. "I'm sorry if I crossed the line the other night. If I truly made you uncomfortable, I'll back off, but tell me the truth. Did you enjoy the kiss?"

Sloane's color heightened. "That's irrelevant."

"I beg to differ. When it comes to kissing, enjoyment is very much relevant."

"For any other pair, maybe. For *us*, it's irrelevant because I refuse to compromise my professional integrity by engaging in inappropriate activities with a client." She stabbed a piece of pancake with her fork for emphasis.

"It's the twenty-first century, and you're your own boss. It's not like you'll get fired."

"My reputation is at stake."

"Your reputation is sterling. No one would dare say a word against you." It was easy to fall back on the work excuse, and in a way, I got it. Sloane had more to lose than I did if we got involved, but in the grand scheme of things, it wasn't a deal-breaker. Other couples in similar situations had figured it out. "Look at Eldorra's royal couple. They had a centuries-old *law* working against them, and now they're happily married."

"I'm not a princess, you're not my bodyguard, and they were in love," Sloane said flatly. "It's different."

"Every love starts with a kiss." I was pushing her close to the limit, but I'd always regret it if I didn't try. Comfort was easy, but I was starting to realize that easy wasn't always the right answer. If it were, I would've taken the CEO position at the Castillo Group instead of formulating an impossible plan to open a New York nightclub in *six months*.

Screw it. If I was going to do this, I might as well go all in.

"Go on a date with me," I said.

Her eyes flared with an unidentifiable emotion before they shuttered. "No."

"Why not? And forget about your job for a second. Give me a real reason, Sloane."

Her fingers curled tight around her fork. Odds were, she was picturing stabbing me with it, but I didn't mind a little hypothetical violence. It kept things interesting.

The noise from the dining room retreated as I waited for an answer. Beneath my casual exterior, my heart fought to break out of my chest.

I'd never felt this nervous over someone, ever.

I knew I was speeding into this with no clear view of the

consequences. I knew I should focus on the club instead of my personal life, and I knew I might've fucked up the tentative understanding Sloane and I had reached in Colombia.

I knew all this, yet I didn't care. I wanted her too much, and I wanted *this*, whatever this was, to work. Even if it didn't, I had to at least try.

She opened her mouth.

I tensed, every muscle poised for—

"Sloane? Is that you?"

An unfamiliar and deeply unwelcome voice fractured the moment. Our heads swiveled in unison toward the interloper.

Buzz cut, tanned skin, bulging muscles. He looked like the type of guy who spent half his life chugging protein shakes and working out. He wore a black T-shirt and jeans and stared at Sloane in a way that made me want to punch him in his generically handsome face.

"Excuse us, but we're in the middle of a conversation," I said. I usually wasn't so rude to strangers, but there was something about this guy that I instantly disliked.

"You haven't answered any of my calls or texts," he said, ignoring me. "What's going on?"

Sloane stared at him, her face frozen. She seemed too stunned to answer.

"I'm sorry, but who are you?" I didn't bother hiding my irritation this time.

Protein Shake glanced at me, his eyes narrowing as he took me in. "I'm her boyfriend, asshole. Who the hell are you?"

CHAPTER 20

Sloane

I'D WORKED WITH XAVIER FOR YEARS, AND I'D NEVER seen him angry. Frustrated, yes. Annoyed, definitely. But angry? No.

Until now.

The shift in his countenance was subtle but unmistakable: The tightening of his jaw. The glint in his eyes. The way his muscles coiled.

He was seconds away from losing his temper, and I needed to take control fast before we landed ourselves on Perry fucking Wilson's blog again.

"He's not my boyfriend." I finally found my words and pinned an annoyed glare at the man standing across from me. "Since you asked, I haven't answered your calls or texts because I already made it clear: We're over."

"I thought you were *joking*. We had such a good thing going. Why would you want to end it?" Mark demanded. He appeared genuinely baffled.

Oh, for Christ's sake. This was what I got for indulging in a regular hookup instead of one-night stands.

I didn't want a relationship, but I had physical needs like

everyone else, and having a consistent booty call was easier than wading into the sewage of online dating or waiting for lightning to strike in real life.

The problem? Men always got so attached. Sleep with them a couple of times and they suddenly thought we were going to ride off into the sunset together.

I didn't even like sunsets. They were depressing.

"I told you our time together has expired." I looked around for our server. There had to be a rule against unlawful loitering at diners' tables. "Now, as Xavier mentioned, we were in the middle of a conversation. Please leave."

My talk with Xavier had been uncomfortable, off-putting, and surprising in a multitude of ways, but I'd rather spend the entire day rehashing our kiss than speak with Mark.

I'd broken things off with him right before Greece. We met when he was bartending at the happy hour spot my friends and I frequented, and we hooked up for a few months until he booked us a *weekend getaway* at a bed-and-breakfast. That was when I knew it was over.

"Oh, come on," Mark wheedled. If I hadn't been sure we were over before, I was now. There was nothing more unattractive than a grown man whining. "If you—"

"She said *leave.*" Xavier cut him off, his voice lethally soft.

He hadn't moved since Mark called himself my boyfriend, but his eyes smoldered with deadly warning.

Despite his relaxed pose, one arm tossed over the back of the booth and the other resting on the table, tension filled every line of his body. He resembled a predator lying in the weeds, waiting to strike.

A shiver breathed cold down my spine.

Xavier wasn't the violent type, but I had a gut feeling that if he and Mark went head to head, one of them would end up on the ground—and it'd be the one standing right now.

"This doesn't involve you," Mark snapped, but he took a tiny step to the right, away from Xavier. "I still don't know who the fuck you are."

"You don't need to know who I am." Xavier's affable smile didn't reach his eyes. "You do, however, need to take a hint. Sloane broke up with you, and you didn't listen. She told you to leave, and you didn't listen. That's two strikes. I highly suggest you don't make a third."

Some people's anger ran hot, exploding in outbursts and impulsive violence.

Xavier's ran cold, smoothing his tone, frosting the air, and sending another breathless shiver over my skin.

I could and did take care of myself. I didn't want to play the damsel in distress, and I didn't need a man barging in to reiterate things I'd already said.

But fuck, sometimes it felt good to have backup, especially when it came wrapped in muscles and devastating charm.

Mark's gaze slid from Xavier to me and back again. Whatever he saw in our faces must've spooked him because he turned tail and fled without another word.

My fork clattered against my plate when he disappeared from view. I'd clutched it in a death grip this entire time, and the metal left a cold imprint against my skin.

Xavier dropped his arm from the booth, tension unwinding from his body like a spool of rope. The dangerous gleam vanished from his eyes, and he observed me for a quiet moment.

"Luna," he said, "you have unequivocally shitty taste in past men."

I groaned, already over this day even though it was only noon.

"Thank you for brunch, but we're done here." I tossed a twenty on the table for tip, grabbed my bag, and stood. "I have..." He knew about my cleared calendar. *Dammit, Jillian*. If she weren't such a great assistant otherwise, I would fire her for sharing that information with Xavier. "Emails to check."

"I certainly hate to keep you from your emails, but we haven't finished our earlier conversation, as you kindly pointed out to Meathead Central." Xavier flagged down our server and paid our bill before following me out of the restaurant. "Give me a good reason why we can't date besides our working relationship."

"That should be enough reason." I purposely turned away from him and scanned the street for a passing cab. A quick phone check told me it would be faster than trying to hail an Uber.

"Working relationships come and go, Luna. Personal ones don't." A small pause. "At least, they shouldn't."

"Are you firing me?"

"No, I'm saying we can work around the publicist-client thing. Hell, we can watch one of those rom-coms you love—er, love to *hate-watch*—so much for inspiration," Xavier amended when I glared at him. "Hollywood must've come up with a dozen strategies for this sort of thing."

"I told you, rom-coms are unrealistic. Hollywood isn't real life." I whirled to face him. "You just told Mark to know when to take a hint. *Why* are you being so insistent about this?"

"Because I want you."

Simple. Matter-of-fact. And a fierce, unexpected blow to my chest.

The air evacuated from my lungs as I stared at Xavier. His eyes and mouth had sobered, wiping away the irreverence and leaving only sincerity behind.

"I don't want a kiss or a one-night stand," he said. "I want *you*. I want to know you outside work. I want to take you on real dates. And I don't know if it'll work out in the end, but I want us to at least try."

For God's sake, Sloane, no one wants to date a block of ice.

A thick sensation crawled into my throat and curled up there.

"Trust me." I strangled my bag strap with one hand. "You don't want to know me outside work."

When I was working, no one blamed me for being cold or direct. They expected it. When I was dating...that was a whole different matter.

"Let me be the judge of that." Xavier's voice softened. "What are you so afraid of?"

A wretched tingle spread behind my eyes and nose. "Nothing."

I averted my gaze to the street, where honking cars and jaywalking pedestrians provided enough stimulation to obscure my real answer.

I'm afraid of letting someone in again.

I'm afraid of getting my heart broken.

I'm afraid that, if you get to know the real me, you'll find me unlovable like everyone else, and it'll hurt so much more because it's you.

My past was my past. I'd been young, stupid, and inexperienced, and I'd dated plenty of other men since my first heartbreak. I hadn't been afraid of giving them a chance because I knew they wouldn't breach my defenses.

Xavier? He had the potential to destroy the entire system.

"Sloane." His light touch seared my arm. "Look at me."

"No." I hardened my resolve and thrust out my arm to hail a passing cab. "We'll go over your PR plan later. I'm taking the rest of the day off."

By that, I meant I was going to catch up on my emails at home, take a nice long bubble bath, indulge in a glass of wine and a movie...and *not* think about Xavier Castillo in any way, shape, or form.

The cab screeched to a halt in front of me. I opened the door and climbed in. Xavier climbed in after me.

"What are you doing?" I demanded. "This is breaking and entering!"

"It's a cab."

"That you're *breaking and entering* into." I rapped my knuckles against the divider separating us from the front seat. "You have an intruder in your car. I don't know this man. Please dispose of him immediately."

The driver glanced in the rearview mirror, unimpressed. "Weren't ya just talking to him a second ago?"

"*He* was talking to me."

"*We* were talking to each other," Xavier corrected.

"I—"

The driver released a huge sigh. "Look, lady, I don't got time to deal with a lovers' spat. You wanna go or not?"

"We're not—"

"She wants to go. Just keep driving around until we say otherwise." Xavier slipped a hundred-dollar-bill through the opening in the divider. "A pre-tip for your service. Thanks, man."

The driver snatched the bill from his hand and sped off.

"This is kidnapping," I said furiously. "You are committing a crime."

"You broke into my room twice in the past month, so consider us even." Xavier smiled, but his eyes remained serious. "You can't keep running from the hard stuff, Luna. Eventually, you'll have to face what you're so afraid of."

"That's ironic, coming from you."

Xavier had spent half his life avoiding responsibility. He was the last person who should lecture me on running.

"True," he acknowledged. "But I'm working on it."

I didn't have a good answer to that.

I slumped against my seat, suddenly exhausted.

It was too much. Spain, Colombia, seeing Pen, getting my

father's email and finding out my sister was pregnant, kissing Xavier...The past month's bombshells had hammered dent after dent into my walls, and I was so tired of holding them up.

"If you truly didn't feel anything during our kiss, I'll stop the car right now, and we'll never discuss this again," Xavier said quietly. "It won't affect our work together, and we can pretend it never happened. But if there's even a tiny part of you that thinks this can work..." He swallowed. "I'm not saying we have to get married or jump into a long-term relationship, but I want us to let each other in. Doesn't have to go all the way to the rooms where we keep our secrets. Even the entrance hall will do for now."

My laugh broke free of its own accord. "My God. That is the *worst* metaphor I've ever heard."

"Hey, I never said I was a poet." He gave me a crooked grin. "So, what do you say? They're just dates, Luna. We'll keep them discreet, and if it works, it works. If it doesn't, it doesn't. No harm, no foul."

The responsible thing to do was shut this down once and for all. Nothing good could come of letting *any* man in, much less one as clever and charming as Xavier, and saying yes went against my vow not to get involved with clients.

But I would be lying if I said I felt nothing for him. Our kiss had made me feel more than anything else in recent memory, and I had the unsettling feeling that if I walked away, the what-if's would haunt me for the rest of my life.

I hope I don't regret this.

"Two months, effective immediately." Just saying the words made my chest tighten, but I pushed back the worst-case scenarios threatening to surface. "We have until the end of December to determine whether this can go anywhere."

"Like a trial period."

"Yes." I lifted my chin. "Do you have an issue with that?"

"Not at all." Xavier's grin deepened as he held out his hand. "We have a deal."

It was my last chance to back out, but fuck it, I hadn't come this far to chicken out now.

I slid my hand into his and tried to ignore the swoop of butterflies in my stomach. "We have a deal."

CHAPTER 21

Sloane

"I WON'T SAY I TOLD YOU SO, BUT I TOLD YOU SO," Isabella said. "I *knew* you and Xavier would eventually give in to your sizzling, delicious—"

"Please stop. I'm in a cab, and I'm going to hurl."

"I hope not, considering you're on your way to a first date." I could hear her grin over the phone. "Have fun. Fill us in on *everything* later, and don't worry about the Perry thing. We got you."

I hadn't forgotten about Perry Wilson's attempt to throw me under the bus. Since I was back in the city, I could focus on taking him down with some help from my friends.

"Thank you." The cab rolled to a stop. "I'm here. Talk to you later."

"Ooh. Send us a picture of—"

I hung up before Isabella said anything else inappropriate. I paid the driver and climbed the steps to Xavier's West Village town house, the nerves in my stomach sprouting teeth and fangs.

It was Saturday, two days after my questionable decision to say yes to *casually* dating him (emphasis on the *casual*). Xavier didn't tell me what he had planned, only that I should wear "cozy clothing," and if it were anyone else, I would've balked the second he told me our first date was at his house. That was how charming serial killers lured their victims to their deaths.

My showing up anyway was either a testament to how comfortable I felt with him or how stupid I was. Honestly, I preferred the latter explanation over the former.

I lifted my hand, but the door opened before I could knock.

Xavier's tousled black hair and lean, sculpted body filled the frame, and I was beset by the strange sensation of my heart sputtering. He wore his version of cozy: jeans and a fine cashmere sweater that outlined his broad shoulders and arms. No shoes.

For some reason, seeing him barefoot at home felt unbearably intimate.

I dropped my arm with a twinge of self-consciousness. "Hi."

"Hi." His smile displayed a flash of his dimples. "Before you think I'm a creep who was waiting at the window, I came out to get this." He picked up a small brown box from the front stoop. "You just happen to have perfect timing."

"That's not a knife you bought to murder me in your secret basement, is it?"

The dimples deepened. "I guess you'll find out."

"Funny."

I hung my coat on the brass tree by the door and followed him deeper into the town house. I'd visited once before to drop off some papers but never made it past the living room.

Xavier gave me a quick tour and explanation of each room we passed.

Contrary to what I'd expected, his house didn't resemble a college fraternity's. It was surprisingly cozy despite its vast layout, and the coastal decor was a refreshing mix of soft whites, moody blues, and dusty yellows. He either had an excellent eye, an excellent interior designer, or both.

"This is where I spend most of my time." He gestured at the second-floor den, which was part TV room, part library, and part home arcade. "It's the jack-of-all-trades in the house."

"Is that a claw machine?" I walked closer to the metal container filled with stuffed toys. It occupied the far-right wall between a vintage pinball machine and a retro popcorn cart.

"Ah, yes." Xavier rubbed the back of his neck, pink tinting his cheeks. "I hated those things when I was younger. I spent a fortune on them but never got the toy I wanted, so I installed this and rigged it so everyone who plays gets what they want."

The boyish explanation was so unexpectedly charming that I didn't bother hiding my smile.

"The scars from our childhood enemies run deep," I said solemnly.

"Yes, they do." Xavier fixed me with a grave stare. "Don't get me started on Doris's old cat. She almost killed me and Hershey in our sleep once."

"Hershey?"

"Childhood pet. He was a brown Lab, hence..."

"The name."

"Bingo."

A mental image of a young Xavier with his dog popped up, and my heart melted the teensiest bit.

Ugh. Our date hadn't officially started, and I was already softening. What was wrong with me?

"Did you have any pets when you were younger?" Xavier's hand brushed mine when we left the den. Electricity sizzled up my arm, and I instinctively jerked it away.

I smoothed a hand over my bun to hide the knee-jerk reaction, my heart pounding. I wasn't sure if he'd noticed, but a tiny grin played at the corners of his mouth as he led me past the third-floor bedrooms and to the rooftop.

"No," I said a tad belatedly. "My father doesn't like any animals except horses." I made a determined effort not to glance at any of the bedroom doors and picture what was behind them.

What did Xavier's room look like? His childhood bedroom in Bogotá had been stripped and transformed into a generic guest suite. Did he display items from his travels? Artwork? Posters? If so, posters of what?

"But I have a temporary pet fish," I said, determined not to dwell on such silly questions. "The person who rented my apartment before me left him behind."

Xavier opened the door to the rooftop. "What's his name?"

"The Fish."

He stopped and looked askance at me. "You named your pet fish…Fish?"

"*The* Fish," I corrected. "Articles of grammar are important, and like I said, he's a temporary pet. There's no use giving him a real name."

"Right. How long have you had this temporary pet?"

"Five years."

His laughter sent white puffs of breath into the chilly fall air. "I hate to break it to you, Luna, but once it passes the one-year mark, pet ownership is no longer considered temporary."

I constructed a whole argument about how *temporary* didn't have a defined time limit. Therefore, if I'd adopted The Fish with the intention of rehoming him one day, it was considered temporary regardless of how much time passed.

However, the words died on my tongue when I stepped fully onto the rooftop and saw what he'd planned for our first date.

Oh my God.

A giant standing TV screen dominated one side of the rooftop, kitty-corner to a table covered with every snack one could think of. There were white ceramic dishes filled with M&M's, pretzels, gummy bears, and other candies I couldn't identify at this distance; plates groaning with chips, cookies, and sundry snacks; massive bowls containing six different types of popcorn; and a full charcuterie board. A champagne bucket sat next to tea, coffee, and three bottles of wine (one red, one white, one rosé). Beneath the table, a glass-fronted minifridge boasted an assortment of water, juice, and soda.

Area rugs and potted plants scattered across the floor, lending the scene a cozy feel. Strategically placed candles and the canopy of lights overhead illuminated the rooftop in lieu of the setting sun while portable heat lamps warded off the cold.

However, the *real* star of the show was the giant mattress laid out in front of the screen. Piled high with pillows, cushions, and cashmere blankets, it looked so cozy I wanted to dive right into the middle and never get up.

The entire setup was so cheesy, it looked like something out of a rom-com.

And I loved it.

Emotion prickled my chest. When was the last time someone put this much thought into something for me?

My exes had taken me to expensive dinners and exclusive shows, which were nice, but they only cost money. Time and care required far more effort, and no one had ever deemed me worthy of those things.

"Since it's Halloween, I figured we could do a double feature," Xavier said. "One witchy rom-com and one Christmas rom-com that doesn't release until the holidays. Friend of a friend is high up at the studio and pulled through for me."

For once, I didn't have a sarcastic reply.

"That..." I cleared my throat of its hoarseness. "That sounds nice."

We filled our plates with food and settled on the mattress. He'd pushed it up against the low brick wall so we had back support, but a mountain of pillows softened the hard surface.

The opening credits rolled across the screen. I tried to focus on the lead actors' names instead of Xavier's presence.

We weren't pressed against each other, but we were close enough that every time one of us moved, something grazed.

His arm against my shoulder.

His leg against my knee.

His hand against my thigh.

Moments of contact so brief they barely counted as touches, but so potent they wreaked havoc on my body. My entire right side tingled from his proximity, and awareness pulsed to life in my veins.

We were on a New York rooftop in late October, and I was burning up. It wasn't because of the heat lamps or the blankets; it was because of him.

"I'm surprised you scheduled this for Halloween." I made conversation simply to divert attention away from the rapid patter of my heartbeat. *Get a hold of yourself, for Christ's sake.* "There are dozens of parties tonight."

"Those are boring. This isn't."

"You would rather watch a rom-com about a witch and a plumber falling in love than attend a costume party with celebrities?"

"One hundred percent. As long as I'm watching it with you."

His answer came out so casually, it took a second to register. Once it did, the patter morphed into a full-blown marching band, drums and all.

Damn him.

Tonight was supposed to be an obligatory date. I wasn't supposed to like it this much.

You know you have to actually give him a chance, right?

Vivian's gentle reminder from our happy hour yesterday floated through my mind. *Don't go through the motions waiting for the trial period to expire. It won't be fair to either of you.*

I hated when other people were right.

"What about you?" Xavier asked. "No Halloween plans with the girls?"

"No. They're with their families." A small pang hit my gut. "Vivian and Dante took Josie to this Halloween thing at the zoo. Kai and Isa have a *Mode de Vie* event, and Dominic and Alessandra are at Valhalla's fall gala." Kai and Isabella technically weren't married yet, but they might as well be.

I was the odd one out. I didn't mind it; I would rather be single and content than in a relationship and miserable. But there were slivers of time when I wondered how it would feel to exist in the world knowing there was someone who loved me totally, unconditionally, and whole-heartedly for who I was instead of who they wanted me to be.

"Speaking of Dante, did you figure out why he's on the inheritance committee?" I asked, eager to think about something—anything—else.

"No, I haven't spoken to him yet. I've been focusing on next week's meetings." Xavier's leg brushed mine again, and there was that stupid *zing* again. He glanced at me, the moving images onscreen throwing his features into light, then shadow, then light again. "He did a lot of business with my father, so I assume that's part of the reason."

"Maybe. I can ask Vivian—"

"Luna." He gently hooked his pinky around mine beneath the blanket, and my knowledge of how to breathe evaporated. "This is a date. No more work talk."

"Right." *In and out. You know how to do this.* "Are you ever going to tell me why you call me Luna?"

"One day." His dimples winked into view. "If you're really nice to me."

I tamped down a smile. "I'm nice to you right now."

"You forgot a word."

"*Really* nice. What does that entail, a blow job?"

My quip trailed off when I realized my mistake. Discussing blow jobs with Xavier? *Bad idea.*

Abort, abort! Alarm bells clanged in my head, but it was too late.

Something intense swallowed the humor in his eyes, and my already-scarce supply of oxygen dwindled to emergency levels.

Neither of us was paying attention to the movie at this point. Unfortunately, that meant *all* my attention had rerouted to 1) the delicious warmth of Xavier's body, which had inched close enough to short-circuit my brain, and 2) a salacious mental gallery of images that revolved around me, him, and a certain activity with the initials BJ.

My blood sang with sudden heat.

"Perhaps, but not tonight." His silky murmur ghosted down my spine. "I don't pass first base on the first date. What kind of man do you think I am?"

"You're telling me you've never done more than kiss someone on the first date." It wasn't a question, but the voice that delivered it was so breathless, I didn't recognize it as mine.

"I have, but that was years ago, we weren't dating, and I wasn't trying to woo them."

Another type of warmth, one that had nothing to do with arousal, pooled in my stomach. "Is that what you're trying to do? Woo me?"

"Depends." A smile played on his lips. "Is it working?"

Yes. "No."

"Liar."

"A suitor shouldn't call the object of his wooing a liar. It's poor etiquette."

"I'm honest when the situation calls for it, and you'd die of boredom if someone simply agreed with everything you said and did." His pinky, still hooked around mine, curled just a bit tighter. I wished I minded.

"You think you know me so well," I whispered, even though he was right.

"Only parts of you." The gentle brush of his thumb against my hand unlocked a colony of butterflies in my stomach. "But we'll get there."

The implication that we would last until that point sent my defenses into overdrive, but the evening was so nice, and his touch felt so good, I ignored it.

It was only when the witch movie ended and the Christmas one began that I realized I'd watched a rom-com without writing a review for the first time in five years.

CHAPTER 22

IF I HAD MY WAY, I'D SPEND THE NEXT TWO MONTHS focused solely on Sloane.

We ended our movie date Saturday night with nothing more than a chaste kiss on the cheek, but it was the best damn date I'd ever had. She was warming up to me, and that was what mattered.

I'll be honest—I wasn't used to chasing women. From the moment I hit puberty, I'd been inundated with female attention. Dating was easy, and sex was even easier, so this whole trial thing with Sloane was uncharted territory.

Were it anyone else, I would simply let them go. But she wasn't anyone else, and I was already making plans for our next date. We had two months, so I needed to make the most out of them.

Unfortunately, I had to deal with the pesky issue of my nightclub. Namely, securing the proper licenses, location, financing, and a million other things that came with starting a business.

That was how I found myself in Valhalla again the Wednesday after my date, face-to-face with the man who could make or break my plans before they even started.

Name number one on Kai's list.

Vuk Markovic, also known as the Serb, sat across from me in his office, his eerie blue eyes devoid of emotion as I explained my idea. He'd eschewed the typical CEO uniform of a suit and tie in favor of a black sweater and pants. A brutal scar slashed his face into two halves, and a coil of burn scars wrapped around his neck.

I tried my hardest not to stare. Luckily, it got easier when I hit my flow. I hadn't pitched a business plan since college, but I was a fast learner and a comfortable public speaker.

I needed a partner for legitimacy, and Vuk was perfect for the job. He was the current chairman of Valhalla's management committee, which arguably made him the most powerful man in the city. He had over a decade of experience under his belt and a sterling reputation for being fair but ruthless when the occasion called for it.

Of course, he needed a compelling reason to go into business with me beyond a mutual acquaintance. Kai had gotten me in the door; it was up to me to close it.

"Markovic Holdings is launching its new nonalcoholic vodka next summer. The timing lines up perfectly with the Vault's launch," I said. I'd named the club the Vault after its (hopeful) location. "We can host an exclusive preview and have a bespoke bar highlighting the drink. Sloane Kensington is in charge of the opening; it'll be the nightlife event of the season. Every tastemaker who matters will be there, and it'll be the first of our Tastemaker Series."

The idea was simple—a monthly event series where attendees would receive early and/or exclusive access to everything from food to performances to fashion previews, all while sipping Castillo beer and Markovic alcohol.

My family specialized in beer, but Vuk helmed a massive liquor empire that ranged from cheap wine any college student could buy to fine champagne so rare, only a handful bottles were produced annually. Next year, they were diversifying into the rapidly growing zero-proof alcohol sector, and the company was putting big money into making it a success.

The signature Tastemaker Series would take place on a separate night from general nightclub revelry, but its purpose wasn't to draw regular parties. It catered to the media and influencers, who always liked being the first to try anything new; their attendance, plus the ever-evolving nature of the events, would create fresh buzz every month and keep the club at the forefront of people's minds.

At least, that was the plan.

Vuk waited until I finished my spiel before firing rounds of methodical questions at me.

Who are your competitors?

Do you have a location under contract?

Do you have any other brands or businesses lined up to participate in the Tastemaker Series?

How the hell will you pull all this off in less than six months?

He didn't say the last part, but it was implied.

Technically, he didn't say anything at all; the questions came in the form of written notes. No one knew much about him beyond his business dealings, but according to rumors, his non-verbalism wasn't due to medical reasons (legend had it he'd once said "thank you" to a Valhalla attendant). He just really fucking hated talking.

I addressed Vuk's concerns as best I could, but my confidence waned in the face of his unchanging stoicism.

"The Vault will be the biggest splash in New York nightlife

since Legends," I said. "I have the connections, the vision, and the drive, but at the end of the day, this business is about instinct. What works, what doesn't, what's the next big thing. You can't buy it or learn it." I leaned forward, keeping my eyes on his. "I have it, and if you sign on as my partner, I'll make us into actual fucking legends."

I'd devised the club as a way to fulfill my inheritance clause while sticking it to my father, but now that I had time to sit with it, I *wanted* to make it work. Not for money, family, or the world, but for myself. I wanted to prove I could do this.

Vuk stared at me, his expression remote.

I understood why most people crapped themselves when they were in the same room as him. There was something deeply unsettling about the Serb. Maybe it was a combination of his silence, his status, and his scars; maybe it was something else entirely.

Either way, nerves rattled in my veins when he started writing. He slid the paper across his desk less than thirty seconds later.

Come back to me when you've secured a location.

Dammit. Securing the location I had in mind was near impossible without Vuk as a partner.

If that was a deal-breaker, why the hell hadn't he said so before we scheduled this meeting?

I swallowed my disappointment, thanked him for his time, and exited his office. On my way out, I passed by a dark-haired man with—holy shit, was that Ayana?

"Hey, is Vuk busy?" the man asked. He must've seen me leaving the Serb's office.

I masked my surprise. Very few people called Vuk by his first name out loud; he reportedly hated it.

"He wasn't when I left."

The man nodded. "Thanks."

Ayana gave me a brief smile in passing. With her luminous dark skin and high cheekbones, the supermodel looked even more ethereal in person, but I felt a grand total of nothing. Not even a flicker of lust or attraction.

Sloane and I had kissed once, and she'd already ruined me for other women.

I should be more alarmed at this development, but I found it hard to summon anything other than a smile when I saw her pacing the library. I'd signed Sloane in before my meeting with Vuk, and while I didn't *need* moral support, I loved having her there.

"What did he say?" she asked when I came within earshot. "Or write. You know what I mean."

"He said to come back to him when I've secured a location."

"Name number two?"

"Name number two," I confirmed.

"Shit."

My sentiments exactly. I had a meeting with the second name on Kai's list this Friday, and I wasn't looking forward to it.

"On the bright side, it wasn't a no. I'll get it done," I said. "How are things going with PW?"

Sloane had filled me in on her plans to take down Perry Wilson. No arguments from me there; the gossip blogger was a massive pain in my ass.

"They're going," she said. "My friends planted the seeds. I'll take care of the rest. I was actually doing a little research for that before you came in."

"Perfect. In that case, it's been a productive day, and we can go to dinner." I needed to reset after my meeting with Vuk, and food always made me feel better.

Sloane's mouth twitched. "Your sense of meal times needs recalibration. It's only four."

"By the time we fight through rush hour traffic, it'll be five, which is happy hour time. You know what comes after happy hour?"

"A shower."

"Dinner." My mouth curled into a grin. "Though I'm not opposed to sharing a shower." I pitched my voice low enough for just her to hear.

She went a teensy pink around her ears, but she cocked an eyebrow and asked, "What happened to slow and steady wooing?"

"Get your mind out of the gutter, Luna. All I proposed was sharing a shower. It'll be perfectly PG-13 except for the two very attractive naked people in it."

Sloane's burst of laughter attracted several disapproving stares before she covered her mouth.

My grin widened. If someone had asked me a year ago what my favorite thing in the world was, it would've been a cold drink on a hot beach. Now, it was making Sloane laugh. Seeing her lower her guard and actually be herself never got old.

"I'm sorry to disappoint, but there'll be no shared showers today or anytime in the near future," she said after she wrestled her amusement under control. "That—"

Her phone lit with an incoming call, and a quick glance at the screen wiped the smile from her face.

Sloane picked up, her skin going pale as she listened to whatever the caller had to say. A minute later, she hung up and grabbed her coat from the back of her chair. "I have to go."

Shimmers of concern threaded through my gut. "What happened?"

I followed her to the exit, and she didn't answer until we were in the hall, away from any prying ears.

"It's my sister." She finally looked at me, her eyes a storm of panic. "She's in the hospital."

CHAPTER 23

Sloane

I DIDN'T ARGUE WHEN XAVIER INSISTED ON ACCOMPA-nying me to the hospital. He'd driven to the club today, and it was easier taking his car than hailing a cab.

Rhea's stressed voice echoed in my head as we sped toward the hospital.

My day off...Penny collapsed on the street...hospitalized...

She hadn't had time to fill me in on the details before a nurse called for her in the background. The lack of context sent my stomach into upheaval and my imagination spiraling down thorny paths.

How badly was Pen hurt? Was this a broken limb or something worse? Would they have to operate on her?

Dread clawed at my insides.

I should've checked in on her earlier. It'd been a month since London, and Rhea gave me the occasional text update, but I should've found time to sneak in a video call. Instead, I'd been buried in work and Xavier.

Logic told me Rhea would've been more distraught if Pen were in serious danger, but logic always cracked in the face of frigid, debilitating fear.

Thankfully, Xavier didn't ask questions or make conversation. He simply gunned through the streets, navigating jaywalkers and traffic with surprising dexterity...until we hit the gridlocked mess that was Midtown Manhattan during rush hour.

The lights were green, but traffic was so backed up, no one could move.

"What happened?" I straightened, trying to make sense of the snarl of cars, pedestrians, and bicyclists weaving through the intersection.

"Looks like an accident." Xavier opened the driver-side, leaned out, and did a quick survey of our surroundings. "We're backed up for blocks."

Shit. My hands curled around the edge of my seat. We could be stuck here for hours, and I didn't have hours.

What if Pen took a sudden turn for the worse? What if I missed out on seeing her for the last time by—

No. Don't go there.

I fought for calm. Devolving into a hysterical mess wouldn't do anyone any favors.

"I'll be right back." Xavier got out of the car fully. "If traffic somehow disappears in the next five minutes, my baby is in your hands." He patted the top of his Porsche.

"What are you...?" I twisted around to watch as he walked down the line of cars behind us and knocked on the window of the last one. The driver rolled it down, Xavier handed him something, and after a short exchange, the car reversed and turned onto a side street.

Thankfully, there were only three cars blocking us, and Xavier repeated this process with the last two until we were clear.

"Change of plans." He slid back into his seat and followed the others' lead in reversing and rerouting. "This next part might be bumpy."

"What did you do?"

"Gave the drivers three hundred bucks each to go the opposite direction." Xavier frowned at the side street, which was also clogged. "Bribery works wonders."

"We need to talk about the dangerous amount of cash you carry—*shit.*" I clutched the door's armrest, my heart leaping into my mouth as the Porsche swerved onto the sidewalk. "This is not a road!"

"I'm aware." He plowed forward, two of the wheels on the sidewalk and two on the street, past a queue of blaring car horns and angry curses. "There are no people walking here, and I can afford the fine."

"You've lost your mind—*fuck*!" My heartbeat ratcheted up another notch when we nearly sideswiped a fire hydrant, and I didn't breathe until we finally, *finally* turned on a new street and returned to proper driving.

As in, no sidewalk, only asphalt.

The incoming rush of oxygen made me dizzy. *Note to self: never get in a car with Xavier behind the wheel again.*

"You need to get to the hospital. This is the fastest way we can get there," he said calmly. He drove with one hand; the other closed around over mine, interlacing our fingers. I stiffened with surprise. "Don't worry, Luna. We'll make it."

I stared at his profile for a second before my gaze drifted to our intertwined hands. His was so large it engulfed mine, and so warm the heat radiated up my arm, through my chest, and into my stomach.

He was focused on the road, and his act of comfort was a casual, unthinking one, but somehow that made it all the more intimate.

Emotion climbed into my throat, thick and sudden.

I missed sex because I hadn't had it in a month, but I hadn't realized how much I'd missed *this*. Non-sexual touches. Easy intimacy. Connection, in one form or another.

Maybe it was because I hadn't had *this* in years, if I'd ever really had it at all.

I faced forward and squeezed Xavier's hand, letting his reassuring strength calm me. I didn't care about displaying vulnerability in that moment; I just needed someone to hold on to.

Luckily, we didn't hit major traffic again, and we arrived at the hospital in relatively short order.

"You go inside," he said. "I'll look for parking."

I didn't argue.

For a random Wednesday afternoon, the hospital was packed, but since I was family, I easily made it past the front desk.

I checked my phone in the elevator. No new messages from Rhea, which I assumed was a good thing. *Please let her be okay.*

The doors slid open. I ran out, turned the corner, and—

My stomach plummeted.

George and Caroline stood in the hall, him in a suit and her in a designer tweed dress. Their backs faced me, but I would recognize them anywhere.

I'd been so focused on seeing Pen I hadn't considered their presence. Honestly, I wouldn't have been surprised if they *hadn't* shown up. They had a habit of ignoring her unless it was absolutely necessary.

They were talking to a nurse and hadn't noticed me yet. Rhea, however, did. Our gazes locked before she deliberately turned, letting me take advantage of George and Caroline's distraction to slip into Pen's room.

I'd deal with the fallout later. Right now, I needed to see her.

Pen appeared to be sleeping, but she stirred when I closed the door behind me.

She turned her head, her eyes widening with surprise. "Sloane?"

"Hi." I mustered a faint smile even as I frantically scanned her for signs of grievous injury. She looked so tiny in the hospital bed, but other than a giant bandage over her forehead, I didn't spot anything amiss. She didn't seem to have any broken limbs, bruises, or contusions. "How are you feeling?"

"I'm okay." Pen's voice was thin but steady. "Don't worry. It's just a cut. Everyone's freaking out over nothing."

"What happened?" The knots in my chest loosened, but worry lingered in the spaces between them.

"It's so stupid," she grumbled, sounding her full nine years of age. "I fell and hit my head on the sidewalk. That's it."

"Pen." I leveled her with a stern stare.

She heaved an aggrieved sigh. "I crashed while Annie and I were taking a walk. I hit my head on the curb and, um, almost got run over by a bicycle."

I bit back a curse and a litany of questions. Annie was Rhea's backup whenever Rhea had the day off. She should've known better than to take Pen out at this time of day, when she was most likely to crash.

Thankfully, it appeared to have been a mild crash or she would've been knocked out instead of talking to me, but still.

I smoothed a hand over her hair, my heart squeezing at how fine and delicate it felt. She was so young, and she'd already been through so much.

"But I'm okay." Pen's eyes drifted closed before she opened them again, her small face filled with determination. She always resisted sleeping when we saw each other. The selfish part of me was thankful for the extra time; the anxious part worried it made her crashes worse. "Annie took me here just in case..."

I could guess why they'd put her in a private room so soon. My father had donated an entire wing to the hospital years ago.

"Where's Annie now?" I asked.

"I don't know. She got fired." Pen looked down. "Rhea left her niece's baby shower early to see me."

"Because she cares about you. We all do," I said gently.

I glanced at the bandage again. It was a relatively minor injury, but even minor injuries could have intense effects on people with CFS. The recovery took longer, and the pain could intensify their symptoms.

"Do Mom and Dad know you're here?" Pen's eyes were closing again.

"Not yet." Dread punctured my relief at the thought of confronting them.

"I'm glad you came. They'll..." Her voice faded into nothing, and she was out.

I lingered for a minute, savoring our last moments together.

Pen and I had both changed since I left my family years ago. We were older, somewhat wiser, and more cognizant of what we were dealing with when it came to George and Caroline. But in some ways, we were the same—still trapped by our circumstances, still helpless to change them.

The adrenaline from Rhea's call dissipated, leaving me with cold, hard clarity. The second I stepped into the hall, George and Caroline would know I'd been secretly seeing Pen. The only way I could've gotten here so quickly was if Rhea had contacted me, and the only *reason* I'd come so quickly was because I loved Pen. Considering she'd been four during our last known-to-them contact, it wouldn't take a genius to figure out we'd kept in touch over the years.

Maybe I'd get lucky. Maybe George and Caroline wouldn't make a big deal out of it, and they wouldn't fire Rhea or lock Pen somewhere I couldn't get to her out of spite.

Yeah, and maybe Satan will repent and give up ruling the underworld to become an elf in Santa's workshop.

I was tempted to hide in Pen's room and wait for my family to leave before I slipped out, but from what I could see through the door window, that wasn't happening anytime soon. It would be infinitely worse if someone came in and found me skulking around.

I was a lot of things, but I wasn't a coward. Whatever the consequences were, I'd deal with them. I only hoped I could shield Rhea from the brunt of the impact. She'd told me about Pen's hospitalization knowing I would show up and she'd probably get fired. She'd done it because she knew Pen would want to see me, and she didn't deserve to be let go over a moment of empathy.

I steeled myself, walked to the exit, and opened the door.

However, I barely crossed the threshold before I came to a dead halt.

George, Caroline, and Rhea weren't the only people outside Pen's room anymore. The nurse was gone, and a slim, perfectly groomed blond stood next to my father and stepmother. Beside her, a handsome man with brown hair and blue eyes looked around with a bored expression.

This time, there was no sneaking past them. Their conversation fell silent as the door shut behind me, and my four (ex) family members gaped at me with varying expressions of shock, disbelief, and confusion.

"Well," the blond said, recovering first. "This is a surprise."

I suppressed a flinch. Her voice, lovely as it was, had the effect of burrowing into my skin and peeling the scabs off old wounds. Seeing *him* was worse. It was like having a Mack truck from the past blindside me from behind and send me flying.

They were the only people who could still make me feel inferior and insignificant.

My sister Georgia and Bentley—her husband, my brother-in-law…and my ex-fiancé.

CHAPTER 24

Sloane

THE HARSH GLARE OF FLUORESCENT LIGHTS PAINTED the hall in stark whites and shadows. Shoes squeaked, medical staff hurried past, and the smell of disinfectant clouded the air.

None of that affected Georgia, who looked like a modern Grace Kelly who'd just stepped out of the pages of *Vogue*.

"Don't tell me you called yourself Penny's family at the front desk so they'd let you up," she said. "That's a tad ironic, isn't it?"

Her skin glowed in a way that shouldn't be possible beneath the unflattering lighting. She wasn't showing yet, and her cashmere sweater and Italian wool slacks fit her Pilates-toned figure like they were custom-made (which they likely were). A four-carat heirloom diamond dazzled from her ring finger.

It was the same ring Bentley had proposed to me with.

Acid gnawed at my gut, but I met Georgia's gaze with contempt. "Pen *is* family," I said. "She was four at the time. She shouldn't be held responsible for the poor decisions made by adults in her life."

"Penelope is a Kensington," Caroline said coldly. "*You* are no longer a Kensington in anything but name, which means she's not your family. You have no right to be here."

"That's rich coming from someone who pretends she doesn't exist half the time." I returned her glare with a chilly smile. "Don't stay too long, Caroline, or people might mistake you for an actual mother."

"You little—"

"Caroline." My father placed a hand on her arm, reining her in. "Don't."

My stepmother sucked in a deep breath and touched the strand of diamonds around her neck. Her glare didn't ease, but she didn't finish her attack either.

George turned to me, his expression unreadable, and pieces of my bravado melted away like iron tossed into a fire.

It was our first face-to-face encounter since our estrangement. If seeing Bentley was akin to getting hit by a truck, seeing my father was like getting trapped in the sands of time. Every shift of grain evoked a different memory.

The timbre of his voice as we walked through Central Park Zoo for my seventh birthday and he pointed out the different animals to me.

The proud smile on his face when I was presented at my debutante ball.

The shock when I told him I was starting my own PR firm instead of settling down and popping out babies like I "should."

The defensiveness when I accused Georgia and Bentley of sleeping together behind my back, the fury when I refused to "take their relationship in stride" and give them my blessing, and finally, the utter coldness when he gave me his ultimatum.

If you walk out that door, there's no coming back.

The weight of our history crushed my lungs. Emotions surged through me in a jumble of old anger and fresh nostalgia, and it took everything I had not to turn and run away like the coward I prided myself on not being.

I'd had many years to imagine what our first post-estrangement meeting would be like. They ranged from ignoring one other (most plausible) to a tearful, joyful reunion (least plausible).

Confronting each other outside my sister's hospital room after she'd almost died was so *im*plausible that it landed fully outside that range.

"Sloane." My father might as well be talking to his driver, for all the emotion he showed. "How did you know Penelope was here?"

The bitter pill of disappointment cracked on my tongue. What had I been expecting, a hug?

"I..." I forced myself not to look at Rhea. "I got a message from Annie."

I felt bad about throwing her under the bus, but she was already fired. Rhea wasn't, and Pen needed her.

Plus, I doubted my family would check with Annie. Once they fired someone, that person didn't exist to them.

Caroline's eyes narrowed. "You've never met that woman."

"That you know of." I arched one brow. "How would I know who she was otherwise?"

"Penelope could've told you."

"She could've. But she didn't."

"This is ridiculous." My stepmother redirected her glare toward my father. "George, kick her out. She stopped being a Kensington the day she *humiliated* this family by leaving it—my God, the number of whispers I had to endure during my charity meetings after that—and she—"

"You can't kick me out," I snapped. "This is public property. You don't own the hospital, no matter how much money you donate to it."

"Perhaps not, but we can get a restraining order against you for lying to the hospital staff and intruding on a private family affair."

"You can certainly try. My—"

"Enough!" my father thundered. Caroline and I lapsed into mutinous silence. "This is neither the time nor place to engage in petty squabbles."

He turned the full force of his flinty gaze on me. "Sloane, you are legally a Kensington," he said. "But you gave up all rights to participate in this family the day you walked out of my office. That includes contacting Penelope in any way, shape, or form. I made that clear."

My nails dug into my palm. "She's a kid, and she needs someone who—"

"What she *needs* is none of your concern. You have no more claim on her well-being than a stranger on the street." Disappointment shadowed his face. "We could've solved this. I gave you an opportunity to make amends, and you ignored it. The consequences are yours to reap."

His dismissal fell like an axe blade, severing my power of speech.

The beginnings of a storm brewed behind my ribcage, but as always, it was all sound and no fury. No rain, no tears. Just an endless, ceaseless pressure that yearned to break but couldn't.

"Rhea, go inside Penelope's room and stay there," he said. "If anyone except myself, Caroline, Georgia, Bentley, or hospital staff try to enter, call security and let me know immediately."

"Yes, Mr. Kensington," she said quietly. She flicked a worried glance at me before she hurried past and disappeared into the room.

"The doctor says Penelope is doing fine and in no danger," my father told Georgia and Bentley. "Stay if you'd wish. I'm heading back to the office."

"And I'm meeting Buffy Darlington at the Plaza." Caroline gathered her coat tight around her. "We have a silent auction to plan."

Neither acknowledged me nor checked on Pen on their way out. I wasn't surprised they'd ignored me, but the way they bypassed Pen pissed me off. I guess I should've expected it; their parenting style was best described by the phrase "doing the bare minimum."

My blood hummed with the aftershocks of our confrontation. After years of picturing the moment, it'd been both overwhelming and underwhelming, but it wasn't over yet.

"I did not expect to see *that* show today." Georgia tilted her head. "What did Daddy mean when he said he gave you an opportunity to make amends?"

Next to her, Bentley remained silent. He hadn't said a word since he saw me, which was for the best. If he opened his mouth, I'd punch him in it. Twice.

"He emailed me about your pregnancy." I smiled over the churn in my gut. *I shouldn't have eaten that chicken salad for lunch.* "I would say congratulations, but I'm the only person here who doesn't lie."

Bentley had the grace to redden. Georgia didn't.

"That's okay," she said with maddening calm. "The new town house Daddy bought us is congratulations enough. He's thrilled he's *finally* getting a grandchild. Speaking of which, are you still single?" She glanced at my bare ring finger, her patronizing tone grating against my already-raw nerves. "I can't imagine why."

Forget punching Bentley. I was inches away from punching my sister in her perfect, heart-shaped face.

"Neither can I." The velvety interjection draped over me like a protective blanket. "That's why I asked her out before those other idiots beat me to it."

Warmth brushed my side. A second later, a strong arm wrapped around my waist, drawing me closer and grounding the storm brewing inside me.

Only one person had the ability to do that.

"Xavier Castillo." Georgia straightened, her gaze sweeping over his tousled dark hair and sculpted body. He wasn't the preppy boarding school type she'd always gravitated toward, but he exuded a raw sensuality few could match. That, plus his family's fortune was triple that of Bentley's.

I tensed, something green and ugly slithering through my veins at the way my sister eyed him.

Beside her, Bentley stiffened and placed a possessive hand on Georgia's hip. She ignored him, her eyes sliding to Xavier's arm around my waist.

"You're dating Sloane?" Her question swam with disbelief.

"Yep," he drawled. "I chased her for months, but she finally agreed to go out with me." He dropped a kiss on the top of my head. "Sorry that took so long, babe. Parking was a nightmare, and the front desk initially refused to let me up because I'm not family. How's Pen?"

"A bit banged up, but she'll be okay." I leaned into him, playing up the girlfriend act. We technically weren't lying; we *were* dating, albeit more casually than Xavier made it seem. "Thank you for coming here with me."

That was a hundred percent honest.

"Anytime, Luna. I'll always be here for you."

I glanced up, my heart stilling for a split second at the sincerity in his eyes. It surprised me no matter how many times I saw it, and it scared the hell out of me.

I knew how to deal with fake people. I interacted with dozens of them every day. But genuine people were rare, and they slipped past my defenses in a way that could be disastrous.

Then again, it might be too late where Xavier was concerned. He—

Bentley cleared his throat, derailing my train of thought and dragging our attention back his way.

"Aren't you his publicist?" he asked, earning a sharp glance from Georgia. My client list wasn't a secret, but it was interesting that he was so familiar with it.

"Seems like a violation of professional ethics to date a client."

We stared at him.

Shit.

Bentley wasn't wrong, but I wasn't going to explain the nuances of our situation to him. To be honest, I feared that, once I went down that road and passed all my justifications, I'd find no good reason for dating Xavier other than I wanted to. He was the kryptonite to my logic, my inhibitions, my rationality, and everything else I relied on to keep me out of quagmires like this one.

Similarly, I'd gotten so caught up in wiping the smug look off Georgia's face that I forgot we were supposed to be keeping our relationship low-key in public. We weren't hiding it, but we didn't flaunt it either. We didn't want to give the city's gossip network any fodder.

"Who I date or how I run my business is none of your concern," I said coolly. "I'd tell you to mind yours, but you don't have a business of your own, do you?" A small tilt of my head. "It's sad that your family can't buy you deals the way they bought your admission into Princeton."

Flags of color burned high on Bentley's cheekbones. He worked in private equity like his father, but he'd gotten the job mostly because of his connections. He also *hated* reminders about being wait-listed at Princeton. The only reason he'd gotten off the list was because his family donated a building.

"This is absurd," Georgia said. Without our father or my relationship status to use against me, she'd clearly lost interest in the conversation. "We won't stand here and let you insult us. Come on, Bentley, let's go. We have dinner reservations at Le Boudoir."

They didn't say a word about Pen before they left. That was

my family in a nutshell. Great at surface-level sentiments like showing up; shitty at actual sentiments like following through.

Honestly, I was surprised Georgia had showed up at all. She and Pen tolerated each other at best and rarely spent time together. Georgia didn't care for children (which was concerning, since she was pregnant), and Pen thought she was "too narcissistic." I didn't know where she'd learned the word *narcissistic*, but she wasn't wrong.

"You have such a wonderful family," Xavier said after Georgia and Bentley were out of earshot. "I can't imagine why you don't want to talk to them."

I huffed a small laugh. "Yeah, me neither."

Now that my family was gone, the string of defiance that'd kept me upright collapsed. My shoulders sagged as adrenaline leaked from my pores, leaving me heavy and exhausted.

I stepped out of Xavier's embrace and sank into one of the chairs lining the hall outside Pen's room. I stared blankly at the opposite wall, my emotions a wreck after the surprise encounter with my family.

Sometimes, I wished I were the type of person who could forgive and forget. If I swallowed my hurt and anger and pretended I was happy for Georgia, that might actually be true one day. Fake it till you make it and all that.

If my sister had been a good sister, and her betrayal with Bentley were a one-off, I could be tempted to consider that route, but Georgia had never been a model sibling. She was used to being the center of attention and getting whatever she wanted. Often, what she wanted was what she couldn't have—the one-of-a-kind porcelain doll my grandmother had gifted me for my birthday, our mother's vintage dress for her debutante ball, and, of course, my fiancé.

She'd put up such a fuss about the doll and dress that my

father "redistributed" them to her. As for Bentley, he bore a fair share of the blame. I believed in greater accountability for the cheater than the person they cheated with, but in their case, they could both jump off the Brooklyn Bridge.

I heard a small rustle of clothing as Xavier sat next to me. He'd let me process silently, which I was grateful for, but I couldn't stay catatonic forever.

"Thank you." I turned my head to face him. "You didn't have to do that."

"Don't know what you're talking about." He lounged in his seat, the position reassuringly familiar against the impersonal hospital walls. "I merely told the truth like I always do."

"Right. What did you tell the front desk to get them to let you up?"

"Nothing." Xavier's grin twinkled with mischief. "I let Benjamin do the talking. Five Benjamins, to be exact. I may have also told them I was your fiancé."

"That has to be illegal, and you *have* to stop walking around with so much cash. It's unsafe."

"Unsafe?" He shifted, his knee grazing mine. "Don't tell me you're starting to care, Luna."

"Starting, no." I'd passed *starting* weeks ago; I just hadn't known it at the time.

A rush of anxiety shot through me. Admitting I cared was akin to getting my teeth pulled out with pliers, but he'd been honest with me about his feelings. I should be honest with him (to an extent).

Xavier's grin dimmed as the implication of my reply hit. Surprise flashed through his eyes, followed by a slow, molten warmth.

"Then we're on the same page," he said softly.

Some of my anxiety abated. "I guess we are."

We sat in silence for a while, watching nurses rush past and strangers come and go. Hospitals bled tears, but it was comforting, in a way. It reminded us that we weren't alone in our grief and that the universe wasn't targeting us. Shitty things happened to everyone.

It was a strange comfort, but it was a comfort nonetheless.

"Is Pen really okay?" Xavier asked.

"Yes. I got to see her for a bit before she crashed and I ran into my family." I picked a piece of lint off my pants. "My father and stepmother were here. They left before you came."

"I saw them on my way up." His voice gentled. "How was that?"

"It was how I expected it to be. The Kensingtons remain divided." My mouth twisted into a sardonic smile. "What'd you think of my sister and her husband? Charming, aren't they?"

"That's not the first *c* word that came to mind."

A small laugh sliced through my turmoil. I didn't know how he did it, but Xavier had a talent for making horrible situations tolerable.

"There seemed to be some tension between you and Bentley," he said. "Beyond your antagonism with your sister."

If he ever gave up the nightclub gig, he should join the FBI. Xavier was terrifyingly observant.

"There would be," I said. "Considering he was my fiancé before he married my sister."

His shocked eyes snapped up to meet mine, and my smile grew more bitter.

"Not a lot of people knew about us," I said. "At least not in New York."

I'd never told anyone the full story, not even my friends. They knew bits and pieces, but rehashing the memories was too painful. I'd rather lock them in a box and pretend they didn't exist.

However, seeing Bentley again had ripped the lock right off, and I needed to share them with someone before I drowned in them.

"We met when we were both studying abroad in London," I said. "I was a junior; he was a senior. He stayed there for a job after graduation, and we dated long-distance for a bit. He worked in investment banking at the time, and because he was always so busy, I often visited him instead of the other way around. Then they transferred him to the New York office, and he proposed a month before I started Kensington PR."

My father had been thrilled when we started dating. Bentley had a good job, knew all the right things to say, and came from a rich, "acceptable" family. He was George Kensington's dream son-in-law. Honestly, my father was probably happier now that the perfect son-in-law was paired with the perfect daughter instead of with me.

"My plans for starting the company had already been underway, so it wasn't like I could push them back to plan my wedding. Even if I could, I wouldn't have wanted to. But those first months after the opening were…stressful, and our relationship became strained. He accused me of prioritizing work over him; I accused him of wanting me to fail. We were both so busy we barely saw each other, and when we *did* see each other, we fought. But I loved him, and I thought the bumps would pass after I got the firm off the ground and we were married."

There was no one except Xavier within earshot, but that didn't stop red, itchy embarrassment from crawling over my skin. I'd been such an idiot. I should've known, if Bentley had been that unsupportive at the beginning of my career, that his resentment would only grow the more success I achieved.

"A few months after he proposed, I flew to London for work. Of course, we fought about it since it was over the holidays, but it was a crisis surrounding my biggest client at the time. I resolved it faster than expected and came home early. When I walked into our apartment, I found him having sex in the living room with my sister. On New Year's Eve."

The scene was imprinted on my brain no matter how hard I tried to scrub it. Her bent over the couch *I'd* picked out, him behind her, their moans and gasps as I stood frozen, trying to process what the fuck was happening. They'd been so caught up in each other, they didn't notice me until after they'd finished.

A fresh wave of humiliation flooded me. Getting cheated on was one thing. Getting cheated on by your fiancé and sister was a new level of betrayal.

Even though Georgia and I weren't close, I hadn't expected her to be so callous. She'd never even apologized.

"Jesus." Xavier let out a string of Spanish curses. "I'm so fucking sorry, Luna."

"It's okay. It was an important lesson," I said flatly. *Don't trust people, and don't let them in.* I couldn't get hurt if I didn't care. "They barely showed remorse. I kicked Georgia out, but not before she blamed my overworking for why he strayed. After she left, Bentley and I got into a huge fight, and he..." My knuckles whitened around the edge of my chair. "He said I was too *frigid.* That I'd always been an ice queen and that I got worse after I started my PR company. He said I couldn't blame him for hooking up with Georgia when she was so passionate and I couldn't even show proper emotion. Needless to say, we broke up that night. He and Georgia started dating officially a week later."

If you weren't such an ice queen all the time, maybe I wouldn't have gone looking elsewhere.

My throat and nose burned. "The worst part was my father took Georgia's side. There was no way his precious perfect daughter would've done that without good reason. He blamed me using the same reasons they did, and when I refused to let it go, he gave me an ultimatum. Get over it or get out. So I got out."

Recounting the story out loud carried the sting of fresh wounds, but as my words dissolved in the sterile air, the initial pain gradually transformed into a therapeutic numbness.

By locking away those memories, I'd given them power. They'd festered over the years, sprouting horns and claws and morphing into a nightmare I constantly ran from, whether I knew it or not.

By sharing them out loud, I'd stripped them of that power. They were nothing but a small man behind a big curtain, trying to convince me they could hurt me.

They couldn't.

It wasn't my fault that Georgia was a terrible sister or that Bentley was an insecure, cheating bastard. Nor was it my fault my father was too blinded by his biases to see what was right in front of him. *They* were the ones who should be ashamed, not me.

"Sloane. Listen to me." Xavier grasped my shoulders and turned me so I faced him. His eyes glittered like dark coals of anger. "You are not fucking *frigid*. You're one of the most driven, passionate people I know, even if you may show it differently than others, and you built one of the best PR firms in the world in five years. You think someone without passion can do that? And even if you were quote unquote 'cold' to your asshole ex, he deserved it. If he doesn't appreciate you for who you are, then he *damn* well doesn't deserve your time or energy."

His expression was fierce, and his touch seared like it was trying to impress his conviction onto my soul.

It happened so suddenly, I would've stumbled had I been standing.

A *whoosh* swept through my stomach, followed by the dizzying, disorienting, but not totally unpleasant sensation of tumbling over an edge. Pieces of me floated alongside his words, little champagne bubbles that shouldn't exist after such a shitty day but did anyway.

Xavier Castillo. Only you.

"You should be a motivational coach." I managed a wobbly smile. "You would kill on the speaker circuit."

"I'll keep that in mind." For once, he didn't match my smile. "Tell me you understand, Luna. None of what happened was your fault. Fuck Bentley, fuck Georgia, and *fuck* your family." He paused. "Except Pen."

Another laugh burbled, elbowing unshed tears out of the way. "I understand."

I truly did.

I'd come to the same conclusion seconds before Xavier's speech, but thinking it and hearing someone else affirm it were two different things.

An anchor unhooked from my shoulders, and for the first time in years, I breathed easier.

Running into my family had started as a disaster and ended up being therapeutic. *Go figure.* Nothing in my life had worked the way it should've since Xavier entered it, though I wasn't complaining.

"Good." He released my shoulders, but a trace of caution lingered on his face. "We should probably get out of here soon unless you want to see Pen again."

"She won't wake up for a while, and I don't want to get Rhea into trouble." I explained my father's instructions. Xavier responded with a *c* word that made me smile. "But I agree. We should leave before the staff starts asking questions."

A quick glance at my watch told me we'd been here for...fuck. *Two hours*? How was that possible?

"We'll pick up dinner. Then I'll drop you off at your apartment," Xavier said as we exited the building. It was already dark outside, and a brisk chill snuck beneath the layers of my coat and sweater. "You must be hungry."

"I'm not that hungry." Despite my recent catharsis, I blanched at the thought of returning to my empty apartment. Well, The Fish was there, but he wasn't exactly stimulating company.

I usually didn't mind being alone. I preferred it. But after the past few hours, I needed a physical release. Something to shake off the day.

"I have a better idea." I stopped next to the passenger side and spoke over the top of his car. "You were telling me the other day about this great club in Greenwich Village. Is it open on Wednesdays?"

Xavier's eyebrows winged up. "Yes, but—"

"We should go."

"Are you sure? It's been a long day."

"That's why I want to go." I opened the door, slid inside, and buckled my seat belt while Xavier took the driver's seat. "You said I should be more spontaneous. This is me being spontaneous."

"It's a little different than the type of club you're thinking of." Xavier searched my face. He must've found whatever he was looking for because a smile slowly replaced his frown. "But if you want to go, we'll go. Just don't say I didn't warn you."

CHAPTER 25

"I CAN'T BELIEVE YOU DID THIS TO ME." SLOANE'S breathless accusation whirled through the air as I spun her out. Her dress flared around her knees in a silky blue cloud before it settled languidly against her skin. "You took me to a *salsa* club. I'll never forgive you."

Amusement kicked the corners of my mouth up. "Why? Because you're enjoying yourself too much?"

"Because I *don't know how to salsa.*"

"You're doing just fine, Luna." I pulled her back in, one hand molding to the curve of her lower back while the other guided us through the music. "Not everything you do has to be perfect. Remember our dance lessons in Spain? Just let go and have fun."

We were at an underground salsa club in Greenwich Village. The clientele ranged from beginners to professional dancers who'd won world competitions. That was the beauty of the club. Everyone was welcome, and no one judged.

We'd arrived two hours ago, and with Jose Cuervo's help, I'd coaxed Sloane into joining me on the dance floor. She'd relaxed enough to follow my lead, but not enough to fully immerse herself in our surroundings.

"Our dance lessons." Sloane tipped her chin up to look at me. Exertion flushed her cheeks, and her eyes sparkled in a way that made my heart hurt. I knew she was guarded, but I hadn't realized *how* much until she let those guards down. "I barely remember them."

"Well, now I'm hurt. After all the effort I put in, you don't remember? Next time, just lie to me." I spun us lazily toward the edge of the room. It was a small club, which meant there weren't many pockets of free space, but I wanted Sloane to myself as much as possible.

"That's not what I meant, you big baby. I meant Spain feels like a lifetime ago, and..." A hitch cut into her breath when I slid a leisurely hand up her spine.

"And?" I prompted.

Her dress was cut low in the back, and silk soon gave way to smooth bare skin. It glided effortlessly beneath my touch, its warmth turning my blood to liquid fire and muddying my thoughts in a way that would've been dangerous if I gave a fuck.

This wasn't the type of club our friends or acquaintances frequented. No one knew who we were, which meant we were free for the night.

"And..." Sloane's eyes closed for the briefest moment when I brushed the sensitive skin of her nape. "I can't believe it's only been a month."

"People can live years in a month if they do it right." I curled my hand around the back of her neck and rubbed a gentle thumb against her skin. "Since you don't remember, we'll need a refresher."

An arch of her brow, paired with wary amusement. "Do we?"

"We do. I take my teaching role *very* seriously." I dipped my head, closing the distance between us until her breaths grazed my lips.

We hadn't kissed since the library. I wanted to take things slow, but when I was near Sloane, what I wanted was irrelevant.

I didn't *want* her. I needed her. Desperately.

I needed her the way the ocean tides needed the moon, and I would give anything for her to feel a fraction of the same way toward me.

"Let go," I repeated softly. "Listen to the music. Lose yourself in it."

Uncertainty wavered across her features.

For Sloane, control was a necessity, not a luxury, but we all had to relinquish control sometime. Otherwise, our world would always be limited by the arbitrary boundaries we drew around it.

"No one's watching." Her back faced the wall, and my body shielded hers from the dance floor. We pressed tight against each other, close enough for me to hear the battle waging between the steady *thump, thump, thumps* of her heart. "It's just us, Luna."

In the background, fast-paced music segued into the smooth, alluring beats of a new song. Smoky vocals wound through the air, and the rhythm of the couples around us slowed to match.

A swallow slid up and down Sloane's throat. "Okay," she whispered.

Her response hit my blood like a shot of vanilla whiskey.

We were talking about dance lessons, but they were the last thing on my mind as I guided her through the steps.

It was an intimate venue, just big enough for a hundred at a time and dim enough to unfasten people's inhibitions in the shadows. Amber lights glowed overhead, accentuating the curves of Sloane's cheekbones and the shiver of her body as my hand drifted from her neck to the small of her back again.

She started off stiff, but she moved with natural precision, her body turning in sync and her feet following mine without missing a beat. However, the longer the music played, the more her movements flowed. Steel melted into silk, and the wariness in her eyes softened into something that sent a rush of heat through my veins.

Lessons were technical. Impersonal.

This? This was as personal as it got.

"You said you don't pass first base on the first date." Her gaze flickered beneath the lights. "What about the second?"

Her question sent a shock through my system, the earlier heat igniting into an inferno that razed every other thought I had to ash.

There was only her, and this, and us.

"I could be convinced." My husky drawl betrayed the desire coiling in my body. My skin stretched too tightly over my muscles, and if I didn't taste her soon, I would implode.

Sloane smiled as if she knew exactly what was going through my mind.

She stood on tiptoes and, after a brief, agonizing moment, brushed her mouth against mine.

That was it.

A single brush, and the leash on my restraint snapped.

One hand dove into her hair, cupping the back of her head while her arms circled around my neck. The other pushed us back against the wall until our bodies molded into each other.

I didn't give a fuck who was watching. No one else except her existed in this moment, and I couldn't get *enough* of her—the softness of her lips, the sweetness of her taste, the little moans and gasps as I explored her mouth with the hunger of a man starved.

If kisses had colors, this one would reflect the tatters of control swirling around us, a symphony of crimson and amber and pure, stunning cobalt. They sank beneath my skin, sending electric currents over every raw, exposed nerve.

In a world of black and white, she was my kaleidoscope.

"Xavier." Sloane's breathless pant slipped through my haze. "We should leave. Go somewhere more private."

A surge of lust outpaced my desire to prolong this moment, and I pulled back, soaking in the sight of her swollen lips and heavy-lidded eyes. Strands of hair fell from her messed-up bun, and a strawberry flush decorated her face and chest.

I'd never seen anyone more perfect.

So fucking beautiful, and so fucking mine.

I leaned down and captured her mouth in another lingering kiss. "I know just the place."

Sloane and I barely made it through the door before the first piece of clothing hit my living room floor.

The drive to my house had been short, but those ten minutes had felt like an eternity when she'd been sitting there, beautiful and willing and wanting. If we'd hit one more red light or meandering pedestrian, I might've crashed the car out of sexual frustration.

But we'd made it, and the air thrummed with urgency as we stripped each other bare.

Dress. Shoes. Shirt and pants.

I unclasped her bra and tossed it to the side. She tugged my boxers down, and I kicked them behind me.

There was neither rhyme nor reason to the ferocity of our desire, but when the last stitch of clothing slithered down her body, I didn't give a damn about rhyme *nor* reason.

Moonlight slanted through the windows and found the curves of Sloane's body, sculpting shadows beneath her breasts and draping silver across her shoulders.

Long legs. Creamy skin. Hair that gleamed pale beneath the

moon's kiss. She looked like a goddess come to earth, but the most beautiful thing about her wasn't her face or naked body.

It was the trust behind it.

She was standing here, in my house, bared and vulnerable, and I wasn't stupid enough to take any second for granted.

Sloane's lips parted as my hand skimmed over her shoulder and up her neck to touch the twist of hair on her head. It was mussed but still intact from our previous activities, and the urge to see it tumble over her skin flared hot and bright in my gut.

"Take your hair down, Sloane," I said quietly.

I expected hesitation, but her eyes didn't leave mine as she reached up and slowly removed the pins keeping the twist intact. Her hair unwound, lock by lock, until it cascaded around her face in a waterfall of pale silk. The tips brushed her breasts, and I couldn't breathe past the tightness in my lungs.

Every time I thought she couldn't get more perfect, she proved me wrong.

"Good girl." I gathered her hair in a fist and tugged her head back. The rise and fall of her chest quickened, and a small smile touched my lips. "I like it better wrapped around my fist."

The air shifted, heady anticipation exploding into raw, unadulterated lust.

Sloane gasped when I pressed her against the wall like I had at the club, only this time there was no one around to witness the way I nudged her thighs open with my knee or hear the moan she released when my fingers brushed her pussy.

Every muscle went taut as my cock gave a painful throb.

Fuck. Me.

She was wet, so wet that I could easily slide inside her right now without much friction, but I hadn't come this far to rush the best part.

I liked to play before eating.

"You're dripping already, Luna," I drawled, swiping a lazy thumb over her clit. My lips curved with satisfaction when her back bowed in time with another gasp. "We've barely gotten started."

Her eyes fluttered open again, and she slanted a narrow-eyed glare at me. "Are you going to keep talking, or are you going to finish what you started?"

A rumble of laughter rose in my chest. *That's my girl.* Sloane wouldn't be Sloane without her sharp tongue, even when she was pinned naked beneath me.

"I always finish what I start." I tightened my fist around her hair and gave it another tug. Her head arched, baring her throat, and a small quiver rippled through her body as I traced the delicate length of her neck with my mouth.

Bit by bit, I mapped her skin with kisses until I reached the flutter of her pulse. I paused, savoring the find, before I slid two fingers inside her and pressed my thumb firmly against her clit.

Her pulse went fucking wild.

"*Oh God*!" Sloane's hips jerked, and a keening cry left her lips as I pushed deeper until I was buried knuckles-deep inside her. Her nails scored deep crescents in my shoulders, but the sting only intensified my pleasure. I loved seeing her like this. Wild, uninhibited, and so damn beautiful that it made my heart ache. "Xavier, I...that...*ah*."

Her words gave way to an unintelligible string of moans and whimpers as I finger fucked her sweet little cunt. She writhed so powerfully, I had to release her hair and hold her down with my free hand.

It wrapped around her throat, not enough to hurt, but enough to prevent her from bucking me off as shudder after shudder wracked her body.

My cock was so hard, it felt like the skin would split. I

hadn't touched it, but I didn't need to when touching Sloane was enough.

"That's it," I murmured. I coaxed her closer to the edge, curling my fingers just enough to hit her most sensitive spot. "Let go, sweetheart. Come for me."

And she did.

Her body stiffened, and a hoarse cry tore from her throat as she came apart beautifully around me.

The convulsions rolled into one another, soaking my hand and prolonging our pleasure until she finally slumped against me, weak and breathless. "*Fuck.*"

My chest muffled her voice, and another laugh shook my shoulders as I withdrew from her.

"I told you I always finish what I start," I teased. "Quite quickly, I might add."

Sloane lifted her head, her eyes sparking with amused challenge. "Don't act so smug when you haven't been tested yet."

My cock gave another painful throb. "Valid point. Test away. I'm your willing guinea pig."

Her laugh followed mine. "Tip: Never use the phrase *guinea pig* in the middle of sex."

"Technically, we're not in the middle—"

The rest of the sentence died when she pushed me off her and onto the couch. I landed on the cushions with a small grunt, but my surprise sharpened into hunger when she straddled me.

"Maybe test was the wrong word." Sloane leaned down so her nipples grazed my chest. An electric spear of need pierced through my body. "I bet I can make you come faster than you made me come."

"Always so competitive." I was too distracted by the delicious proximity of her breasts to my mouth to come up with a wittier reply. "What does the winner get?"

"Bragging rights." Sloane drew my bottom lip between her teeth with a gentle nip. "Loser lives with the eternal knowledge the other is better."

"Deal." I pulled her head back so she looked straight at me. "Stop talking and sit," I said, paraphrasing her earlier question into a command. "I want to see you ride my cock."

Fire blazed in her blue depths. She planted her hands on my shoulders and pushed herself up, her eyes locked on mine as she positioned the tip of my cock at her entrance.

"I'm on birth control," she said. "And I'm clean."

"Me too."

That was all I managed to say before the murky waters of lust closed overhead, amplifying the thunder of my heartbeat as she sank onto me, inch by inch, until I was buried deep inside her.

Her mouth opened in a small gasp, but the noise that came out of me was so raw and guttural, it sounded more like beast than man.

Tight, hot, and so fucking wet.

We fit so perfectly it was like God himself had custom carved us for each other, and when she moved, it was like sliding home into heaven.

She started slow and sinuous, but her rhythm soon picked up, and I had to grit my teeth and mentally run through my pitch presentation for the Vault just so I didn't embarrass myself by coming too early.

"You feel so damn good." I groaned, my head falling back so I could drink her in.

Sloane bounced up and down on my cock, her hair a mess, her face flushed with exertion. The sounds of flesh slapping against flesh filled the room, and I was so lost in this, in her, that I didn't give a fuck about the bet.

I grabbed her hips and slammed her down, eliciting a sharp

squeal. I thrust up to match her pace, and the volume of our grunts and moans intensified until I came with blinding force.

My vision whitened, streaks of lightning racing behind my eyes, and I vaguely heard Sloane cry out in pleasure before I regained some form of control over my senses.

When my vision finally cleared, she was just coming down from her own orgasm. She smiled down at me, her expression a mix of post-coital bliss, triumph, and something else I couldn't identify.

"I won."

"You did." I pulled her down and gave her another kiss. "Bragging rights for life."

I didn't mention how neither of us had timed the encounters, so who really knew who'd won? That wasn't important.

A warm, heavy blanket of contentment draped over me as we lay in companionable silence and waited for our pulses to return to normal.

I'd spent my whole life chasing the next high. When you had everything, everything got boring fast. I wanted bigger, better, faster. I wanted something that would last, and when Sloane rolled to the side and curled up against me, I knew I'd I found it.

This was my greatest high. Her, sated and happy, in my arms.

Nothing in the world could ever beat this moment.

CHAPTER 26

Xavier

I COULD'VE STAYED IN MY HOUSE WITH SLOANE forever and been happy, but unfortunately, I had real-life responsibilities that required my attention.

On Friday, two days after my night with Sloane and one day after I almost made her late to work with a morning quickie (she still hadn't forgiven me for that), I sat in a glass-and-chrome office atop one of DC's most coveted addresses.

Icy green eyes regarded me with impersonal scrutiny. "Xavier Castillo." Alex Volkov's voice matched the man: cool, distanced, pitiless. "You're the last person I expected to ask for a meeting."

Name number two on Kai's list.

I shrugged. "Things change. People change."

As CEO of the Archer Group, the country's largest real estate development company, Alex owned half the real estate in Manhattan—including my dream location for my club. The turn-of-the-century, honest-to-God bank vault was located in the basement of one of Alex's skyscrapers, and if there were two things my target clientele liked, it was bank vaults and hidden gems.

Alex leaned back and tapped a finger on his desk. He was the only person who hadn't told me he was sorry for my loss following my father's death. I appreciated it; I was getting sick of the pity.

"You're aware of how much that location costs." It wasn't a question.

Eight figures.

"Yes. It's not a problem." I didn't have access to my full inheritance yet, but thanks to my last name and Kai's introduction, I was in the process of securing financing from Davenport Capital, Dominic Davenport's company. *Name number three.* I'd sent Alex documented proof prior to our meeting.

"Permits and licenses?"

"Silver & Klein is handling it. They don't foresee any issues." The prestigious law firm was based in DC, but it represented corporate clients across the country. *Jules Ambrose, Silver & Klein. Name number four.*

Alex peppered me with more questions. I answered them gamely, but I knew his decision hinged on one factor—the one I *didn't* have in my pocket for this meeting.

"Your pitch is impressive. Your paperwork is in order. But I'll be honest," he said after I addressed his concerns about potential competitors on the market. "I don't buy that you've changed so much, so fast. You've never owned, started, or operated a business, and you have a well-deserved reputation for reckless partying."

"I don't know about *reckless*..."

"I'm also aware your inheritance hinges on this club," he continued, ignoring me. "What happens if it doesn't pass muster during its first evaluation?"

It was a good question, one I tried not to think about too often. The prospect of failing so spectacularly in the public eye was like falling off that bridge in my nightmares: terrifying, out of my control, and damn near inevitable.

"I understand your concerns." I covered the sudden lurch in

my stomach with a confident smile. *Fake it till you make it.* "But what I did in my past doesn't define who I am now. Yes, I've spent the better part of my twenties engaging in...other activities besides entrepreneurship, but as the progress I've already made proves, I'm serious about this."

Alex stared at me, unmoved.

Dammit. Talking to the man was like talking to an iceberg—a low-key hostile one.

I searched for an argument that didn't rehash what he already knew, and my eye caught on the single framed photo adorning his desk. In it, he stood next to a beautiful woman with long black hair and a sunny smile. Each held a baby in their arms; one was swaddled in pink, the other in blue.

Alex wasn't smiling, exactly, but his face contained more warmth than I'd thought him capable of. He'd been married for a while, but I distinctly remembered a time when the cold, seemingly unfeeling CEO's relationship with his now wife had made waves.

No one had thought he was capable of falling in love—until he did.

"You say you don't buy that I've changed so much, so fast, but not all change is gradual," I said slowly, forming my words as I went. "Sometimes, an unexpected event forces us to step up in ways we haven't before, or we meet someone who changes our outlook. It happens every day. My father's death was one of those triggers for me." Sort of. But I wasn't about to discuss my inheritance or my mother's letter with a near stranger. "I'm not proud of the time I've wasted, but I'm trying to make up for it now." I met Alex's gaze with a steady one of my own. "Have you ever done something you regretted? Something you were desperate to fix but relied on someone, somewhere taking a leap of faith on you for it to change?"

He didn't move, but a tiny glint of emotion flickered in his eyes.

"We don't know each other well," I said. "But I promise, if you take this leap of faith on me, I'll do the location justice. Because it's not just your name and reputation riding on this—it's also mine."

The ensuing silence stretched taut beneath the quiet hum of the heater. It was impossible to read Alex's face, and just when I thought I couldn't take it anymore, his chin dipped a fraction of an inch.

"Bring on a business partner. If I deem them acceptable, the vault is yours."

My heart soared and crashed in the span of five seconds.

It was a bigger concession than I'd expected from Alex, and it was exactly what I didn't want to hear.

Vuk wanted the location confirmed before he signed on. Alex wanted Vuk or someone like Vuk attached before he confirmed. It was one hell of a catch-22.

The universe truly loves fucking with me.

"I'm way ahead of you." I smiled, projecting assuredness I absolutely did not have. "I'm in the process of bringing Vuk Markovic on as a silent partner."

"Good. Then producing a signed contract with him shouldn't be a problem." Alex checked his watch. "I expect the contract before Thanksgiving, Mr. Castillo. I've already received multiple offers on the vault, but since I'm intrigued by your proposal, I'll give you a grace period. My offer expires on November 26 at midnight."

"Noted." I did a quick calculation of my odds between Vuk and Alex. I had an infinitesimally better chance of getting Vuk to bend than Alex, if only because he lived in New York and I could badger him more easily. "Thanks for your time. I appreciate it."

Mental note: Go back to Vuk and figure out how the hell to get him on board. Not necessarily in that order.

I exited Alex's office, my mind spinning with fragments of ideas and strategies. A flat wall-mounted screen played silently while I waited for the elevator. The big story of the day was the birth of Princess Camilla, Eldorra's newest royal baby.

I envied her. Babies didn't have to worry about bars and business. They just cried and slept and ate, and people still loved them.

Once I made it downstairs, I instructed the driver I'd hired for the day to take me to Harper Security headquarters. Every nightclub needed security, and Christian Harper provided the best.

Name number five.

I hoped my meeting with him went better than the one with Alex.

Upside: my meeting with Christian did, in fact, go better than the one with Alex, probably because he got paid whether my club sank or swam. If he didn't, he'd simply pull his services.

Downside: I had no clue how to get Vuk to sign a binding contract in eighteen days without a location.

I *could* try to secure another space. I had a list of backups in case the old bank vault fell through, but my gut told me they weren't the right fit.

People's first impression of a nightclub was its location. I wasn't going to water it down and go with any old spot.

After my meeting with Christian, I swung by Silver & Klein's offices to meet with Jules. She was their youngest senior associate, and she was handling all my legal paperwork, including licenses, permits, and contracts. She assured me she'd have a silent partner contract drawn up and ready to sign by early next week.

Instead of staying the night in DC, I took the train back to New York and spent the weekend devising methods to convince Vuk, ranging from aboveboard to, uh, ethically questionable.

The charges for temporary kidnapping couldn't be that bad, right? It wasn't like I was going to keep or kill the guy. He might kill *me* after, but once I made him a shit ton of money, perhaps he'd forget I hired someone to hold him hostage until he signed on the dotted line. Hypothetically.

The fact I was even considering that course of action, however jokingly, spoke to my desperation.

The weekend's only bright spot winked into existence on Sunday. I'd convinced Sloane to meet me in Queens for a surprise, and the concrete weighing on my chest eased when I saw her at our designated meeting spot.

Queens was out of the way for both of us, but that was necessary given the circumstances.

She stood near the building entrance, resplendent in a white dress, coat, and boots. Her hair was back up in a bun, but a smile played on her lips as I approached.

"This better be good," she said. "I'm missing brunch with the girls."

I gave her a kiss hello, savoring her softness before I pulled back. "Consider this a Story Sunday." At her questioning brow, I clarified, "A Sunday where you do something so exciting, you'll have a story to tell at your next brunch."

Her laugh unlocked a rush of dopamine, like a song I'd heard once and loved but never discovered the name of, only to stumble upon it again years later.

"That's not a thing," she said, following me inside. "But since we're here, can you tell me what all the cloak-and-dagger stuff is about? Why are we in Queens on a Sunday morning?"

"You'll see." I took her down the hallway toward our reserved room. I'd checked in earlier, and I *may* have bribed the staff into letting us enter through the back entrance. "How's Pen?"

Sloane sobered at the mention of her sister. "According to

Rhea, she's recovering quickly from her crash, which is good. And her injuries will heal in time. But…" She sighed. "I'm still worried, especially since Pen tries to brush these things off. She's afraid it'll make us coddle her more, which she hates."

"And you can't visit her again?"

"She's been discharged from the hospital, and I can't visit her at her house without alerting my father and Caroline." Storm clouds rolled in, turning Sloane's eyes blue gray. "Part of me is waiting for them to ship her off to a distant cousin in Europe. They'd do that just to spite me and make it harder for me to see her."

I would say it was hard to imagine a parent doing that to their child, but as someone who'd practically been raised in boarding schools, I knew better.

I stopped in front of our room.

"But they won't do that until they're back from DC" I'd picked up some useful intel during my Friday meetings in the city: George and Caroline were both currently in DC for a big fundraiser.

Surprise rippled across Sloane's face. "How did you know that?"

"I had to confirm their whereabouts before I did this." I opened the door.

Sloane stepped inside, but she only made it two steps before her jaw dropped. "*Pen*?"

The brightest, most precious grin lit Pen's face. "Surprise!"

She sat on the couch with Rhea, a bowl of complimentary snacks on her lap. Her nanny kept glancing at the open door like she expected George Kensington to storm through it at any second, but at least she was here. That was what mattered.

"What are you doing here?" Several long strides took Sloane to her sister. She hugged the tiny blond, her expression stunned. "How did you…?"

"It took some coordinating, but I had a friend pick up Rhea and Pen and drive them here." The *friend* had actually been Harper Security personnel who could extract them from their penthouse without alerting the doorman, concierge, or anyone who might snitch on them to the Kensingtons.

We had a backup in case George and Caroline found out about Rhea and Pen leaving—specifically, movie tickets—but the plan was going smoothly, thank God.

"Before you worry, I also checked with Pen's doctor," I said, closing the door and taking a spot on the second couch. "He said it was okay for her to come, provided we keep physical exertion to a minimum."

Sloane glanced at Pen, who affirmed my words with a solemn nod. "What he said."

Apparently, her crash on Wednesday had been relatively mild. It'd seemed worse than it was due to her accident, and she'd recovered enough to make today feasible.

"Rhea?" Sloane turned her attention to the nanny. "Are you...?"

"I'm okay." The other woman gave her a weak smile. "Mr. and Mrs. Kensington bought your excuse about Annie. Thank you for doing that."

"You don't have to thank me. You wouldn't have been in that situation if it weren't for me, and I should be the one thanking you." Sloane's voice caught. "For everything you've done for me and Pen over the years."

Rhea had been nervous about my plan given how close she'd come to being found out. However, she possessed an unwavering sense of loyalty to Pen and Sloane, more than she did to her employers, and she'd eventually agreed.

The look she gave Sloane now was that of family—soft, touched, and full of love.

Then the moment passed, and everyone broke eye contact before the fun outing turned into an emotional spiral.

"So where are we, exactly?" Sloane cleared her throat and took in the room, which was sparse save for the two couches, two tables, a media console, and a giant screen with a bunch of monitors and equipment hooked up to it. A smattering of artwork decorated the walls with primary colors.

"We're at the best sports simulation center in Queens." I opened one of the console drawers and took out four controllers. I held on to one and passed the others around. "You said Pen likes soccer, so we're playing soccer."

"I don't like soccer. I *love* soccer," Pen corrected. She was already flipping through the different games, searching for the perfect one.

"My apologies." I suppressed a smile. Her sassiness reminded me of a certain other blond. "Who's your favorite player?"

"Asher Donovan," she answered without hesitation.

Typical. Girls of every age loved him, even if they weren't into soccer the way Pen was, but I'd give credit where credit was due—the dude was talented.

It was just annoying as fuck that someone who looked like a Greek god could also play *that* well and, based on the few interactions I'd had with him, be *that* nice. It was even more annoying that he was Sloane's client.

Whatever. As long as he wasn't her favorite, I didn't care. Much.

After I playfully riled Pen up a bit by informing her that Vincent DuBois was, in fact, more talented than Asher, we settled on a Euro Cup simulation. Sloane and Rhea dropped out halfway through, leaving me and Pen to battle it out for victory.

I didn't consider myself a kid person. I liked them fine, but I couldn't relate to people more than half my age.

However, Pen was awesome. She was more mature than half the grown-ups I knew, and she was a kick-ass player. She scored three goals on me in the first half, when I wasn't even letting her win on purpose.

For a kid who looked so sweet, she was also pretty damn scary, as I soon found out the hard way.

When Sloane excused herself to use the restroom, Pen paused the game, turned to me, and asked with absolutely no preamble, "So. What's going on with you and my sister?"

I almost choked on my Coke while Rhea tried and failed to hide a smirk.

"We're hanging out," I said vaguely. I wasn't sure how much detail I should share with a nine-year-old about my love life, but I had a feeling I should err on the side of caution.

"No, *we're* hanging out." Pen gestured between us. "You and Sloane are doing more."

Jesus Christ.

I glanced at the door, willing Sloane to walk through it and put me out of my misery.

No such luck.

"We're dating," I clarified. I hoped like hell Pen wasn't going to ask me what *doing more* entailed. I wasn't going to touch *that* conversation with a fifty-foot pole.

"For how long?"

"Officially? A little over a week, but—"

"Are you seeing other people?"

"No."

"Are you in love with her?"

"I..." A bead of sweat trickled down my back. I couldn't believe I was getting interrogated by someone who came up to my hip. "I care about her a lot."

I care about her more than I've ever cared about anyone. But

I didn't know if it was love. I'd never been in love, so I didn't know what it felt like, but I should recognize it when it showed up, right?

A surge of anticipation leaked into my bloodstream, tempered by uncertainty.

"That wasn't my question." Pen pierced me with deceptively innocent-looking blue eyes. Behind her, Rhea's shoulders shook with mirth. She wasn't even bothering to hide her laughter anymore. "Sloane has never even *mentioned* her ex-boyfriends, much less let me hang out with them, so she must really like you."

A jab to my chest killed the jolt of electricity her words elicited.

She must really like you.

"Don't hurt her," Pen warned, her little face fierce. "If you do, I'll sic Mary on you."

"I would never hurt her," I said, and I meant it. The thought alone made my heart clench. After a short pause, I added, "Who's Mary?"

"Show him, Rhea."

Rhea, still laughing, pulled up something on her phone and handed it to me.

A Victorian doll stared up at me from the screen with unblinking blue eyes. She had black hair, a frilly white dress, and a smile made of pure evil.

It was the creepiest fucking toy I'd ever seen.

"My mother got her at an antiques shop," Pen said. "She belonged to an English aristocrat's daughter who was murdered by an unknown killer. Legend has it the girl's spirit lives on in her favorite doll."

"About ten years ago, someone tried to steal her from her old owner because she's so valuable, but they died of mysterious stab wounds in their sleep," Rhea added.

I couldn't tell if she was joking.

Also, what the fuck? Who bought their daughter a *possessed killer doll*? Then again, I wouldn't put it past Caroline Kensington.

"Ah." I shoved the phone back into Rhea's hand before Murderous Mary climbed out of the screen and stabbed *me*. "No need to call in Mary. I'm not a doll person, and like I said..." My tone gentled, turning serious. "I would *never* hurt Sloane. She means..." *The world*. "Too much to me."

Pen's frown remained for another beat before it melted into something more vulnerable. "Good," she said, her voice small. "Because she's been hurt enough already."

I hadn't planned on getting punched in the gut by a nine-year-old today, but Pen's aim was even better than her virtual soccer skills.

A burn spread from my gut to my chest, for Sloane *and* Pen. Both of them deserved better than what they got from the people who supposedly loved them.

"What did I miss?" Sloane's voice punctured our bubble. I'd been so caught up in my thoughts, I hadn't heard her return.

"Nothing," Pen and I chorused.

"We were just taking a break," I added.

"Because I was kicking his a—his butt." Pen giggled when I sent a mock glare her way. "It's okay. You're the Vincent to my Asher. I'm just better than you."

"Okay, that's it." I rolled my sleeves up. "No more going easy on you. Now it's *really* on."

We traded insults and banter as the second half ticked down. I was too into the game to pay attention to much else, but once or twice, I caught Sloane staring at us with a strange expression. She averted her gaze every time I turned in her direction, but not before I picked up on the suspicious brightness in her eyes.

The four of us stayed at the simulation center for another half hour before Pen's energy visibly flagged. She didn't want to leave, but I could tell the day's activities had taken their toll on her. I promised we'd come back in the future, and by the time the Harper Security guy picked her and Rhea up, Pen could barely keep her eyes open.

She did, however, muster enough energy to hug both me and Sloane goodbye. I never thought I'd get so attached to someone I'd just met, but a ferocious wave of protectiveness swept over me as I returned her hug.

Thank God she had Rhea and Sloane because the rest of Pen's family could go straight to hell for ignoring her.

Sloane murmured something to Pen, who nodded, her chin wobbling, before she followed Rhea into the car.

"Thank you," Sloane said as we watched their car disappear down the street. "That was...You didn't have to do that."

"I wanted to." My mouth flicked up in a smile. "Though I might've changed my mind had I known how badly she'd kick my ass."

Pen had won the game, seven to three.

Sloane's small laugh lightened the heaviness following Pen's departure.

"Also, before you heap too much praise on me, I have a confession to make," I said, earning a questioning arch of her brow. "I..." *I don't want this day to end. I don't want you to leave. I don't think there'll* ever *be a day when I want you to leave.* "I made us dinner reservations at a restaurant nearby. They're not until seven, so I guess we'll have to spend the rest of the day in this area."

"We do, do we?"

"I'm afraid so. We'll have to entertain ourselves before I ply you with so many carbs, you'll dream of pizza and noodles."

Amusement glinted in her eyes. "I can live with that. I've had worse dreams."

"Good." I laced my fingers through hers and led her toward the main street. "Seb told me about this great ice cream place we have to try."

"Seb?"

"Sebastian Laurent. He's like a walking food guide."

He was name number six on Kai's list, but I already knew him, so it'd been an easy ask to have his team design and execute the Vault's menu.

"Right." Sloane's palm was warm against mine. The breeze carried her scent into my lungs, and I instinctively squeezed her hand in response.

Sometimes, things got awkward after sex, but not for us. If it hadn't been for Wednesday night, I might've not taken the leap and organized today's outing with Pen. Something between us had shifted that night, and I wasn't talking about the sex.

Are you in love with her?

Pen's question echoed in my head. It lingered for a beat before it dissolved into the memory of Sloane sleeping in my arms. She'd curled into me, her body pressing against mine, her face free of any waking worries. I'd forced myself to stay awake just a bit longer so I could listen to her breathing.

I didn't know why, but it brought me the most overwhelming sense of peace and something else I couldn't quite put my finger on.

A loud rustle yanked me back to the present. It was the type only a large animal could make, but when I searched the overgrown bushes surrounding the simulation center, I didn't see anything.

Huh. Weird.

I shook my head, blinking away phantom sounds and the ghosts of Wednesday night. What would a large animal be doing in the middle of Queens anyway?

Whatever it was, I must've imagined it.

CHAPTER 27

Sloane

"WHY ARE YOU SMILING SO MUCH?" JILLIAN ASKED. "It's freaking me out."

"I'm not smiling. I'm exercising my mouth." I took the proffered coffee with one hand and finished sending my email with the other. I glanced up when I didn't get a reply. "That was a joke."

It wasn't a great one, but hey, I was out of practice. I deserved some slack.

"I know," she said with a shudder. "That freaks me out even more."

"Hilarious," I said dryly. "When you're done with your stand-up routine, connect me with Asher. If he's late to a meeting again, I'm adding a waiting fee to his monthly bill."

"Sure." She gave a dreamy sigh. "Asher days are my favorite."

I shook my head and waited for the door to close before I logged on to my private video-conferencing system.

Jillian wasn't wrong. I *was* smiling a lot, to the point where I annoyed myself, but I was still riding high from the past week.

Last Wednesday had been a rollercoaster of emotions. Pen's

hospitalization and seeing my family were unpleasant shocks, but my night with Xavier, both at the club and his house, smoothed the jagged edges of an otherwise epically shitty day.

I hadn't planned on sleeping with him. Part of me actively resisted it because I *knew* it was a bad idea. But there was something about the way he held and looked at me...He posed the greatest danger to my perfectly constructed world, yet I'd never felt safer than when I was in his arms.

Take your hair down, Sloane.

It was a simple request, but when I did it, it'd felt like more.

It'd felt like trust.

I stared at my screen. Asher wasn't on yet, which was just as well. Once they got rolling, my memories couldn't stop replaying the past few days—the way Xavier felt inside me, the way we moved together, the way he'd planned the outing with Pen and how great he was with her. I didn't have much of a maternal instinct, but my ovaries had almost exploded when they hugged goodbye.

There was nothing sexier than a man who was good with children.

He'd chosen an activity she would like that wouldn't aggravate her symptoms, but he also treated her like a normal kid, not a porcelain doll. That was what Pen wanted, and it was probably the reason she'd gotten attached to him so fast. My only worry was—

"Sorry, boss." Asher's perfect face filled my screen, his smile as roguish and charming as his British accent. Despite his words, he appeared unrepentant about his latest mishap. "Before you say anything, know it won't happen again."

I almost jumped before I caught myself. I'd gotten so wrapped up in my thoughts, I'd nearly forgotten about the call.

I straightened, brushing aside concerns about my personal life to focus on my most high-profile client.

Asher was in his house in Blackcastle. He wore an old gray T-shirt, and his hair was damp from either sweat or a shower. He must've come straight from his daily workout.

I wished he were as dedicated to maintaining his reputation as he was to his fitness. You'd think the most famous soccer player in the world would be too busy with and protective of his career to engage in illegal street races, but this wasn't the first time I'd had to clean up his mess before the press got wind of it.

"I'm not your boss. If I were, you wouldn't ignore me every time I tell you to do something," I said evenly. "Let me make something clear, Donovan. I don't care *how* great your scoring record was at Holchester. You're the new kid in the club at Blackcastle. You have a nine-figure contract riding on your ability to control your impulses so keep your head down, obey the speed limit, and for God's sake, stop fighting with Vincent DuBois. He's your teammate."

Asher's $200-million transfer earlier this year had made headlines worldwide, but it came with a unique stipulation: a two-year probationary period, during which he must uphold the contract's ironclad morality clause, among other things. If he didn't, his contract would be terminated, and he'd have to pay back half of his first two years' earnings.

Asher's face clouded at the mention of his rival. Vincent was the only player who came close to matching his fame and talent.

"Vincent's an asshole," he said.

"I don't care. Your rivalry is whipping the tabloids into a frenzy, and we don't need that right now. Shape the hell up, Asher, or I will personally hire a mercenary to repossess every car in your garage *and* make sure Rahim never sells you another vehicle. That upcoming limited-edition Bugatti you have your eye on? Gone to the next highest bidder."

Asher was famous, but I was determined, fed up, and pissed

off. Plus Rahim, his luxury car broker, owed me for the sheer number of referrals I'd sent his way (for people who were more responsible drivers than a certain athlete).

Asher swallowed at my threat. "Come on, Sloane. That's not—"

"Take care of it. Now."

I ended the call. Some clients required tougher love than others; Asher required freaking titanium.

I had a few minutes before my next meeting, so I quickly checked my phone.

Xavier: Black coffee, two sugars?

A smile touched my lips, easing my frustration over Asher.

Me: I'm working
Xavier: That wasn't the question, Luna
Me: …
Me: No sugar today. I've had too much already

I blamed the doughnuts Jillian had brought for breakfast.

I didn't get an immediate answer from him, so I turned to my group chat with the girls.

Isabella: Operation PW is in full swing ;)
Isabella: I MAY have gone to PW's favorite cafe to write today, and I MAY have overhead him discussing an upcoming blog post

My heart skipped a beat.

Me: Is it…

Isabella: Mmhmm. He didn't name names, but I'm almost positive it's what we planted
Vivian: Do you think he'll actually run it?
Vivian: She's one of the few celebs he's been too afraid to go after
Alessandra: I'm not sure "celeb" is the right term
Vivian: You know what I mean
Isabella: He might need an extra push
Sloane: I'll take care of it

My office phone rang, interrupting me from the chat.

"Sloane, your next appointment is here," Jillian said.

"Bring her in, please."

Two minutes later, Ayana entered my office, a striking vision draped in marigold silk and shoulder-grazing earrings.

"Thank you for meeting with me on such short notice." She folded herself gracefully into the chair opposite mine. Her skin glowed beneath the lights, and she had cheekbones that could slice through diamonds. No wonder she'd taken the modeling world by storm over the past year.

"You're my client. I'm happy to help in any way I can," I said.

Ayana was my last new client for a while. My roster was technically closed, but Alessandra's mother was Ayana's modeling mentor. I'd met with her earlier this year as a favor, and I liked her so much I'd signed her that day.

"Good." She hesitated, her lovely face shadowed with nerves. "Because I might be in trouble."

For the next forty-five minutes, I listened as Ayana laid out her situation. I kept my expression neutral, but every cell in my body blanched when she reached the *marriage* part.

"I don't know what to do," she concluded. She stared at her lap, her anxiety palpable. "I owe him so much, but..."

"But nothing. It's your life," I said firmly. "Listen, as your publicist, I'll tell you this would be *great* publicity. There's nothing the public loves more than a celebrity wedding. But as a woman, as a human, I'll tell you to follow your gut. Is gratitude worth five years of your life?"

When Ayana left, the question lingered.

I couldn't answer it for her, and my job was to spin her decision into media gold, no matter what it was. I just hoped she made a choice she wouldn't regret later.

I opened my inbox, but I didn't get a chance to read anything before Xavier appeared at the door.

"Was that Ayana I saw coming out?" He strolled in, his hair tousled by the wind and his sweater molding to his form in a way that was positively sinful. "I didn't realize she was still in town."

A sizzle of awareness ran beneath my skin, chased by something darker that I ignored. It must be my lunch. Tuna salad was hit-or-miss on a good day. "Do you know her?"

"Not personally, but she's a friend of a friend, and I've seen her around a few times," Xavier said with a shrug. "Luca mentioned she was supposed to be shooting a Delamonte campaign in Europe this week, but I guess not."

"Ah."

His eyebrows arched. "What happened? Did the meeting not go well?"

"It went fine." I stared at my screen, willing myself to get over whatever was roiling in my stomach. "She's great. Obviously. Since she's the first thing you mentioned when you walked in."

Silence greeted my curt response.

When I looked up again, Xavier wasn't staring at me in shock like I'd expected. The bastard was *laughing*.

Great, rolling waves of silent laughter shook his body and sent a rush of heat to my cheeks.

"Luna." Mirth gleamed in his eyes. "Are you jealous?"

"No," I snapped. "It was merely an observation."

I returned to my screen and glared at the lines of text until they blurred. Prickles bloomed behind my nose and eyes.

It was stupid and irrational because I didn't *really* think Xavier was interested in Ayana, but I couldn't fix the valve leaking inside me. The one that held back a flood of insecurity, which I thought I'd turned off until little moments like this dripped self-doubt into my stomach.

Too cold. Too dispassionate. Too unlovable.

Xavier was the opposite of me—full of warmth, easy to like, and a charmer at his core. He'd been honest and committed since we'd started dating, but a part of me was waiting for him to run.

One day, he'd wake up and realize I wasn't the person he wanted me to be, and he'd leave.

"Sloane." He didn't sound amused anymore. Soft footsteps preceded the clean scent of his cologne; firm hands turned me around. "Look at me."

I fixated stubbornly on his neck. One of his tattoos peeked from beneath his sweater, and it was the only thing that kept me from falling apart.

What the hell happened? One second, I was working and smiling so much I scared Jillian. The next, I was on the verge of a breakdown over a *man*.

Past me was disgusted with myself, but past me didn't know what current me knew: this trial period I'd proposed had backfired spectacularly.

I'd thought we could have fun for two months and say we tried. I'd thought I could walk away at the end of this and be okay.

But I couldn't. Not when jealousy gnawed through my insides at the mere thought of Xavier with someone else.

"*Look at me.*" Fingers grasped my chin and notched it up. Xavier's eyes bored into mine, stripping me bare. "You have nothing to be jealous of. I mentioned Ayana because I was just talking to Luca and that was at the top of my mind. It doesn't have anything to do with how I feel toward her because I *don't* feel anything."

"She's a supermodel. Everyone feels something toward her."

"I don't," he said. "I don't care how beautiful or famous someone is, Luna. None of them hold a candle to you."

If he were anyone else, I would've dismissed his reassurance as empty words. But this was Xavier, and *because* it was Xavier, his reply had the effect of a thousand fluttering wings. Their velvety tips brushed my heart, sealing the leak and soaking up the insecurities.

I managed a smile over the steel drum of my heart. "You always know what to say."

"It's easy when it's the truth. Now..." He leaned down and gave me a soft, lingering kiss. He tasted like coffee and warmth. "*That's* a proper hello."

I laughed, my skin tingling from either our kiss, the end of our previous conversation, or both. I was a bit embarrassed by my uncharacteristic outburst of jealousy, but I was too pleased to see him to care.

"Do we have a meeting today?" I asked, trying to shift back into work mode. "I thought we were going to talk on the phone."

Xavier had said he had a plan for getting Vuk to sign on as his business partner without a location first, and he wanted to run it by me.

"We don't, and we were. But I'm not here for business. I'm here to see you." Xavier nodded at the coffee cup he'd set on my desk. "Black, no sugar."

I took a sip and narrowed my eyes at him over the rim. "I have a lot of work to catch up on."

I'd been so distracted since we started dating that I wasn't ahead by two weeks like I usually was. I was *on schedule*, which was unacceptable.

"It's lunchtime, and Jillian said you don't have any meetings until two."

"Jillian needs to stop telling you my schedule, and I'm not hungry."

"No." Xavier's voice turned to silk. "But I am."

I didn't get a chance to react before he picked me up and set me on the desk in one smooth, swift motion. He shoved my skirt up around my hips and slipped his thumb beneath the edge of my underwear to find me already slick and wanting.

"Xavier," I hissed, glancing behind me at the *un*locked door. "Someone will hear."

Despite my protest, my clit throbbed with need. Heat gathered like a firestorm in my lungs as those strong, deft hands caressed me, molding to my hips and thighs, stoking the fires higher and hotter until they incinerated my reservations.

"Good." Xavier sank to his knees and pushed my knees wider, granting him an unfettered view of my soaked arousal. His eyes gleamed up at me, dark and bright as volcanic glass. "Then they'll know exactly who you belong to."

A humiliating little whimper left my mouth when he bent his head and closed his teeth around delicate silk. A woozy, breathless second of anticipation sent my pulse skyrocketing, followed by something between a cry and a gasp when he ripped my underwear off and dived in.

Bursts of light exploded behind my eyes at the sudden switch from lazy sensuality to feral, untamed hunger. My brain couldn't catch up, so it ceded all power to my body. The buck of my hips;

the grasp on his hair; the arousal that raced through me, so fast and potent it was almost painful.

I tried to close my legs, scoot backward, do *anything* that would let me catch my breath before I exploded from pure pleasure, but Xavier's iron grip forced me to stay in place. He was merciless in his assault, his mouth and tongue and teeth pinpointing every sensitive spot with devastating accuracy.

I wasn't sure if I was screaming or sobbing or utterly silent. I wasn't sure if my staff was standing at the door right now, watching him tongue fuck my brains out while I lost all semblance of control.

I wasn't sure of anything at all, really, except for the fact I never, ever wanted this to end. Not with him, and not with us.

The firestorm inside me finally erupted, and this time, I *heard* my cry before a hand clamped over my mouth, muffling my scream.

My orgasm was so intense that I disintegrated immediately, bits and pieces of me falling, floating, *burning* until the smoke cleared, and a hazy shadow of my senses returned.

The hand over my mouth dropped, replaced by a punishing kiss. I tasted my arousal, and my nipples tightened again like I hadn't just come so hard, I couldn't breathe properly.

"That was a preview. The next time you doubt how much I want you..." Xavier drew my bottom lip between his teeth and nipped. The sting traveled straight to the emptiness pulsing between my thighs. "Remember this."

He gripped my hips again, pulling me off the desk and bending me over so I was bared to him. My skirt was still bunched around my hips, and my underwear lay in tatters on the floor.

I heard my desk drawer open, followed by the rasp of a zipper and the distinctive tear of tape.

My mouth dried. "What—" A piece of duct tape sealed over my lips, cutting me off.

"In case you scream again. You don't want people hearing, remember?" Xavier's dark velvet reply promised all sorts of wicked intent. "And I need my hands for something else."

Lust and fear surged through me in equal measure, one indistinguishable from the other. He'd left my hands free, so I could easily tear off the tape—but I didn't.

I lay there, legs spread, mouth taped, wetness dripping down my thighs at the obscene picture I must've made.

My fear didn't stem from what he was about to do to me; it came from how much I wanted it. How much I *liked* the tiny loss of control because it meant I didn't have to think; I could just feel.

"Hold on to the desk." Xavier's warning shivered down my neck.

I barely had time to obey before he slammed into me, my back instinctively bowing from the force of his thrust. I tried to scream, but the duct tape prevented me from making anything except incoherent moans as he fucked me senseless, one hand holding me down, the other delving beneath my blouse to play with my breasts.

I clung to the edge of the desk, reduced to one giant raw, exposed nerve. Sweat coated my skin, and my clit throbbed in time with his thrusts, each pulse so powerful that it sent dark clouds across my vision.

Every time my pleasure seemed to plateau, another pinch, another squeeze, another thrust drove it higher to the point of being unbearable. My brain could no longer process the overwhelming sensations racking my body, and I seemed to slip out of myself for a second, seeing the filthy scene we presented to the world.

My hair had fallen from its bun. Wisps of it stuck to my flushed skin, and drool leaked from beneath the duct tape as Xavier pistoned in and out of me, his deep groans sinking into me as deeply as anything else.

I loved the sounds of his pleasure. I loved the way I felt right then, helpless and ravished yet so very safe. I—

My entire body tensed. Pinpricks of light dotted the drifts of black clouds, and I shook uncontrollably as I climaxed, bucking and jerking against his cock. My pussy spasmed again and again, sending lightning bolts of pleasure through my stupefied brain. I heard Xavier give a final, guttural grunt before he came too, but the waves kept coming, rolling through my body like a ceaseless ocean of electric, mind-numbing pleasure.

I didn't know how long we stayed there, me sprawled bonelessly across the desk, him still buried inside me, but when we finally moved, it was almost two.

"Just in time for your meeting," Xavier teased. I was a mess, but other than his ruffled hair and ruddy cheeks, he looked like he'd just stepped out of a magazine. Bastard. "I have impeccable timing."

He cleaned me up and fixed my clothing with gentle hands before pulling the tape off my mouth.

"Hilarious." My voice didn't sound like mine; it was too hoarse from...A blush worked its way over my skin, and Xavier's satisfied grin widened. "I'll have to postpone my meeting. I can't discuss media strategy looking like I've..."

"Been freshly and thoroughly fucked?"

My blush deepened at Xavier's smoky drawl. "I wouldn't put it quite that way," I said with as much dignity as I could muster considering my underwear was in shreds.

What I'd done—what *we'd* done—was so out of character for me that I couldn't quite wrap my head around it.

I wasn't the type of person who mixed business and pleasure, which...well, okay, that horse had left its gate weeks ago. But I was hyperaware of my surroundings at all times, and I never engaged in compromising activities at the office.

Xavier was the only person who could make me forget about my rules and *like* it. It was disturbing.

God, I hoped no one had heard us. Everyone should be at lunch, but you never knew when an enterprising assistant chose to stay in and catch up on work (and catch her boss having sex in the process).

"You can put it any way you want, Luna, but it's the truth." Xavier's lips touched mine. "For the record, you look beautiful when you're freshly fucked."

"How charming." I should pick up the phone and reschedule my two-o'clock meeting, but I wanted to stay in his arms a while longer. "They should create a makeup tutorial for it."

"I'm sure one already exists." He drew back, examining me. "How are you feeling?"

"Good. A little sore, but...good." I couldn't find a better term to describe the weightlessness I felt. *Good* wasn't adequate, but unlike other words, saying it didn't freak me out.

"Good," Xavier repeated.

His palms braced the desk on either side of me, and as we smiled at each other, the silence soft with contentment while we savored our last moments before reality intruded, another word surfaced in my mind.

Happy.

Simple, basic, but no less true.

CHAPTER 28

Sloane

BY SOME MIRACLE, NO ONE SAID A WORD WHEN XAVIER and I emerged from my office after our, uh, session yesterday. People were still trickling in from lunch, and the staff members who *were* there were too busy oohing and aahing over pictures of Princess Camilla to pay us any mind.

Thank the Lord for small favors.

I'd rescheduled my meeting and forgot about Xavier's Vuk plan until we met up for dinner the next night. He hadn't mentioned it beyond his initial text about it.

"Two questions," I said as we meandered through downtown. "One, what's the plan for Vuk? And two, where are we going for dinner? I'm starving."

"Oh, now you're hungry," Xavier teased, wrapping his arm around my shoulders. The warm weight sent a swarm of butterflies diving and whirling in my stomach. "Yet you kicked me out when I tried to take you to lunch."

"Because I remember what happened *yesterday* during lunch. I got zero work done." I attempted a haughty look but ended up blushing at the sly glance he sent my way.

I did that a lot more these days, blushing. It was enough to drive a blush hater like me mad.

"I'm aware." Xavier's drawl went molten with desire. "You look good bent over your desk, Luna. Especially when your pussy is dripping with my—"

"*Xavier*." The flush escalated to a five-alarm fire.

I glanced around us, convinced every other person on the sidewalk could hear his filthy words. I wasn't a prude, but I didn't want all the random Janes and Joes to know about my sex life either.

He laughed. "Fine. I'll save the dirty talk for the hotel."

The hotel? "Where exactly are we going?" I asked, my voice rife with suspicion.

"You'll see. Ask me another question."

"I hate your evasiveness."

"You love it because you love surprises."

"I'm a Virgo. I hate surprises." Except for the Sunday meetup with Pen, but that didn't count.

"Ask me another question, Luna," Xavier said, ignoring my perfectly serviceable astrology argument. I was a firm supporter of hard science, but astrology was too fun to give up.

"Fine," I grumbled. I *was* intrigued by what he had planned, but I'd never admit it. I didn't need him springing surprises on me left and right. "The one you skipped. What was the Vuk plan you came up with?"

"The Vuk plan. Right." We turned left onto a quiet street. "What are the driving forces behind every successful businessman? Why do they do what they do?"

Easy. "Money, power, and fame."

"There's one more."

A furrow dug between my brows. "Ego? No, that falls under the other three. Revenge? Ambition? Spite?"

Xavier side-eyed me. "Passion."

"Oh." I wrinkled my nose. "Not as good as spite."

That was what had driven me to build Kensington PR into what it was today. Yes, I was passionate about what I did, and yes, I needed the income, but during my darkest moments and most sleepless nights, spite was the fire that kept the darkness at bay.

I'd wanted to prove I could thrive without my family's money or support, and I had. They wanted me to fail and ask for their help; I would rather tie the last brick of my business to my feet and jump into the Hudson before I gave them that satisfaction.

That was just me though. Maybe other people were different.

"Perhaps not," Xavier said dryly. "But I've been doing some research into Vuk, and he has an interesting history. Do you know how Markovic Holdings started?"

I shook my head.

"Vuk worked for a small distillery in his hometown in high school. He loved the place but hated how it was run, so he hustled and saved until he had enough money to buy it outright after college. He studied chemical engineering, and after he took over the distillery, he revolutionized the vodka-making process to create..."

"Markovic Vodka," I finished, naming the world's most popular vodka brand.

"Exactly. Obviously, he's come a long way since then, but the point is, this wasn't a man who went into the business for money or fame. He saw something he loved, thought he could do it better, and *did* do it better. It took years and a shit ton of work, but he did it. That's passion." Xavier shook his head. "That was my mistake. I appealed *solely* to his business side and forgot about the heart."

I smiled. Vuk wasn't the only passionate one; I'd never heard Xavier so fired up about something until the club.

"Appealing to his other side is a good idea," I said. "When's your next meeting with him?"

"Tomorrow. The problem is, I don't have a frame for my pitch. I didn't exactly grow up dreaming of being a nightclub owner."

"No, but I distinctly remember a pile of discarded bar sketches in Colombia. They're a start."

"They're also in the trash. In Colombia," he pointed out.

"I'm guessing if you had them there, you'll have some lying around here." I arched an eyebrow. "I've seen your house. You still have a trophy for winning Biggest Flirt at prep school."

"Hey, that trophy is made of solid fake gold. It's worth its weight in sentimentality." Xavier's teeth flashed white against his tanned skin. "But you might be right about some old sketches lying around."

"That's why people pay me the big bucks," I quipped.

We walked for another five minutes before we turned onto a quiet side street and stopped in front of a charming brick building. Ivy blanketed its walls, and a peek through the glass door revealed an elegantly appointed lobby filled with plants and rich fabrics.

"It's a new family-owned boutique hotel," Xavier said. "It opened just a few months ago, but its restaurant serves some of the best Thai food in the city."

My stomach rumbled at the mention of food. "Sold."

"One more thing before we go in." His face sobered with a touch of nerves. "I booked the hotel for the night in case you'd rather stay here. With me. Their suites are beautiful, and—"

"Okay." My heart thudded out another response.

Yes. Yes. Yes.

Surprise flashed in his eyes, followed by a slow smile that sent a cascade of tingles down my spine.

"Okay," he repeated.

That was all we needed to say.

"Good evening, Mr. Castillo." The front desk recognized him on sight. "Which of our suites would you like to stay in tonight?"

"We'll take the Royal Suite and dinner by the pool. Please send pajamas and toiletries as well. We didn't bring any luggage."

"Of course. If you change your mind, any of our other suites are at your disposal."

I paused, turning over her words. "Wait." I fixed Xavier with a disbelieving stare. "When you said you booked the hotel, you booked the *whole* hotel?"

"I like supporting family businesses." His dimples twinkled with mischief. "I also like privacy."

The businesswoman in me said he shouldn't be splashing money around like this when the fate of his inheritance hung in the air.

The romantic in me said to shut up and enjoy the experience.

For the first time in my life, the romantic won.

The concierge gave us a quick tour of the hotel's amenities before taking us outside, where dinner would be served.

"If you'd like to order more food, swimwear, or any other amenities, you can do so using these cards," she said, handing us each a slim gold card. They had several white buttons embedded in them for various purposes, including housekeeping, dining, and general services. "Enjoy your evening."

"Thank you," I said.

The door closed behind her, I turned, and…

My heart skipped an awed beat. *Wow.*

I'd stayed at many luxury hotels in my life. Most were pretty generic in the way all luxury hotels were, but this place was *beautiful.*

The turquoise lagoon pool featured a miniature waterfall at one end and a hot tub on the other. Lush foliage and custom rockscapes enhanced the tropical vibes, while a cushioned, candlelit cabana infused the scene with dreamy romanticism. Overhead, a glass dome protected the entire space from the elements, and the temperature was a perfect, balmy seventy-five degrees.

We weren't in Manhattan; we were in the freaking Garden of Eden.

Xavier laced his fingers through mine and pulled me toward the cabana. When we got closer, I noticed the low wooden table was covered with food.

Correction: it was covered with a *feast*. Coconut puff sticks sat next to grilled and marinated chicken skewers; classic pad Thai noodles starred alongside pineapple fried rice served in an actual hollowed-out pineapple, and an array of soups and curries perfumed the air with lemongrass, ginger, cumin, and a dozen other mouthwatering spices.

My stomach rumbled again with eagerness.

"There's no way we'll finish all this," I said, sinking onto one of the giant cushions that doubled as a seat.

"Probably not," Xavier admitted. "I didn't know what dishes you like best, so I ordered a bit of everything." Another peek of his dimples. "None with walnuts though."

Those butterflies in my stomach were getting out of hand; I needed pest control or something.

"I don't think walnuts are usually featured in Thai cooking," I said, trying to hide the swell in my chest.

"You never know. What do you have against those poor nuts anyway?"

"They look like brains. It creeps me out...*Stop laughing*."

"I'm not laughing," he managed through gusts of laughter. "I just didn't expect that to be the reason."

I attempted to hold on to my indignation—my reason for hating walnuts was perfectly valid, thank you very much—but Xavier's amusement was too infectious, and a smile eventually cracked my frown.

Our rapport took on an easy rhythm as we ate our way through the feast. Talking to Xavier was like talking to one of my best friends. I didn't have to scrounge for topics or worry he'd take something I said the wrong way. He understood me, and as our conversation wound from food, film, and music to travel, I relaxed to the point where I forgot about everything outside this moment.

"Thailand," Xavier said when I asked about his favorite places he'd visited so far. "I went after college, fell in love, and stayed there for an entire summer. It was hot as hell, so I spent most of my time at the beach." A hint of wistfulness flickered over his face. "My mom was a fan too. When I was young, she would tell me about her adventures abroad and how she always went back to Thailand. The culture, the nature, the food..." He nodded at the half-empty dishes in front of us. "She loved it all."

I remained quiet lest I spook him into withdrawing. Xavier never talked about his mother, and I was fascinated by the glimpse into their relationship.

I knew they'd been close. They'd had to be, considering how devastated he'd been by her death, but I didn't know the details—the little things that transformed Patricia Castillo from an amorphous piece of the past to a concrete memory.

"Maybe that was why I stayed so long," Xavier said. "It made me feel closer to her."

My chest tightened, mirroring the weight he bore. I'd had a few more years with my mother than he'd had with his, but I understood the desire to connect to someone who was no longer there. Their presence, no matter how brief, left an emptiness that could never be truly filled.

"My mother wrote me a letter when I was born." Xavier's mouth twisted in a wry smile when my gaze jerked up to his in shock. "I didn't know about it until last month. My father told me about it during our...during our last conversation. He said he'd forgotten about it because my mom placed it in a safe. I don't know if I believe him, but I guess it doesn't matter now. He's dead, and I have the letter."

His shrug looked forced. He could pretend it wasn't a big deal, but it was. We both knew that.

"Did you read the letter?" I asked softly.

His Adam's apple slid up and down his throat. "Yes."

I waited, not wanting to push him on such a sensitive topic. I was curious about the letter, but I was more concerned about Xavier. Dealing with his father's death and a long-lost letter from his mother in such a short period of time must've taken a huge toll, especially since he didn't have anyone to talk to about it. I was the closest thing he'd had to a confidant in that house.

The tightness in my chest compounded.

"It's funny," Xavier finally continued. "When I read that letter, I could *hear* her voice. It was like she was right there, watching over me. She said she couldn't wait for me to discover my favorite places in the world and that, if I were ever at a loss as to where to go, I should choose a place by the beach. I went to Thailand long before I knew the letter existed, but coincidentally, the beach was one of the reasons I chose to go there. It was far away from my father, surrounded by water, and it reminded me of my mother." A faint smile. "It was a triple win. I just wish..." The smile faded beneath a shadow of melancholy. "I wish I would've found that letter sooner. I might've lived my life a little differently. Done things I'd be more proud of."

"You're not a bad person, Xavier," I said, my voice gentle. "You didn't do anything egregious that you should be ashamed of. And you may not have read her letter until recently, but I think a part of her was always there with you, guiding you. Besides..." My mind slipped to five years ago, when I'd walked away from the only family I'd ever known at the time. "It's never too late for change. If you're unhappy with the road you're traveling, you can choose a new one at any time."

Xavier stared at me, his eyes a hurricane of emotions I couldn't decipher.

"I wish she could've met you," he said, so quiet that I felt more than I heard his words. "She would've loved you."

The tightness behind my ribs morphed into a raw, pervasive ache. It spread everywhere—my throat, my nose, behind my eyes and in the deepest grooves of my heart.

I didn't cry, but this was the closest I'd come to doing so in a long, long time.

"She left this with the letter." Xavier reached into his pocket and retrieved an antique gold pocket watch. He set it on the table and ran a pensive thumb over the case. "It's a family heirloom. I'm not a watch person, but I've been carrying it around because...I don't know. It felt right."

"It's gorgeous." I picked the watch up gingerly and opened it, admiring the sapphire accents and exquisite craftsmanship. Whoever made it obviously did so with love; every element was hand tooled to perfection, including the faded but legible engraving: *The greatest gift we have is time. Use it wisely.*

I studied it, careful not to rub against the time-worn letters.

"The quote is a good reminder, isn't it?" The corners of Xavier's mouth flicked up without humor. "I wasted years doing nothing with my life. I was so resentful of my father and so scared of fucking up that I didn't even try. It made sense to me at the time but..." His voice caught. Stalled. Then the conversation turned in a direction I didn't expect. "Do you know why my mom died?"

I closed the pocket watch and returned it to the table, my heart pounding. "It was a house fire. She didn't make it out in time."

"No, that's *how* she died, not why." The hurricane in his eyes brewed into something darker, stronger, beyond the confines of categories. "She died because of me."

Nothing could've prepared me for the punch of his words. Air evacuated from my lungs, and a bruise blossomed where the impact hit, unexpected and agonizing. "Xavier..."

"Don't," he said harshly. "Don't try to say it's not my fault until you hear the whole story."

I lapsed into silence, my eyes burning with unshed emotion.

"I was ten. My father was away for business, and my mom was volunteering at an event. She loved art, so she donated a lot of money and time to local galleries." Xavier swallowed. "My father's birthday was the day after his scheduled return. She wanted to surprise him with a party, and she put me in charge of the decorations. It was my first time being in charge of something so important. I wanted to make them both proud, so I went all out. Balloons. Piñatas." His knuckles whitened. "Candles."

An invisible anchor dragged my heart through my stomach. *No.*

"I did a test run to see how everything would look," Xavier said. "But I thought I heard a noise in another room, and I got distracted. I accidentally knocked one of the candles over." His eyes were bleak. "I tried to put it out, but there was wood and cardboard everywhere. The fire spread too quickly, and I got trapped. Luckily, we didn't have a lot of staff back then, just a housekeeper. She was outside checking the mail, and when she saw the flames, she called the fire department. But my mom came home right then, and when she found out I was inside, she didn't wait for the firefighters. She ran in and pulled me out. We almost made it to the front door before a beam fell and trapped us again. I don't remember much of what happened after that. I passed out from too much smoke inhalation. When I woke up, I was outside with the medics. I survived. She didn't."

I didn't think; I just reached out and closed my hand around his, wishing I could do something, anything, except listen helplessly.

"My father rushed home when he heard the news. I don't think he truly believed my mother, his wife, was gone until he saw her body. And when he did...I'd never heard anyone cry like that. Sometimes, I can still hear it. It was almost inhuman." Xavier brushed his fingers over the pocket watch, his expression taut. "He *loved* my mother more than anyone else in the world. They'd met in college, the aspiring businessman and the heiress who fell in love with his charm, his ambition, his loyalty. She was the reason why he worked so hard to build the Castillo Group, and when she died, a part of him died with her."

Xavier lifted his head again, his gaze clouded with decades-old anguish. "He blamed me. After her funeral, he told me he wished I were the one who'd died instead of her. He was drunk at the time. Really drunk. But I've never forgotten those words. The truth always comes out when our inhibitions come down."

I couldn't breathe through the knots in my chest.

I had a shitty family, but I couldn't imagine a parent saying that to their child. Xavier had been *ten*. He'd been just a kid.

"The thing is, I didn't blame him," he said. "Not at first. It *was* my fault. If I hadn't been stupid enough to light that *one* damn candle, there wouldn't have been a fire, and my mother would still be alive. But the older I got, the more I..." Xavier faltered. "I don't know. I got angry too. It was easier to swallow than guilt, and my father was right there, taking his rage out on me. Physically, mentally, emotionally. He still wanted me to take over the company because he had no other choice. I was his only heir. But outside of that obligation, he hated me, and I hated him back." He tapped a tattoo on his bicep. It featured the family crest for the Castillos' biggest rival and had set social media ablaze when he first got it. "One year, I came home with this, and I left with scars."

My stomach roiled at his matter-of-fact tone.

"My father was the only parent I had left," Xavier said. "It should've brought us closer, but it drove us apart. Every time we were together, we were reminded of who was missing, and it hurt too much. So we lashed out in our different ways, and by the time I graduated college, I was done. I didn't want anything to do with him or the company—except when it came to money. It doesn't reflect well on me, but it's the truth."

Heavy silence descended, punctuated by the soft burble of water and faint music from inside the hotel.

Xavier stared at where my hand rested over his, a thousand emotions passing over his face before he shook his head.

"I'm sorry." He let out a rueful laugh. "This was supposed to be a beautiful dinner, and I dragged you into the most morbid conversation possible." He tried to pull his hand away, but I stopped him with a firmer grip.

He'd been there for me at the hospital, in Spain after my father's email, and in a dozen other situations and ways he didn't know mattered as much as they did.

It was my turn to be there for him.

"This *is* a beautiful dinner. Coconut puffs are the way to my heart," I said, earning myself a shadow of a smile. "But before I say what I'm about to say, I want you to know two things. One, I'm terrible at comforting people. I have no talent or desire to do so, and tears make me uncomfortable. Two, I hate platitudes. They're fake and stupid. So I want you to listen carefully when I say this: It wasn't your fault. You were a kid, and it was an accident." I squeezed his hand, wishing I could imprint my sincerity into his skin because I meant every word. "*It wasn't your fault.*"

Xavier's eyes gleamed bright and turbulent. Playboy, heir, hedonist, flirt—those masks were gone, leaving only the man in their place. Raw in his vulnerability, flawed in many ways, and marred by cracks and bruises beneath a deceptively polished facade.

I looked at him, and I'd never seen anyone more beautiful.

His hand curled around mine and squeezed. Just once. Just enough to jump start a piece of my heart I'd never known existed.

Then the cracks sealed, the bruises faded, and he stood, withdrawing his hand from mine to pull his shirt over his head.

I was so thrown by the sudden shift in atmosphere that I didn't find my voice until he was halfway to the pool. "What are you doing?"

"Skinny-dipping." His pants joined his shirt on the ground.

"You can't skinny-dip here," I hissed, glancing around. "There are security cameras, and someone could come out any second."

"No one will come out unless we call them. Even if they do, they can't see anything if we're in the pool." Xavier shed his boxers, his smile containing equal parts challenge and amusement. "Come on, Luna. Don't make me do this alone."

He stood in front of the pool, all bronzed skin and sculpted muscle, as naked and unabashed as a Greek statue come to life. Soft lights spilled over the hard contours of his body, tracing the ridges of his abs and the strong, lean sinew of his legs.

A hot ripple wavered through me, coupled with a surprising pinch of envy.

What would it feel like to be *that* carefree and spontaneous? To do something I wanted without worrying about the consequences?

Oh, what the hell. It wasn't like he hadn't seen the goods before.

I made an impulse decision and stood before I changed my mind. Xavier's eyes darkened as I walked toward him, shedding my dress, tights, and underwear with each step.

By the time I reached him, I wasn't wearing a stitch of clothing, and it felt *good*. More than good. It felt freeing.

"Stunning," he whispered, and I felt that one word from the top of my head to the tips of my toes.

We sank into the pool, our movements languid as we relished the silky, heated waters. We didn't talk; we simply floated there, unburdened by the weight of our clothes and long-hidden secrets, our fingers interlacing more out of habit than thought.

It was impossible to see stars in the city sky, but the quiet, the warmth, and the fragrance of exotic blooms jeweling the air transformed our little pocket of New York into a magical secret world, at least for tonight.

Our lives weren't perfect, but here, together, we were at peace.

CHAPTER 29

I HADN'T PLANNED ON TELLING SLOANE ABOUT MY past. I'd never told *anyone* what happened with the fire, but there was something about last night, the way she looked at me, and the ease I felt around her that pulled the words out of me before I processed what was happening.

Once they were out, it was like a giant weight had been lifted off my shoulders. I hadn't realized how much the poison from my past was eating me up inside until I expunged it, and not only did Sloane listen without judgment, but she'd comforted me afterward.

Sloane Kensington didn't comfort people, but she'd comforted me. If I'd ever thought I could walk away from her before, last night confirmed I couldn't.

Thanks to her, I also showed up to Vuk's office on Friday morning armed with my new strategy. I didn't bring slide decks or shiny handouts; I didn't even bring my old bar sketches. I simply told him the truth. My fractured relationship with my father, my refusal to take over his company out of fear and spite, his death and my mother's letter...everything I shared with Sloane, I reframed into a story that wasn't just about numbers; it was about the heart behind them.

"You're worried the club will crash and burn if my inheritance committee doesn't rule in my favor come May," I said. "I would be too if I were in your shoes. But here's the thing: I'm no longer doing it for my inheritance." Vuk's eyebrows notched up. "I'm no longer doing it *just* for my inheritance," I amended. "My entire life, I relied on what other people gave me. I lived off something I didn't build, and I told myself I was okay with it because I didn't have the courage to stray from that path. But this club? Everything I've achieved so far? That's mine, and I'm fucking proud of it."

I'd had help along the way because no one built an empire alone. But the vision and execution were mine, and I hadn't fucked them up so far. Things were going *well*, as well as starting a new business in the city could possibly go, and it made me think I could do this—take the Castillo name and make it my own.

"I would love to have you as a partner," I said. As expected, Vuk hadn't said a word during my spiel, but his eyes appeared marginally warmer than they had when I arrived. Either that, or I was delirious from lack of sleep. "But if you say no, the club will still open. If I don't secure the vault, I'll find another location. It's not ideal, but business isn't always about the ideal. It's about getting things done, and I'll get it done with or without you." I paused, letting my words sink in. "However, I'd much rather do it with you. So." I nodded at the contract on his desk. "What's your answer? Are you going to take the risk, or are you going to play it safe?"

It was a gamble, provoking Vuk like that. Without him, my path to opening the club would be that much harder, but I *would* figure it out. I hadn't realized it until I'd said it out loud, but I wasn't lying when I'd said I could do it on my own. I'd have to fight like hell, and I probably wouldn't sleep from now until May, but people had overcome worse obstacles to achieve their goals.

If they could do it, so could I.

Vuk studied me, his eyes so pale they were nearly colorless.

He didn't move. He didn't smile. He didn't speak.

I maintained his gaze, my heart pounding to an ominous rhythm.

Then, after an endless, agonizing silence, and without saying a single word, Vuk Markovic slid the contract toward him, picked up his pen, and signed on the dotted line.

I did it.

I fucking did it.

Vuk was officially my business partner, and with his stamp of approval, the rest of the pieces fell into place. That night, Sloane and I celebrated with food, wine, a so-bad-it-was-good rom-com, and lots of sex (obviously).

I also had the personal pleasure of delivering the news to Alex over the phone. He greeted the update with as much emotion as a block of granite, but he did sign off with something that made me smile.

"Delivered two weeks early," he said. "You might survive the industry after all."

It was the closest to a compliment one could expect from Alex Volkov.

But most importantly? The bank vault was mine.

Jules had fast-tracked my permits and licenses and was currently working with Alex's lawyers on the commercial lease. My relationship with Sloane was developing into something more than I'd thought possible, and the financing from Davenport Capital was in the final stages of approval.

Opening a nightclub this big this fast required a ton of capital, and with my inheritance tied up and Vuk unwilling to pour *too* much cash into an untested venture, I was relying on the Davenport money to cover the shortfall. I was confident it would go through, especially with Vuk on board.

Overall, life was good. Really good.

But as someone wise once said, all good things came to an end, and this particular streak of luck came to a sudden, crashing halt the following Monday.

Luca: Did you see this?

His next text included a link to a Perry Wilson blog post.

I grabbed my coffee from my usual spot and tucked a twenty-dollar bill in the tip jar before I clicked on the link. Perry was always talking shit, and people knew better than to take half the stuff he said too seriously.

What was it this time? Did I have an orgy with models in the middle of Fifth Avenue? Get into a brawl with someone at a club? By now, it was semipublic knowledge that Sloane and I were seeing each other. It'd elicited some disapproving whispers and controversy among the more conservative crowd, but people weren't as scandalized as she and Perry had originally expected.

One, there wasn't concrete proof. Two, it was New York—more salacious things happened every day. And three, she was too damn good at her job for her clients to drop her over such a small "scandal."

However, my disinterest exploded into shock when I saw Perry's blog post. It was about me and Sloane, but it wasn't what I'd expected.

Kensingtons not so estranged?? What's going on with New York's most famously dysfunctional family?

There was barely any text, but there were photos. *Dozens* of them.

Sloane and I entering the simulation center in Queens. Us leaving with Rhea and Pen. Me hugging Pen goodbye. So on and so forth, our perfect, secret day captured in high-definition detail for the world to see.

I scrolled to the end, the roar of my pulse drowning out the car horns and sounds of traffic from the street.

If there were photos of us at the hotel, and he'd published nudes of Sloane...

Rage prowled beneath a slick of panic, followed by a tingle of relief when the post ended without mentioning our night at the hotel. I didn't know how long Perry's photographer had followed us, but obviously, it hadn't extended to the rest of that week.

However, my relief soon hardened into ugly, gnawing guilt.

Pen. Sloane. Rhea. All of them had been fucked over by *my* decision. I'd been so confident I could arrange the meetup without detection, and I'd done it without consulting Sloane despite knowing the risks. She'd been so worried about her sister, and I'd wanted to surprise her with something nice. I'd worried she'd talk me out of it if I told her, and dammit, she would've been right.

Because I might've just killed any chance she had of seeing Pen again in the future.

Fuck. I made an abrupt turn away from my house and toward her office.

Her family must've seen the blog post by now. No one liked to admit it, but everyone read Perry Wilson, if only to ensure they weren't his latest target.

"Come on, Luna, pick up," I muttered as I dodged an angry cab driver and crossed the street while the light was still green. The call went to voicemail, as did the next one and the one after that.

Luckily, I was only a few blocks away from her office, and

I made it there in record time. I'd pissed off half the drivers in Midtown along the way, but I didn't give a shit. I needed to see her and make sure she was okay.

"Xavier!" Jillian half stood, her eyes widening when I burst in like a madman. "What are—"

"Is she in a meeting?"

"No, but she's sitting in on a magazine interview with Asher Donovan. Silent observ—"

I was already gone before she finished her sentence.

Sloane was sitting at her desk when I entered her office. She was polished as always in a blouse and pencil skirt, her hair gathered in a perfect bun, but I knew her well enough to pick up on the tiny signs of tension—the ramrod-straight posture, the subtle clench of her jaw, the rhythmic tap of her pen against her desk.

She looked up from her computer at the sound of the door opening and closing. She must've read the unspoken question on my face because she clicked something on her computer, and Asher's answer about his workout routine faded into silence.

"I saw it," she said. A tinge of pink colored her cheekbones and the tip of her nose. "I got a call from Rhea this morning. They fired her."

"Shit." The jagged rocks of guilt multiplied, weighing down my stomach and feet as I crossed the room. "I'm so fucking sorry, Luna. I shouldn't have brought them to the center. I wasn't thinking—"

"Don't be sorry. You had good intentions, and you did everything you could to minimize our chances of getting caught." Sloane gave me a wan smile. "It was a perfect day, Xavier. I'll never be sorry that I got to see Pen, and she was happier than I'd seen her in a long time. That was because of you. It's not your fault George and Caroline would rather prioritize their pettiness over their daughter's well-being." Her grip around her pen tightened at the mention of her father and stepmother. "This is on them. Not you."

Her reassurance eased only a smidge of guilt. The rest continued to fester like a nest of vipers, their serpentine coils slithering through my gut and squeezing tighter with each *what if* and *shouldn't have.*

Yet another case of me fucking up.

But I could self-flagellate later. I was here to check on Sloane, not wallow in self-pity.

"How's Pen?" I asked. "Do you know?"

Sloane shook her head. "They kicked Rhea out before she woke up. She didn't even get to say goodbye. Rhea has taken care of her since she was born, and I can't imagine..." Her voice hitched. "Anyway, with Rhea gone, I have no intel into what's happening. They could've already shipped her off to a distant cousin in Europe for all I know. I wouldn't put it past them."

She maintained a brave front, but I saw past the matter-of-fact replies to the fissures underneath. She was breaking, and it fucking killed me to know I was the cause of it, however indirect.

She may not blame me, but that didn't stop me from blaming myself.

However, something she said sparked an idea. *With Rhea gone, I have no intel into what's happening.* Sloane didn't have intel, but I knew someone who could get it. For the right price, they could get anything.

I kept the plan to myself for now. I didn't want to raise her hopes without confirming with my contact first.

I'd started this mess. It was up to me to fix it.

"We'll figure it out. I promise." I managed a crooked smile. "Between you and me, we can figure out anything. We're geniuses."

Sloane released a half sob, half laugh.

Her eyes were dry, but when I opened my arms, she came

around the desk and buried her face in my chest without protest. Her shoulders shook, and I kissed the top of her head, wishing I had the power to take her pain away even if it meant shouldering it myself.

We didn't speak. She didn't shed any tears.

But I held her all the same.

Sloane

Some people wallowed after a disaster. Others threw fits of temper.

Me? I planned.

I had a week to swallow my shock, anger, horror, and the thousand other emotions that exploded after Perry's post. I could dwell on Rhea's unfair firing or work myself into a state of panic over being cut off entirely from Pen, but that wouldn't do anyone any good. Instead, I did what I did best: I figured out how to solve a crisis.

It started with taking down Perry.

I'd already planted the seeds for my revenge; it was time to harvest them.

I tapped my pen against my knee and stared at my laptop. It was the Wednesday before Thanksgiving, and I was working from home again. I'd already filled five pages of notes on Operation PW (Operation Perry Wilson).

Perry's power stemmed from two things: information and the platform to disseminate that information. Over the years, the little weasel had cultivated a network of spies from New York to L.A. who fed him juicy tidbits about the rich, famous, and misbehaving. Some of them were true; many were embellished.

It was impossible to fully cut off his sources because *anyone* could be a leak. Hotel maids, gardeners, chauffeurs, random passersby on the street...there were no limits to who could send in an anonymous tip.

Since I couldn't eliminate his sources, I had to eliminate the reason why people *wanted* to send tips to him specifically. He didn't pay them, but for anyone who wanted to expose a celebrity, get back at someone they felt had wronged them, or simply gain the satisfaction of seeing their tip used, they turned to the biggest fish in the pond. People *knew* Perry had the means to bring their tips to a huge audience, which brought me to the second pillar of his power: his platforms, specifically his blog and his social media.

They were concrete. Tangible. Which meant they could be taken down.

I couldn't do it on my own. I needed an army, and luckily, I knew exactly where to find one.

A new message popped up in my encrypted server. My heart skipped a beat as I read and reread it.

Confirmed.

For the first time since I'd seen Perry's blog post, I smiled.

I knew Xavier blamed himself for what happened, but it wasn't his fault. I didn't resent him for organizing one of the best days I'd had in a while, but the blog post *did* light my fire when it came to Perry fucking Wilson.

Next to me, The Fish swam leisurely in his aquarium. Most people preferred cuddly pets like cats and dogs, but I liked having a fish. Our roles were clear, and our worlds never crossed. He stayed in his house; I stayed in mine.

Still, it was nice to have an animate being to talk to when I was home, even when they couldn't talk back.

"He's toast," I told the oblivious goldfish. "I will not rest until that man's career is reduced to writing cat-food copy for *Fast and Furriness.*"

The Fish stared at me for a second before swimming away, indifferent to my scheming.

My phone rang, and I was so distracted by visions of Perry sobbing over a bowl of wet cat food that I didn't check the caller ID before I answered.

"Hello?"

"Sloane."

The familiar voice dripped ice down my spine. Images of Perry's bad highlights and signature pink bow tie vanished, replaced by floppy brown hair and blue eyes.

I straightened, my hand closing tight enough around my phone to elicit a small crack.

"Don't hang up," Bentley said. "I know I'm the last person you want to hear from right now, but we need to talk."

CHAPTER 30

Sloane

I SHOULD'VE TOLD BENTLEY TO FUCK OFF, BUT MY curiosity won out over anger.

That Sunday, four days after his call, I got out of a cab and walked into a nondescript bar in a remote area of town. It was half past noon, and the bar was empty thanks to the early hour and holiday weekend.

Xavier and I had spent a quiet but cozy Thanksgiving at his place. I'd been nervous about celebrating the holiday together—I hadn't spent any holiday with any man since Bentley—but thankfully, Xavier didn't make a big deal out of it. We ate, drank, watched movies, and had sex. On one occasion, he convinced me to play strip poker, which ended with us naked on the floor in about two point five minutes (and it had nothing to do with the cards). Overall, it was exactly what I needed.

The only damper was my meetup with Bentley. I hadn't told Xavier about it because there was nothing *to* tell until I figured out what my ex wanted.

So here I was, on a freezing Sunday in the middle of a bar that looked like it hadn't been cleaned since Reagan was in office, just to meet the man who'd cheated on me and broken my heart.

I'm an idiot.

Bentley was already waiting for me in a corner booth, his blue polo and clean-shaven face a startling contrast against the grunge decor.

He rose when he saw me. "Thanks for coming. I appreciate it."

"Get to the point." I took the seat opposite his and kept my coat on. I wasn't planning on staying long. "I'm busy."

Bentley's brow pinched as he sat down again. The son of a big-time financier, he possessed the preppy, all-American good looks of a Ralph Lauren model and the arrogance of someone who'd been rich, popular, and good-looking his entire life. He wasn't used to being treated like an inconvenience, which was too fucking bad because that was what this was.

"It's Georgia." To his credit, Bentley recovered from my insult remarkably quickly. "She's having...difficulties with her pregnancy."

Of everything I'd expected him to say, that hadn't been one of them.

I cocked an eyebrow, confusion mingling with a smidge of concern. I despised Georgia as much as one could despise their sister, but I wasn't a monster.

I was, however, confused as to why her husband was telling me instead of literally anyone else in her orbit.

"Has she seen a doctor?" I asked.

Bentley blinked, then laughed. "No, not *medical* concerns," he said. "She and the baby are fine. She's just been so temperamental. You grew up with her. You know how she can be. She's constantly screaming at me over the stupidest things, like the other day when I didn't get her a frozen hot chocolate at three in the morning and she threw a Lalique vase at my head. A *Lalique* vase. Do you know how expensive that was?"

Any sympathy I had vanished, replaced by an urge to knock Bentley's head against the wall until an iota of common sense rattled in that thick skull of his.

"Let me get this straight," I said. "You called me out here on a holiday weekend to *complain about being yelled at?*"

"I could've died from that vase," he said defensively. "She's out of control."

"She's pregnant, Bentley, which means she's growing an entire *human* inside her. It's understandable if her hormones get a bit out of control." *Especially when her husband is a shithead.*

I couldn't believe I was defending Georgia, but Bentley had his head so far up his own ass, he could give himself a root canal—preferably *without* Novocain.

"Yes, well, I didn't expect the pregnancy process to be so messy," Bentley said, as if he were discussing a misbehaving pet instead of his wife and unborn child. "But that's not all. Ever since we saw you at the hospital, she's gotten more paranoid. She accused me of checking you out and said I still had feelings for you. She said she was my second choice and that I'm always comparing her to you. The thing is..." He learned forward, his face earnest. "She's not wrong."

Pin-drop silence.

I gaped at him, sure I'd heard wrong. There was no way he was bold enough and *stupid* enough to say that to my face.

Our server approached before I could respond. Bentley ordered a beer, and after a small pause, I ordered a glass of red wine.

After the server left, Bentley continued. "I didn't mean for things between us to blow up the way they did. You have to understand, you were working all the time. When you *were* home, all you talked about was Kensington PR. We barely had sex. I felt like I was living with a roommate instead of my fiancée. I needed more of a human connection, you know? Georgia was there, and she was so understanding of my concerns, and...well, she reminded me of you. Except she was a little warmer at the time." He let out another laugh.

A muscle beneath my eye spasmed as our drinks arrived. Our server gave me a sympathetic look—people who worked in bars had a finely tuned asshole radar—but I didn't say a word.

Let him dig his own grave deeper.

"I thought she was what I wanted," Bentley said. "But things aren't the same as they used to be. After we got married, she became so demanding. She's always complaining about this or that, and we don't have sex as much as we used to. Plus, she's obsessed with tracking your every move. Did you know she set up a news alert for your name? It's unhealthy. When we saw you at the hospital and she found out you were dating Xavier Castillo, she lost it."

"I see." I didn't touch my wine.

The news alert revelation was a surprise, but it was exactly the type of thing Georgia would do. She was a huge believer in monitoring her "competition."

"I miss you, Sloane." Bentley gave me a mournful look. "You were always so calm and rational about things. You'd never throw a vase at my head. I didn't appreciate it at the time, and I should've."

"Interesting," I said coolly. "Because I distinctly remember you calling me an *'ice queen'* and telling me that dating me was like dating a block of ice."

He blanched. "I said that in the heat of the moment. I was upset that you seemed to care more about your work than our engagement, so..."

"You fucked my sister on our living room couch and tried to gaslight me into thinking it was my fault? Then you *married* her a year after you proposed to me and didn't say a single word to me for years until you ran into me and magically realized you were still into me?"

This wasn't about me or his relationship with Georgia. Maybe there was trouble in paradise, but at the end of the day, Bentley was driven by his ego. He'd seen Xavier, who was a better man than him in every single way that counted, and he'd seen Georgia's reaction to him.

He felt threatened, so he was trying to claw back power by 1) seducing me away from Xavier 2) proving he *could* get me back despite what he'd done, and 3) secretly sticking it to Georgia for whatever slights she'd committed against him.

He was more transparent than a poorly stitched web.

"It wasn't like that," Bentley said, his cheeks red. "You have *no idea* the pressure I was under at the time. I had a lot riding on my transfer to New York, which I'd insisted on so I could be closer to *you*. Then I got there, and you weren't even paying attention to me. I was insecure, I admit it, but I've been paying for my mistake since." He gave me the same puppy-dog eyes my younger self could never resist. "We were so good together once. Do you remember London? Us walking by the Thames, eating at the best restaurants every night, checking into a hotel, and staying there all weekend...it was perfect."

I ran a hand over the stem of my wineglass, silently taking in the man who'd broken my heart and destroyed my relationship with my family. My father and Georgia weren't blameless, but Bentley had been the trigger.

Once upon a time, I'd thought he was the love of my life. I'd been so swept up by his good looks, his deceptively sweet words, and the magic of falling in love abroad like in the rom-coms I watched so often. His proposal was supposed to mark the start of our happily ever after.

But happily ever afters didn't always end so happily, and now, after age and experience stripped the rose tint off my glasses, I saw him with crystal clarity.

His hair was too perfect, his clothes too pressed, his smile too fake. His words dripped with entitlement instead of a teasing lilt, and what I'd mistaken for charm was simply manipulation wrapped in shiny clothing.

He was so utterly boring, so nauseatingly fake, that I couldn't believe I'd ever fallen in love with him.

Most of all, I couldn't believe I'd let *this* asshole scare me away from relationships for so long. He didn't deserve the power I'd given him over me, and I was done letting him ruin my life.

"I do remember London." I smiled. He smiled back, clearly taking it as a sign that I was warming to his advances. "What exactly are you trying to say?"

"I'm saying we can have that again." He paused and glanced around. "I can't leave Georgia while she's pregnant, but I know we won't work out in the long term. However, you and I can still rekindle things in the meantime. I know you miss me as much as I miss you."

"I'm dating someone, Bentley."

"Who, Xavier?" He snorted. "Come on, Sloanie. We both know that loser isn't good enough for you."

"I see," I repeated. My expression didn't waver at my much-hated nickname—*Sloanie*. It was so damn condescending. "I'm... flattered, and obviously, there's really only one answer."

"Obviously," he said with enough smugness to power an entire fraternity house.

"Take your proposition, and go fuck yourself with it."

Bentley blinked. My words registered, and his smile disappeared beneath a mottle of red. "You—"

"Let me make a few things clear." I spoke over him. "One, I would rather sleep with a leprosy-infected ogre before I *ever* let you touch me again. You are a disgusting, misogynist pig whose brain is inversely proportionate to the size of your giant ego, and you're lucky I was too young when we met to know otherwise. Two, Georgia has *many* faults, but she and every other woman who's unlucky enough to cross your path deserves better than you. I hope the next time she throws a vase at you, she doesn't miss. Three, Xavier is ten times the man you could ever hope to be. He's smarter, kinder, and better in bed." I cocked my head. "News flash, Bentley, you're not the sex god you think you are. Your technique is shit, and you couldn't find a clit if the woman drew you a map and marked it with a giant X."

A burst of laughter punctuated the end of my rant. A group of twenty-something women had taken over the neighboring booth, and they were listening to us with rapt attention.

Story Sunday indeed. I hoped one of them recognized Bentley and told everyone they knew about his shortcomings. It was a long shot, but it was what he deserved.

I stood, my smile widening at his indignant sputters. "All that to say, I disrespectfully decline your offer to be your mistress. Don't contact me again, or I'll slap you with a restraining order and make sure every single person in your workplace and social circle knows you can't take *no* for an answer."

"You fucking bitch—"

I'd ordered the biggest glass of the darkest red wine, and I didn't wait for him to finish his trite insult before I tossed the full contents in his face and walked out. Once I was outside, I stopped the recording on my phone and saved it to my files.

I hadn't decided whether to send it to Georgia yet. She deserved to know what her husband was doing and saying behind her back, but our relationship was complicated, so I held on to it for now.

Bentley didn't follow me, though I hadn't expected him to.

My lips curled into a smile at the memory of his mouth hanging open while wine dripped from his hair and chin.

I'd written many film reviews excoriating the cheesy power move of throwing a drink in a guy's face, but as I hailed a cab to go home, I concluded I'd been wrong.

The move may be cliché, but it was damn satisfying.

Sometimes, the rom-coms got it right.

CHAPTER 31

Xavier

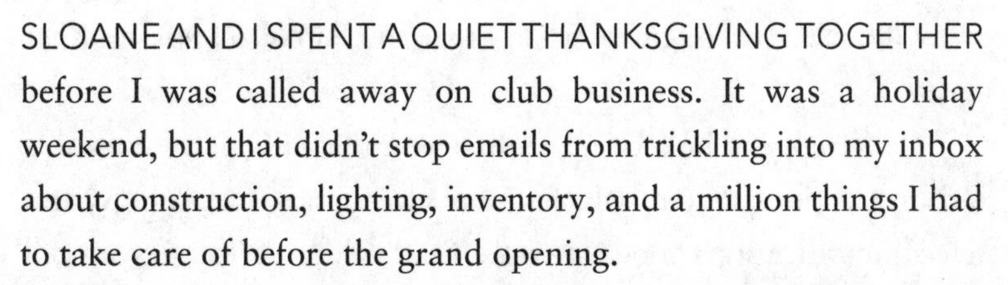

SLOANE AND I SPENT A QUIET THANKSGIVING TOGETHER before I was called away on club business. It was a holiday weekend, but that didn't stop emails from trickling into my inbox about construction, lighting, inventory, and a million things I had to take care of before the grand opening.

She slept over at my house on Thursday and Friday, but we parted ways on Saturday to take care of our respective work. She acted a little strange when we said goodbye, but I had a feeling spending such a big holiday together had freaked her out, so I didn't pry. I didn't want to drive her away by pressing too hard, especially given the week's events.

I was still torn up about Rhea and Pen, but at least I'd confirmed with my contact about getting the intel I needed. He'd have the first batch ready soon so I could (hopefully) set Sloane's mind at ease.

Besides Sloane, the only person I saw over the weekend was Luca. He seemed to have gotten over his Leaf spiral and was back to working at his family's corporate office in the city. Either that, or Dante had put the fear of God in him enough to kick his ass into shape.

I still didn't know why my father had put Dante on the inheritance committee, and my attempts to ask the man in question had so far been rebuffed.

Maybe Dante was still upset about the time I'd roped Luca into hosting a Vegas penthouse party that ended with the cops shoving us into jail for the night. If so, that didn't bode well for a favorable vote during my first evaluation, but I'd worry about that later.

I had more pressing matters at hand.

"Our Void system is perfect for this space," my newest contractor said. "It doesn't hit the market until late next year, but I'm happy to give you early access."

"Out of the goodness of your heart, I assume."

Killian Katrakis gave me an enigmatic smile. *Name number seven.*

Half-Irish and half-Greek, Killian was the CEO of the Katrakis Group Corporation, an international electronics, technology, and telecommunications conglomerate. They sold everything from cell phones and computers to TVs and commercial sounds, the latter of which was the reason for his visit today.

Normally, this type of meeting was reserved for the account executives, not the CEO of the entire company. However, Kai had given me a direct line to Killian's office, and Killian had been surprisingly intrigued when I mentioned where the club was located. He'd insisted on seeing the space and matching it with one of his systems himself.

"I'm a businessman, Xavier," he said. "I don't do anything out of the goodness of my heart." He nodded around us. "The grand opening for this will make headlines around the world because it's attached to your name. Every club owner out there will take notice and try to compete."

"That includes buying the same sound system we used on

opening night." I cocked an eyebrow. "You have a lot of faith in my ability to pull this off."

The reasoning he offered for granting me early access to the Void was a simple one, but I didn't buy Killian's concern over publicity for his company's latest sound system. The entire product vertical made up a fraction of the Katrakis Group's revenue compared to phones and laptops, but perhaps it was a passion project or a pride thing.

Billionaires were eccentric, and if the rumors were true, the notorious bachelor was eccentric in many ways.

"I have faith because I recognize the same quality in you that I've seen in every successful entrepreneur," Killian said. "Hunger. You don't want this to work; you *need* this to work because the club is a reflection of you. If it fails, you fail, and you would do anything not to fail."

Unease crawled over the back of my neck.

Killian had me pegged to a tee, and we'd met less than an hour ago. Was I really that transparent, or was he really that good?

We finished our walkthrough of the vault. It needed work, but the bones were there—stone floors, original crown moldings, teller enclosures that could be transformed into bottle displays. Once I cleaned it up and installed my design elements, it was going to be a hell of a space.

"Who's in charge of the design?" Killian asked, savvy enough to steer the conversation toward safer waters after his uncanny psychoanalysis.

"Farrah Lin-Ryan from F&J Creative." *Name number eight.* She was the city's premier interior designer for dining and hospitality spaces.

"Good choice," Killian said with an approving rumble. "We've worked together on a number of projects."

I knew Farrah was good, but it was reassuring to hear it from someone else.

After a few more questions about the design and a handshake deal, Killian promised to send a contract over and left for another meeting.

I stayed, soaking it all in.

It was my second time in the vault after Alex had handed over the keys, and I was still wrapping my head around the fact that it was *mine*. My place to shape, mold, and design as I saw fit (with some professional input). It was my responsibility, which was both thrilling and terrifying.

A familiar chime reverberated through the empty space.

I glanced down, my high melting into concern when I saw who was calling. I had a lunch date with Sloane soon, but I was too anxious to let the call roll to voicemail.

"Is everything okay?" I asked without preamble after picking up.

Eduardo wouldn't call me in the middle of the day unless something was wrong. Then again, it wasn't like I had any more parents left to lose.

A brief, humorless smile flicked into existence at my dark humor. Coping mechanisms were coping mechanisms, no matter how morbid.

"I wanted to see how you were holding up and how the nightclub is going," Eduardo said. "I've heard good things from Sloane, though she may be a bit biased considering the, ah, recent developments."

So news of our relationship had made its way to Bogotá. I wasn't surprised. I bet the inheritance committee was watching me like a hawk.

"We didn't start dating until after I came up with the idea," I said. "If you're worried about it compromising Sloane's judgment, don't be. She's not that type of person. She'll be honest regardless of our relationship status."

Even if she were the type to go easy on me because we were

dating—which she wasn't—I wouldn't want her to. I'd succeed on my own merit or not at all.

"I know that, *mijo*, but not everyone does. There are growing whispers of her conflict of interest. She's your publicist, *and* she's one of your evaluators come May, yet you two are...involved," Eduardo said delicately. "It doesn't look good."

"I don't care how it looks." Stubbornness set into my jaw. "We're consenting adults. What we do in our free time is our business, and my father's will didn't say a thing about conflicts of interest, nor did it forbid me from dating a committee member. If anyone has a problem with us dating, they can take it up with the executor of his will. Sloane is one judge out of five, Eduardo. She won't make or break the decision."

"Unless there's a tie, but I see your point." A long pause preceded his next words. "I've never heard you so fired up over a woman."

"She's not just any woman. She's..." *Everything*.

I almost said it. The word came so easily, it would've slipped right off my tongue had its potential implications not hit me at the same time like a hollow-point bullet.

Sloane couldn't be my *everything*.

Yes, I cared about her deeply, and no, I couldn't stop thinking about her. She set my blood on fire whenever she was near and when she hurt, I hurt. She was the only person with whom I felt comfortable enough to share the secrets I'd shared, and if a genie popped out of a bottle this very second and asked me to change something about her, I wouldn't change a single thing.

But all that wasn't the same as her being everything, because if she were everything, then that meant she...that meant I...

"Ah." Eduardo's voice softened. "I see."

I didn't know what he heard in my silence, but I wasn't ready to face it. Not yet.

"How's the CEO search going on your end?" I asked, abruptly switching subjects. I needed something to take my mind off my Sloane spiral, and the Castillo Group's seemingly eternal CEO search was as good a distraction as any.

"It's fine. The board probably won't make a final decision until the New Year. There's strong contention over which of the candidates is better suited for the role."

"They should choose you." I meant it as a quip because Eduardo had never wanted to be CEO, but the more I thought about it, the more it made sense. He was included on the shortlist as a courtesy, but why *wouldn't* they choose him? I'd seen the other names; he could run circles around them. Plus, he wasn't an asshole like ninety percent of the list.

His shocked laugh rolled over the line. "Xavier, you know this was always supposed to be a temporary arrangement. My wife would kill me if I took it on permanently."

"She might be more open to it than you think." Eduardo's wife was unyielding when it came to family time, but she was also a lawyer. She understood how to balance work and her personal life, and I bet Eduardo did too. "You care about the company, you have the institutional knowledge, and you're good at the job. You helped my father build it into what it is today. What external candidate could *possibly* beat that?"

Silence reigned for several beats. "I don't know. It's a big decision. Even if I want it, I can't guarantee the board will go for it."

"Just think about it. I bet the board isn't pushing it because they think you *don't* want it."

"Maybe." He sighed, the sound edged with sadness and frustration. "Alberto had to go and leave us with this mess, didn't he?"

"He always did like fucking people over." I leaned against a pillar and stared at the wall of old safe-deposit boxes across from me. The sight transported me back to Colombia—my father's room, my mother's letter, the scent of old books and leather during the reading of the will. "You know what I don't understand? How and why my father failed to catch the loophole in his will. He didn't stipulate the company I should be CEO of, Eduardo. Does that sound like Alberto Castillo to you?"

"No. At least not the Alberto Castillo I knew before his diagnosis. But impending death changes people, *mijo*. It forces us to confront our mortality and reevaluate what's important."

I snorted. Eduardo always liked to sugarcoat things when it came to my father. "What are you saying? That he had a sudden change of heart while lying on his deathbed?"

"I'm saying that in the last days of his illness, he had a lot of time to think. About the past, about his legacy, and most of all, about his relationship with you." Another, heavier pause in which I could *hear* Eduardo turning words over in his mind. "He found your mother's letter at the beginning of the year when he was getting his affairs in order. Alberto wanted to tell you about it in person, but..." He hesitated. "That's why I was so insistent that you visit him. I didn't know how much longer he had, and some things are meant to be shared face-to-face."

Wisps of cold stole through me and pulled my chest tight. "Don't put that burden on me, Eduardo," I said harshly. "You know why I didn't want to come home."

"Yes. I'm not blaming you, Xavier," Eduardo said, his voice gentle. "I merely want to share the other side of the story. But for what it's worth, your father didn't read the letter. That was for your eyes only. He knew Patricia enough to know that was what she would've wanted. But seeing that letter from your mother...I think it forced him to think about what she would've said if she saw the two of you after her death. How she would've hated the way your relationship fell apart, and how it would've broken her heart to see him blaming you for what happened. She loved you and your father more than anything else in the world. Your rift would've devastated her."

The gut punch from his words cracked the concrete wall I'd built around my chest, making my ribs ache and my throat close. "Did he tell you all that, or did you put the words in his mouth?"

"Half and half. Your father and I were friends since we were children, and we'd confided in each other enough that he didn't always have to express his thoughts out loud for me to understand them."

The safe-deposit boxes blurred for an instant before I blinked the haze away. "Fine. Let's pretend everything you said is true. What does that have to do with the will?"

"I can't say for sure. He didn't tell me he was changing his will until after the fact," Eduardo admitted. "I didn't know about the new inheritance clause, nor did I know I would be on the evaluation committee. But you're right. Alberto Castillo was not a man who would've overlooked such a glaring loophole, which meant he put it in there on purpose. I suspect..." This time, his hesitation carried a hint of caution. "It was his way of simultaneously extending an olive branch and pushing you closer to your potential. He could've easily cut off your inheritance unless you followed whatever terms he dictated, or he could've written you out of the will altogether. But he didn't."

An olive branch from my father. The idea was so absurd I wanted to laugh, but Eduardo wasn't wrong. My father *could've* cut me off. It would've been his last big *fuck you* before passing.

I thought he'd changed my inheritance terms so he could manipulate me into doing what he wanted even after his death. That was definitely part of it, but...maybe there was more to the story.

Or maybe I'm naive and delusional.

"He didn't sound like he'd had any change of heart during our last conversation," I said.

Grow up, Xavier. It's time for you to be useful for once.

My phone slipped in my grip before I tightened it.

"I'm not saying he was a saint. He had his pride, and I also suspect he thought you would've rebuffed any overtures he made. The last thing a dying man wants is another fight with his son," Eduardo pointed out. "You don't have to take everything I said as gospel. Those are my conjectures, not the hard truth. But allow yourself the possibility that it *is* true, and let that be your closure. Your father is gone, Xavier, but you're still here. You can hold on to your grudge forever and let it consume you, or you can put the past where it belongs and move forward."

Eduardo's words echoed long after I hung up.

My first instinct was to reject his interpretation of events. I loved him like a father more than I did my own, but he was too biased when it came to his oldest friend and business partner.

However, what he'd said made a strange, twisted sort of sense, and it scared the crap out of me. I'd clung to my resentment toward my father as a lifeboat through the storms of our relationship. Without it, I might drown beneath a sea of regrets and what-ifs.

Billows of uncertainty followed me out of the vault and onto the street, where they dissipated beneath an onslaught of noise and activity. I knew they would coalesce again when I was alone, but for now, I happily pushed them to the side as I walked to my lunch date with Sloane.

People could say whatever they wanted about the city, but it provided distractions like no other.

Sloane was already waiting for me at the restaurant when I arrived. It was her turn to pick, and she'd chosen a tiny family-run restaurant nestled in the heart of Koreatown. It smelled incredible.

"Sorry I'm late." I gave her a soft kiss hello before taking the seat opposite hers. "Eduardo called, and our conversation ran long."

"It's okay. I got here not too long ago." Her eyes sharpened with knowing. "Did he call about your inheritance?"

"Sort of." I gave her a brief summary of our conversation. When I finished, her face had softened with sympathy.

"How are you feeling about what he said?"

"I don't know." I blew out a long breath. There was one thing my mother had forgotten to tell me in her letter: how complicated life got when we grew up. Every year on earth added another layer of twists and drama.

Life was easy when there was only black and white. It was when the line between them blurred that things got murkier.

"I'm conflicted," I said. "The easy path is to continue hating my father, but I have to…I can't think about that right now. There's too much going on. Speaking of which, I have something for you." I slid a manila envelope across the table. Christian Harper had had it hand delivered by messenger this morning, and I'd been carrying it around all day. "I hope I didn't overstep."

Thankfully, Sloane didn't call me out on my obvious deflection of topic. She opened the envelope and scanned the documents, her eyes widening with each word.

When she finished, her gaze snapped up to mine. "Xavier," she breathed. "How did you…?"

"I know someone who specializes in information retrieval." I tapped the envelope. "Pen's still in the city, she hasn't had any major health issues, and she's with a new nanny. Hopefully, that means George and Caroline aren't planning on shipping her abroad."

It wasn't much, but I hoped it was enough to put Sloane's mind at ease. Sometimes, uncertainty was worse than the pain of any knowledge.

"Hopefully." Sloane's eyes gleamed bright with emotion. "Thank you. This was...you didn't...anyway." She cleared her throat and slid the papers documenting Pen's whereabouts and well-being back into their envelope. Pink decorated her cheeks and neck. "You didn't have to do this, but I appreciate it. Truly."

"You don't have to thank me. I was happy to do it."

Our gazes lingered, the noise from the restaurant fading beneath the weight of unspoken words.

Sunlight streamed through the windows, throwing shadows beneath her cheekbones and highlighting the fine blond strands framing her face. The glacial-blue pools shielding her eyes cracked, revealing a sliver of vulnerability that grabbed hold of my heart and squeezed.

She was so fucking beautiful it almost hurt to look at her.

I wondered if she knew that.

I wondered if she knew how much she occupied my thoughts and how I counted down the minutes to seeing her again when we were apart.

I wondered if I'd upended her life the way she had mine, to the point where the pieces would no longer fit if she weren't there, because she wasn't a pit stop; she was the destination.

The bullet from earlier dug deeper.

I opened my mouth, but Sloane blinked and looked away before I said something I regretted—not because I wouldn't mean it, but because it would've been too much, too fast for her.

Disappointment and relief swirled in equal measure.

"Speaking of calls, I got one from Rhea last night," she said, effectively breaking the moment. She tucked a stray strand of hair behind her ear, the pink on her cheeks darkening to a dusky rose. "She said a check mysteriously showed up in her mailbox yesterday. The sender kept their identity anonymous, but the money is enough to cover at least one year's worth of food and living expenses."

"Really?" I maintained a neutral expression. "That's pretty lucky. I guess good things do happen to good people."

"I guess they do." Sloane paused, then said pointedly, "I mentioned Rhea's address over Thanksgiving, didn't I? When I said I would send her money to tide her over while she finds a new job?"

"Did you?" I picked up the menu and scanned it for something to eat. We should order soon; I was starving. "I don't remember."

"Hmm." Sloane's mouth twitched. "I'm sure you don't."

A small grin curled in response to her knowing tone, but neither of us pursued that line of conversation. Instead, we switched to something even more satisfying: revenge.

"Are we still on for Dante and Viv's party this weekend?" she asked.

She'd told me her plan for Operation PW, and the party was crucial to its execution. It would also give me an opportunity to talk to Dante and hopefully get some answers. Most importantly, I'd get to spend more time with Sloane and her friends—not that I was angling for her friends' approval or anything. But having them on my side couldn't hurt, could it?

I smiled. "I wouldn't miss it for the world."

CHAPTER 32

Sloane

OPERATION PERRY WILSON WENT INTO FULL EFFECT that Saturday at Dante and Vivian's annual holiday gala.

Before Josephine was born, they'd hosted it at their house, but since they didn't want to disturb the newborn, they rented out the Valhalla Club's ballroom for an "intimate" gathering featuring three hundred of Manhattan's richest and most powerful.

One of those three hundred was Kai Young.

"I know that look," he said when I approached him at the bar. I'd brought Xavier as my date, but we'd split to take care of our respective businesses first—me with Kai, him with Dante. "Who are you planning to destroy?"

Next to him, Isabella gave me a grin and a thumbs-up when he wasn't looking. She'd offered to broach the subject with Kai, but I'd declined. This was my fight, and she'd already gone above and beyond.

"I think you know," I said. "He's a mutual thorn in our sides."

"Let me guess." Kai glanced at his fiancée, who quickly averted her gaze and pretended to study her drink. "Initials PW?"

"Yes."

"He's a disreputable blogger. I know you're upset about recent posts he's published"—Kai's tone indicated Isabella had ranted to him about it on more than one occasion—"but as the CEO of a media company, I can't get involved in my friends' personal fights."

"This isn't personal," I said. "He may be a disreputable blogger, but you've been battling him for web traffic and clicks for *years*. Plus, you despise the man. He's everything that's wrong with journalism."

"What he does isn't journalism," Kai said immediately. I arched an eyebrow, and after a small beat, he shook his head with a wry smile. "Point taken."

For someone like Kai, who operated by the rules and an innate sense of honor, Perry's sleazy methods were akin to smearing shit all over the business the Youngs had spent decades building. One bad apple could ruin the entire bunch.

"What if I told you there was a way you can beat him *and* make sure he won't be a problem in the future?"

"I'd say if something sounds too good to be true, it is." Kai finished his drink and set it down. "But I'm listening."

I told him my plan. He listened without interruption, but when I finished, he shook his head.

"He won't agree to that," he said.

"He won't have a choice."

"Amendment: Why would *I* agree to that? I want to be less associated with him, not more."

"Because it *won't* be him. It'll be his property, but the man himself will be gone." My voice turned coaxing. "Think of how great a story that would be: Kai Young transforms popular but controversial gossip blog into a shining beacon of respect in the dirty celebrity-news industry. No one else would even *attempt* to clean up the blog's reputation. You pull it off, and you'll be a legend."

Kai studied me in that quiet, thoughtful way of his. Isabella's face popped up over his shoulder again; this time, she gave me a double thumbs-up.

Nailed it, she mouthed.

"Isa, love, stop talking to Sloane behind my back," he said without turning around.

Her face fell. "How do you *always* know? I swear you're not human," she grumbled. "But fine, I'll hang out with Ále until you're done. She and Dom better not be hooking up in the library again..."

She kissed him on the cheek and wandered off. Kai's gaze followed her affectionately for a second before it returned to me.

"Between this and Xavier's club, you know how to sell a pitch," he said.

"That's my job." I inclined my head. "Thank you for helping him, by the way. Your list has been incredibly helpful."

"I merely gave him my contacts. It was up to him to close the deals, which he did. Securing Vuk Markovic as a business partner is no small feat." A smile flickered over Kai's mouth. "I should've known not to underestimate him after Spain."

My senses went on high alert. "What do you mean?"

"The blog post about you in Spain," he said. "He reached out after it was posted and asked if I could throttle its reach. I didn't know him well, but he was quite insistent. Obviously, I couldn't guarantee anything since the Young Corporation doesn't own Perry's blog, but I could stop our outlets from picking up individual posts."

What he didn't say was that his company owned almost every major news website and media outlet. By suppressing pickup, he'd effectively killed the post. People could share it on social media, of course, but the story hadn't been juicy enough for that. Without oxygen, the embers died a quiet death.

Xavier hadn't said a thing about it. I'd assumed people weren't interested in the personal lives of publicists, even if Xavier was involved. Maybe that was true, or maybe it had become a nonstory because of what he'd done *before* we even started dating.

Emotions swelled in my chest, and I fought to marshal them into some semblance of order.

"As for your proposal, it's an intriguing one, but I can't commit to it quite yet," Kai said, oblivious to the chaos his casual statement had incited. "I'll have to discuss it with my team."

That was what I'd expected, and it was better than an outright no. I was confident his team would see things my way after they weighed the pros and cons because the pros *far* outweighed the cons.

After Kai left to find Isabella, I ordered a double shot of whiskey and let it burn away the tingly lightheadedness that accompanied any thoughts of Xavier.

Now was not the time to blush and swoon over him. I had a revenge plan to finish enacting.

Armed with fresh determination and a stomach full of hard liquor, I sauntered over to the gift table, where Tilly Denman and her friends were giggling over something. I'd bet my color-coordinated closet that Tilly had already swiped one of the gifts, but I wasn't here to police her kleptomaniac tendencies.

In our world, Tilly and Co. spread gossip faster than a wildfire through dry brush, and I was counting on them to do exactly that when I turned my back to them and pretended to take a call.

"Hi, Soraya...what's wrong?" I paused for dramatic effect. "Calm down. Tell me what's wrong."

The giggles behind me immediately dwindled to silence.

Soraya (one name only) was one of the biggest influencers on the planet. Famous for her chatty vlogs, sexy outfits, and striking good looks, she had over 150 million followers across her platforms, and they were *rabid*. As in, someone once paid two thousand dollars for a napkin she'd used at the Met Gala.

Anything she did was news, and any scandal she was involved in was *big* news.

"No, listen to me. You can't go to his house. He's *married*." I lowered my voice enough to make eavesdroppers think I was discussing confidential matters but not enough that they couldn't hear me. "If people find out you and Bryce..." I walked away, suppressing a smile at the cliff-hanger I'd dangled in front of Tilly and Co.

Bryce was another influencer with a rabid fanbase. He'd recently gotten married in a splashy wedding, every second of which was documented on his YouTube channel, but there'd been rumors about him and Soraya for years.

My friends had stoked those rumors through various channels leading back to Perry, and it was only a matter of minutes before "confirmation" of Bryce's alleged affair with Soraya reached the blogger's ears.

A rational person would ask why an experienced publicist would discuss sensitive client matters in the middle of the season's biggest party, but Tilly and her friends didn't care about logic. They simply wanted drama and gossip.

I'd done my part. Now I just had to sit back and watch Perry take the bait.

Since my work for the night was finished, I did a quick lap around the room to say hi to clients and important players before meeting up with Vivian. Xavier and I had agreed to reconvene at the bar when we were done with our tasks; since he wasn't there, I assumed he was still talking to Dante.

"Great party, as usual," I said, handing Vivian a glass of champagne. She was the city's most coveted luxury-event planner, so I hadn't expected anything less. "You outdid yourself."

"Thanks." She smiled, faint lines of exhaustion fanning across her face. Nevertheless, she glowed in a red gown and jewels that would make the late queen of England jealous. "I'm just glad the planning is over and done with. Remind me never to host a gala months after giving birth again. I don't know what I was thinking."

Vivian and Dante could afford plenty of help with Josie, but they preferred to be more hands-on with the parenting. I didn't understand it, but I didn't have a kid, so what did I know?

"Done," I said. I glanced around the room. "Where's Isa and Ále?"

"Isa and Kai disappeared somewhere. I figured it was better not to ask. Ále wasn't feeling well, so Dom took her home early."

"By not feeling well..."

Vivian arched a perfectly shaped brow.

"Right," I said with a small smirk.

Good for them.

Alessandra and Dominic's marriage had gone through a long rocky stretch due to Dominic's workaholism and neglect. They even briefly divorced last year after he missed a major anniversary, but after some time apart and major remorse and lifestyle changes on his part, they'd worked things out and were stronger than ever.

"Speaking of couples..." Vivian glanced over my shoulder. "Incoming."

My pulse tripped when a warm hand rested on the small of my back. I didn't have to look to know who it was. The shape and feel of Xavier's touch was so ingrained in me, I could pick it out while blindfolded.

"Hey, Vivian," he said easily. "I'm sorry to interrupt, but do you mind if I steal Sloane away for a minute?"

"Not at all." Her eyes glinted with amusement. "I assume my husband is now free to talk?"

He responded with a grin that was all charm and a hint of bashfulness. "He's all yours. Sorry for hogging him all evening. We had quite a lot to discuss."

"I imagine you did." Vivian winked at me on her way past. "Enjoy the rest of the party."

"You are such a kiss-ass," I said when she left.

"Me?" Xavier placed a hand over his heart. "I prefer to think of it as being charming."

"A charming kiss-ass."

"I'm simply trying to ingratiate myself with your friends," he said. "Unfortunately, Alessandra left before I could work my magic on her, and I'm not sure where Isabella went. I think Vivian likes me though."

"Not after you monopolized Dante's attention all evening," I quipped, swallowing a bubble of laughter. "Speaking of which, how did the conversation with him go?"

"It went." Some of Xavier's good humor slipped. "He was vague about why my father named him in his will. Just said that they respected each other as businessmen, and my father trusted his judgment. He did give me an earful about the time I got Luca arrested though."

"So he didn't answer," I surmised.

"Basically."

It wasn't like Dante to be so evasive. Perhaps he didn't know why Alberto had put him on the committee either.

I would ask Vivian to do some digging for us—if Dante was honest with anyone, it was his wife—but this wasn't her problem, and she was busy enough with Josie and work. I didn't want to add to her plate.

"I guess it doesn't really matter except to slake my curiosity. He's a judge whether or not I know the reason," Xavier said. "How did your talk with Kai go?"

I filled him in as we meandered toward the exit. We hadn't planned on leaving early, but Vivian and Dante were busy entertaining guests, and an unspoken understanding drew us away from the crowd and into the quiet hall next to the ballroom.

"So it went a lot better than mine," Xavier quipped when I finished. "You think he'll say yes?"

"I'm ninety percent sure he will." Kai was a businessman, and my proposal made perfect business sense.

However, my Perry plan wasn't the takeaway from that conversation.

The blog post about you in Spain. He reached out after it was posted and asked if I could throttle its reach.

The tingles from earlier returned in full force, especially now that Xavier was standing right there, looking more delicious than any man had a right to look with his tuxedo and rumpled hair. He'd eschewed a tie, breaking dress code, but it worked on him.

Everything worked on him. He was the epitome of effortless charm.

His eyebrows shot up when I grabbed the front of his shirt and pushed him into the nearest bathroom.

Like everything else at Valhalla, it was spotless. Marble floors, gleaming mirrors, custom-made scents piped through hidden diffusers—it resembled a celebrity dressing room more than it did a public facility, and it would do just fine for what I had in mind.

"Remember our office meeting the other week?" I locked the door behind us. "The one we had right after Ayana left."

Xavier leaned against the counter, his gaze darkening around the edges as he realized why I'd brought us here.

The air shifted, growing heavier, denser, *hotter.*

"I might recall a thing or two about it." Desire strung taut beneath his languid drawl. He didn't move, but his eyes tracked me like a predator's, dark and hungry, as I slunk toward him.

"Well..." I stopped in front of Xavier, the toes of my heels kissing the tips of his dress shoes. I hooked my fingers through the loops of his belt and pulled him an inch closer. "I thought tonight might be the right night to return the favor."

My husky whisper didn't sound like me, but dragging someone into a bathroom so I could have my way with them didn't *feel* like me, so it was a night of firsts.

Xavier's breath quickened, but still, he didn't move when I undid his belt and dragged the teeth of his zipper down. Electric anticipation hummed in my veins, but I didn't rush.

I wanted to savor this, and there was something so arousing about the wait—about the ravenousness of his gaze and the subtle tightening of his muscles, like it took all his willpower not to bend me over and take me any way he wanted me.

Heat ignited between my thighs at the thought.

I sank to my knees as I peeled his pants and briefs down, my mouth watering when I saw the thick, throbbing erection waiting for me. He was so fucking big, and hard enough to make my pulse spike. Beads of pre-cum dripped from the tip, and when I flicked my tongue out for a taste, a whole-body shudder rippled through him.

That was all the encouragement I needed.

I sealed my mouth around the head of his cock and sucked, teasing the sensitive underside with my tongue while I stroked his length with both hands.

"*Fuck.*" Xavier let out a hiss, his head falling back as I worked my mouth down to where my hands were.

I was technically giving him pleasure, but my skin flamed like I was the one being teased. Every suck went straight to my clit, every twist and stroke coiled tight in my belly until I moaned with need.

I took him deeper, hoping it would satiate my gnawing hunger. The wet, sloppy sounds of the blowjob mingled with his loud groans as he grasped fistfuls of my hair to steady himself while he panted and bucked against my mouth.

The gentle tug against my scalp sent goosebumps scattering across my skin. My nipples hardened to painful points, but I didn't get a chance to relish the sensation before his cock hit the back of my throat.

I gagged, my eyes watering and drool leaking from the corners of my mouth as I struggled to take him all the way.

Xavier's hands gentled, but my whimper of protest had them tightening again. Rough amusement laced his chuckle.

"You like that, don't you?" He tugged, bringing my gaze to his. Lust carved grooves beneath his cheekbones and etched lines of tension between his brows. "Fuck, Luna, you look so good on your knees, choking on my cock."

My thighs clenched at his filthy words. Tiny flutters disrupted my stomach as he held my head and pushed the final inch down my throat. I choked again, his cock so deep that my nose grazed his stomach, and just as little pinpricks danced across my vision, he pulled out until only the tip rested on my tongue.

I managed to suck in a gasp of air before he drove into me again, and again, and again, harder and faster each time, until the brutal rhythm matched the painful pounding of my heart.

The knot of need in my stomach coiled tighter. I was so flushed, I was sure water would steam if it touched my skin, and despite the rawness of my throat, I couldn't stop one hand from drifting between my legs.

"Not with your hand." Xavier's harsh command stopped me a second before I made contact. I let out another whimper of protest, but this time, he was unrelenting. His body shifted, but he didn't let go of my hair as he nudged his shoe between my legs. He ground the tip against my most sensitive spot, eliciting a muffled yelp.

I was so desperate for more friction I didn't think. I simply did as he asked, and straddled his shoe. I spread my legs wider, the beautiful pressure and rub of leather against silk and tender, sensitive flesh making me ache all over.

My moans built in intensity as I picked up speed, grinding shamelessly against his shoe while he fucked my mouth.

I didn't care how obscene this was or whether there were people on the other side of the door; I was too lost in a haze of sensation.

The bumps and ridges of the laces scraped against my swollen clit and sent sharp lightning bolts of pleasure through my body. I couldn't believe how wet I was; I was dripping all over the floor, like this was the first time I'd ever come close to orgasm.

Still, it wasn't enough. I wanted, I *needed* more friction, and I held on to his thigh to steady myself as I sucked and ground harder. His face fucking picked up speed to match mine, and my mind went fuzzy, my hips jerking, my movements frantic as the need built and built and—

The pressure inside me exploded at the same time warm, thick ropes of cum splashed down my throat. Xavier's loud, guttural groan mixed with my strangled cries as the fuzziness fully blanked into a haze of white.

Shudder after shudder racked my body while I rode out my orgasm mindlessly. Everything was so warm and slick and *nice*, and when the haze finally cleared and Xavier's fingers unknotted from my hair, I slumped against his leg, too exhausted to stand.

Strong hands unwound my arms from his thigh and picked me up. Xavier set me on the counter, his movements smooth and fluid as he cleaned me up.

After he finished, he straightened my dress, his eyes gleaming with amusement and lingering desire.

"Well," he drawled, his voice husky. "If you need another favor, anything at all, I'm right here and willing."

My laugh melted into a smile when he kissed me.

I'd ruined my dress, underwear, and makeup as well as his shoes and pants, and I didn't know how we would get out of here without people knowing exactly what we'd been up to, but I didn't care.

I was too sated and content, and for tonight, at least, none of my worries could touch me.

CHAPTER 33

Sloane

AFTER SATURDAY, I COULD ADD THE VALHALLA CLUB bathroom to the list of places I'd never look at the same again (after my office, my kitchen, Xavier's living room, and well, pretty much every place we'd had sex).

It was a great cap to the night, but blowjobs and orgasms aside, the gala also kicked off step two of Operation Perry Wilson, which officially commenced that Monday.

I had just stepped off the elevator and into my office when a breaking-news alert popped up on my phone.

Soraya engaged in scandalous sex affair with MARRIED influencer?! the headline screamed. It was a rhetorical question.

One click took me to Perry's blog, which expounded breathlessly on the alleged affair using details my friends had fed into the grapevine: the gifts, the secret weekend getaway in upstate New York, the airplane bathroom blowjob during a brand trip both Soraya and Bryce had participated in over the summer.

It was salacious and dishy and completely untrue, but Perry wasn't known for his fact-checking. His post was chock-full of allegations without proof.

I smiled. He'd bought the whole story hook, line, and sinker.

"Is it true?" Jillian asked breathlessly. She was already at her desk, her coffee mug full and her computer zoomed into a photo of Soraya and Bryce on their brand trip. Perry's blog branding was splashed across the top of the screen. "Is Soraya *really* sleeping with Bryce? I totally shipped them together before he got married, but—"

"Jillian." I fixed her with an arch stare. "Is Soraya our client?"

She sighed. "*No.*"

"Focus on our clients, please. What's the status on magazine profile pitches for Ayana?"

After some minor grumbling, Jillian updated me on the pitches. I sent a quick text during her tangent about how much she hated a certain editor.

Me: Your turn
Soraya: On it 😈

Soraya may not be a client, but her publicist and I were friends and we'd come to a mutually beneficial agreement, locked into place by an ironclad NDA.

Like I'd said, I needed an army to take down Perry's social media accounts, and Soraya happened to have one of the largest, most terrifying fanbases on the internet. They'd once taken down a huge makeup brand's website for forty-eight hours after their director of marketing said they'd never work with Soraya because her "image" wasn't the "right fit."

Luckily for me, Soraya was venturing into music and launching her debut album soon. She wanted a big PR splash, and a sex scandal meant *major* PR. No such thing as bad publicity and all that. The fearless social media star also wasn't afraid to go head-to-head with Perry, whom she already hated after he'd invented a nasty nickname for her best friend, another influencer, and driven the poor girl into rehab.

Soraya was one of the very few public figures he'd been cautious about attacking directly due to her fans. However, thanks to a few pushes from me, he'd finally caved when the juiciness of the story seemed to outweigh his sense of self-preservation.

I entered my private office, my steps lighter than they'd been in weeks.

Bryce knew the story was coming too. I wouldn't drag an innocent into my schemes without their knowledge, but he and his wife had been okay with the plan. The furor over their wedding had died down, and they were interested in keeping the public's attention on their relationship.

After Soraya posts her denial video later (accompanied by photos and receipts showing her in Europe during her alleged upstate getaway with Bryce), it was only a matter of time before her followers ripped Perry apart.

Taking Perry down wouldn't solve my Pen dilemma, but it gave me a semblance of control, which I desperately needed. Between dating Xavier and Perry's sabotage, my life had spun out of control after Spain.

I turned on my computer and resisted the urge to check the updates Xavier had given me about Pen again. Things could've changed after he'd handed me the files, but I hoped that the upcoming holidays meant George and Caroline wouldn't do anything too rash. They kept Pen out of the spotlight as much as possible, but they'd still get questions if their youngest daughter was mysteriously shipped abroad right before Christmas.

The only force stronger than their desire to spite me was their desire to keep up appearances. That meant I had until the New Year to figure out a solution because never seeing Pen again was *not* an option.

I spent the morning and better part of the afternoon taking calls and closing email chains before the holidays. I was reviewing the *Sports World* interview with Asher when the door flew open.

I lifted my head, expecting to see Jillian or maybe Xavier. Shock rippled through me when I saw my sister's slim form instead.

"You bitch."

My eyebrows winged up at her scathing greeting. Georgia was usually subtler than that.

"That's a matter of opinion, but I'm only a bitch to people who deserve it," I said, overcoming my initial jerk of surprise to offer a cool smile. "For example, people who show up uninvited to my workplace and attack my character before I've even had my second coffee."

Georgia came to a stop in front of my desk. Red splotches mottled her flawless skin, and a muscle twitched beneath her eye. I'd never seen her so upset, not even when our grandmother left her vintage Chanel collection to me instead of Georgia in her will.

"Bentley told me what you did," she snapped.

"Really?" This was going to be good. "Please, what did I do? Enlighten me."

"You tried to fuck him. You called him, pretended you had something important he *needed* to know, and asked him to meet you at the same time as the Windsor Rose Society's annual post-Thanksgiving ladies' brunch because you *knew* I'd be occupied that day." Her blue eyes flashed with animosity. "Trying to seduce your pregnant sister's husband? That's low even for you."

"Not any lower than fucking your sister's fiancé in their living room on New Year's Eve."

Georgia's mouth thinned. "Oh, please. That was *years* ago, and Bentley had a good—"

"Spare me your bullshit, Georgie." She hated when people called her that, which was why I did it as often as possible. "I'm not rehashing the same conversation we've had multiple times in the past, but I'll tell you this: we're not the same people we were back then, and I wouldn't touch Bentley again if you paid me a million dollars." I returned to my computer. "You want him so bad? You can keep him."

"You're many things, Sloane, but I didn't think you were a liar." Georgia tossed her phone on my desk. "You met up with him on Sunday. Don't deny it."

I glanced down. *Motherfucker*. Bentley had somehow snapped a photo of me at the bar when I was ordering my drink and distracted. His hand was also in the frame, displaying his favorite Rolex.

I didn't know what had possessed him to do that—insurance, maybe, or blackmail—but the man was truly dumber than a box of rocks. The photo was more damning for him than it was for me.

"I did meet up with him—after he called *me* and said he wanted to talk." I slid the phone back across the desk. "He's the one who propositioned me, Georgie." I didn't go into detail about what he'd said—yet.

It happened so fast I almost missed it. A flicker crossed Georgia's face, just long enough to make me think there'd been trouble in paradise before Bentley and I ever met up.

"You're lying."

"Am I lying about the Lalique vase you threw at his head?"

She went deathly still.

The vase was a small, specific detail that I would've never come up with on my own unless Bentley told me—Georgia hadn't made a habit of throwing expensive housewares growing up.

"That doesn't mean anything," she said, her complexion several shades paler than when she'd entered. "It could've just come up during your conversation."

"Believe me, don't believe me. It's not my job to convince you of your husband's infidelity." My voice cooled another degree. "But there's an old saying, Georgie: if he cheats with you, he can cheat *on* you." I paused, letting pettiness take the wheel. "There's also another saying: karma's a bitch."

The splotches from earlier made a glorious return, spreading across Georgia's face and neck and blanketing her skin with a mask of bright red.

"This is why no one wants to be around you, Sloane," she hissed. Whenever she felt threatened, her claws came out, and right now they gleamed sharp and deadly beneath the lights. "You're a coldhearted snake; you always have been. You didn't even cry when Mom died. What kind of sick, heartless monster doesn't shed a single tear when their *mother's* gone?"

Ice rushed to fill my veins, freezing me from the inside out.

I could handle anything she said about us, Bentley, or the estrangement, but in true Georgia fashion, she'd zeroed in on the one weakness I had left—the idea that there was something wrong with me, that I was broken somehow because I didn't *feel* the way "normal" people should feel. The fear that I was a monster in human clothing, devoid of compassion and unable to form genuine connections.

I knew that wasn't totally true. After all, I loved my friends and Pen, and I connected with Xavier more than I had any man in the past, including Bentley. But fear often overrode fact, and Georgia had ripped the stitches off my wounds with alarming alacrity.

I stood, taking comfort in the way I towered over her. My sister had an uncanny ability to make me feel small, but I would rather die before I let her see it.

"Get out of my office." The quiet command lashed out once in warning.

Georgia ignored it.

"Thank God we got rid of Rhea." When she sniffed

weakness, she was like a shark hunting blood. "She was a terrible nanny anyway, and I would hate for Penny to grow up with a lying traitor in the house. How much money did you bribe her with?"

"Get. Out. Of. My. Office."

"Speaking of getting rid of people, you know Xavier's going to leave you." Georgia pivoted to another soft spot with unerring accuracy. "I'm sure dating you is a novelty in the beginning. Everyone wants to melt the so-called ice queen; Bentley says that's the only reason he proposed. He liked knowing *he* was the one who tamed you, but he quickly realized his mistake, didn't he?" She tilted her head, her beautiful face vicious. "Now let's take Xavier. Rich, gorgeous, used to having *fun*. How long do you think a guy like that will stay with someone like you before he gets bored? He doesn't—"

"Ever since we saw you at the hospital, she's gotten more paranoid. She accused me of checking you out and said I still had feelings for you." Bentley's voice played from the recording on my phone. Georgia froze, her smirk withering at the sound of her husband's words. "She said she was my second choice and that I'm always comparing her to you. The thing is...she's not wrong."

I didn't take my eyes off my sister's rapidly paling face as the replay of my conversation with Bentley continued. There was a reason I hadn't sent her the audio right after I left the bar; I'd wanted to see her reaction, and it was as glorious as I'd imagined.

For once, Georgia was speechless.

Part of me had considered keeping the audio to myself, but that was before she stormed into *my* office, flung accusations in *my* direction, and ignored *my* requests to leave.

If she wanted to stay so badly, then she could do so on my fucking terms.

Her earlier words still hurt, but the satisfaction at seeing her tremble with outrage was enough to temporarily numb those wounds.

"Worry less about my relationship with Xavier and more about your own marriage," I said, my voice cold and calm. "It took one chance encounter for Bentley to try come crawling back to me. I don't want him anymore, of course, nor will I ever want him again. Unlike other people, I prefer partners who understand the concept of loyalty, but I can easily walk away and never give that man another thought. You, on the other hand, are stuck with him." I offered a casual shrug. "Perhaps try marriage counseling or therapy. I imagine being someone's second choice is difficult, but you should be used to that by now. You seem to want only the things I've had first."

Georgia's skin grew increasingly mottled the more I spoke. This was the worst-case scenario for her—not only hearing the shit Bentley had been saying behind her back but knowing I, specifically, was privy to her humiliation. She hated losing face in front of her "competition," and as much as she and her friends tried to one-up each other on a regular basis, I'd always been her biggest competitor in her mind.

If there was one thing Georgia Kensington did not tolerate, it was coming in second place.

"Now, if there's nothing else, I have work to do." I leaned back in my chair. "Xavier and I have dinner plans at Monarch, and I don't want to miss them."

Monarch was one of the most exclusive restaurants in the city. Even my father had issues getting a reservation.

"Whatever," Georgia snapped. "Monarch is over anyway. No one eats there anymore."

It was as weak a comeback as I'd ever heard from my sister, and I merely looked at her until she spun on her heels and stormed out without another word.

I waited until the door closed and several beats had passed before I let the disdain slide off my face.

What kind of sick, heartless monster doesn't shed a single tear when their mother's gone?

Thank God we got rid of Rhea.

You know Xavier's going to leave you.

In her absence, Georgia's taunts rushed to fill the void, and without my pride to keep me upright, I was suddenly so, so tired.

I closed my eyes and tried to breathe through the rapid patter of my heart. I hated how I'd taken her bait before I cut her off with the Bentley recording. I hated how transparent I was to her, and how deeply her words cut when I should've been immune.

I'd known she was trying to hurt me, and I'd let her do it anyway.

My hands closed around the edge of my desk. It reminded me of Xavier, which reminded me of what Georgia had said.

Everyone wants to melt the so-called ice queen.

How long do you think a guy like that will stay with someone like you before he gets bored?

The deadline for our two-month trial period loomed at the end of the month. I'd avoided thinking about it because I wasn't sure what I would do—stay in a relationship that made me terrifyingly happy and risk it ending one day, or run back to the comfort of my solo bubble? That was, of course, assuming I had a choice and Xavier wanted to be with me after the trial period concluded.

What if he didn't?

That would make things easier for me. I wouldn't have to choose, and I could slide back into my old life like it'd never happened. Like we'd never kissed or floated in a pool beneath the city skies. Like he'd never held my hand during a race to the hospital or set up a rooftop movie screening on a beautiful fall day. Like I'd never comforted him, trusted him, and—

The world blurred for an instant.

It was so unusual and disorienting, I couldn't comprehend it. When I did, a reckless shock of hope darted through me, and I reached up, my breath stuck somewhere between my throat and lungs.

My fingers touched my cheeks. They were dry.

I blinked, and the world was clear.

Of course it was.

Disappointment and relief amplified the pressure crowding my chest. My office suddenly felt too small, the air too thin. I could still smell my sister's perfume, and it made my stomach roil.

I needed to get out of here before I suffocated.

Jillian was waiting outside my door when I exited. "Sloane, I'm so sorry," she said, her expression stricken. "I tried to stop her, but she got past me, and once she was inside, I didn't want to—"

"It's fine." At least my voice was clear. *Thank God for the small things.* "Please call building security and ask them to place Georgia Kensington-Harris and Bentley Harris on the guest blacklist. I want them to call the police if either comes within a thousand feet of my office."

"Consider it done." Jillian worried her bottom lip. "Are you okay? Do you, um, want a doughnut?"

She believed sugar was the answer to all problems.

I almost smiled, but my facial muscles didn't have it in them. "No, thanks. I'm working from home for the rest of the day. Assign Tracy to oversee the *Curated Travel* interview with the Singhs instead." I gave her a few more instructions before I left and walked to my apartment instead of taking a car.

Nothing cleared my head like a good walk.

I missed Pen. I missed Rhea. I even missed the tiny sliver of hope that my sister and I could reconcile one day, which was ironic considering I'd never felt like I truly belonged in my family.

But there'd been a time when I could pretend, and on days when I was too tired to fight, pretending was enough.

What happened in my office had effectively killed that hope. It'd drawn too much blood.

As for Xavier...

I entered my building's lobby and slid into the elevator right before the doors closed.

As for Xavier, he hadn't given me any indication that he wanted us to end. He'd been nothing but supportive and caring since we started dating; I'd be stupid to doubt him. Right?

By the time I got off the elevator and unlocked my apartment door, I'd successfully pushed Georgia's taunts to the back of my mind. I couldn't control how good she was at pushing my buttons, but I *could* control my reaction to her, and I'd already given her more energy than she deserved.

Forget what she said. Focus on work.

I flipped on the lights and kicked off my shoes. I had a solid hour and a half to work before I had to meet Xavier for dinner. Part of me wanted to ask for a raincheck, but seeing him always made me feel better. I needed him after this shitshow of a day.

Needed.

I'd never needed anyone, and the idea that I needed him sent a little shiver down my spine—from fear or pleasure, I wasn't sure.

I tossed my tote bag on the couch and was about to slip into something more comfortable when I paused. The hairs on the back of my neck prickled as I looked around.

Something was wrong.

The apartment was still. *Too* still.

I slowly retrieved the bottle of mace I always kept in my bag while my eyes roved over the TV, the bookshelves, and the door to my bedroom. Everything was as I'd left it that morning, so why...

My gaze snagged on the side table.

The Fish's aquarium rested there, clean and clear.

In the aquarium, The Fish usually swam at his leisure, his orange scales beaming a hello every time I walked through the door.

Not anymore.

The Fish floated upside down in the tank, his eyes sunken, the pupils cloudy.

My mace clattered to the ground, the sound muted beneath the sudden roar of blood in my ears, but I couldn't bring myself to pick it up.

Dead. He was dead. *He was dead.*

I didn't understand the wellspring of grief that sprang from my chest or the tremble weakening my knees. I had no proper explanation for the burn in my eyes or the sudden, overwhelming sense of *emptiness* that invaded the apartment.

I wasn't prepared for any of those things because The Fish wasn't a cute, cuddly pet I'd bought for myself. He was my pet by default, abandoned by a stranger and housed here temporarily while I waited for the right time to rehome him. He'd never laid his head across my lap when I was sad or brought me a toy to play fetch with because he was a fucking fish.

But I'd lived with him for five years, and for five years, in this sterile apartment, we were all each other had.

I sank onto the couch and willed myself to cry, to expel the pressure mounting in my chest.

Once. I wanted that relief just *once*, but as always, I didn't get it.

And an eternity later, when the pressure became unbearable and my will to fight eroded to nothing, I simply curled up on the couch, squeezed my eyes shut against the pain, and pretended I was someone, somewhere else because that was the only thing I'd ever been able to do.

CHAPTER 34

SOMETHING WAS WRONG.

My and Sloane's dinner reservation was at seven, and it was currently seven fifteen. For most people, running fifteen minutes late wasn't the end of the world, but this was Sloane. She was *never* late.

She hadn't answered any of my texts, and when I called her, it went straight to voicemail.

I checked my watch again, my worry escalating by the minute. When I'd gotten in touch with her office earlier, Jillian said she'd left two hours ago to work from home. Had she fallen asleep? Been the victim of a mugging? Gotten into a car crash and rushed to the hospital?

A cold spike of terror pierced me at the prospect.

"Fuck it." I ignored the scandalized glare from the couple next to me and grabbed my coat from the back of my chair. I wasn't going to sit here like an idiot while Sloane was potentially bleeding to death somewhere.

I tossed a fifty-dollar bill on the table for the trouble and headed straight to the exit. Perhaps I was overreacting and Sloane would show up right after I left, rolling her eyes and huffing about my jump to conclusions, but I didn't think I was.

Even if she wasn't fatally wounded, she was hurt. I could *feel* it, an insistent cocktail of instinct and intuition that drove me into the back of a cab and toward her apartment.

My phone rang right after I gave the driver her address.

My pulse skyrocketed, then crashed. It wasn't Sloane; it was Vuk's office.

"Good afternoon. This is Willow, Mr. Markovic's assistant. I'm following up on the email you sent this morning." A smooth feminine voice flowed over the line. "Mr. Markovic would like to schedule a joint walkthrough of the vault at your earliest convenience, as well as discuss a few matters regarding your partnership. Is now a good time to connect?"

"Hey, Willow. That's great to hear, but—" The cab shuddered to a halt at a stop sign, then ambled along at the speed of a groggy snail. How the hell did I get the only slow taxi driver in Manhattan? "I'm in the middle of a personal emergency, so I can't talk right now."

A long pause greeted my answer. "To clarify, you're refusing the meeting?"

"I'm postponing the meeting due to the aforementioned emergency." I covered the phone with my hand and leaned forward. "Get me there in ten minutes, and I'll tip you a hundred bucks."

The cab lurched forward with sudden speed.

Sloane always complained about how much cash I carried around, but it was damn handy in times like this.

I returned to my call. "Please give Mr. Markovic my apologies. I'm happy to talk any other time except now. As for the walkthrough, please email me his availability, and I'll put something on the schedule."

I hung up before she could protest. I was too on edge to argue or engage in professional small talk.

I might've just shot myself in the foot by insulting Vuk so soon after he'd signed on as my partner, but the only thing I cared about right now was making sure Sloane was okay.

The cab pulled up in front of her building. I shoved the fare plus an extra hundred bucks at the driver and hurtled out of the car. It was my first time visiting her apartment—we'd always stayed at my place or a hotel—but two hundred dollars, a picture of me and Sloane on my phone, and a call up to her apartment with no answer persuaded the concierge to let me past.

She wasn't answering her phone. *Why wasn't she answering her phone?*

Images of Sloane unconscious on her bedroom floor or drowning in her tub or…fuck, I didn't know, gushing blood after she'd accidentally sliced a crucial artery open in the kitchen filled my mind.

Sometimes, I really hated my imagination.

The elevator stopped on her floor. I sprinted into the hall and blew past a row of apartments until I reached hers.

"Sloane!" I pounded on the door. "It's Xavier. Are you in there?"

Obviously, she couldn't answer if she was unconscious. I should've asked the concierge to accompany me so they could open the door in that very scenario.

I knocked again while my mind raced through my options. I could stay and wait another minute for her to answer. I could race downstairs and grab the concierge. I could *call* the concierge and ask him to come up, but my chances of convincing him to leave his post were higher face-to-face.

Every second counted, and—

Was that a sound coming from behind the door?

I froze, willing my heartbeat to slow so I could listen more carefully. That was definitely a rustle, followed by the click of a lock sliding free.

Then the door opened, and there she was. Blond hair, blue eyes, alabaster skin unmarred by blood or bruises.

Relief punched through my panic, but it nosedived a second later when I noticed the haunted look in her eyes and the lines of tension bracketing her mouth.

"Hey." I reached for her but stopped halfway, afraid she might shatter beneath my touch. Sloane was always so strong, but in that moment, she looked brittle. Fragile. "What's wrong?"

"Nothing." She stepped aside so I could enter, avoiding my gaze the entire time.

"Sloane." It was a question, plea, and command wrapped into one.

She disliked sharing her problems, but if she kept them bottled up all the time, they'd eventually explode.

Whatever she heard in her name made her chin wobble, but when she finally answered, her voice was devoid of emotion. "The Fish died."

"The..." *The Fish*. Her pet goldfish. My stomach twisted. "Oh, fuck. I'm so sorry, Luna." She hated platitudes, but I meant it.

When Hershey had died, I'd been inconsolable. It was one of the reasons I hadn't gotten another pet. I didn't want to go through the pain of losing one again.

"It's fine." Sloane turned her head, and I followed her gaze to a sheet of paper on the coffee table.

A closer look revealed a neatly typed list of instructions for taking care of The Fish.

1. Feed him one sinking pellet once a day every day

except on Sundays. Do NOT feed him more than the allotted amount or he will overeat.

2. On Sundays, feed him frozen brine shrimp for enrichment.
3. The water must maintain a temperature of 73 degrees Fahrenheit at all times.

The rest of the list was obscured by another paper, but she'd obviously put a lot of thought into it.

"He was just a goldfish." Sloane picked up the instructions, ripped them in half, and tossed them in a nearby wastebasket. "He wasn't even really mine. He couldn't leave his tank or make noise or do anything other pets do. He's not the smartest or cutest, and he probably doesn't..." Her chin wobbled again. "I mean, he probably *didn't* know or care who I was as long as I fed him."

"You had him for years," I said gently. "It's normal to feel grief over a pet passing."

"For other people. Not for me." She took in my jacket and pants. I usually didn't dress so formally, but the restaurant had a strict dress code. Realization wiped some of the stoicism off her face. "We had dinner reservations, didn't we? I'm sorry. I was going to do some work before I left, but I saw him when I got home, and I had to figure out what to do with his body. Then I had to clean out the aquarium because there's no use keeping it there when he's dead, and when I was in the kitchen, I saw all these bags of unused fish food that I obviously don't need anymore, so I—"

"Sloane. It's okay. They're just reservations." I tipped her chin up so her eyes met mine. "They're not important."

She swallowed, a tinge of pink blooming around her eyes and nose. "No," she said thickly. "I guess they're not."

She didn't resist when I pulled her into my chest, and when

she curled into me, just a little bit, I wanted to hold her tight and never let go.

"What did you do?" she asked. "When Hershey..."

"I cried," I said truthfully. "A lot. He was my best friend. Luckily, he'd been outside with our housekeeper during the fire that..." I faltered at the memory of Hershey running up to me after I'd woken up. He'd refused to leave my side for weeks after the accident, as if he knew I would break if I didn't have something to hold on to. "If it weren't for him, I don't know how I would've made it through those first few months. I went to grief counseling for a while, but it didn't work as well as just having Hershey there."

Some of the stiffness melted from Sloane's shoulders as I recounted my experience. After I finished, she stayed in my arms before she said, very quietly, "Having The Fish around helped too. I didn't realize it at the time, but when I was upset, it was nice to have someone—something—to talk to." She buried her face deeper into my chest, as if ashamed of what she was about to say. "I'm sad he died. I never even gave him a real name."

"Well, he's a goldfish," I said practically. "There are worse things you could've called him."

Her muffled laughter made me smile. I knew how difficult it was for Sloane to admit her feelings out loud, so her seemingly small confession was actually a huge step for her.

"Anyway, that's why I was late," she said. "We've missed our reservations, but if you give me fifteen minutes, I can get ready—"

"Forget about dinner. We'll order takeout and watch the new Cathy Roberts movie." I'd rather be here than at some stuffy restaurant anyway.

Sloane lifted her head. "The one where the big-city rich girl is forced to move to the Australian countryside and falls in love with the surly but handsome ranch hand?" she asked hopefully.

"Yep. I'll even let you write your scathing review in peace

without questioning your unfair harshness toward the poor actors or screenwriter."

Her eyes gleamed. "Deal."

While I ordered the food, Sloane pulled up the movie and grabbed her review notebook and pen.

However, she hesitated as the film studio's opening credits played onscreen, and a secret battle waged across her face before she spoke again.

"There's one more thing," she said. "Georgia came to see me at work today. She accused me of trying to seduce Bentley."

My eyes snapped toward hers. Her admission had come from so far out of left field that I couldn't do more than stare, stunned, as she explained what'd happened with her sister as well as with Bentley over the holiday weekend.

But the more I listened, the more anger seeped beneath my skin, slow yet *scorching*. I kept a tight rein on it for now, but there was no fucking way I'd let anyone to talk to her the way Georgia and Bentley had.

"I should've told you about his call earlier, but I didn't know what he wanted, and I didn't want to put a damper on Thanksgiving." Sloane tapped her pen against her knee. It was a nervous tic I'd picked up on years ago, shortly after we started working together. It'd been one of the few cracks in her perfect facade at the time. "Georgia really pissed me off, and I was too upset to stay in the office, so I came home. That's when I saw... well." She cleared her throat. "I don't know why I'm telling you this, but I figured you should know. Just in case anyone tries to make my meeting with him into anything more than it was."

Warmth rushed to fill my stomach, calming my fury. I swallowed the choice words I had for her ex and simply said, "You can tell me anything."

Sloane's pen stilled.

"I know," she said, even softer than before, and a tiny, crucial brick crumbled from around my heart.

We didn't say much else after that, but later that night, after the movie ended and our half-eaten food had grown cold, I carried a drowsy Sloane to her bedroom and tucked her in beneath her comforter.

She fully passed out before her head hit the pillow. It'd been a long, emotionally draining day for her, but I didn't take for granted how comfortable she felt falling asleep while I was here.

As I smoothed a stray lock of hair from her face, revealing the curve of her cheekbone and the shadow crescents of her closed lashes, Pen's question from the simulation center echoed in my ears.

And I wondered, my mind flipping from the first time we'd met in her office to this moment right here, right now, just how in the hell I'd fallen in love with Sloane Kensington.

CHAPTER 35

Xavier

I DIDN'T CONFESS TO SLOANE. NOT YET.

I wasn't sure she reciprocated my feelings to that degree, and I needed to figure out a way to tell her without potentially scaring her off.

I did, however, stay with her Monday night through Tuesday morning, when she left for work and I called Vuk's office back, apologized, and confirmed a walkthrough of the vault later in the month. I spent the rest of the day dealing with club obligations.

On Wednesday, I took care of more unofficial business.

The Arthur Vanderbilt Tennis Club was one of the oldest private tennis clubs on the East Coast. A favorite haunt of the polo-wearing, polo-playing crowd, it charged an obscene amount of money for annual access and was famous for the time visiting tennis superstar Richard McEntire attacked a ball boy with his tennis racket and knocked several of his teeth out. I hadn't known it was possible to knock someone's teeth out with a racket, but apparently it was, because McEntire and the club settled the case for a cool two million dollars.

As a Castillo, I was granted automatic admission, so on

Wednesday afternoon, at the tail end of lunch hour, when old-money bankers flocked to the indoor courts for a workout and boys' talk, I strode through the halls toward the men's locker room.

A cacophony of noise greeted me when I stepped inside. Steam thickened the air, partially obscuring the mahogany panels and crowd of finance bros as they prepared to return to work. Nevertheless, it didn't take me long to find who I was looking for.

Bentley Harris II held court in the coveted center aisle. He was busy laughing and joking with several guys who looked like carbon copies of him: clean-cut, clean-shaven, and half-dressed in business formal.

He had his back to me, so he didn't notice my approach.

"Our new receptionist is hot, but she's blond," he said. "I get enough of that at home. Georgia's been a real bitch lately. She came home Monday all pissed about something—what?"

One of his friends had noticed me and nudged his arm.

Bentley turned, his expression souring when he saw me.

"Harris." I donned an affable tone, the type I'd use to greet an old classmate or a friendly acquaintance.

"Castillo," he said stiffly. "I didn't realize you were a member of the club."

"They offered me a courtesy membership when I first moved to New York," I said lazily, my smile hiding the flicker of rage in my gut. "Of course, I don't use it often. Why come here when I could go to Valhalla?"

A wave of embarrassed discontent rippled through the air, subtle but distinctive.

I barely used my Valhalla membership either, but everyone knew the tennis club was a consolation prize for people who couldn't get a Valhalla invite—like Bentley and company, for example.

Bentley's jaw ticked. His eyes darted to his friends before he forced a laugh. "How lucky of us to see you here then," he mocked. "Are you slumming it, or did Valhalla finally kick you out after they realized your spot could go to someone more worthwhile?"

"You mean like you? Sadly, their roster's still full," I drawled. "As for slumming, you're right. I came by to see you."

The noise from the rest of the locker room dwindled as everyone tried, and failed, to pretend they weren't eavesdropping. Brewing aggression crackled like static before a storm, and the steady *drip, drip, drip* of water from the showers sounded unnaturally loud in the tension-laced air.

Bentley took a step toward me, his face all smiles but his eyes hot and bright with humiliated anger. "If you want to see me, make an appointment," he said with a misplaced sense of bravado. He thought he was safe here, surrounded by his friends and the reek of privilege. "I don't talk to jobless losers."

My rage from Monday night reignited—not at his jab toward me but at the vision of him speaking to Sloane with that same snide condescension.

"That's where you're wrong," I said, still with my affable tone. "I'm not here to talk."

Then I drew back my arm and slammed my fist into his face.

There was a satisfying crunch of bone, followed by a howl of pain. Blood fountained from his nose as he staggered backward and the brewing storm broke, loosening a frenzy of shouts and jeers as the other locker room occupants shoved one another for the best view of the fight.

None of them intervened, but the ruckus fueled the anger burning swift and hot through me.

I wasn't a violent person. I rarely had to resort to physical brawls to solve a problem, and in Bentley's case, I didn't *have* to; I wanted to.

He recovered enough to rush at me, fists clenched, but I was ready for him.

With a swift side step, I dodged his wild swing and took the opportunity to deliver a powerful punch to his midsection.

He doubled over from the impact and clutched his stomach, gasping for breath. I didn't give him a chance to catch it before I hauled him up by his collar and slammed him against a nearby locker.

"That was your first and final warning," I said, my words quiet enough to reach only his ears. "Touch, talk, or even *think* about Sloane again, and I'll make what Richard McEntire did to that ball boy with his tennis racket look like a walk in the fucking park. That includes any indirect contact. If you make her life difficult in *any* way, you'll be blacklisted from New York society so fast, it'll make your head spin."

"You don't have the power," Bentley sneered, but a glint of fear swam beneath his murky eyes. For someone like him, getting blacklisted was even worse than getting beat up.

"No?" I said softly. "Try me."

I didn't abuse my family's wealth or last name often, but I was still a Castillo. Even with my inheritance tied up and my reputation as a hedonist, I could crush Bentley Harris II like a fucking bug.

He knew it as well as I did, which was why he didn't say a word when I dropped him on the ground like a sack of potatoes.

"Pass the message along to your wife," I said, my face hardening. "The same goes for her."

I wouldn't touch Georgia. Sloane's relationship with her sister was her domain, but that didn't mean I had to stand by and watch while Georgia tried to tear down the woman I loved.

Loved.

It was a strange concept, and not one I'd had experience with in the past. But now that I'd identified it, I couldn't believe it had taken me so long to recognize it.

The way my mind mapped every detail about Sloane, both consciously and unconsciously, like I would drown if I didn't inhale enough of her. The comfort I had in sharing my secrets with her, and the spike in my pulse whenever she was near. The warmth; the jealousy; the fierce, overwhelming protectiveness.

I *loved* her, totally and completely, and I'd be damned if I let anyone hurt her.

Bentley must've heard the vicious resolve edging my voice because he didn't attempt to save face in front of his peers. The others' shouts had died down to grumbles of disappointment at how quickly the fight had ended, but I hadn't expected it to drag on.

At the end of the day, people like Bentley Harris were cowards. Cowards never lasted long in the face of those willing to call their bluff and I knew, with bone-deep certainty, that he and Georgia would never bother Sloane again.

I stepped over Bentley's sprawled legs and walked out, leaving him bleeding and humiliated on the floor.

I didn't bother acknowledging the other club members or taking advantage of the empty courts on my way out.

My business here was done.

CHAPTER 36

Sloane

I SHOULD'VE BEEN EMBARRASSED ABOUT BREAKING down over a goldfish, of all things, but it'd been surprisingly cathartic, at least with Xavier. I suspected I would've felt differently had I opened the door and seen anyone else.

But I hadn't, and he'd been here, and he'd stayed.

Overnight.

That was already a big deal for me because I didn't let random men in my personal space. But he wasn't a random man; he was *him*, and the house felt so much more vibrant when he was there that I'd thrown caution to the wind and invited him over for the weekend.

That was right. I, Sloane Kensington, had willingly invited someone to stay—count them—one, two, *three* nights with me, and I didn't dread it.

Who even am I?

In keeping with the mushy-sentimental-aliens-abducted-my-body theme, I also tried to play Martha Stewart on Friday night. The results were...mixed.

"Have you ever baked before?" Xavier leaned against the

doorframe and arched an eyebrow at my attempt to make chocolate chip cookies while a batch of cupcakes baked in the oven. Amusement played in his gaze, along with a hint of concern.

I'd barely used my appliances before tonight. I usually ate out or ordered in; the kitchen was there for show and the occasional cup of coffee.

"No, but I'm a fast learner." I frowned at the recipe I'd printed out.

Cream together butter and sugars. What the hell did that mean? Was I supposed to stir the ingredients so they were mixed? If so, why didn't the writer say *stir* instead of the maddeningly vague *cream?*

"Are you?" Xavier sounded skeptical, which I didn't appreciate.

"Yes." *Fuck it.* I was stirring. You couldn't go wrong with a good stir.

"Not that I don't believe you, darling, but your cupcakes are burning."

The wail of the smoke alarm drowned out the last piece of his sentence, and an acrid smell filled my nostrils.

"Shit!" I spun in time to see smoke billowing from the oven. I opened the door and coughed as a cloud of pale gray fumes enveloped me.

One burned hand, one opened window, and several fans of a magazine later, the alarm cut off, plunging us into silence.

We stared at the tray of blackened cupcakes on the table.

Xavier dropped the magazine he'd used to fan the smoke into the recycling bin. "Crumble & Bake delivers," he said carefully. "Perhaps we should order in."

My shoulders slumped. "I guess we should."

Half an hour later, we curled up on my couch with a Nate Reynolds movie and a box of Crumble & Bake's cupcakes. I'd abandoned my cookie batter in the kitchen, which was for the best, though I wasn't happy about it.

"I wanted to try something new," I grumbled. "Baking is an essential life skill."

I was too embarrassed to admit I'd been trying to impress him. It was so stupid and backward, the notion that a woman had to be good in the kitchen. Hello, wasn't that what food delivery was for? But I liked Xavier so much, and baking had seemed like a nice, domestic activity to add some life into the apartment.

I tried not to look at the side table where The Fish used to reside. I'd tossed the aquarium days ago, but I still felt its absence.

"You know what else is an essential life skill? Living," Xavier teased. "I'm concerned any future baking attempts will result in your kitchen burning down."

"Very funny." I tossed a balled-up napkin at him. "Next time, *you* try to bake."

"I'm good. I know where my talents lie, and it's not in the kitchen." His arm rested on the back of the couch, his fingertips grazing my shoulder. "But you don't need to cook for me, Luna. I'm happy ordering in."

"Because restaurants do it better?"

"Well, yeah." He laughed when I knocked my knee against his in reproach, but a smile broke through my disgruntlement.

If I put enough time and effort in, I was *positive* I'd kick baking's ass. There was no way a little sugar and flour could beat me, but I didn't like baking, and I didn't have to be good at everything (even though I could be if I wanted).

"In better news, Perry's social media accounts got banned," I said as Nate Reynolds engaged in a shoot-out with a group of mercenaries onscreen. Xavier always watched rom-coms with me, so I suffered through the action thriller for him. It wasn't as bad as

I'd expected. It was actually pretty good, and Nate was delicious eye candy.

Xavier's eyebrows shot up again, this time in surprise. "When did that happen? They were working last night."

"Less than an hour ago, right before the smoke alarm went off," I said. "I saw Isa's text on my lock screen."

I'd eagerly googled the story while Xavier paid the delivery guy.

After Soraya posted her denial video earlier this week, her fans had swarmed Perry's accounts with vicious determination and successfully gotten *all* of his social media banned. Apparently, the platforms had denied his appeals, and he'd already uploaded a new blog post begging for help reinstating his accounts.

It wouldn't make my father rehire Rhea or help me see Pen, but it was deeply satisfying.

"So revenge has been served," Xavier said.

"Not yet. There's still the matter of his blog." I tapped my phone. "A little birdie told me Bryce is suing him for libel and the emotional distress it caused in his marriage."

"Plenty of people have sued him for libel before. It's never stuck."

"This time is different. There's proof Perry acted with reckless disregard and published that post without verifying any of the 'facts.'"

"Perry Wilson in court. That would be a sight to see," Xavier drawled. "I'm surprised he was foolish enough to do that. Say what you will about the man, but he's usually more careful about these things."

I shrugged. "Man's ego is always his downfall." A tiny smile crept across my mouth. "Plus I may have planted a rumor that an upstart blog was about to scoop him on the scandal of the year."

Besides his general mean-spiritedness, Perry was famous for his paranoia over someone usurping his throne.

"His advertisers are already spooked," I added. "If this libel suit has legs, which I think it does, there'll be an exodus, which means he'll need money, which means..."

"It'll be primed for a takeover," Xavier finished. "Kai Young?"

"He emailed me yesterday. He said he's open to it if the price and conditions are right." I didn't doubt Kai's ability to squeeze the best deal out of Perry's soon-to-be-dying blog.

"So you'll be rid of Perry Wilson the man, and you'll ensure his only remaining platform will be in friendlier hands." Xavier whistled. "Remind me never to get on your bad side."

"I don't do stuff like this often, but he deserves it," I said. It wasn't about just me or Xavier; it was about the entire culture Perry had propagated. Gossip and rumors had always existed, but he'd taken them to a new nasty, underhanded level.

And yeah, okay, it was also a *little* personal. My blood boiled every time I thought about his blog post on Pen. Attacking adults was one thing; dragging a child into it was another.

"If I had access to my inheritance, I'd buy it out and save you the trouble," Xavier said. "I've always wanted a little slice of the internet kingdom."

I laughed. "I appreciate the sentiment, but the thought of you running a news blog is terrifying."

"You don't think I can do it?"

"I think you can do it *too* well." Except instead of celebrity news, he'd probably use it to document his adventures, many of which would land him squarely in the middle of the press's crosshairs.

I tore off a piece of cupcake, my mind churning. *If I had access to my full inheritance...*

"If I ask you a question, will you answer truthfully?" I asked.

Xavier glanced at me, then grimaced and paused the movie. "Uh-oh. Nothing good ever comes after that opening."

"It's nothing bad," I reassured him. "I'm just curious. Why do you want your inheritance so badly? It can't be about just the money."

At first glance, it seemed obvious why someone would want billions of dollars. But Xavier had his hang-ups about his father's money, and while he blew through cash the way certain celebrities blew through cocaine, he didn't strike me as someone who'd sit on that much money simply to have it.

"Why not?" he asked lightly. "Maybe I'm a greedy bastard, plain and simple."

I merely looked at him without saying anything, and after a long, tense silence, his irreverence dissolved into a sigh.

"I'm giving half of it to charity."

I almost choked on my cake. That wasn't what I'd expected. *At all.*

"Not that I don't think giving to charity is admirable, but isn't that exactly what your father's will stipulates will happen to the money if you don't pull off this CEO thing?" I asked.

"Yes."

"So why…" My question trailed off at Xavier's smirk. My eyes narrowed and drifted to the tattoo of the Castillos' rival family's crest on his bicep. It represented the duality of Xavier: his stubbornness and resentment, but also his dedication and passion. He was the type of person who'd ink a permanent symbol of his war against his father on his body, and I suddenly knew exactly what the catch was. "You're donating to charities your father hated, aren't you?"

His smirk widened into a grin. "I wouldn't say he hated the charities themselves," he said. "But he certainly wouldn't have approved of donating to some of their causes."

He handed me his phone. The Notes app was open, and I scrolled through the list of charities he'd put together. Most of them focused on civil and human rights, with a few arts and music causes thrown in. I'd bet my apartment those were for his mom.

She loved art, so she donated a lot of money and time to local galleries.

I also flashed back to the organizations listed in Alberto's will. All of them had been business or commerce oriented.

I reached the last name on the list and laughed out loud. "The Yale endowment fund?"

"My father was a Harvard guy; he hated Yale with a passion. School rivalry and all that." Xavier's dimples played peekaboo. "I'll make sure he gets a nice library on campus."

"You're evil but genius." I handed his phone back, still laughing. "You're an evil genius."

"Thank you. I've always aspired to be both those things. Evildoers have way more fun, and geniuses are, well, geniuses." Xavier pocketed his phone. "To be fair, I would've donated to those causes anyway. The fact my father would've disapproved of ninety percent of them is the cherry on top."

I lifted my half eaten cupcake. "To revenge."

"To revenge." He tapped his chocolate against my lemon raspberry. He chewed and swallowed before adding, "Don't get me wrong though. I'm definitely keeping some of the money. I like my cars and five-star hotels."

"You mean you like trashing five-star hotels."

Xavier pointedly ignored my allusion to his birthday weekend in Miami. "But I don't need *all* of it. It's more than any reasonable person could spend in a lifetime." His expression turned pensive. "Once I get the club off the ground, I'll make my own money, and I won't have to rely on his. It'll be a clean break, once and for all."

He didn't mention Eduardo's theory about the will's loophole, and I didn't bring it up.

"You'll succeed," I said simply.

Xavier's answering smile was pure warmth, and later that night, when we lay sweaty and sated in each other's arms, I still felt the brush of it against my skin.

For the first time since The Fish died, I fell into a dreamless sleep.

CHAPTER 37

BAD LUCK COMES IN THREES.

I'd been exposed to that superstition since I was a child, but no one ever defined the time period for when those three bad things happened. It could be a day, a week, a month or, in my case, three months.

My father's death and new inheritance clause in October.

Perry exposing our outing with Pen in November.

That was two, but the relatively smooth period after the blog exposé lulled me into a false sense of complacency. The issue with Pen and Rhea still hung over our heads, but at least Pen was in the city for the foreseeable future and Rhea was taken care of until she found a new job.

After Perry's social media takedowns and the unspoken but significant shift in my relationship with Sloane—namely, the realization that I loved her but couldn't tell her lest I send her running for the hills—life resumed its normal pace. That was to say, it was batshit busy.

Despite the upcoming holidays, work on the club was in full swing. I'd hired a construction crew, plumbers, electricians, and everyone else I'd need to get it up to speed before Farrah could start on the actual design, and I was already knee-deep in grand opening plans by the time late December arrived.

We were making good progress on the club, but it wasn't *enough.* The clock ticked down toward my thirtieth birthday, and every passing day amplified my anxiety. Whenever I thought about my endless to-do list, my breath ran short and a tidal wave of overwhelm crashed over me.

However, I kept all that to myself as I took Vuk and Willow on a tour of the vault.

"We're preserving the original floors and windows, but we're turning the teller enclosures into bottle displays," I said. "The bathrooms will be where the private counting rooms are, and safe-deposit boxes will be painted over so they form an accent wall."

Vuk listened, his face impassive. Instead of the designer suits favored by most CEOs, he wore a simple black shirt and pants. Beside him, his assistant took copious notes on a clipboard.

Willow was a fortysomething woman with bright coppery hair and a no-nonsense attitude. Either she could read minds or she'd worked for Vuk long enough to read *his* mind because she asked all the questions he would've asked had he, well, actually talked.

"When's the construction going to be finished?" she asked.

Since it was an active construction site, all three of us wore personal protective equipment, but I could picture her eagle eyes drilling into every detail behind her safety glasses.

"End of the month," I said. "Farrah's already sourcing most of the furniture and materials we need so we can hit the ground running as soon as this is done."

I swept my arm around the vault. Workers bustled back and forth, hammering nails, installing wiring, and shouting to one another over the whir of drills and saws.

Having so many contractors here at the same time wasn't ideal. It increased the risk of accidents, but given the ticking clock, I had no choice. I needed the basics in place before the New Year so we could focus on the design. That took the most time, and I wasn't even counting other things I had to do like hiring and marketing.

Vuk was a silent partner. His primary contributions were his name and money; the rest was up to me to figure out.

I tamped down a familiar swell of panic and answered the rest of Willow's questions as best I could. I wasn't an expert on the nuts and bolts of construction, but I knew enough to satisfy her curiosity for now.

"Hey, boss." Ronnie, the lead electrician, approached me halfway through my tour. He was a short, stocky man with eyes the color of old pennies and a face like a rock, but he was the best in the business. "Can I talk to you for a sec? It's important."

Shit. That tone of voice didn't bode well for my blood pressure.

While Vuk and Willow examined the teller enclosures, I followed Ronnie to the back of the club, where a mess of wires crisscrossed in some sort of nightmarish Gordian knot.

"We've got a small problem," he said. "This wiring hasn't been updated in decades. The situation isn't dire—you've probably got a year or so left before a rewire is no longer optional—but I figured you might want to get this done before you open."

"What's the catch?" An update was simple enough. Ronnie wouldn't have called me over unless there was something else.

"Can't get it done before the New Year" he said. "A full rewire of this scale will take at least ten days, and that's not counting the necessary finishing decoration works."

There were fourteen days left in the year. Ronnie went on holiday starting Wednesday. I opened my mouth, but he shook his head before I uttered a single word.

"Sorry, boss, no can do. My wife has been planning our

Christmas trip since *last* Christmas. If I cancel or postpone, she'll cut off my balls, and I'm not being figurative. No amount of money is worth my balls."

"It's a matter of timing. I'll cover all the expenses for your trip if you take it after the New Year."

Ronnie grimaced. "She'll cut off *one* ball for even suggesting that. Christmas is her thing."

I could tell there was no swaying him, which left me with limited choices.

Choice #1: I could try to find another electrician who could get the job done in time (possible, but the quality of their work might be lacking and would lead to bigger headaches down the road).

Choice #2: I could wait until the New Year to rewire, but that would mean pushing the design plans back. Considering the timeline and all the scheduling and labor that went into *that* process, it was the least desirable option.

Choice #3: I could stick with the current wiring and update once the club was up and running. Again, it wasn't ideal, but nothing about my situation was.

"You said the situation isn't dire, right? So we don't *have* to rewire before the club opens," I said.

"No, but..." Ronnie hesitated. "The insulation has worn off on a few wires, so there's a safety issue."

Double shit.

I rubbed a hand over my face, a headache setting in at the base of my skull. "How big is the safety issue?"

"It's not an emergency, but it's something to keep an eye on. Gotta make sure the wires are handled properly and don't overheat, or you're in for a nasty shock."

I summoned a half smile at his pun.

"Have you been running into any electrical issues?" he asked. "Flickering lights, power outages, or the like?"

I shook my head.

"Then I think you're okay *for now.* Again, I recommend rewiring as soon as possible, but I know you have a deadline. I'll try to do as much as I can before I leave for the holidays." Ronnie nodded at the wall. "So, what'll it be?"

Part of running a business was making hard decisions, and I made mine before I could overthink it.

"We'll rewire after the design is finished. Who knows? Maybe we'll get it done before the opening," I said with more optimism than I felt.

"Maybe." Ronnie shrugged. "You're the boss."

With that behind me, I rejoined Vuk and Willow, who'd tucked her clipboard into her car-sized purse.

"I'm afraid we have to leave early," she said. "Mr. Markovic has a personal emergency he must attend to."

I flicked my eyes at Vuk, who didn't appear particularly concerned about his alleged personal emergency. Perhaps he and Alex were related. They possessed roughly the same range of emotional expression.

"We'd like to finish this walkthrough another time," Willow said. "Mr. Markovic is...indisposed for the rest of the year starting on Sunday, but we can come by Saturday morning. He has a few more questions regarding your plans for the club."

Sloane and I were supposed to go ice-skating on Saturday, but I didn't want to insult Vuk again by postponing. If I finished the walkthrough in the morning, that left the afternoon and night free for our date.

I smiled. "Saturday it is."

Saturday morning dawned bright and clear.

Sloane had stayed over last night, and she was still in bed

when I slipped out to meet Vuk. She rarely slept in, but I'd kept her busy all night so I didn't wake her before leaving.

The city was already awake and busy when my cab dropped me off at the skyscraper housing the vault. A family of tourists in matching Christmas sweaters blocked the building entrance, and I had to endure their impromptu daytime caroling as I skirted around them.

At the same time, someone came around from the other side and bumped into me. A baseball cap shadowed half his face, but he looked vaguely familiar. Before I could investigate further, he disappeared around the corner, and my curiosity about his identity became an afterthought when I entered the vault to find Vuk and Willow waiting for me.

He wore the same black shirt and pants; she'd changed into a red dress that matched her hair.

"Add some green accessories and you'll give the Rockefeller tree a run for its money," I quipped.

Willow was not amused.

I'd paid the construction company a shit ton of money to work weekends; even then, they could only spare a skeleton crew this close to Christmas.

There were only three workers inside, which made this walkthrough much easier than the first one. Actually, it was more than easy.

It was smooth.

Perfect.

Until it wasn't.

I'd just finished answering Willow's last question about the security measures when her head jerked to the left. Beside her, Vuk tensed, his nostrils flaring with the first iota of emotion I'd seen in him.

"Is something wrong?" I asked.

"Do you smell that?" Willow's voice and body were drawn as tight as the strings of a violin.

I paused, my senses pushing aside the overwhelming construction-site scents of wood and metal to focus on the whiff of something harsher.

Smoke.

The realization hit right as the drills died and a panicked shout reverberated through the room.

"Fire!"

What occurred next happened so fast, my brain didn't process it until the back wall burst into flames.

More shouts. Running. Movement. *Heat.*

So much fucking heat. It was the bad kind, the kind that hit you like a sudden power outage, plunging crucial corridors of your mind into darkness and short-circuiting the pathways between your brain and muscles.

Choking, paralyzing, life-stealing heat.

Sweat enveloped my skin.

Xavier! ¿Dónde estás mi hijo?

She was trapped...couldn't get past the front door...

Died of smoke inhalation...

Lucky we recovered her body...

It should've been you.

My mind seethed with visions better left buried. Reality wavered, switching from past to present and back again.

It should've been you.

An attempt at air drew in smoke instead of oxygen. I coughed, my lungs burning, and ironically, that was what snapped me out of it.

The smells, the heat, the panic. I'd been here before.

I'd almost died when I was ten, but I wasn't ten anymore, and I'd be *damned* if I let another fire finish what the first one had started.

I blinked, and my surroundings rushed back in horrifying

clarity. Flames danced around me with malevolent glee, spreading faster than my eyes could track them. Their red and orange tongues reached hungrily for anything in their path and cast a surreal glow on the vault's stone floors and ribbed ceilings. The temperature soared to such unbearable heights that every inch of my skin screamed for relief.

Still, my feet remained rooted to the floor.

My mind was back, but my body remained frozen until a loud *crack* finally, thankfully shattered my numbness and spurred me into motion.

I didn't waste time checking to see what had caused the sound.

I simply ran, dodging abandoned tools while covering my mouth and nose with my forearm. Flames rushed toward me like ants streaming toward an overturned picnic basket, and I made it halfway to the exit before a wave of dizziness slowed me down.

I stumbled but didn't stop moving. I was already lightheaded from the smoke; if I stopped moving, I would die.

I made it another ten or so feet when a flash of black caught my eye.

My heart stopped. *Vuk.*

"Markovic!" I coughed from the effort of shouting amid a scarcity of oxygen. "We have to get out of here!"

The fire was closing in fast. If we didn't leave soon, we'd get trapped.

Vuk didn't move. He stood there, his eyes blank, his body so still I couldn't even see him breathe. If he weren't standing, I would've thought him dead.

Willow was nowhere in sight.

"Vuk!" I didn't give a shit if he hated his given name. I only cared if it got through to him.

It didn't.

Dammit.

I silently cursed using every English and Spanish expletive I knew as I closed the distance between us and forcefully hauled him toward the exit.

I was in excellent shape. I worked out regularly, and I packed a good amount of muscle, but trying to drag two hundred and thirty-five pounds of uncooperative Serb through a fire was like trying to pull a freight train with a toy car.

Sweat poured into my eyes. My muscles weakened and turned slack. The distance between us and the door stretched endlessly, each step akin to climbing a different Mount Everest.

Part of me wanted to give up, lie on the floor, and let the flames burn away the pain and worries and regrets.

But if I did that—if I didn't get us to the exit—we'd die. I'd never see Sloane again, and I'd be responsible for yet more death.

I couldn't let that happen.

Through sheer force of will, I dragged us inch by inch across the floor. I wasn't breathing so much as gasping now, and bursts of darkness peppered my vision.

But somehow, I did it.

I didn't know how. Maybe it was the same superhuman strength that allowed mothers to lift entire cars off their children, or maybe it was my body's last rallying cry before it collapsed.

Whatever it was, it pulled us through the vault exit and toward the stairwell. The door flung open, and suddenly black and yellow streamed past my vision.

I glimpsed the letters *FDNY* before someone pulled Vuk off me, and someone else grabbed hold of me, and we were moving, ducking, hurrying up the stairs while other crew members battled the encroaching fire.

I let them guide me, too dazed and disoriented to do more than follow, but I looked back once—just long enough to see the vault, my dream, and everything that came with it burn.

CHAPTER 38

IT'D BEEN THE WIRING.

After the smoke cleared and the first responders' questions were answered, I sat in the back of an ambulance, watching the activity around me with dull eyes.

The cause of the fire wouldn't be official until the city and insurance company investigated it, but I'd overheard snippets from the firefighters.

Electrical fire. Outdated wiring—the same wiring *I'd* told the electrician to keep a mere two days ago.

A small, logical part of me said it wasn't my fault and the fire would've happened anyway because he wouldn't have finished the rewiring even if I'd given him the go-ahead. A larger, more insidious part asked why I hadn't taken the proper safety measures before I'd opened the vault to dozens of contractors and put them in harm's way.

I should've made sure everything was up to code before I rushed into construction, but I hadn't because I'd been so fucking focused on meeting the deadline.

One mistake, and people had gotten hurt.

The lingering burn in my throat reignited. The immediate symptoms of my smoke inhalation had cleared after the medics had treated it with high-flow oxygen, but I still felt raw and bruised, like someone had turned me inside out and kicked me till I bled.

Luckily, no one had died, but two of the construction workers had been transported to the hospital with severe burns. The remaining worker made it out with some bruises and a broken hand after something fell on it. I hadn't seen Vuk since the firefighters rescued us, but I had seen Willow waiting outside, her face the color of snow. By the time I finished answering the medics' questions, Vuk and Willow were gone.

I was lucky there hadn't been more people inside and that the fire hadn't spread to other floors or damaged the structural integrity of the building. I was even luckier the fire hadn't happened *after* the club opened and was packed with people.

But I didn't feel lucky; I felt like I was drowning.

My fault.

This was all my fucking fault again.

I scavenged for a scrap of emotion—anger, sadness, shame—and found nothing but a terrible, all-encompassing numbness. Even my guilt was hollow, like the fire had sucked the essence out of it and scattered its ashes throughout my body. It no longer manifested as sharp knives piercing my conscience; it was just *there*, pervasive and intangible.

Why had I thought I could do this? Opening a nightclub in six months was madness, and I should've never tried. I should've *known* rushing things would lead to disaster, but I'd been too blinded by pride and ego.

"It should've been you." My father glared at me, his eyes bloodshot from grief and alcohol. "You should've died, not your mother. This is your fault."

He'd been right. He'd always—

"Xavier." A new voice penetrated my fog of memories. It sounded far-off, like something out of a dream.

Cool, smooth, feminine.

I liked that voice. I had a sense that it'd brought me great comfort in the past, but it wasn't enough to rouse me from my stupor.

"Xavier, are you all right?" Ripples of concern disrupted the smoothness. "What happened?"

Pale blond hair and blue eyes filled my vision, blocking my view of the skyscraper, medics, and curious passersby.

Sloane.

One out of a thousand knots loosened, but that was enough.

The world snapped back into crystal clarity. Car horns blared from the street, first responders wrapped up their work, and the ugly phantom of smoke snaked through my lungs.

It was a crisp December day, but the acrid fumes clung to me like Saran Wrap, sinking into my skin and suffocating me from the inside out.

"*Xavier.*" Warm hands framed my face. "Look at me."

I did, if only because I didn't have the strength to argue.

Worry etched across Sloane's features. Her gaze roved over me frantically, and when she spoke again, her voice was softer than I'd ever heard it. "Are you okay?" she repeated.

She was bundled up in a cashmere turtleneck, coat, and pants. It was an odd thing to notice given the circumstances, but it reminded me we were supposed to go ice-skating today. At this very moment, we were supposed to be at Rockefeller Center, people watching over hot chocolate.

It was funny how days, plans, *lives* could change just like that. One blink, and everything was different.

"I'm fine," I said. My voice sounded as hollow as my guilt.

That was the thing. I was always fine, and it was always the people around me who suffered.

I lived; my mom died. I came out of the vault without a scratch while two men had to be treated for third-degree burns.

"What happened?" Sloane asked, her voice still soft. "How did…?"

"It was an electrical fire," I said flatly. I laid it all out for her—the wiring, the electrician's warning, my decision to push off the update and, most importantly, my lack of foresight in taking care of these things before construction had started.

"This wasn't your doing." Sloane had always possessed an uncanny ability to read my mind. "The electrician himself said the wiring wasn't an emergency. You—"

"Maybe not, but it was my *job* to think about things like that." I set my jaw. "I can't cut corners like that. Imagine if this happened *after* the club opened. It would've been another Cocoanut Grove." The 1942 fire at Boston's Cocoanut Grove was the deadliest nightclub fire in history.

"But it didn't." Sloane stood firm. "I talked to one of the responders. No one died, and the physical damage isn't as bad as you think. The vault has a lot of fireproof elements. It'll be tight, even tighter than before, but with the right crew, you can rewire the club, fix the fire damage, and open in time. Maybe it won't be—"

"What?" I stared at her, trying to process her words. They made sense individually, but together they formed a jumbled mess. "What are you talking about?"

"The club. I did some quick calculations. It'll take two months to clean up the damage, which throws off your initial design timeline, but if we scale back the interiors and focus on the experience, it's doable."

I couldn't believe what I was hearing. "We're not scaling back anything because the club is done. It's not happening."

Shock registered on Sloane's face. "Xavier, the vault is salvageable. It—"

"No, it isn't." The loosened knot from earlier twisted into an unbreakable coil. "I gave it my best shot, and *this* is what happened." I gestured around us. "If this isn't a fucking sign to quit, I don't know what is."

"This isn't a sign of anything." If I was stubborn, she was unyielding. "It'll be harder, but if—"

"Dammit, Sloane!" A torrent of pent-up emotions punched through my numbness. Pain, fury, frustration, regret—they all poured out, eating away at my rationality and restraint until I was nothing but pure, unadulterated instinct.

And right now, my instinct was to lash out at the closest target.

"I don't give a *shit* about the club or its design," I said, low and vicious. "People almost *died* because of me. Because of *my* oversight and decisions *I* made. I survived a fucking *fire* this morning, and you think I want to plan a fucking party? That's the *last* thing on my mind."

Sloane's mouth trembled for a split second before she squared her shoulders and raised her chin. "I understand you're upset, and you're right," she said with infuriating calm. "Now isn't the time to discuss business. We can do it later, after we get you—"

"We aren't discussing it later or ever." I couldn't breathe past the pressure choking me. "I told you, the club is *done.* Do you hear me? As in, it's never happening. Why don't you get it?"

"Because I know this is your emotions talking!" Her composure finally snapped. "You went through a lot today, and I'm not trying to downplay that. But you can't make a decision about your entire future based on—"

"Yes, I can!" I stood, needing to move, needing to do *something* to feed the ugly beast prowling inside me. "Trying to secure my fucking 'future' almost got people *killed.* This project was impossible from the start, and I can't sit here and run business calculations when there are men lying hurt in a hospital because of me. Not all of us can go through life pretending they don't feel, Sloane!"

Unlike you.

I didn't say it, but I didn't need to; that was the problem with us knowing each other so well.

Sloane's skin leeched of color. She'd taken a step back when I stood, and she stared up at me with something I'd never seen from her before: raw, undisguised hurt.

Hurt *I'd* put there—intentionally, callously, and maliciously. I knew her weak spot, and I'd attacked it without thought.

Emptied of fuel, the beast inside me deflated, leaving only regret in its wake.

Fuck. I reached for her, my throat clogged with the bitter residue of my words. "Luna..."

"You're right." She shied away from my touch, her eyes still glossy with hurt. "Not everyone can."

"I didn't—"

"I have to go." Sloane turned away, her chest rising and falling with rapid breaths. "We'll talk after things have calmed down."

Don't go.

I'm sorry.

I love you.

Words I should've said but didn't. *Couldn't.*

The only thing I could do was watch her walk away as my world went down in flames for the second time that day.

CHAPTER 39

Sloane

HE HADN'T MEANT IT.

I knew he hadn't meant it because at his core, Xavier wasn't cruel or malicious. He'd been upset about the fire and lashed out.

In hindsight, I shouldn't have pushed him so hard about rebuilding the club after the fire. It'd been the wrong time, but when I saw him sitting there, looking like a shell of himself, I'd panicked and defaulted to what I did best—solving crises. I hadn't known how to assuage his guilt, so I'd tackled the concrete issue of his club instead.

Logically, I understood all that, but emotionally, I couldn't dig out the barbs of his words. They'd embedded themselves in old wounds, tearing through scabs and sutures to pour salt into raw flesh.

Not all of us can go through life pretending they don't feel, Sloane!

If anyone else had said what Xavier said, it would've stung, but I would've brushed it off in short order. After all, I'd been accused of worse over the years.

But coming from him, the sentiment devastated me. He wasn't entirely wrong, which was *why* it hurt so much. No one liked hearing the sting of truth from the person they cared about most, especially when it was delivered in anger.

Even a week later, even knowing he hadn't meant it, it hurt so much I couldn't breathe. That was what terrified me the most—the fact someone else had that much power over me.

"More popcorn?" Alessandra nudged the bowl into my lap.

I shook my head, watching our fourth holiday rom-com of the day without really seeing it. My review notebook lay empty in my lap; every time I tried to write something, I pictured Xavier playfully teasing me about it, and I lost my words.

"This movie is boring." Isabella yawned. "Maybe we should switch genres. Watch a thriller instead."

"That's fine," I said without enthusiasm. I wasn't in the mood to see fictional couples get their happily ever afters anyway. The concept of a happily ever after was a total scam.

My friends exchanged glances. It was the day after Christmas and a full week after the fire. The accident had made headlines, but everyone had been distracted by the holidays, and it hadn't generated the same media firestorm it would've had it happened any other week of the year.

I'd told my friends what happened and declined Alessandra's offer to spend Christmas with her and Dominic. The only thing worse than being alone on Christmas was being a third wheel.

Isabella and Kai had been in London, and Vivian, Dante, and Josie had gone to Boston to visit Vivian's mother, so the last thing I'd expected when my doorbell rang that afternoon was to see my three best friends crowded in the doorway, armed with enough popcorn and wine to fell an elephant.

It'd been the only bright spot of my week.

While Isabella searched for a new movie, Vivian regarded me with quiet concern. "Have you talked to Xavier since Saturday?" she asked gently.

The question scraped against exposed wounds, and I shook my head, refusing to meet her eyes.

"Do you *want* to talk to him?"

Again, I shook my head, this time with less conviction.

Xavier and I hadn't talked or messaged since I walked away after the fire, not even to wish each other a merry Christmas. Part of me had been tempted to reach out first, make sure he was okay, and apologize for overstepping, but pride and self-preservation stopped me every time I picked up my phone.

Maybe our not talking was for the best. Obviously, I didn't know how to comfort him properly, and my presence made things worse instead of better.

"You have to talk to him eventually." This time, Alessandra was the one who spoke. "Your dating trial is expiring soon."

Pain cleaved through me. "I know."

I wouldn't win awards for my eloquence today, but I was afraid that if I uttered more than a handful of words at a time, it would destroy my already-tenuous grip on my emotions.

I hadn't allowed myself to fully *feel* the implications of what happened with Xavier and the silence that'd followed, and if I had my way, I never would. Some things were better left repressed.

Isabella paused her search for the perfect thriller, and there was another exchange of glances around the room.

"What are you going to do when the trial ends?" Isabella asked cautiously.

I set my jaw against the pressure swelling in my chest. "I don't know."

Except I did.

I just didn't know if I had the strength to go through with it.

Xavier

I could describe the week after the fire in one word: hell.

The paperwork? Hell. Visiting the hospital and seeing the workers' burns up close? Hell. Speaking to the workers' agonized families? Hell.

Not seeing or talking to Sloane while knowing how much I'd hurt her the last time we spoke? Hell times a fucking thousand.

I should've run after Sloane and apologized right after she left, but I'd been worried I'd make things worse. I hadn't been in the right frame of mind to do anything except go home, pour myself a glass of whiskey, and pass the hell out.

The days after that had been filled with phone calls, meetings, paperwork, and a million other things I didn't want to do. I'd tried to contact Vuk but couldn't get through, and I'd spent Christmas at home, torn between calling Sloane and avoiding our inevitable confrontation like a coward.

The coward won out.

I wasn't proud of it, but our trial dating period ended soon, and I didn't need a genius-level IQ to know I'd blown it.

As long as we didn't talk, I could live in denial and pretend we were going through a minor hiccup, which was how I ended up at Valhalla's bar the Sunday after Christmas, drowning my sorrows with Lagavulin.

I finished my drink and motioned the bartender for another one. He slid a fresh glass of whisky across the counter as someone settled on the stool next to mine.

"Save it," I said without turning my head.

"This is quite sad." Kai ignored my preemptive dismissal, his tone mild. "Have you considered other methods of coping besides drinking by yourself at"—he checked his watch—"three in the afternoon?"

"I'm not in the mood for your judgment, and I'm not the only one sitting at the bar at three in the afternoon." I cast a pointed glance in his direction. "Aren't you supposed to be in London right now?"

"We flew back early at Isabella's insistence." A delicate pause. "Apparently, one of her friends needs 'major cheering up.' Her words."

It was obvious who she'd meant.

My gut twisted at the indirect mention of Sloane, and it took everything in me not to interrogate Kai.

Has Isabella talked to Sloane already? What did she say? How is she doing? How much does she hate me right now?

"Her friend isn't the only one." Kai nodded his thanks when the bartender brought him a strawberry gin and tonic. He had a strange affinity for that particular cocktail. "I'm sorry about the fire. Truly." He sounded sincere, which made it worse.

The past week hadn't done much to ease my guilt, and I felt like I didn't deserve people's sympathy.

"Have you talked to Alex yet?" Kai asked.

I grimaced. "Not yet. We're meeting tomorrow."

I wasn't looking forward to it. Alex's assistant had scheduled the meeting, so I didn't know his thoughts regarding the fire in his building, but I imagined they weren't pleasant.

"I haven't talked to Markovic since the fire either." I flashed back to the wild look in Vuk's eyes and the old burn scars around his neck. "He disappeared when we got out of the vault. Do you think…?"

"The Serb does what he does," Kai said. Most people referred to Vuk as the Serb, per his preference, but I couldn't shake the habit of calling people by their, well, actual name. "No one knows what goes through his head, but if he hasn't dissolved your partnership yet, I assume everything's fine."

My shoulders tensed.

Kai's eyes sharpened behind his glasses. "*Is* everything fine?"

"Besides the small matter of the fire? Sure." I tossed back my drink. "Because I'll dissolve the partnership myself after the New Year. The club isn't happening."

"Why not?"

Another headache set in behind my eyes. I was sick and tired of explaining the same thing over and over again.

I clipped out the same reasons I'd given Sloane; like Sloane, Kai seemed unimpressed.

"People make mistakes," he said. "Entrepreneurs make even more. You can't succeed in business without failing, Xavier."

"Maybe not, but I bet most mistakes involve a disrupted cash flow or media mishap, not a fire that could've killed people."

"Could've but didn't."

"By some miracle."

"I don't believe in miracles. Everything that happens, happens for a reason." Kai turned to face me fully. "That list of names I gave you? Those are some of the sharpest people in business. They believed in you enough to invest their time, money, and resources into the club, and they wouldn't have done that if they didn't think you were capable of pulling it off. So stop using your martyr act as an excuse and figure out how to finish what you started."

The heated reprimand was so out of character for Kai, it stunned me into silence. We weren't friends, exactly, and maybe that was why his words successfully cut through me. There was nothing quite so humbling or clarifying as getting lambasted by an acquaintance.

I opened my mouth, closed it, then opened it again, but nothing came out because he was right. I *was* acting like a martyr. I'd taken the fire and made it all about me and my guilt, and I'd used that as an excuse to walk away from the club.

Despite my success in getting the process started and the best of the best onboard, I was afraid I'd still fail. The fire gave me an opportunity to walk away without admitting to that fear.

I'd downed three glasses of whisky before Kai arrived, but the realization sobered me up quickly.

First Sloane, now this. I really was a coward. *To think I accused Bentley of being that very thing when I'm worse.*

I swallowed the golf ball that'd lodged itself in my throat and tried to think logically.

Kai might've been right, but it didn't change the fact that pulling off a grand club opening by early May was nearly impossible from a logistical perspective. I could throw together something smaller, but whatever I did needed to pass muster with the inheritance committee.

Basically, I could try harder, but my chances of failure had increased exponentially.

I rubbed my temple, wishing not for the first time that I'd been born into a simple, normal family with regular jobs and regular lives instead of this *Succession*-esque mess.

"Isabella put you up to this, didn't she?" Even in my current state, I was clearheaded enough to recognize that Kai's appearance in this particular place, on this particular day, wasn't a coincidence.

He didn't respond, but the small twitch of his mouth said it all.

"How'd you know I'd be here today?" I asked.

"Educated guess. This bar has seen its fair share of comfort drinking." He nodded at the glittering display of expensive bottles and crystal glasses. "I may have also asked security to alert me if and when you check in."

I snorted. "I'm flattered you went to the trouble."

"Don't be. I didn't do this for you," Kai said dryly. "I did this for my reputation and for Isa. I was the one who connected you with the people on my list, and it'll reflect poorly on me if the club doesn't succeed. Plus..." His gaze flicked to his phone. "Isa would never let me hear the end of it if I didn't get you to pull your head out of the sand."

Sloane.

My hand flexed around my glass as another wave of regret crashed into me. She'd tried to help, and I'd driven her away. Then I couldn't be bothered to say a simple *I'm sorry*, not even on Christmas, because I'd been too wrapped up in my own mental bullshit.

God, I was an idiot.

I stood abruptly and grabbed my coat from the hook beneath the counter. "Listen, this was a good talk, but—"

"Go." Kai returned to his drink. "And if anyone other than Isa asks, this conversation never happened."

I didn't need him to tell me twice.

I sprinted out of the club and into one of Valhalla's chauffeured town cars. I gave the driver Sloane's address.

It'd been eight days, two hours, and thirty-six minutes since we last spoke.

I only hoped I wasn't too late.

CHAPTER 40

Xavier

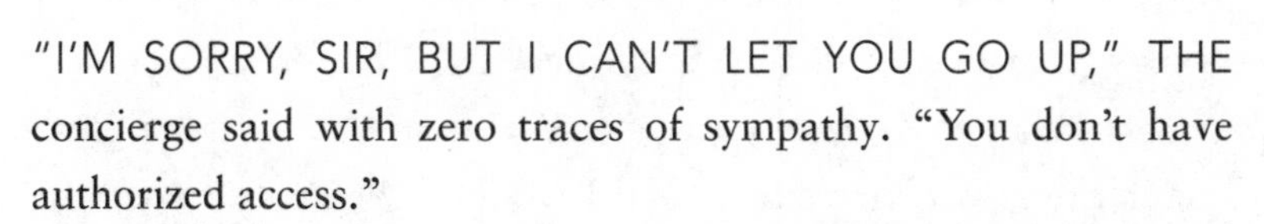

"I'M SORRY, SIR, BUT I CAN'T LET YOU GO UP," THE concierge said with zero traces of sympathy. "You don't have authorized access."

"I've been coming here for weeks." I tamped down my frustration in favor of a smile. Catch more flies with honey than vinegar and all that. "Apartment 14C. Call her. Please."

"I'm sorry, sir." This concierge was different from the one who'd let me up when I thought something had happened to Sloane, and he proved remarkably resistant to my powers of persuasion. "Ms. Kensington specifically left instructions stating that no guests are to be admitted without her explicit written approval."

"She's my girlfriend. I have written approval," I said. I wasn't *technically* lying. We were dating, and I didn't know for sure that she *hadn't* added my name to her list of approved guests. "Perhaps you lost it."

"I didn't."

"Perhaps another concierge lost it."

"They didn't."

I gritted my teeth. Fuck honey. I wanted to shove this guy's head in a bucket full of raw vinegar, but I didn't have the time for petty violence *or* arguments.

"Let me up, and this is yours." I slid a hundred-dollar bill across the counter.

The concierge stared at me, stone-faced. He didn't touch the money.

I added another hundred to the pile.

Nothing.

Three hundred. Four hundred.

Goddammit. What was wrong with him? No one said no to Benjamin.

"Ten thousand cash." That was all I had in my wallet. "That's tax-free money if you let me up for just a few minutes."

I could bypass him physically, but without a resident key card, the elevator wouldn't budge, and I wouldn't be able to open the door to the stairwell.

"Sir, this is unnecessary and inappropriate," he said calmly. "I do not accept bribes. Now, I must insist you vacate the premises, or security will have to escort you out."

He nodded at the pair of Hulk-sized security guards who'd seemingly popped up out of nowhere.

Sloane's building *would* be guarded by two stone mountains and the only incorruptible concierge in Manhattan.

However, I wasn't leaving without seeing her, which meant I needed a plan C. I scanned the lobby, searching for another plausible avenue when my eyes fell on a small plaque mounted on the wall.

The Lexington: An Archer Group Property.

My pulse jumped. *Archer Group.*

There was only one person who could help me in that moment.

Asking him for a favor wasn't the smartest idea considering I'd just burned down one of his properties, but beggars couldn't be choosers.

One call to an annoyed Alex Volkov and one very bitter concierge later, I stepped out into Sloane's hall.

Surprisingly, Alex hadn't given me a hard time, though I suspected he was saving that for our meeting. But I'd worry about that tomorrow; I had something more urgent to attend to.

I rapped my knuckles against Sloane's door.

No answer, but she was in there. I could feel it.

Another knock, my gut contorting into more and more knots as the minutes passed. It wasn't like her not to answer the door. Perhaps the concierge called up to warn her I was coming?

I was about to call her just to see if I could hear her phone ring when I heard it—a tiny rustle of movement that cut off as quickly as it'd started. If I'd shifted, or if the elevator had dinged in that moment, I wouldn't have heard it, but I did, and it was enough to pour fresh energy into my efforts.

A third, harder knock. "Open the door, sweetheart. Please."

I wasn't sure if she heard me, but an eternity later, footsteps approached and the door swung open.

My heart stuttered beneath the blow of seeing Sloane again. The past week had felt like months, and I drank her in like a lost wanderer stumbling onto a desert oasis. She was bare-faced and in silk pajamas, her hair twisted into a bun, her eyes wary as she kept a hand on the doorknob.

"Hi," I said.

"Hi."

The seconds ticked by, tainted by the bitterness of our last conversation.

"Can I come in?" I finally asked. It'd been a long time since we were this uncomfortable around each other, and the tension cast a shadow over the entire hall.

"Now isn't a good time," Sloane said, avoiding my eyes. "I have a lot of work to do."

"On the Sunday after Christmas?"

Silence.

I rubbed a hand over my face, trying to piece together the right words in the right way. There were a thousand things I wanted to tell her, but in the end, I opted for simple and honest.

"Sloane, I didn't mean what I said last week," I said softly. "About you having no emotions. I was frustrated and upset, and I took it out on you."

"I know."

I faltered; I hadn't expected that. "You do?"

"Yes," Sloane said stiffly. She went a teeny bit pink around her ears. "I should apologize too. I shouldn't have pushed you so hard right after the fire. That was...that wasn't what you needed at the time."

"You were just trying to help." I cleared my throat, still feeling ill at ease. "And I'm sorry for not reaching out on Christmas. Honestly, I was too ashamed to just call you like nothing had happened, and I figured you wouldn't want to discuss the fire during the holiday..." It wasn't the best excuse, but none of my recent actions could be classified as smart.

"You weren't the only one who didn't reach out. It's a two-way street." Sloane slid her pendant along its chain.

"Maybe we can have a belated celebration," I said. "The ice rinks are still open."

"Maybe." She was so quiet, I almost didn't hear her.

I paused, trying to paint why this whole thing felt wrong. At first glance, we were on the same page. I'd apologized, she'd apologized, everything was great. So why was tension still hanging over us like a storm cloud? Why wasn't Sloane meeting my eyes? Why did she sound so fucking sad?

The only thing I could think of was…

No. A surge of panic seized my limbs, but I covered my suspicions with a forced smile. "So we're okay. I know we have a lot of stuff to figure out regarding the club, but you and me, we're okay?"

I searched her face for a hint, *any* hint, that she agreed.

I didn't find it, and when she opened her mouth, a part of me already knew what she was going to say.

"Xavier…"

"Don't." I clenched my jaw. "It's not time yet."

"Our trial period ends in two days." Sloane's eyes finally met mine, and it was like looking at a sea of stars in the night sky. They gave the illusion they were within reach, but if I extended my hand and tried to grasp those fleeting emotions, they'd slide through my fingers like whispered taunts. "What happens then?"

"Then we end the trial and start dating for real." I didn't bother playing coy. "That's what I want, Luna. Tell me that's not what you want too."

I didn't know a lot of things, but I knew her. I knew she had feelings for me. I'd tasted them in her kiss, heard them in her laughs, felt them in the way she'd pressed her body to mine. They weren't the hallucinations of a man in love; they were real, and I'd be damned if I let them slip away.

But when Sloane straightened her shoulders and her expression cooled, I had a sneaking suspicion that the feelings I'd thought would bring us closer would end up being the very things that drove her away.

"I didn't want to do this today, but since you're here, we might as well." Her knuckles whitened around the doorknob. "We had fun; I'm not denying that. But our trial period is all but over and we won't..." She swallowed. "We won't work in the long term."

A strange roar erupted in my ears. "What are you saying?" I asked quietly.

I knew exactly what she meant, but I wanted to hear it from her mouth. I wasn't giving her an easy way out on this.

"I'm saying there's no extension." Sloane's mouth wavered for a split second before firming. "I want to break up."

Sloane

I was freezing.

The heater was running at full strength, but goosebumps coated my arms and legs, and the doorknob felt like ice in my hand.

Or maybe the cold was coming from the hallway, where Xavier stood still as a winter night, his face carved with shock.

As I watched, the sharp edges hardened into determination, and he shook his head. "No."

I closed my eyes, wishing I were anywhere but here, that his plea through the door hadn't weakened my defenses so much, I'd abandoned my original plan to break up with him over the phone.

That wouldn't have been the bravest thing to do, but it was preferable a dozen times over to witnessing Xavier's hurt disbelief in person.

I opened my eyes again and steeled my resolve against the voice banging inside my head, screaming *don't do this*.

I had to. If we didn't break up now, we'd have to break up someday, and I'd rather cut ties before I was in too deep.

You're already in too deep, the voice snarled.

I ignored it.

"Don't make this any harder than it has to be," I said. "The terms were clear. We date for two months, then decide whether we're going to work. Well, those two months are over, and I've decided we won't."

"*You* decided. I remember you saying something about this being a two-way street." Xavier's cold stillness fell away and revealed a blaze of emotion in his eyes. "Give me a good reason why we won't work."

"We're too different."

"That wasn't a problem when we were dating. Opposites have long-term relationships all the time, Luna. It's not a deal-breaker."

"It is for us." Something large and jagged had taken up residence in my throat, and every word scraped painfully on its way out. "I'm not meant for long-term relationships, okay? I get bored. Things don't work out. What we have is already complicated because we work together, and it's easier for both of us if we break up before we're forced to."

I'd rehearsed my speech a hundred times over the past two days, but it rang as false now as it had the first time.

I *did* have a good reason for why we wouldn't work, but I couldn't tell him because I was terrified—of him, of this, of *us*.

He wouldn't knowingly hurt me, not right now, but if I gave him an inch, he'd take a mile. I'd succumb to his promises, his power over me would solidify, and one day, I'd wake up and realize he could break me into more pieces than anyone else. His offhanded comment, delivered in the heat of the moment last week, had sent me reeling. What would happen if he *tried*?

Everything was fine during the honeymoon phase of a relationship, but that phase had to end eventually, and I refused to leave myself vulnerable when that happened.

No matter how much it hurt in the short term, breaking up was the best thing to do in the long term.

"Forced?" Xavier's eyes flashed at my reply. "Who's going to force us, Sloane? Your family, our friends, the world? They can all fuck themselves."

"Stop. This is the smart—"

"I don't give a damn about smart. I give a damn about us and the fact you're lying to me."

Heat seared my cheeks and chased away the bone-rattling cold. "I am *not* lying," I snapped, trying to hide the waver in my voice. "Do you remember when we ran into Mark at the restaurant? You said he couldn't take a hint. Don't repeat his mistake."

It was a low blow, and my chest wrenched at Xavier's resulting flinch.

I didn't want to hurt him, but if that was what it took, that was what I'd do—no matter how much it destroyed me in the process as well.

"Maybe, but there's a crucial difference between me and Mark." Xavier stepped toward me, and I instinctively took a step back. His broad shoulders filled the doorway, and though he hadn't officially entered my apartment, his presence permeated every molecule of air until all I could see, smell, *taste* was him.

His earthy scent grabbed hold of my lungs and squeezed, and the memory of his skin beneath my touch was so vivid that, for a moment, I felt as though I could reach out and trace the echoes of our shared moments in the air.

"Let me tell you a secret," he said quietly.

I crossed my arms, but it did nothing to stave off a cascade of shivers when he spoke again.

"You kept asking me why I called you Luna. I didn't tell you because I was afraid it would send you running for the hills. Even before we kissed, before we were *anything* other than a publicist and her client, you were a light in my life. A persistent, sometimes scary one, but a light all the same." Xavier's throat bobbed with a hard swallow. "Luna is short for *mi luna*. My moon. Because no matter how dark the nights got, you were always there, shining so brightly that I always found my way through."

Prickles swarmed behind my eyes. My chest was a tightly wound spool of emotions, but I didn't touch it, afraid that a single unraveled thread would send me crashing down.

"I don't know when it happened. One day, you were someone I was stuck with if I wanted to keep my current lifestyle. The next, you were…*you*." A sad smile touched Xavier's lips. "Beautiful, brilliant, and so damn caring beneath that mask you present to the world. You can try to hide it, but it's too late. I've seen the real you, with all its perfect and broken pieces, and I love every single one of them."

The prickles reached the point of unbearable. They danced in front of my vision, blurring Xavier's face and turning my world into a watercolor of emotions. Every dot stabbed at me, and I was sure that if he kept talking, and I didn't escape, I would bleed out right here on my living room floor.

"Stop," I whispered.

He didn't.

"I've been falling in love with you day by day for years, and I didn't even know it," he said, his voice thick. "Well, now I know it."

"Don't." The room constricted around me, squeezing the air from my lungs, and the simple act of breathing became an arduous task.

My head swam. I wanted to hold on to something for steadiness, but Xavier was the only thing within reach, and touching him would obliterate me.

He pressed on, uncaring that he was flaying me alive.

"I love *you*, Sloane. Every fucking inch of you, and I want you to look me in the eyes and tell me you don't feel the same. Tell me you aren't running because you're scared of getting hurt again. Tell me you *truly* believe we can't work when the past two months have been the best of my life. Even with my father's death, and Perry, and a dozen things that went wrong, they were still perfect because you were there."

Trembles racked my body. The pressure was getting worse, and I couldn't contain it for much longer.

"That doesn't matter." The lie tasted so bitter I almost choked on it. "I want you to leave. Please."

"That's not what I asked you," he said fiercely. "You've *always* been honest with me. Don't—"

"I am being honest!" Something heavy and frantic seized control of my body and pushed at Xavier's chest. He couldn't be here. He couldn't see me when I broke, and I knew with bone-deep certainty that I was on the razor's edge of breaking. "I *don't want you here*. You love me, and I don't feel the same toward you. So *go*!"

Pushing him was like shoving a brick wall, but a tidal wave of panic imbued me with superhuman strength.

I didn't see it happen. I just knew that one second, he was in the doorway; the next, I'd slammed the door in his face. The lock had barely clicked shut before I sank to the floor, my limbs quaking as I tried to tune out his knocks and pleas.

The prickles coalesced into a sheet of white and gray, and the hollow ache that yawned inside me was so overwhelming, it felt like my very core had crumbled into dust.

I'd never felt this level of despair, not even when I walked in on Bentley and Georgia all those years ago.

I give a damn about us and the fact you're lying to me.

I couldn't see Xavier through the blur in my eyes at the end, but I'd heard the anguish in his voice and felt it in the air. It'd mirrored the same pain rushing in to fill the emptiness in my chest because he was right. I *had* lied to him.

I cared. More than cared.

He made me feel everything when I'd thought I could feel nothing, and that realization led to an undeniable truth: I *loved* him, so much so that I couldn't breathe, and I'd pushed him away because I knew love would only end in heartbreak.

The journey wasn't worth the destination.

I didn't know how long I stayed there, my back to the door and the weight of what I'd done anchoring me to the ground, but it was long enough that Xavier's pounding had faded into silence.

Something warm and wet slid down my cheek.

It was such a foreign sensation that I didn't touch it, afraid of what I'd find, until it dripped from my chin.

I pressed my fingers to my face. A drop of the substance trickled onto my lips, and it wasn't until I tasted its salty grief that I realized what it was.

A tear.

CHAPTER 41

MY FAMILY HADN'T CALLED ME *PEQUEÑO TORO* FOR nothing.

Last night, I'd stayed outside Sloane's apartment until her neighbor came home and threatened to call the cops. Normally, that wouldn't have deterred me—the worst they could do was charge me with loitering—but Sloane wasn't going to change her mind and throw herself into my arms the same day we broke up.

I needed a new strategy.

I spent the entire train ride to DC that morning agonizing over it. Sloane said she didn't love me, but her reaction hadn't been that of someone who didn't care. I'd never seen her so distraught, and as much as it killed me to know she was hurting, her pain was a good thing. It meant she felt *something*; if she didn't, she would've simply dismissed me the way she had Mark.

Ironically, the stronger her feelings, the more likely she was to shut down and pull away. Sloane was afraid of getting hurt again, but no amount of reassurances on my part could convince her she wouldn't get hurt somewhere down the line thanks to Fuckface Bentley. She had to come to that conclusion herself.

The question was, how could I get through to her?

Because there was no way in fucking hell I was taking our breakup at face value. Not when it looked like it'd destroyed Sloane as much as it had me.

I don't want you here. *You love me, and I don't feel the same toward you. So* go*!*

A vise squeezed my chest. I rubbed a hand over my face, trying to wipe the image of Sloane's tortured expression from my mind.

"Would you like another moment to daydream about frivolity, or can we commence our meeting?" A cold voice dragged me back to the present. It was as welcoming as a sea of cacti, but at least it successfully banished thoughts of my breakup—for now.

Alex Volkov observed me from the other side of his desk. He radiated displeasure, but he was here, which was a semi-good sign.

"I had to postpone a family trip to the zoo to be here, so let's make this quick," he said. "You have ten minutes."

I tried to imagine Alex pushing a stroller around the zoo, but the only way I could see him stepping foot in the place was if he was magically transformed into one of those vicious jungle cats they kept in locked enclosures.

"Look on the bright side," I said, attempting levity. "I'm sure the zoo will still be there in ten minutes unless the Smithsonian *really* pissed someone off."

He stared at me, expressionless, but I could've sworn the temperature dropped thirty degrees.

Right. I forgot Alex possessed roughly the same amount of humor as a rock.

I gave him a quick overview of what happened with the fire. He knew all this already, but the recap provided an opportunity to gauge his reaction in person.

He'd been oddly calm about the destruction of one of his most valuable properties. Granted, he wasn't exactly an emotive person, but I'd expected *something*. A strong rebuke, a sniper across from my townhouse...hell, even a frown.

He didn't give me any of that.

"I see," he said after I finished. The bitter residue of guilt lingered in my mouth, but it vaporized at his next words. "I looked into it. The fire wasn't the result of a freak electrical accident. It was sabotage."

Sabotage. The word detonated like an atomic bomb.

Shockwaves rippled through the room, and I stared at Alex, sure he was joking if it weren't for the fact he didn't joke. Ever. "What are you talking about?"

"My team investigated the fire since I can't trust those insurance idiots to produce a single ounce of competence," Alex said. "The wiring was old, but it didn't explode by itself. Someone gave it a hand."

"There was no one in there except me, Vuk, Willow, and the construction crew," I said. "The crew members were thoroughly vetted by Harper."

"No, it wouldn't have been one of them. Whoever did it snuck in before the workers arrived, shaved off the insulation on the remaining good wires, and repositioned them to maximize their chances of exposure."

Christ. It was like I'd gone to sleep and woke up in the middle of a Nate Reynolds movie. "Your team managed to ascertain all that from a burned-down vault?"

Alex's smile didn't contain a single trace of warmth. "I hire the best."

If he was worried about the saboteur targeting another one of his buildings, he didn't show it.

Sabotage. I turned the word and its implications over in my head.

"That doesn't make sense," I said. "Who would want to

sabotage the vault to the point of committing arson?" The nightlife industry was cutthroat, but most of the players shied away from outright crimes unless they were in the mob. If they *were* in the mob, the type of establishment they ran was vastly different from mine; there was no threat there.

"I have my fair share of enemies. So does Vuk. So do you." Alex sounded bored, like we were discussing the weather instead of arson. "Hunting down the culprit will take time, but I will find them."

Finally, there it was—a speck of icy rage that belied Alex's outward composure. Whoever the culprit was, they were in for a world of pain once he tracked them down.

"I don't have enemies," I said. Competitors, sure. People who didn't like me, absolutely. But enemies? I wasn't in the mafia. I didn't have people who wanted to kill me or hurt the people close to me.

"Everyone that's rich and in the public eye has enemies, even if they don't know it," Alex said. He tapped his watch; it'd been ten minutes. "I'll take care of the saboteur. You take care of repairing the damage."

I'd forgotten about my impending decision regarding the club's future; I'd been too distracted by Sloane and this meeting with Alex.

Kai had a point about my martyr act, but unless I discovered a way to freeze time, I would never get the club up and running by the deadline.

I told Alex as much.

"That bears no relevance to our situation," he said, checking his watch again. "Were you not the one who told Markovic you'll get it done, no matter what? 'If you say no, the club will still open. If I don't secure the vault, I'll find another location. It's not ideal, but business isn't always about the ideal. It's about getting things done, and I'll get it done with or without you.'"

I grimaced. It was eerie hearing my conversation with another person quoted back to me verbatim.

"You wanted something of your own; well, this is your chance," Alex said. "Unless, of course, you lied and only started the club for your inheritance. If that's the case, I gravely misjudged you, and I do not like being wrong." His green eyes glinted with warning. "Make a decision by noon on January first."

He stood and left me alone in his office, his words hanging like a guillotine ready to fall.

There was nothing like being reprimanded by a man who did not give one flying fuck about you to put things into perspective quickly.

Alex may have been invested in the club, but he wasn't personally invested me, and he'd cut straight to the heart of the matter.

He was also right. The Vault started as a necessity because of my inheritance but it quickly became a passion project. I *liked* building a business. I loved the thrills, the challenges, and the creation of something that was mine. Was I really going to let an arbitrary deadline ruin that for me?

I didn't need until January first to get my answer; I had it by the time I returned to New York later that day.

However, I held off on telling Alex; I had another, much more urgent matter to attend to. My trial period with Sloane officially ended tomorrow, and I needed to get through to her before then.

My meeting with Alex had preoccupied me enough to dull the pain of last night, but when Sloane's office building came into view, a gut-wrenching ache resurfaced.

I want to break up.

You love me, and I don't feel the same toward you.

The ache sharpened into a knife and twisted. Other men might've given up after being so thoroughly dismissed, and I would've had I thought she meant it. But the only thing worse than hearing those words come out of Sloane's mouth was seeing her face when she said them. Her anguish had mirrored mine, and I hated how much hurt she had to have experienced to be so afraid of love.

Or maybe I was just fucking delusional.

Either way, it wasn't over yet. There were minutes left until the buzzer, but I still had a chance to turn the tide and score a comeback victory. That shred of hope was the only thing that kept me going because the thought of losing Sloane...

It's not going to happen. You won't lose her.

I couldn't. Not when I'd just found her. Not when losing her meant losing a crucial piece of myself in the process.

My heart pounded painfully as I entered the building, but anxiety melted into confusion when I arrived at Kensington PR and found Jillian and several junior publicists crowded outside Sloane's office, their ears literally pressed to the door.

"What...?"

"Shh." Jillian placed a finger over her mouth. *Perry,* she mouthed.

Oh, fuck.

I came up beside her and snuck a peek through the window. Sloane hadn't fully closed her blinds, revealing a glimpse of the drama unfolding inside.

Perry Wilson, the gossip guru himself, gesticulated wildly. It was only the second time I'd seen him in person, and once again, I was struck by how ordinary he looked.

Signature blond highlights and pink bow tie aside, he could've passed for any random man I passed on the street. He couldn't be taller than five-five or five-six, his scrawny frame squeezed into a blazer and jeans. For someone with so much bravado behind the keyboard, he was awfully small in person.

His voice, however, was loud enough to bleed through the door. "I know it was you. *You're* the one who planted those false tips for me."

Sloane sat behind her desk, observing him with a bored expression. "Perry, darling, I have no idea what you're talking about. I'm a publicist with legitimate business concerns. I don't have time to engage in the type of subterfuge you're accusing me of." She tapped her phone. "You're already being sued for libel. Don't add slander to the mix."

Perry's face turned the same color as his tie. "I have eyes and ears everywhere, Sloane. They told me Tilly overhead *you* discussing the affair at the Russos' holiday party. Now Soraya's stupid minions have gotten me banned from social media, and that libel suit is bullshit."

"Good. Then you shouldn't be concerned about it," Sloane said. "As for your eyes and ears, perhaps they should've fact-checked for you before you uploaded that post. This is the twenty-first century, Perry. If you can't handle a twenty-two-year-old and her fans, you might want to switch careers. I hear *Fast and Furriness* is looking for a new copywriter."

Perry quaked with indignation. "You won't get away with this."

"Please, spare me the cliché villain lines." Sloane sighed. "I have clients to attend to, and you have advertisers to appease before they all flee your sinking ship."

The blogger was so furious his voice dropped to near inaudible levels, and I only heard snippets with what he said next.

Bitch...check in with your star client...not talking about the one you're fucking.

Jillian and the other publicists scattered from the door. A minute later, Perry stormed out in a tornado of pink and cologne.

"Hey, man." I clapped my hand on his shoulder hard enough

to make him stumble as he passed. "Sorry to hear about your troubles. Good luck at *Fast and Furriness.*"

Perry squawked with outrage but was smart enough not to confront me physically. He stomped toward the elevator, looking not unlike a child throwing a temper tantrum, and I couldn't believe *this* was the man who'd caused so many powerful people so much distress over the years.

It was like peeking behind the curtain and seeing the real Wizard of Oz. Disappointing.

Jillian giggled and didn't stop me when I walked into Sloane's office and closed the door behind me.

With Perry gone, the stiffness eased from her shoulders, but they tightened again when she saw me.

Sloane was obviously exhausted, but even with faint purple smudges beneath her eyes and lines of tension bracketing her mouth, she was the most beautiful woman I'd ever seen. It had nothing to do with her looks and everything to do with who she *was.*

Smart, fierce, and so damn mine.

I should've recognized it sooner, and I would wait forever until she did too.

"So, Perry's really done, huh?" I asked.

It was odd to talk about something as banal as Perry when the devastation from last night's conversation hadn't fully settled. The wreckage floated around us, each shard a silent reminder of what was at stake.

However, jumping right into the reason I was here would be a surefire way to make Sloane shut down. I needed to ease into things, and honestly, I'd take any excuse to talk to her again, no matter the topic.

"For now, but people like him always find a way to survive." Sloane tapped her pen against her desk, her eyes wary. "We don't have a meeting scheduled for today."

"No, we don't."

Tap. Tap. Tap.

The nervous rhythm mirrored the tension dripping in the air. It was so potent I could taste it in the back of my throat, and while I wanted nothing more than to grab her and kiss the hell out of her, I had to be smart about this.

I had one last chance, and I wasn't going to fuck it up.

Sloane's throat bobbed with a swallow. "Xavier..."

"Don't worry. I didn't come to make a scene." I pushed my hands into my pockets and fisted them to keep myself from reaching for her. "I came to tell you three things. One, I met with Alex this morning about the fire. He said it was sabotage."

The tapping stopped. I could practically see the wheels in her head spinning as she processed this bit of information. "Sabotage. By who?"

"Still unclear." I summarized the meeting for her. "It's Alex, so he'll figure it out and put in safeguards to ensure something similar doesn't happen again while I repair the club."

Sloane stilled, her eyes flaring with surprise and a wary hope that poured fresh fuel into mine. Hope meant she still cared, and if she still cared, that meant an infinitesimally larger chance of winning my upcoming gamble.

"That's the second thing," I said more quietly. "I'm going ahead with the Vault. You and Alex were both right, and I don't care if I pass the deadline and don't get my inheritance. That's no longer what the club is about. I just needed a kick in the ass to realize it." A sardonic smile crossed my mouth. "Or two."

Sloane's gaze flickered with another emotion I couldn't name before she slammed a steel gate over it. "Good. There's no use wasting the effort you've already put into it."

"Final thing." I took a step closer, my eyes trained on hers.

"Our trial period doesn't end until tomorrow, which means we're not over yet. Not officially."

Sloane's grip on her pen tightened. "I already made my decision."

"It doesn't count when there's still time to change your mind."

Her mouth quivered for a split second before flattening into a straight line. "Don't make this harder than it has to be."

Pain laced her voice, and that was enough to spur me on. I hated seeing her hurt, but if that meant I was getting through to her, I would bear it.

"I'll make it as hard as I can," I said fiercely. "I love you, Sloane, and if you think I'm letting you go that easily, you're mistaken. I've spent half my life running from the hard stuff and taking the easy way out because I'd never wanted anything enough to *work* for it." I swallowed. "Then I met you, and I finally understood what people meant when they said love is worth fighting for. I know it sounds like a cliché, and if you heard this is a movie, you'd probably write a scathing review about it"—Sloane choked out a laugh—"but I mean it. I've learned to fight for what's important, and there's *nothing* in this world that's more important to me than you. Not the club, not my inheritance, not my reputation."

I took another step closer, desperate to touch her but knowing I couldn't.

"I know you're afraid," I said. "Hell, I am too. I've never been in love, and I've never *wanted* to be in love. I have no idea what people do in these situations, which is probably why I'm here, making an ass of myself." A hint of self-deprecation slipped into my voice. "If you truly don't feel anything for me, then I accept that." *Even if it kills me.* "But if you do, even the tiniest bit, then don't do what I used to do. Don't run away from what could be because you're afraid of what *might* be."

It was blunt, but Sloane had always responded best to directness. It was one of the many things I loved about her.

"I won't lie and say I know what our future looks like. No one does. But I *do* know that whatever happens, we'll figure it together," I said softly. "We always do."

Sloane didn't move, didn't speak, but her eyes shone with suspicious brightness.

I took a deep breath and braced myself for what I was about to say. "Tomorrow, top of the Empire State Building. Meet me at midnight." That was when our trial period officially expired. "If you don't show…" I swallowed past the glass shards in my throat. "I'll know what your answer is, and I'll never mention this again."

Sloane let out another watery-sounding laugh. "Are you *Sleepless in Seattle*-ing me?"

"*Gossip Girl*, actually. Doris was a big fan," I said with a fleeting smile. Then my face sobered, and my voice softened into something more tender. "I know you think happily ever afters are unrealistic, Luna, but they don't have to be. You just have to believe in them enough for yourself."

She didn't respond. I hadn't expected her to, but when I walked out, my heart knotted in my throat, I couldn't help but second guess my strategy.

I'd taken a huge gamble by giving Sloane an ultimatum, but we were the same in as many ways as we were different. She needed that push.

I just hoped that in doing so, I hadn't made the worst mistake of my life.

CHAPTER 42

Sloane

I COULDN'T STOP CHECKING THE TIME.

It was one in the afternoon; there were eleven hours until my trial period with Xavier expired, but the looming deadline killed my appetite as I pushed my salad around my plate.

If you don't show up, I'll know what your answer is, and I'll never mention this again.

The end of our relationship aside, what would happen if I didn't show up? Would we stop working together? Would I never see him again? Would the past two months disappear into the past like they'd never happened?

I should be happy about that. That was what I *wanted*, but if that were the case, why did I feel nauseous?

The few forkfuls I'd forced down earlier churned in my stomach. Cutting all ties with Xavier would be the smartest thing to do. We couldn't return to our old working relationship when I knew how his lips tasted, and how he felt inside me, and how he held me like—

"Hellooo. Earth to Sloane." Isabella waved her hand in front of my face, severing my spiraling thoughts. "Where are you?"

"Sorry." I attempted another bite of food. It tasted like cardboard. "I was just thinking."

"About tonight?" Alessandra's eyes gleamed with knowing concern. "Have you decided what you're going to do?"

I usually grabbed takeout for lunch on workdays, but I'd asked my friends to meet me at a proper restaurant because I needed their advice. I'd filled them in on Xavier's ultimatum, and their reactions had run the gamut.

Isabella wanted me to meet him, no questions asked. Vivian said I should go with my heart, which wasn't helpful, because my heart had a habit of making terrible choices. Alessandra was surprisingly neutral, but out of everyone at the table, she understood how important it was to make a decision on my own time, not anyone else's.

The problem was, I didn't have much time; I had hours at most.

"No." I flicked a piece of walnut to the side; I'd forgotten to tell the server not to include them in my salad.

I didn't know what dishes you like best, so I ordered a bit of everything. None with walnuts, though.

Unshed emotion crowded my throat. I hadn't cried since last night, and I hadn't told my friends about the tears. They weren't relevant; they were a physical symptom, that was all.

I didn't let myself examine what they were a physical symptom *of*.

"I shouldn't go. I'm not going to go," I said with half-hearted conviction. "Meeting him would be stupid, right? We'll break up eventually, and it's better to rip the Band-Aid off now than later down the road."

Isabella frowned, Alessandra quietly cut her chicken, and Vivian took a sip of her water without meeting my gaze.

Ugh. I loved my friends, but obviously, they were biased. They were all disgustingly in love, and while they'd gotten *their* happily ever afters, they didn't count. They *wanted* to be in love, and they didn't self-sabotage just by virtue of who they were. I would never be the soft, loving type that did well in relationships, and I was perfectly happy being alone.

Perfectly. Happy.

I stabbed at a strawberry with so much force the plate wobbled. "Anyway, enough about my dating life," I said. "Did I tell you about Perry's visit to my office yesterday? He was *fuming*."

I regaled the table with Perry's satisfying breakdown, and they made all the right noises of encouragement, but I could tell they were still stuck on my Xavier dilemma.

If I were honest, so was I.

My voice petered out toward the end when I remembered what happened after Perry left. Xavier had shown up, and my heart had slammed against my ribs like it was desperate to break free.

I know you think happily ever afters are unrealistic, Luna, but they don't have to be. You just have to believe in them enough for yourself.

My stomach roiled again, and I stood abruptly, startling my friends from their food.

"I'm going to the restroom," I said. "I'll be right back."

I ducked my head and speed walked to the ladies' room. The farther I walked, the easier it was to breathe and block out memories of Xavier—the warmth in his eyes, the rawness of his voice, the brief glimpse of his dimples after my *Sleepless in Seattle* comment. The dining room chatter helped, too. There was nothing like a little white noise to repress unwanted thoughts.

I'd chosen to meet my friends at Le Boudoir, which had cleaned up its reputation after a guest died at its soft opening last year. The coroners had ruled it a natural death, and the morbid event added a strange mystique to the restaurant, which bustled with surprising activity for this time of year.

In one corner, Buffy Darlington reigned over a table of distinguished old-money socialites. In another, Ayana sat with her date, a good-looking man with dark hair and an intense expression. They appeared to be having a heated discussion so I didn't say hi; I wasn't in the mood for small talk, anyway.

I pushed open the door to the restroom and used the facilities. My skin was cold and clammy, but by the time I washed my hands and reapplied my lipstick, I'd gotten my nausea under control. Sort of.

I checked my phone again. *Ten and a half hours.*

I swallowed the bile rising in my throat. That was plenty of time. Surely I'd—

"Sloane."

My head snapped toward the door. I recognized that voice, and of all the people I didn't want to see now or ever, she ranked in the top five.

My stepmother walked toward me, wearing a Chanel tweed suit and the expression of someone who'd just swallowed a lemon whole.

I wiped my face of any inner turmoil. "Caroline."

I'd never subscribed to the idea that women needed to visit the restroom in packs, but I wished one of my friends were with me, if only so I didn't get charged with aggravated assault for clawing Caroline's eyes out.

She'd fired Rhea, kept Pen from seeing me, and was an all-around terrible human being. Given my current mood, she was lucky if I didn't stab her with my heel.

Her own heels clacked against the tile floors as she came up beside me. She reached into her bag and fished out a lipstick.

"I didn't expect to see you here on a Tuesday afternoon," she said, reapplying the understated mauve color with precision. "Aren't you supposed to be at that little job of yours?"

"My little *job* happens to be one of the top PR firms in the country." I gave her a brittle smile. "Not everyone marries up for money. Some of us are smart enough to earn it."

"How quaint." Caroline recapped her lipstick and dropped it in her purse. "As much as I love hearing about your *plebeian* adventures..." She wrinkled her nose. "I have something else I'd like to discuss."

"I don't know where you can polish your horns. Perhaps you should google *demon services* and go from there."

She pursed her mouth. "Honestly, Sloane, this is why you're better off *working* than trying to find a proper husband. No respectable man would tolerate such juvenile humor."

"It's a good thing I don't like 'respectable' men, then. They have a habit of saying one thing and turning around and doing the opposite—sometimes with your sister."

Caroline's eyes narrowed at the Bentley reference, but she didn't take the bait. "This is about Penelope," she said, and just like that, my snarky quips vanished.

I hadn't gotten any updates about Pen since the one Xavier gave me. I didn't want to give Caroline the satisfaction of begging for information, but my pulse beat a frantic rhythm while I waited for her next words.

"She hasn't been acting like herself lately," Caroline said after a pause. "She barely eats, and her transition to a new nanny has been...difficult. She's normally so well-behaved."

How would you know? You barely talk to your own daughter.

I bit back the stinging retort so I didn't alienate my stepmother when she was giving me firsthand insight into what'd happened after Perry's bombshell post. The revelation that Pen wasn't eating concerned me, but I couldn't believe Caroline sounded shocked by the developments. She should *know* what the cause was.

"She misses Rhea," I said. "Rhea has been with her since she was born. She's practically a mother to her, and you sent her away in the middle of the night without a word. Of course she's upset."

Caroline tensed. I didn't think she cared about anything other than her clothes and social status, but I could've sworn I saw a flash of hurt at the *mother* comment.

"Yes, well, perhaps we were a bit hasty in our actions in that regard," she said stiffly. "However, Rhea conspired with you to sneak visits to Penelope while George and I were gone. She's untrustworthy, and her actions couldn't go unpunished."

"Untrustworthy?" I would've laughed had I not been so incensed. "If you're worried about untrustworthiness, you should look to a few other people in your household. Yes, Rhea lied by omission, but she did that for Pen. You may be happy to keep your daughter at home and pretend she doesn't exist because she's not *perfect* enough for you, but she's a child. She needs someone who cares about her, and you just took away the one person in your household who fits the bill."

Caroline's lips formed a thin slash of mauve. "Be that as it may, you understood the gravity of the situation when you walked away and *humiliated* this family years ago. Because of you, the Kensington name will forever be tainted by scandal. No one in our world forgets estrangements, Sloane, and you *chose* to give up Penelope along with the rest of your privileges. You couldn't get past your pride then, and you dragged Rhea down with you now. You have no one to blame but yourself."

"The fact that you consider access to Pen a *privilege* like she's a credit card or bank account is exactly why you're not fit to parent her," I said, my voice quiet with fury.

"Oh, get off your sanctimonious high horse," Caroline sneered. "If I weren't 'fit to parent her,' I wouldn't be talking to you right now. Trust me, I have better uses of my time than chatting up my *ex*-stepdaughter in a restaurant bathroom." She took a deep breath before saying more calmly, "As I mentioned, Penelope has been acting up. She's also been asking for you. Incessantly. And contrary to what you think, I'm not a heartless monster. She's my only daughter. I *do* care about her wants and needs."

I didn't buy the sudden loving mother act. Maybe Caroline cared a bit about Pen's wants and needs, but she cared about herself much more.

"So much so that you've ignored her since she was diagnosed with CFS," I said. I couldn't help it; I'd been dying to read Caroline the riot act for ages, and now that I had the chance, it was impossible for me to let it go.

I must've hit a nerve, because her face instantly flushed red.

"I haven't ignored her," she snapped. "I kept her at home to protect her. I hardly think she should be gallivanting around town with her condition, and you of all people should know how our world treats anyone they deem 'different' or 'not good enough.'" Her mouth twisted. "Lord knows I had a difficult time after I married George. They wouldn't let me onto any good charity boards for *years*."

"My condolences. I can't believe you survived such a terrible hardship."

"Make all the wisecracks you want, but this isn't about me or you," Caroline said through gritted teeth. "The only reason I'm even talking to you is because we've tried everything else to help Penelope, and it didn't work. We even had Georgia talk to her."

"Asking Georgia to make someone feel better is like asking a scorpion for a hug."

To my surprise, my stepmother snorted in agreement. "I've never liked your sister. She always thought she was better than me."

"She thinks she's better than everyone, and you never liked me either."

"No, but you're the only one who can get through to Penelope.

This is more than your typical child's tantrum. If she continues acting the way she has, it'll have a serious impact on her health." Caroline's gaze flitted around the bathroom. "George doesn't know I'm doing this yet, but I'm willing to make a deal. Penelope says she wants to see you, and I can make that happen if she gives up her hunger strike."

My heart stumbled at the possibility of seeing Pen again without having to sneak around, but a part of me remained wary. "What's the catch?"

Caroline wasn't altruistic enough to do this solely for Pen's benefit.

"So young yet so cynical." My stepmother produced a humorless smile. "There's no catch. Believe it or not, not everyone is out to get you all the time. Keep an eye out for a message once I've talked to George. Until then, tell *no one* about this conversation."

The echo of her offer followed me back to the table, where my friends were finishing up their lunch.

"Is everything okay?" Vivian asked as I retook my seat. "You were gone for a while."

"Yes." I reached for my glass, desperate to alleviate the uncertainty clogging my throat. Xavier, Caroline, Pen...it was too much all at once, and my head throbbed with an impending migraine. "Everything's fine."

CHAPTER 43

Sloane

WHEN IT RAINED, IT POURED.

Apparently, bad news didn't observe the holidays, because after I returned to the office, I'd gotten slammed with crisis after crisis. Jillian had checked into Perry's parting warning about Asher and found a video of Asher and Vincent DuBois getting into a fistfight. It hadn't hit the wider internet yet, and I'd spent a good two hours ensuring it never would.

Once I put out *that* fire, I'd had to deal with panicked calls from a CEO who'd been caught banging a restaurant hostess in a bathroom stall, a movie star who'd been arrested for attacking a paparazzo, and a socialite who'd left her limited-edition Dior bag somewhere between Paris and New York (I'd redirected her to her assistant. I didn't get paid enough to hunt down transatlantic luxury bag losses).

It was my busiest workday of the year, and by the time I caught my breath, it was ten at night. I'd sent Jillian home hours ago, so it was just me, a sad dinner of instant ramen, and the ominous countdown to midnight.

Two and a half hours.

I swallowed a mouthful of greasy noodles. My migraine had worsened since lunch, but that didn't stop me from doom scrolling on social media to avoid thinking about Xavier.

Yesterday, his presence had filled the room. Today, the office felt empty without him, like a film stripped of its soul.

Two hours and fifteen minutes.

I gave up eating and tossed the remaining cold noodles in the trash. I'd finished my work, so why was I here instead of at home, enjoying a nice movie with a glass of wine?

Because the Empire State Building is a twenty-minute walk away.

Because going home means you've made your choice.

Because this is the last place you saw him, and you feel closer to him here than anywhere else.

I groaned and dug the heels of my palms against my eyes.

If only I had a magic eight ball to tell me what to do. I'd always prided myself on my decisive nature, but when it came to Xavier, I was a mess.

He drove me up the wall sometimes, but he challenged me like no one else did. He pushed me outside my comfort zone while making me feel safe enough to do so, and he'd made me laugh, cry, and *feel* more than anyone else I'd ever met.

Younger me had been convinced that what I'd had with Bentley was love, but it wasn't until Xavier that I realized Bentley had been a mere prologue to the real story.

Me and Xavier, the most unlikely of couples. Opposites in so many ways, yet similar in so many others. He knew every part of me intimately—mind, body, and heart—and he loved me not despite but *because* of my flaws.

We'd seen each other at our worst, yet we'd fallen in love anyway.

A marble fist grabbed my chest and squeezed.

There's no catch. Believe it or not, not everyone is out to get you all the time. Caroline's voice wormed its way into my consciousness.

I never thought there'd be a day when she said anything helpful, but sitting there alone, in my dark office, while the man I loved waited for me minutes away, her words struck hard.

There's no catch.

I was afraid it'd hurt more if Xavier and I broke up down the road, after I'd gotten more attached, but I was *already in love with him*, and it already hurt so much I couldn't think straight. I'd cried for the first time in my life, and I was eating instant ramen alone in my office at night, for Christ's sake.

The same office where we'd met.

The same office where he'd given me the ultimatum.

The same office where I'd told Georgia the truth about Bentley. I thought I'd broken free of the hold Bentley's betrayal had on my decisions, but clearly I hadn't. I was still so afraid of getting hurt that I was willing to let a hypothetical scenario drive away the one man that I could see myself having a future with.

Don't run away from what could be because you're afraid of what might *be.*

If I were honest with myself, I knew we could work. Xavier was the only one who got me, who fit into my life seamlessly yet somehow made it better, and without him, *all* my days would be like this.

Lonely, alone, and aching for something I could've had but let slip through my fingers.

"God, I'm an idiot," I breathed.

My body made the decision a split second before my brain did. I grabbed my coat and rushed out the door before I'd truly processed what I was doing. I just knew that I had to get to the top of the Empire State Building. Right now.

Luckily, the late hour meant I didn't have to wait for the elevator to stop on every floor during the ride down. I had plenty of time to—

The lights flickered once, and the elevator came to a shuddering halt. The panel display flashed to *4* and stayed there.

"You've *got* to kidding me."

In all my years of working in the building, I'd never *once* had an elevator issue. The universe must be punishing me for my earlier indecision because there was no freaking way this was a coincidence.

I jabbed furiously at the lobby button again. Nothing.

I checked my phone. No service, and it was down to the last two percent. I'd been so caught up with work that I'd forgotten to charge it.

Dammit.

My only remaining option was to press the emergency button and pray that 1) someone was on call this late at night during the holidays, and 2) help got here quickly.

After a seemingly interminable wait, a gruff voice answered my call and promised me help was "on the way." He didn't respond to my requests for an exact time estimate.

I paced the tiny metal box and checked my watch again. *10:30 p.m.* That was fine. Even if the rescue crew took an hour, I'd make it to the Empire State Building before midnight.

God, I hoped it didn't take them an hour.

Someone somewhere out there must've heard my prayers, because two technicians showed up twenty minutes later and got me out. I stayed just long enough to thank them before I was off again.

11:05 p.m.

The late December air was a welcome breath of cold after the claustrophobia-inducing elevator, and I made it all the way to Thirty-Fourth Street, where the Empire State Building was located, before I came to a screeching halt. Metal barricades lined both sides of the street, preventing me from crossing. I'd seen them on my way here and assumed they'd end before I reached my destination; clearly, I'd been wrong.

I approached a nearby police officer and forced a polite smile. "Hi, can you tell me what's going on?" I gestured at the maddening makeshift fortress. "I'm trying to get to the Empire State Building."

"Annual Snowflake Parade." The bored-looking officer jerked a thumb over his shoulder. "Whole avenue's shut down. If you want to go to the other side of the street, you gotta go around."

I stifled a groan. How had I forgotten about one of the city's worst traditions? I'd assumed the crowds were your typical tourists flocking to the city for the holidays, but no, it was a whole parade for a completely uninteresting natural phenomena.

"Go around where?"

He told me, and I almost cursed out loud when I calculated how long it'd take me to reach the closest open cross street.

The building was *right there*. I could see it glittering across the way, its spire piercing the night sky. It would take me at least forty minutes to get there via the alternate route—maybe more, considering the crowds—but I had no choice; the parade had started, and there was no way I'd make it over the barriers without being tackled by a member of NYPD's finest.

Instead of wasting more time by arguing, I turned and booked it toward uptown. I wasn't a mathematician, but even I knew that three-inch heels plus throngs of slow-moving, selfie-taking loiterers did not equal speed *or* comfort.

When I reached the cross street, I was sweaty, frazzled, and wheezing for breath.

New Year's resolution: do more cardio. Yoga and Pilates

had not prepared me for trekking through the city in Manolo Blahniks.

The other side of the avenue was equally as crowded, but at least I didn't have to clear an entire parade. Whoever came up with the concept of parades in general deserved to be shot.

I elbowed my way past the crush of people. Halfway through, someone slammed into me so hard my teeth actually rattled. I looked up, ready to rip the guy a new one.

Green eyes, brutally handsome face. He looked oddly familiar, enough so that it gave me pause, but he disappeared before I had the chance to say a single word.

It was just as well. I didn't have time to get into it with a stranger, no matter how rude he'd been.

11:47 p.m.

I picked up my speed and nearly knocked over a woman in a white snowflake hat.

"Hey! Watch it, blondie!" she yelled.

I ignored her. Cars, people, and shop windows blurred until I finally, *finally* reached the Empire State Building's entrance.

11:55 p.m.

I sped through the security process and prayed the elevator here, at least, worked properly.

11:58 p.m.

The sleek glass lift whisked me up to the eighty-sixth floor. Up, up, up, so fast my ears popped, and then…

I was there.

Midnight.

I spilled onto the outdoor observation deck, my skin drenched in sweat and my heart pounding hard enough to break my ribs. Normally, I'd be self-conscious about the way I looked right now, but that wasn't the most important thing.

The most important thing was finding Xavier.

I scanned the deck. It was nearly empty, and for good reason. The heaters were no match against the wind, which whipped against exposed skin with vicious ferocity, and the cold was so biting, it gnawed through layers of wool and cashmere to burrow deep within my bones.

My breaths formed tiny white puffs as I circled the outdoor space. My face was numb after one lap, but that didn't compare to the ice trickling through my veins after the second check.

He wasn't here.

He'd either left—or he'd never showed up at all.

I stopped somewhere between the exit and the edge and stood there, shivering. I was so tired I was surprised my legs still worked, and the blanket of city lights beneath me took on a surreal quality, like scattered stardust waiting for a wish.

If you don't show up, I'll know what your answer is.

I'd gotten here exactly at midnight. If Xavier had left after the hour, I would've seen him. Had he gotten held up or left early for an emergency?

No. If he said he'd be here, he would—unless he'd changed his mind.

I didn't blame him. If I were him, I'd change my mind too because why would anyone…why would they…

A sob racked the air.

I'd never heard such a thing claw its way out of my throat, and it took me a minute to recognize the sound came from me.

Once the first one escaped, the rest followed, and I could no more stop them than a sand wall could stop a tsunami.

Sunday night, I'd cried silent tears, but there was nothing silent about these. They were guttural, chest-heaving sobs, the type that echoed across the deck and made the very air tremble with sympathy. They would've been humiliating had anyone seen me, but at this point, I didn't care.

I'd fucked up my relationship with the only man I'd ever truly loved, and I had no one to blame but myself.

"Luna."

Another sob shook my shoulders. I pressed a fist to my mouth, but the sound bled through anyway, and when I squeezed my eyes shut, I could feel the phantom of Xavier's warmth brushing my back.

It was worse than the cold because it wasn't real; it was my mind conjuring things to torture me.

"Luna."

I needed to get out of here. If I stayed here for a second longer, I'd either freeze to death or lose my mind, but I couldn't bring myself to move.

It's not him. It was a figment of my imagination, and—

Firm hands grasped my arms, turning me around, and there he was. Inky black hair falling carelessly over his forehead, full mouth sculpted with concern, eyes that carved a trail of warmth through my frozen tears as they examined me.

He was still holding me. His body heat seeped through my clothes, and another set of shivers rippled down my spine—this time from warmth, not the cold. Perhaps my mind could evoke sounds and images and sensations, but it couldn't create *this*: the total, all-encompassing peace that I felt only when I was with him.

Not a figment. He was real.

I cried harder.

"Hey." Alarm brightened his gaze. "It's okay. Don't cry." He rubbed away one of my tears with a gentle thumb. "Shh. It's okay."

"I thought you'd left." I hiccupped embarrassed but too relieved to do anything about it.

Understanding dawned on Xavier's face. "There was an old couple here earlier. One of them fell, so I helped them downstairs. I sent you a message in case you showed up while I was gone."

"My phone died." I hiccupped again. "I forgot to charge it."

"Ah." Xavier's voice hoarsened as he pulled me toward him. "I'm here, Luna. I didn't leave. I'm here."

His words should've reassured me, but they threw the floodgates wider. I buried my face in his chest as years of pent-up emotion poured out.

Every fear, every frustration, every heartbreak. They'd waited a lifetime to break free, and once they did, they didn't stop until every last drop of moisture had evaporated and I sagged against Xavier, emptied and exhausted.

Throughout it all, he held me, even when I ruined what was probably a very expensive sweater and made a general mess of myself.

"I'm sorry," I said through a lingering sob. "I didn't…when I…"

I wasn't the type for heartfelt speeches or flowery prose, and it was a testament to how well Xavier knew me that he didn't need either of those things to understand what I was trying to say.

"You don't have to apologize. I know." His arms tightened around me. "All that matters is you're here."

I lifted my head, my heart aching as I looked at the man who'd always been there for me, in one way or another, since he entered my life.

"I love you," I said quietly. I'd said the words before, many years ago, but this time they felt different. This time, they felt right. "I'm sorry it took me so long to admit it, and I'm sorry for pushing you away. I just…" My voice dropped even lower. "I'm scared."

I liked structure and routine. My life was built around the safe harbor I'd constructed for myself since I broke up with Bentley, and what Xavier and I had was completely uncharted waters. They could either take us to the greatest place we'd ever seen or toss us over a hundred-foot cliff with no life raft.

"I am too, but that's what makes this worth it." He pushed

a stray lock of hair out of my eyes, his touch impossibly tender. "Life would be pretty boring if we knew what was going to happen every day."

I sniffled. "Actually, that sounds wonderful. I would love that."

"Well, you color coordinate your office supplies, so I'm not surprised."

My watery laugh chased away some of the heaviness. "Smartass."

"I'm guessing that's one of the things you love about me." Xavier gave me one of those crooked, dimpled smiles I loathed and adored so much. "And your dedication to making sure your green highlighters are *always* lined up to the left of the blue ones is one of the things I love about you." He dipped his head, pressing his forehead against mine. "Love isn't about perfection, Luna; it's about imperfect people creating their own version of happily ever after. And while I don't know everything, I do know this: Every version of my happily ever after will always include some version of you."

Fresh tears welled in my throat. *Oh, God.* I'd spent twenty-something years unable to cry, and now I couldn't stop.

Xavier leaned in to kiss me, but I pulled back in an uncharacteristic bout of self-consciousness. "You don't want to kiss me right now. I'm a mess."

I purposely avoided looking at my reflection in a nearby glass pane, but I knew what I'd find—swollen eyes, red nose, mascara tracks running down my face and hair matted with sweat. Not exactly kissing material.

Xavier framed my face with his hands, stilling me. "I always want to kiss you, and you're perfect exactly the way you are."

If he were anyone else, I wouldn't have believed him, but when his mouth touched mine, every other thought melted away. The wind, the half-dried tears, the fucking journey I took tonight to get here...none of that mattered as I twined my fingers through his hair and returned his kiss with abandon.

Everything I'd gone through was worth it for this moment.

And yeah, a couple kissing on the top of the Empire State Building after their big reconciliation was such a movie cliché, but like I said...

Sometimes, the rom-coms got it right.

CHAPTER 44

Xavier

WHEN I REENTERED THE OBSERVATION DECK AND SAW Sloane standing there, my relief had been so overwhelming I couldn't move for a good five seconds.

I'd waited there for hours, and there'd been a moment—*many* moments—when I thought she wouldn't show. I'd been convinced I'd fucked up by giving her an ultimatum and that I'd ruined my chances of winning her back in the future.

But by some miracle, she *had* showed, and that was all I needed to never let her go again.

We didn't stay at the Empire State Building long. For one, it was way too fucking cold. For two…well, we had better things to do.

Sloane and I stumbled into her apartment without taking our hands or mouths off one another.

We knew each other's bodies so intimately, the buildup was almost thoughtless in its precision—a nip on the sensitive spot behind her left ear, a sliding caress from my stomach to chest and shoulders.

Our clothes left a trail from her front door to her room, where

I pushed her onto the bed and paused, taking a moment just to drink her in.

Sloane stared up at me, her lips swollen from my attentions and her eyes shining in a way that made my heart squeeze.

I love you.

Three words, uttered countless times by countless people over the centuries. Yet coming from her, they had the power to bring me to my knees.

I kissed her again, leisurely mapping a path from her mouth to her neck and shoulders. I took a prolonged detour to her breasts, where I grazed my teeth gently across her hard nipples. A shudder rolled through her body, and her moans became pleas as I licked and sucked and teased until she was begging me to fuck her.

"Please," Sloane gasped. "I need you inside me. *Xavier.*" She whimpered again when I finally released her breasts to kiss my way down her stomach to her arousal. She was so damn wet for me that it made my mouth water.

I wanted to touch her, taste her, fill her up. I wanted every single inch of her against every single inch of me, and I couldn't wait a second more.

I dove in like a man starved, licking over and inside her, tasting her deeply. My fingers worked in tandem with my mouth, and when I ran my tongue over her needy little clit, her moan shot straight to my already aching cock.

I sucked her tender flesh gently into my mouth before I flattened my tongue against her, letting her set the rhythm as her writhing took on a frenzied pace. She ground against my face, her hands tangled tight in my hair, her hips moving faster and faster until—

Sloane let out a cry of protest when I pulled away.

"Not yet, sweetheart." I grabbed a condom from the top drawer of her nightstand, rolled it onto my cock, and lined the tip up with her entrance. "I want to feel you come around me."

She narrowed her eyes, her face flushed from exertion and her denied orgasm. "Then fuck me already."

Laughter rumbled through my chest, but it devolved into a groan when I gripped her hips and finally sank inside her.

Christ. I swore I could feel every millimeter of her cunt as it took me to the hilt, and she was so tight and wet and *perfect* that I would never believe she wasn't made for me. Not when being inside her felt like sliding home after years of aimless wandering.

I fucked her with long, slow strokes, giving her time to adjust and myself time to regain control before I picked up the pace. A squeal fell out of her mouth at the first hard thrust, followed by a breathy gasp when I found the exact angle that made her claw at my back with abandon.

Her hips bucked up to match my rhythm, and the headboard slammed against the wall as I fucked us into a mess of sweat and cum. The slap of skin against skin, the sounds of Sloane's moans, the way her body shook from the force of my pounding…

It was too much.

I bit back another groan. I was about to come, but I'd be damned if I didn't take her with me.

I kept my pace steady as my fingers found her clit. It was still swollen and sensitive from my earlier attentions, and I'd barely grazed it before her muscles stiffened and her pussy squeezed around me.

Sloane's nails dug painful grooves in my skin as she came with a loud cry. I *felt* her contractions in every cell of my body, and it pulled my own climax forth in a powerful burst.

I couldn't put a name to the sound I made if I tried, but my orgasm was so intense, so all-consuming, that my mind blanked for a full minute before reality slowly returned.

I touched my forehead to hers, my chest heaving, and stayed inside her until every twitch and throb of my cock finally stilled.

It was only with the utmost reluctance that I withdrew and disposed of my condom before I settled beside Sloane again. I curled an arm around her waist and brought her close, taking comfort in the steady rhythm of her breathing.

"My neighbors are going to hate me," she murmured.

I laughed, pushing her hair back so I could admire every inch of her flushed, content face. "Only because they're jealous."

"Even ninety-year-old Irma?" She sounded skeptical.

"*Especially* ninety-year-old Irma." I paused. "But if you ever want a third..."

"*Xavier*." Sloane shoved at my chest, her laugh mingling with mine. "You're terrible."

"That's what you love about me."

"It is." She sighed. "I have questionable taste."

"I would take offense to that if I weren't so confident in my good looks and dashing personality." I pressed my lips to hers. "And if I didn't love you so much."

Sloane's face softened.

We sounded like one of those cheesy couples she loved to lambast in movies, but I didn't care, and judging by the way she pressed closer to me, neither did she.

We didn't speak again before she drifted off. My eyes were getting heavy too, but I forced myself to stay awake a while later so I could soak in the moment—my arms around Sloane, her head against my shoulder, the rhythm of our breaths rising and falling in unison.

And as my gaze traced the delicate fan of her lashes and the content curve of her lips, there was only one word running through my head.

Mine.

CHAPTER 45

Xavier

SLOANE AND I SPENT THE REST OF THE HOLIDAYS in orgasmic bliss, interrupted only by the occasional food delivery and twenty-three minutes of a so-bad-it-was-almost-good movie involving feuding families, leprechauns, and a one-eyed dog named Tobey. By the twenty-fourth minute, we'd abandoned the movie for more interesting activities.

After the new year though, we hit the ground running. She got caught up in the whirlwind of Ayana's engagement announcement, and I threw myself into getting the vault repaired as quickly as possible without cutting corners.

My birthday was no longer the end all, be all date, but I would try my damn hardest to open the club by then anyway. It was my challenge to myself.

If I accomplished it, fantastic. If not…well, my father had built his empire from pennies. I could too.

I consulted with half a dozen contractors, and the general consensus was that the damage wasn't as dire as I'd feared. Sloane had been right—the vault possessed a lot of fire-proof elements, and though it needed major work, the right team for the right price could get the job done in two months.

I happily paid that price out of my own pocket.

The new timeline meant I had to change my original design plans, but Farrah was the city's best hospitality interior designer for a reason. After several brainstorming sessions, we came up with a new concept that would take less time to implement but still fit my vision for the club. It threw *her* sourcing completely off schedule, but the hefty bonus I paid her made up for the trouble.

However, there was one more loose end I needed to tie up before I immersed myself completely in my new plans.

The second Tuesday of the year, after the city had recovered from its holiday lull and resumed its usual breakneck pace, I entered Vuk's Upper East Side mansion.

From the outside, the sprawling building resembled a fortress more than it did a home. There were enough security measures to make Fort Knox look like child's play, but the inside was the epitome of old-school luxury. Spiral staircases, arched windows, and gothic influences abounded. Every room was bigger than the last, and marble busts glared at me from their dedicated display tables as I followed the butler into Vuk's office.

The butler announced me and disappeared in a discreet flash of silver hair and starched white cotton.

Vuk's office was as dark and gloomy as the rest of the house. Black paneling, black desk, black leather furniture. The only specs of color were the emerald glass lamp on his desk and his wintry blue eyes as they tracked my approach.

It was my first time seeing him since the fire. His remote expression was a far cry from the terror I'd glimpsed before I dragged him out of the vault, but I'd never forget that look in his eyes.

Frozen. Despairing. *Haunted*.

"How are you?" I ditched my default irreverence for true concern. Vuk and I weren't friends, but he was my business partner, and he'd taken a big chance on me. Plus, he'd been caught in the fire because of me, so I felt partially responsible for whatever he'd gone through the past few weeks.

He dipped his chin, which I took as a sign he was doing well enough.

"What about Willow?" I asked.

Another dip of his chin.

"Right." I'd forgotten how difficult it was to hold a conversation with someone who refused to speak. He didn't seem inclined to express any further thoughts, so I gave him a quick summary of my revised plans for the club and an update on the opening party.

It felt strange, talking business when we'd almost died the last time we saw each other, but Vuk didn't strike me as the type who liked discussing emotions or past traumas (or much of anything, really).

He made a noise of approval when I finished and scribbled something on a sheet of paper.

Who's on the guest list for the opening?

Interesting. Of everything I'd said, that was the part I least expected him to focus on.

"I'm finalizing the invites this week," I said. "I'll email you a full list once I'm done."

I wasn't confident about pulling off the club by my birthday, but I *was* confident in my ability to throw a kick-ass party. Even if people were dubious about my business acumen, they'd show up to see me sink or swim and have a damn good time in the process.

"If there's anyone you want me to include, just let me know," I added.

I'd asked out of courtesy. Vuk didn't date, didn't have a close social circle, and didn't care about public appearances, so I didn't expect him to have anyone in mind.

However, he proved me wrong when he wrote something else on a fresh sheet of paper.

It contained only one word—specifically, one name.

Ayana.

The same Ayana who'd just gotten engaged.

My gaze snapped up to Vuk's stoic one. He didn't offer an explanation for the name, and I didn't ask.

"She's already on the list, but I'll triple check," I said, rearranging my own expression into one of neutrality.

He nodded, I left, and that was that. It was the quickest, easiest meeting I'd had since I came up with the idea for the Vault.

Honestly, it could've been a virtual meeting, but I'd wanted to check on Vuk in person and make sure he was doing okay after the fire. Obviously, he was.

I exited the mansion and flashed back to the sight of Ayana's name written in bold, black strokes. He'd pressed the pen so hard it'd punctured a tiny hole in the paper.

Then again, maybe he wasn't okay, but that was none of my business.

I had enough on my plate without taking on other's troubles, so I put Vuk's strange interest in the supermodel aside and simply made a note to myself to ensure Ayana attended the grand opening, no matter what.

Sloane

Being in love was strange.

The overall rhythm of my day to day stayed consistent—I still went to work, hung out with my friends, and dealt with wild client demands—but the details had changed. They were softer, more fluid, like moonlight slipping between the rigid blinds of my life.

I was quicker to smile and slower to anger. The air smelled fresher, and my steps were lighter. Everything seemed more tolerable with the knowledge that, no matter what happened, there was someone out there who called me his and who I called mine.

Some mornings, I lazed in bed with Xavier instead of waking up early for yoga; some nights, at his suggestion, I dipped my toe into horror films (hilarious—horror protagonists were almost uniformly dense) and slapstick comedy (not for me). Afternoons were either spent eating at my desk (on particularly busy workdays) or at a string of increasingly adorable bistros that Xavier found.

Routine became suggestion, and every suggestion became a touch more magical when Xavier was involved.

I was disgustingly happy, but even so, there were still a few rough patches of my life that needed smoothing over.

One of them was the situation with Pen and Rhea.

Two weeks after I ran into Caroline at Le Boudoir, I received a curt email requesting I meet her at my family's penthouse. Xavier had gone to see Vuk, so I showed up alone, my heart giving a little twist at the sight of the building I'd called home for half my life.

It looked exactly the same as the last time I was here, down to the hunter green awning and potted plants by the entrance.

"Miss Sloane!" The doorman greeted me with a surprised smile. "It's nice to see you again. It's been a long time."

"Hi, Clarence." I smiled back, oddly touched that he'd remembered me after all these years. He used to sneak me little pieces of candy every time I came home from school. My father had forbidden me from eating too many sweets, and he'd been furious when he found some of the wrappers in my room. I'd lied and told him I'd gotten the candy at school. "It *has* been a long time. How's Nicole doing?"

"She's great." He beamed brighter at the mention of his daughter. "She's in her first year at Northwestern. Journalism."

We chatted for a few more minutes before another resident came down, asking for a cab. I said goodbye to Clarence and took the elevator straight up to the penthouse. I didn't recognize the housekeeper who answered the door, but when I followed her through the halls, I had to battle a surprising bout of nostalgia.

The oil paintings. The cream marble floors. The scent of calla lilies. It was like someone had preserved my childhood home in a gilded time capsule, and while I didn't miss living here, I missed the happy moments I *did* have growing up.

Of course, there hadn't been many of them, and they'd been overshadowed by my father or sister in one way or another.

That was all it took to bring me back to reality.

I shook my head and brushed off the last bits of understandable but unwelcome sentimentality before I entered the living room, where my father and Caroline waited for me.

Obviously, Caroline had talked to him as promised, but neither looked too happy to see me. That was fine; I wasn't thrilled to see them either, though I was a bit surprised to see my father at home on a weekday afternoon. I supposed that was a perk of running your own company.

I sat on the couch across from them and arched a cool brow. I was dying to ask a thousand and one questions about Pen, but I wouldn't give them the upper hand by speaking first.

Tension dripped around us for several minutes before Caroline caved.

"I've discussed Penelope's situation with George," she said without preamble. "He's agreed that it's untenable. Therefore, we've decided that, despite the original terms of your departure from this family, it would be...beneficial for all parties involved if you resumed your correspondence with Penelope." Caroline sounded like someone was peeling strips of her skin off with each word.

"But let us be clear. This isn't a free pass for you to worm your way back into this family." My father's eyes blazed beneath thick, gray brows. "You disrespected us, embarrassed us, and ignored us when we gave you an opportunity to make amends. However..." His glower deepened when Caroline glared at him. "Penelope is clearly attached to you, so for her sake, we're willing to give you some leeway provided you act appropriately."

"I have no intention of *worming my way* back into this family," I said coolly. The very idea was laughable. "I'm doing perfectly fine on my own, so let *me* be clear. The only reason I'm here is because of Pen. She's the only Kensington I want anything to do with, and I have zero interest in drudging up the past. You betrayed me, I embarrassed you...I don't care. Now, let's get to the real reason why we're here, shall we?"

I wasn't worried about them kicking me out. They'd swallowed a massive amount of pride just by asking me to come, and they wouldn't throw that away before they said what they wanted to say.

My father's face turned a fascinating shade of purple. He'd thrown me off-balance at the hospital, but I hadn't planned on seeing or confronting him then. This time, I was prepared, but I no longer cared enough to engage more than I had to.

Sometime between Pen's hospitalization and now, I'd healed enough to not let him get to me by the mere fact of his existence.

"We're willing to let you see Penelope on our terms," Caroline said stiffly, drawing my attention back to her. I bristled at her choice of words, but I kept my mouth shut until she finished. "Specifically, once a month at a predetermined time, date, and location of our choosing."

"Once a week, at a predetermined time and date of *our* choosing." I shook my head when she opened her mouth to argue. "Pen is nine. She's homeschooled, which means she doesn't get many opportunities to interact with kids her age. You and George are rarely home, and you've fired the only person in this household who treats her normal. The least you can do is let her have some say in her own life."

Silence engulfed the room.

Caroline glanced at George. A telltale vein throbbed in his forehead, but he gritted out an acquiescence.

"Fine. Once a week at a time, date, and location of your choosing." He stood abruptly, his frame radiating barely suppressed anger. "We're done here."

He left without another glance at me or his wife.

Caroline took his sudden departure in stride. "In the future, you and Penelope will meet elsewhere," she said, flicking her eyes over me. "I have no interest in bringing you into our home again. As you can see, your presence has a way of creating strife."

I ignored her jab and focused on the first part. "In the future?"

Does that mean...? My stomach flipped with a sudden surge of hope.

Caroline smiled thinly. "You may want to stay in the room for a bit longer."

Then she, too, left, but she'd barely departed before a familiar girlish voice squealed, "Sloane!"

I turned my head in time to get tackled by a small blond blur. Pen's arms wrapped around my waist, and a rush of pure, indescribable relief filled my lungs.

I hugged her back, my chest so tight it hurt to breathe.

"Hey, Pen." I smiled past the swell of emotion in my throat. "I missed you."

"I missed you too." She looked up at me, her eyes

shimmering with tears. She looked a lot thinner than the last time I'd seen her. While I was glad to see her again, we needed to have a talk about her hunger strike—after I finished squeezing the hell out of her. "I didn't think I was going to see you or Rhea again," she said in a small voice.

My heart broke at the vulnerability in the words.

"Trust me. I would've found a way to see you again, one way or another." I meant it. My father and Caroline couldn't have stopped me from seeing Pen forever. I would've found a way around their stonewalling, though this was a much better alternative than other, perhaps less ethical alternatives.

I didn't think I was going to see you or Rhea again. The last part of Pen's sentence registered, and a furrow dug between my brows. What did she—

A flash of movement caught the corner of my eye. I turned, taking in the woman hovering in the doorway.

"Rhea!" I gasped. "You're back."

Pen's old nanny smiled, looking tired but satisfied. "I'm back," she confirmed. "Mrs. Kensington called me after the new year. Penny put up such a fuss that the nanny they'd hired after me quit."

"That new nanny sucked," Pen said. "She didn't even know that Blackcastle is a soccer team."

The remaining tension broke, and there were hugs and tears all around as the three of us reunited for the first time since November. Well, not tears from me—I hadn't been able to cry again since I reconciled with Xavier. I suspected I'd emptied the well so thoroughly it'd take another twenty-odd years before the phenomenon happened again.

However, the joy of seeing Pen again didn't stop me from scolding her about her hunger strike. It wasn't healthy, especially not for someone with her condition.

"What's this I hear about you refusing to eat?"

She slunk down in her seat. "I didn't *refuse* to eat. I simply skipped a few meals and threatened to skip more unless they let me see you."

"You shouldn't do that, Pen," I said gently. "Your health is the most important thing, and skipping meals can be seriously harmful."

"But they took you and Rhea away, and the threats worked!" she protested. "See? Look at us." She gestured at our trio. "Honestly, I should've tried that tactic sooner. Then we wouldn't have had to sneak around for so many years."

I sighed while Rhea shook her head. There was no arguing with Pen; she won every time.

"What do you want to do today?" I asked, switching topics. As long as she ate regularly going forward, there was no use dwelling on what was already done. "I took off work, so I'm all yours." I'd planned on going into the office that afternoon, but I'd just emailed Jillian to tell her I wouldn't be in.

Pen pursed her lips, her little face scrunched in thought. "I want to watch a movie."

My eyebrows shot up. She rarely wanted to do something as calm as watching a movie. She watched soccer games, but that was different. "A movie? Are you sure?"

"Yes." She gave a definitive nod. "I don't want to get tired too fast."

"Then a movie it is."

We decamped to the screening room, where I put on a cartoon about fairy princesses and filled her in on what'd happened since we last talked. I omitted the non-kid-friendly parts; there were some things about my life that Pen never needed to know.

"Did Xavier hurt you?" she asked. "Because I told him I'd sic Mary on him if he did."

"He did briefly, but he didn't mean it, and he apologized." I paused, my brow creasing. "Who's Mary?"

"A haunted Victorian doll."

I narrowed my eyes. "You don't *have* a Victorian doll. They creep you out."

"I know." Pen's grin was pure mischief. "But *he* doesn't know that."

I couldn't help it; I burst into laughter. She was *definitely* going to be a handful when she grew up.

Pen made it through the entire movie before her energy flagged. Now that our visits were out in the open, she didn't protest as much as she usually did when we said goodbye.

I told Rhea to call me in the next few days so we could schedule our next visit, and I waited for them to disappear into Pen's room before I left.

I made it halfway through the foyer when the front door opened, and I came face-to-face with my *other* sister.

Georgia and I froze at the same time.

She was impeccably groomed, per usual, but I detected shadows beneath her slightly bloodshot eyes. Her baby bump was finally showing, but that hadn't stopped her from wearing three-inch heels or blitzing through Madison Avenue; her arms were laden with shopping bags from a dozen designer stores.

"Moving back home into the viper's nest?" I asked. "How sentimental."

Georgia sniffed and tossed her hair, but her eyes darted left and right like she'd rather be anywhere else except here. "I'm staying here while our townhouse is getting renovated. The fumes are bad for the baby," she said, emphasizing the last word like I cared that she was pregnant and I wasn't.

Bullshit. She was too much of a control freak not to nitpick renovations from as close quarters as possible. But if the townhouse wasn't getting renovated, then why...

"Is Bentley staying here too?" I asked on a hunch.

Georgia's eye twitched, proving my hunch correct.

I didn't know what happened after I sent her the audio recording, but obviously, it was enough for her to move back home for however long. She still wore her wedding ring, but that didn't mean much. Plenty of people wore their wedding rings long after the love behind them had dissolved.

Instead of feeling triumphant or vindicated by the evidence of their relationship troubles, I felt…nothing. Because, simply put, I didn't care. Not anymore.

"You might think you did something by playing that audio in your office, but you didn't," she said when I brushed past her. "Bentley and I are weathering a few issues at this time, but we'll never leave each other. I will *always* be the one he chose over you."

I looked at her, with her perfect hair and expensive clothes and diamond ring, and felt something I never thought I'd feel toward her: pity.

I'd grown up jealous and resentful of Georgia for being our father's favorite and for playing the perfect daughter and socialite so well when I'd struggled to do the same. She'd always gotten what she wanted, and I'd thought that was something to be envied.

It wasn't until now that I realized my jealousy had been misplaced because Georgia was never *happy* with what she had; she was only happy when she took things away from other people. She spent her life trying to win invisible competitions with others because it made her feel superior when, in reality, her power plays were the ultimate sign of insecurity.

If I still cared enough about her as a sister, I would try to help her, but I didn't. That bridge had burned long ago.

"You're wrong. I *did* do something," I said calmly. "I proved your husband is a lying scumbag, though I'd correctly guessed it wouldn't matter if it took you *that* long to recognize his faults. If you want to stay with him, stay. If you want to divorce him one day, then do that. There's no need to tell me because I truly don't care. But I hope for your unborn baby's sake that he treats them better than he's treated anyone else in his life. Otherwise, he'll learn that children aren't always as forgiving as wives."

Georgia sucked in a sharp breath, but I didn't wait for a response.

I walked out the door and didn't look back.

CHAPTER 46

Xavier

THE NEXT FOUR MONTHS PASSED IN A WHIRLWIND OF meetings and construction during the day and dates out or evenings in at night.

During that time, Sloane and I fell into an unspoken rhythm of staying at each other's houses. One week, I'd crash at her apartment; the next, she'd take up residence at my town house. I gave her her own closet so she didn't have to keep lugging her belongings across town, and she added my favorite brand of espresso to her pantry so I could get my caffeine fix without leaving her place.

They were quiet milestones that passed without fanfare, but they kept me going during the most hectic, gray-hair-inducing season of my life. Contractor delays, customs issues, a nearby steam pipe explosion that cut off our access to the vault for a full week—problems abounded throughout the repair and construction process, and that wasn't counting the massive egos I had to deal with on the marketing side of things.

"The vault is underground," I told a certain rock star's second assistant. "It doesn't have an attached helipad...No, unfortunately, we cannot build one before the opening. Yes, I will make sure we have security in place so he doesn't get mobbed by fans in the ten feet between his car and the entrance."

I cast a warning glare at Sloane, who smirked from her spot next to me on the couch. She was handling the RSVPs for the party, but I'd insisted on sharing the guest relations duties because I had personal relationships with a lot of the attendees.

I deeply regretted that decision.

However, construction issues and self-important guests aside, the run-up to the Vault's opening went mostly according to plan. There were no more fires, thank God, nor were there any major accidents or injuries. The steam pipe explosion cut into our already tight timeline, but my crew pulled through by the skin of their teeth.

The day before my thirtieth birthday, we were still putting finishing tiles in the bathrooms, but...

We got it done. All of it.

The following evening, after dozens of sleepless nights and crushing self-doubts, the Vault officially opened before the clock struck midnight and I turned the big three-oh.

Two hundred and fifty of the city's wealthiest and most influential filled the renovated space, sipping cocktails next to the original six-inch steel walls and admiring the hundred-year-old brass chandelier.

Every single person had RSVP'd yes. There was Ayana and the fashion crowd, Isabella and the publishing heavyweights, Dominic and the barons of Wall Street, and more. Every major entertainment and society outlet was present for coverage because tonight, more titans of business, politics, celebrity, and art had converged in one place since the last Legacy Ball.

I'd never been so proud.

The night was young, and there were still a hundred things that could go wrong, but the fact that I got this far meant everything.

No matter how the inheritance committee ruled tomorrow, I'd created my own business and legacy, and no one could take accomplishment away.

"Have you seen the owner? I have a message for him."

I turned, my mouth curving into a smile when Sloane came into view, breaking me out of my pensive mood. I was taking a moment for myself in the back before I started mingling, but the guests could wait a bit longer. They had plenty to entertain them.

Sloane sauntered toward me in a shimmery silver-white dress and heels that made her legs look miles long. Her hair fell in loose waves around her shoulders, and her eyes sparkled with a hint of mischief as she came up beside me.

It didn't matter how many mornings I woke up to her or how many nights I fell asleep beside her; she never failed to take my breath away.

"I'm not sure where he is, but I'm happy to pass the message along," I drawled. My blood burned a little hotter when she pressed her hand against my chest, but I maintained a deceptively casual stance while I waited.

"Good." Sloane threaded the fingers of her other hand through my hair, brought my mouth down to hers, and pressed her lips softly against mine.

One second. Two seconds. Three.

The kiss lingered on the third beat before she pulled away, leaving behind the taste of mint and strawberries.

"Pass that along to him," she murmured. "Tell him happy birthday, and congratulations on a job well done."

Warmth flickered in my chest, but I couldn't resist a little tease. "I'm happy to, but do you mind repeating that from the top? I want to make sure I get it *exactly* right."

Sloane rolled her eyes, but she was smiling. "Only because it's such a big night." She kissed me again, deeper this time. "You did it," she said, abandoning her earlier pretense. "How does it feel?"

"Pretty incredible, and *we* did it," I said. "I couldn't have done this without you."

Publicity work aside, her faith in me had kept me going through the many setbacks and frustrations of the past four months.

She shook her head. "I helped, but this was all possible because of *you*. Don't undersell your accomplishments. The Vault is your baby. Own it."

The flicker of warmth ignited into a roaring flame. "Have I ever told you how much I loved you?"

"Once or twice, but I'm not opposed to hearing it again."

"I love you," I murmured. "*Más que cualquier otra cosa en el mundo.*"

This time, I kissed her, and I let it last.

Time with Sloane always melted away, and we might've stayed in our little corner in the back forever had one of the guests not spotted us and interrupted to give me his well wishes.

"We should probably join the party," she said after he left. Her cheeks were flushed from our embrace, but I could see her kicking back into work mode. "Everyone is here for you. We'll celebrate privately later."

"Looking forward to it," I said with a wicked grin that turned her cheeks from pink to red.

But Sloane was right, so after one last tiny kiss—hey, it was my birthday; I could take my time—we took to the main floor, where a crowd had already formed around the bespoke bar featuring Markovic Holdings' first alcohol-free vodka. Mixologists worked their magic, conjuring stunning mocktails of pink and blue and green and serving them in frosted glasses adorned with various garnishes. Across the room, the alcoholic bar catered to an equally large crowd.

Vuk commanded his own table in the space between the two bars. He sat by himself, and it was difficult to tell if he was happy, annoyed, or indifferent. He wasn't even paying attention to his latest product launch—he was too busy glaring at something.

I followed his gaze to where Ayana stood with her fiancé, a fashion CEO who, according to the rumors, also happened to be one of Vuk's old college friends.

That can't be good.

Before I could ask Sloane what she knew about the relationship between Vuk and Ayana, Isabella popped up, purple mocktail in hand.

"Hey, guys!" she bubbled. "Great party, and happy birthday, Xavier. This place is a *hit*."

I smiled at her enthusiasm. "Thank you."

"So, I was looking for you because I have an idea for your Tastemaker series." Isabella's eyes gleamed. That, combined with Sloane's sudden grin, set off every alarm in my head.

"How do you feel about hosting a book preview for Wilma Pebbles's upcoming dinosaur erotica?" Isabella asked. "I met her at a recent event, and she gave me an advanced copy of *Penetrated by the Pterodactyl*. It's *amazing*, and she has a huge fanbase."

I blinked, unsure whether she was fucking with me or deadly serious. It was always hard to tell with Isabella. "Um..."

"Think about it." She glanced to the side, clearly distracted by the arrival of another movie star. "I'll send you her backlist so you can get a feel for her books. I really think it'll be a fun event!"

Then she was gone, leaving me to shake my head. "I thought she was going to ask me to host a preview of *her* new book, not Wilma Pebbles's."

"Oh, Isa's love for dino erotica runs far deeper than her own career ambitions," Sloane said, her grin widening. "Trust me."

For my own sake, I declined to ask for further information.

Halfway through the night, Sloane and I split to mingle with different guests. I personally thanked everyone who'd helped me get the Vault off the ground, including Dominic Davenport, who seemed to be surgically attached to his wife's side, and Sebastian, who'd pulled through with the catering.

"You pulled this off, man." Sebastian clapped a hand on my shoulder. "Now I owe Russo ten grand."

"You bet against me?" I asked with mock offense.

"I had faith in you, but Luca's usually wrong." He laughed. He glanced over my shoulder, and his smile turned into a smirk. "Speaking of Russos, I'll leave you to this one. Good luck."

He disappeared before I could respond, and Dante took his place.

We hadn't talked since his holiday gala, but he appeared much more at ease tonight than he had at Valhalla. Perhaps he was finally settling into the rhythm of parenthood, or perhaps it was the near-empty glass of scotch in his hand.

"This is impressive," he said, skipping the standard greetings. "I had my doubts about you, but you pulled it off."

"Everyone keeps saying that," I grumbled, but it was hard to stay annoyed when the night was going so well. "Thank you."

Dante inclined his head, his gaze flicking to the bar where Vivian was talking to Sloane, Isabella, and Alessandra. It lingered on his wife for a soft moment before it returned to me and hardened.

"I have to admit, part of me was hoping you'd fail," Dante said with surprising frankness. "I haven't forgotten about Vegas, Miami, or the dozens of questionable situations you've dragged Luca into. However..." His voice turned dry. "If my brother can clean up his act after years of useless partying, I suppose you can too."

Dante Russo, the king of backhanded compliments.

"I wouldn't say the partying was useless," I drawled. "It gave me the experience I needed to do *this*." I gestured around us.

Dante's eyes narrowed a fraction of an inch. Then, to my shock, he let out a genuine-sounding laugh.

"Keep that same energy tomorrow," he said, brushing past me to rejoin Vivian. "You'll need it."

Tomorrow. My first evaluation. The fate of eight billion dollars.

I would be lying if I said my stomach didn't sink an inch at the reminder, but tomorrow was tomorrow. I'd done my best, and there was nothing I could do between now and morning that would move the needle in a meaningful manner.

So instead of worrying, I grabbed a drink from a passing server's tray, tossed it back, and simply enjoyed the rest of the night.

I'd earned it.

Judgment Day took place the following morning via videoconference. Considering the pomp and circumstance that surrounded the reading of my father's will, it seemed pretty anticlimactic for the fate of eight billion dollars to be decided over Zoom, but everyone was too busy to travel to Bogotá for an in-person gathering, so Zoom it was.

Sloane and I were both at my house, but for optics reasons, we took the call in separate rooms. I was in the library; she was in the living room.

Five faces stared back at me from the screen as I explained my business plan, my rebuilding efforts after the fire, and the opening's smash success. The only thing I didn't tell them was the fire sabotage part. Alex had sworn me to secrecy, and it'd raise more questions than it answered, especially after he told me he found the saboteur but "couldn't disclose their identity at this time." All he said was they had ties to a mercenary group that was targeting certain members of the business community for "confidential reasons."

Part of me wanted details so I could take revenge on the person who'd caused so much strife, but a larger part was happy to keep the fire in my past and let the professionals deal with it.

General rule of life: don't go looking for more problems than you already had.

After I finished my spiel, Mariana spoke first. "Before we proceed with our evaluation, we would be remiss if we didn't acknowledge the biases of certain committee members."

The chairwoman of the Castillo Group's board was petite and sturdy-looking with glossy black hair and an air of authoritative competence. She'd never liked me; she thought my behavior reflected poorly on the company, and while she wasn't exactly wrong, I wasn't going to let her railroad this meeting or slander Sloane's character.

Obviously, that was who she was talking about; Mariana was staring straight at Sloane's square on the screen. To her credit, Sloane didn't blink an eye at the scrutiny, but I was less forgiving.

"I assume you're referring to my relationship with Sloane. If so, that's a non-issue," I said coolly. "Were it an *actual* issue, you or another committee member should've raised your concerns beforehand."

Mariana gave me a thin smile. "I'm not accusing anyone of anything," she said, her tone matching mine. "I'm simply reminding all those present that you two are, in fact, dating, and anything Ms. Kensington says will be *influenced* by that relationship."

"You're right." Sloane cut in before anyone else could respond. Her eyes glinted, and I hid a sudden smile. Mariana was about to get her ass handed to her. "What I say *will* be influenced by our relationship. I've worked with Xavier for three and a half years, and I'm the *only* person on this call that has watched him build the Vault from the ground up. I've watched him grow from a hedonistic degenerate—"

Whoa, a bit harsh, but okay.

"To someone with passion, pride, *purpose. That's* the man I fell in love with, and when I cast my vote, those will be the reasons behind it. My vote won't be biased because I'm dating him; it'll be biased because I know firsthand how hard he's worked to launch the Vault. If he wasn't the type of man who'd do that, we wouldn't be dating in the first place." Sloane pinned Mariana with a steady gaze. "Alberto's will stated Xavier 'must fulfill the chief executive officer position to the best of his abilities.' In my opinion, he's done that and more." She addressed the rest of the committee. "It should come as no surprise, then, that I vote yes."

My hidden smile blossomed into a full-fledged grin.

In five minutes, Sloane had undercut Mariana's sneak attack, redirected the committee's attention to the purpose of this call, and added the first tally in my column.

That's my girl.

Mariana looked like she'd swallowed a gallon of raw lemon juice, but there was nothing else she could say on the topic.

The vote proceeded apace.

"I agree with Sloane's judgment," Eduardo said. "What Xavier has accomplished in six months is extraordinary, and the coverage has been glowing. I also vote yes."

My heart rattled in anticipation.

Two out of five. One more vote, and I was in the clear.

"The timeline is impressive, but I'm not convinced of the Vault's longevity," Mariana said. "Nightclubs come and go, and in my opinion, it's a lazy concept to start with. Despite having a silent partner, you answer largely to yourself. There's no board, no shareholders, nothing you're truly the CEO *of*. Fulfilling CEO duties to the best of your ability means choosing something that isn't an easy win. I vote no."

Easy win? I locked an acerbic reply behind clenched teeth. Arguing wouldn't be smart, but she was voting in bad faith. I'd also addressed her later concern in my presentation, which included plans for expansion if the New York location was successful enough.

But I hadn't expected Mariana to vote yes anyway, so I didn't push back.

The next vote, however, *did* shock me. "I'm sorry, Xavier," Tío Martin said. A feeling of dread curdled in my chest. "As proud as I am personally, Mariana made some good points. I also vote no."

He didn't elaborate or meet my eyes, and I knew with sudden certainty that, for all his fairness, he wasn't immune to domestic manipulation. He'd obviously voted no to placate Tía Lupe.

Two versus two. It was a tie, and there was one vote left.

All eyes swung toward Dante.

He rubbed his thumb over his bottom lip, his expression pensive. Our short conversation last night gave me some hope, but I had no idea whether it was enough to overcome his long-seated dislike toward me.

The minutes ticked by.

Tío Martin shifted in his seat.

Eduardo's brows wrinkled with concern.

Mariana's mouth pursed so tight it resembled a prune.

Sloane and I were the only ones who didn't give anything away, though a bead of sweat cut down my back despite an air-conditioned breeze.

Dante lowered his hand and said, so casually he sounded like he was discussing the weather instead of a seven point nine-billion-dollar fortune, "Yes."

That was it.

No explanation, no grand flourish after keeping us on tenterhooks for so long. Just a simple, resounding yes.

That was all I needed.

Relief exploded behind my ribcage, leaving me lightheaded. A grinning Eduardo started saying something about follow-up paperwork, but his words blurred beneath the weight of my elation.

I did it. I fucking did it.

I didn't *need* their validation, but honestly? It felt good to have it.

The call ended minutes later, and I took great satisfaction at the sight of Mariana's frown before she signed off.

"I screenshotted an image of Mariana's face so you can look at it if you ever feel down."

I turned, another smile taking over my face when Sloane entered the room. She wore a perfectly pressed silk blouse and pajama shorts.

The biggest perk of taking work calls at home? No one could see below your waist.

"You take such good care of me," I teased, pulling her into my lap. "Thanks for casting the first vote, by the way. What you said..."

"Was true. I didn't say anything I didn't mean." Sloane's face softened for an instant before mischief sparked. "Just don't forget that when you're drafting your own will. I'm only doing this for your money."

"Are you now?"

"Yea—aah!" She let out a yelp of surprise when I stood abruptly and maneuvered us so I straddled her on the floor.

"What was that you were saying about my money?" I threatened, pinning her wrists above her head with one hand. I reshaped my grin into a stern frown.

Heat and laughter glittered in her eyes. "That it makes you seven point nine billion times hot—*oh God.*" The rest of her sentence dissolved into a gasp when I slid a hand beneath her shirt and palmed her breast.

It was the weekend, I'd just pulled off the biggest night of my life, and I had a long, free day ahead of me.

If Sloane wanted to tease me, I could return the favor a hundredfold.

"Not God, Luna." I dipped my head, my mouth brushing hers with each word. She tasted sweet, warm, *perfect.* "God has no hand in what I'm about to do to you."

It was for the best, considering our activities in the library, and my bedroom, and the rooftop for the rest of that day were decidedly unholy.

Sloane and I didn't talk about work, money, or anything else, not even when the sun set and we lay, sweaty and exhausted, in my bed.

That was the best part about being with the right person.

Some days, we could talk all night; other days, we didn't need words at all. Just being with each other was enough.

EPILOGUE

Xavier

Eighteen months later

PER THE TERMS OF MY FATHER'S WILL, I RECEIVED AN installment of my inheritance every time I passed an evaluation. I'd just aced my third one last week, and the number before the zeroes in my bank account ticked up exponentially, even after I donated half the payment to various charities.

Ironically, the Vault was doing so well I didn't *need* my inheritance anymore, but it was nice to have that cushion. After its smash opening night and *Mode de Vie*'s subsequent profile of me in its Movers and Shakers section, the club skyrocketed into fame. I was already making plans to open a new location in Miami, but first, I had an even bigger change to settle at home.

"I think that's it." Sloane planted her hands on her hips and looked around the living room. "Everything is unloaded and accounted for."

Piles of cardboard boxes covered the floor, each one neatly

labeled with its contents. *Clothing (fall/winter). Clothing (spring-summer). Books. Office supplies.* So on and so forth.

Movers had spent the day transporting those boxes from Sloane's old apartment to my town house. Just when I thought there couldn't possibly be more stuff, another truckload arrived.

"Are you sure?" I asked. "You packed so light."

"Very funny," she huffed. She patted one of the boxes. "I couldn't leave my Louboutin collection or my review notebooks."

"You have an *entire* box of review notebooks?" Jesus, how many had she written?

"Don't be ridiculous," Sloane said. "I couldn't fit them into one box. I split them up into two."

I shook my head with a mock appalled expression. "I changed my mind; you can't move in anymore. You're clearly not human, and that's a dealbreaker for me."

"Fine." She turned and started unpacking a box labeled *Candles*. "I'd planned on christening every room in this house to celebrate my move-in, but if you don't want me around..." She squealed when I wrapped an arm around her waist from behind and pulled her toward me.

"You don't play fair," I growled. "But who am I to disrupt your plans for such a thorough christening? I take back what I said. You can move in again."

"How generous of you." Sloane was still laughing when I turned her around to kiss her.

Since we started dating, we'd dined at the finest restaurants, enjoyed the most exclusive shows, and luxuriated in weekend getaways everywhere from St. Lucia to Malibu, but these types of moments were my favorite—the casual, comfortable ones where we could be ourselves and nothing else.

We were taking things slow, but moving in together felt like a natural progression after dating for so long. Honestly, I'd been ready a long time ago, but I'd waited until Sloane felt comfortable enough to give up her apartment and, in turn, a piece of her independence.

It was a big move for her, so I hadn't taken it for granted when she told me she'd rather move into the town house than stay in her old building.

An alarm chimed on Sloane's phone, breaking our kiss.

"Shoot." She pulled away and silenced the sound. "I didn't realize it was six already. We have to get ready soon, or we'll be late for Isa's party."

Isabella and Kai had gotten married shortly after the Vault's opening, and she'd taken a short hiatus from writing to enjoy their honeymoon. However, she'd recently finished her latest novel and was celebrating its publication with a book launch party that night.

"Luna, *Isabella* will be late to Isabella's party," I said. "And before we start getting ready, I have a housewarming gift for you."

"You've lived here for years; the house is already warmed." Sloane's eyes sparkled at my sigh of exasperation. "But I love a good gift. What is it?"

"It's in here." I guided her to the hall next to the living room.

I'd been sure it was the right gift when I bought it, but a ripple of anxiety ran down my spine when we turned the corner and the latest member of our household came into view.

Sloane drew a sharp inhale of breath. "Is that…?"

"A goldfish," I confirmed.

My worry that I'd overstepped melted when she touched the mini aquarium, her eyes suspiciously bright. The bright orange-yellow fish inside swam toward her hand and examined it for a second, his fins wagging, before he returned to the little pagoda the pet store had set up in the middle of his habitat. Apparently, he was more interested in exploring his new home than the humans hovering over him.

"I didn't think I'd miss having a goldfish ignore me so much," Sloane said, her voice thick. "He's perfect. Thank you."

"I'm glad you like him. The store said he was the feistiest one." We stared at the fish as it lazily circled the pagoda. "But they didn't define what they meant by *feisty*."

"Feisty." Sloane pursed her lips in thought. "That should be his name."

Feisty the Fish? My God.

"If the store said he was the goldest one, would you have named him Goldie?" I asked, my cheeks hurting from the force of my grin.

Her pensive expression gave way to a stern glare. "Very funny," she said, her cheeks pink. "I'm not great at naming pets, okay?"

"No, no, I think Feisty is a great name. A proud name. A literal name!" I called after her as she stalked back to the living room. Laughter warped around me as I followed her.

"Shut up before I throw a lamp at you," she threatened. "If you're so great at names, *you* choose one."

"Nope, he's for you and whatever name you choose is the one that sticks. At least Feisty is a better option than The Fish 2.0." I corralled my face into some semblance of seriousness. "Every fish deserves a name, and his is Feisty."

I almost made it through the entire sentence without cracking up again. Almost.

My failure resulted in Sloane throwing a cushion at my head, but it was worth it.

Feisty the Fish. I chortled.

"If I tell Dr. Hatfield about this and she says break up with you, I'll do it without hesitation," Sloane warned.

"Aw, come on, Luna, I'm just poking fun." I swallowed another bubble of laughter. "Besides, Dr. Hatfield would never say that. She loves me."

"She doesn't know you."

"She knows me by proxy."

Dr. Hatfield was her new therapist.

Sloane and I had both resumed therapy last year with different practitioners who specialized in (extremely dysfunctional) family issues. It took a few tries before we found the right fits, but I'd forgotten how, well, therapeutic it was to discuss my problems with a stranger whose job was to listen to those problems.

Therapy had been Sloane's idea. She would never patch things up with her father or Georgia, but Pen was still part of that family. Sloane thought therapy would help her better navigate her relationship with Pen versus the rest of the Kensingtons now that she was seeing her sister on a weekly basis, which meant increased contact with George and Caroline. Sometimes, I accompanied her to see Pen; other times, I left them to their sisters-only bonding.

Surprisingly, therapy helped me more this time around than when I underwent it as a teenager. Maybe I was more open to it now that I wasn't mired in resentment and guilt. Whatever it was, my bi-weekly sessions had helped me come to terms with my past and my relationship with my father. At the end of the day, it didn't matter why he'd put the loophole in his will or why he did any of the things he did.

That chapter was behind me, and I was ready to move on to the next one.

"I forgot to tell you. Guess who I ran into the other day?" Sloane asked after we got past the Feisty episode and walked upstairs to shower and change. "I had a meeting with a columnist from *Modern Manhattan*. They have the same parent company as *Fast and Furriness,* and when I was in the elevator up..."

"Don't say it." I grinned, already anticipating her next words.

"Perry Wilson walked in." Sloane laughed. "You should've seen his face. He tried to leave, but the doors had already closed. We spent ten floors pretending the other didn't exist."

Perry had lost his libel lawsuit last year, and Kai bought out his blog soon after. He'd renamed it Confidential Matters, deleted every trace of Perry from the site, and installed a professional team of writers and fact checkers. It was currently pulling in double the traffic Perry had attracted during his peak. People were tired of clickbait articles and baseless mudslinging, and an increasing number were gravitating toward better-quality news.

Meanwhile, Perry had been reduced to manning the phones at *Fast and Furriness*. I couldn't say I felt sorry for him.

Sloane and I entered our room.

Our. It didn't sound as strange as I'd expected. I guess in my mind, I'd already considered the house ours before she moved in.

That being said, it wouldn't be proper to skip an official celebration, would it?

"So," I said casually as Sloane stripped off her clothes in preparation for a shower. "Did you mean—"

"No." She knew what I was going to say before I said it. "We don't have time. We'll be la—*aaaate*!" Sloane shrieked with laughter as I grabbed her and hauled her onto the bed.

She was right. We did show up late to Isabella's party, but we'd also christened the first of many rooms in our house.

I couldn't think of a better way to start the next chapter of our lives together.

Sloane

Six months later

"You were right. This was exactly what I needed." I stretched my arms over my head with a content sigh. "I could stay here forever."

"Say that again," Xavier said.

"What?"

"The first three words. *You were right.*"

I rolled my eyes, but I couldn't restrain a smile. "You're insufferable."

"Yet you're here with me. What does that say about you?" he teased. A breeze swept through his hair, ruffling the black strands as we walked along the beach.

"That I'm a masochist."

"Ah. I knew there was a reason why I loved you."

I laughed, unable to keep up my pretense when he looked so relaxed and happy, and I *felt* so relaxed and happy.

We were nearing the end of our month-long trip to Spain. Xavier had surprised me with the tickets last Christmas, but we'd waited for the weather to warm up before we came.

Our housekeeper was taking care of Feisty, the Vault was finally running smoothly enough on its own for Xavier to take that much time off, and I'd left Kensington PR in Jillian's capable hands. I'd promoted her to my Director of Office Operations last year, with a matching pay raise, and I had full confidence in her ability to run the ship while I was gone. I still checked my email compulsively whenever Xavier was in the shower or getting us drinks, but I no longer felt the need to control everything that came across my inbox.

After all, I was on vacation.

So for the past three and a half weeks, Xavier and I had eaten, slept, and drank our way through Madrid, Seville, Valencia, and Barcelona before ending in the place that'd started it all: Mallorca.

The island had marked the first big turning point in our relationship. Since our first vacation here had been cut short, it seemed appropriate to return and finish what we'd started.

"What do you want to do tonight?" Xavier asked, lacing his fingers through mine. "We can go dancing again, or we can stay in."

"Let's stay in. If I dance anymore, my feet are going to fall off." We'd gone to a different club every night for the past three nights, often staying out until the sun rose, and my body was ready to sue.

At least my dancing skills had improved, thanks to Xavier.

We lapsed into comfortable silence as the sun dipped below the horizon, transforming the sky into a palette of tangerines and lavenders. The clouds seemed to catch fire at the edges, a spectacle captured by the tranquil mirror of the ocean.

I waited for a familiar stab of sadness, but it never came. In hindsight, I hadn't felt it for a while, but I'd never noticed its absence until now.

"Penny for your thoughts," Xavier said. "You look like you're surprised about something."

A smile touched my lips. He always knew me so well.

"I used to hate sunsets," I admitted. "I thought they were depressing. Sunsets represented endings, and they reminded me that every good thing comes to an end. I always felt sad when I saw one, but now...I don't think they're so bad." I shrugged. "I like nights better than days, anyway."

Nights meant dinners at home, beneath the chandelier we'd fallen in love with during our last trip to Paris. They meant crackling fires and conversations in bed, the type that meandered easily until one or both of us fell asleep. Nights were love and warmth and moonlight, my safe haven from the world.

Without sunsets, there would be no nights, and just like that, my decades-old animosity toward the otherwise beloved phenomena dissolved as quietly as if it'd never existed.

"Good," Xavier said softly. "I like nights better, too."

Later that evening, when we curled up on the couch to watch a movie, I didn't bother retrieving my review notebook.

I just wanted to enjoy the film, and I did. The office meet-cute the montage of cute dates, the hero running through the airport for his grand gesture, even the happy ending featuring a pet dog and a ring—I loved it all.

I had no business judging others' clichés.

After all, I was on a romantic European getaway with my long-term boyfriend, who'd started as a client I hated before we gradually fell in love—only I'd been too stubborn to admit it—and I'd almost lost him before I came to my senses and reconciled with him at the top of the Empire State Building.

Now we lived together in a town house with a pet fish and a rooftop movie theater, and we were nauseatingly, disgustingly blissful.

Who said happily ever afters were unrealistic?

Thank you for reading *King of Sloth*! If you enjoyed this book, I would be grateful if you could leave a review on the platform(s) of your choice.

Reviews are like tips for authors, and every one helps!

Much love,
Ana

P.S. Want to discuss my books and other fun shenanigans with like-minded readers? Join my exclusive reader group, Ana's Twisted Squad!

Want more Ana Huang?

Read on for a peek at book one in her If Love series.

PROLOGUE

THIS WOULD KILL HIM.

It didn't matter how much he prepared; these next thirty minutes were going to rip his heart out and pulverize it.

It was inevitable.

"We haven't talked in a while." She sounded equal parts accusing and uncertain.

He didn't blame her. If he were in her shoes, he would've given up on himself a long time ago. She hadn't, which made him love her even more, but her loyalty made this conversation all the harder.

He rested his forearms on his knees and clasped his hands together. He focused on the grain of the wood floors beneath his feet until it swirled in front of his eyes.

"I've been busy."

"With?"

"Classes. Bar plans. That sort of thing."

"You'll have to do better than that."

His head snapped up at the sharpness in her voice. Looking at her turned out to be a mistake.

His chest squeezed at the sight of her face and the hurt swimming in those beautiful brown eyes. It'd been two weeks since they were last alone together, but it may as well have been two lifetimes.

His dread mixed with a strange exhilaration at being alone with her again, and it took all of his willpower not to sweep her up in his arms and never let go.

"Tell me the truth." Her voice softened. "You can trust me."

It would be so easy to pretend everything was fine. To give her the reassurances she wanted to hear and go back to the way things were.

He did trust her—but the truth would shatter her.

So he did the only thing he could do: he lied.

"I'm sorry." He wiped the emotion from his voice and funneled it into the pit of despair swirling in his stomach. Could she hear it? The panicked *thump-thump-thump* of his heart beating against his rib cage, screaming at him to stop? "I didn't want to do it like this, but I don't think we should see each other anymore."

Farrah's face paled. His heart beat louder.

"What?"

He swallowed hard. "It was fun while it lasted, but the year is almost over and I—I'm not interested anymore. I'm sorry."

Liar.

"You're lying."

He flinched. She knew him well. Too well.

"I'm not." He tried to sound nonchalant when all he wanted to do was fall to his knees and beg her not to leave him.

"You are. You said you loved me."

"I lied."

He couldn't look her in the eyes.

Her sharp inhale twisted his heart into a painful knot.

"You're full of shit." Her voice quavered. "Look at you, you're shaking."

He clenched his hands into fists and forced his body to still. "Farrah." *This was it.* His breath came out in short, shallow bursts. "I got back with my ex-girlfriend over the holidays. I didn't know how to tell you. I love her, and I made a mistake here, with us. But I'm trying to fix it."

Her sob ripped through the air. Tears stung his eyes, but he blinked them back.

"I'm sorry." Such a stupid, inadequate thing to say. He didn't know why he said it.

"Stop saying that!"

He flinched at the venom in her voice. She clutched her necklace with one hand, betrayal swirling in her eyes.

"It was all a lie then, this past year."

He dropped his gaze again.

"Why? Why did you pretend you cared? Was it some sick joke? You wanted to see whether I'd be gullible enough to fall for you? Well, congratu-fucking-lations. You won. Blake Ryan, the champion. Your father was right. You shouldn't have quit. No one plays the game better than you."

So this was what dying felt like. The pain, frozen inside like a lump of jagged black ice. The regret over words he couldn't say and promises he couldn't keep. The loneliness as he slid into dark, starless oblivion with no one left to save him.

"I'm sor—"

"If you say, 'I'm sorry,' one more time, I'll go to the kitchen, come back, and cut your balls off with a rusty knife. In fact, I may do that anyway. You're a fucking asshole. *I'm* sorry I wasted all this time on you, and I'm sorrier for your girlfriend. She deserves better."

God, he didn't want her to leave hating him. He wanted, more than anything, to tell her it was all a joke and that he was messing with her. He wanted to grab her and breathe in that orange-blossom-and-vanilla scent that drove him crazy, to confess how head over heels he was for her and to kiss her until they ran out of breath.

But he couldn't. The first part would be a lie, and the second... well, that was something he could never do again.

Farrah walked to the door. She paused in the doorway to look back at him. He expected her to hurl more venom at him—he deserved it. But she didn't. Instead, she turned away and closed the door behind her with a soft click that echoed in the silence like a gunshot.

His shoulders sagged. All the energy drained out of him.

It was over. There was no going back.

It was the right thing to do, and yet...

He squeezed his eyes shut, trying to block out the pain. He couldn't get the image of her face out of his mind, the one that said she thought so little of him she didn't want to waste any more energy yelling at him.

Because of her, he believed in love. The kind of knock-you-down, once-in-a-lifetime love he used to dismiss as a fantasy concocted by Hollywood to sell movies. It wasn't a fantasy. It was real. He felt it to his core.

If only they'd met sooner or under different circumstances...

He'd always been a practical person, and there was no use dwelling on what-ifs. Duty bound him to someone else, and sooner or later, Farrah would move on and meet a guy who could give her everything she deserved. Someone she would love, marry, and have kids with...

The last intact piece of his heart shattered at the thought. The shards pricked at his self-control until he could no longer hold back the tears. Huge silent sobs wracked his body for the first time since he was seven, when he'd fallen out of a tree and broken his leg. Only this time, the pain was a million times worse.

All their moments together flashed through his mind, and the boy who'd once sworn he would never cry over a girl...cried.

He cried because he'd hurt her.

He cried because it kept his mind off the desperate loneliness that weighed on his soul the moment she left.

Most of all, he cried for what they had, what they lost, and what they could never be.

CHAPTER 1

Eight months ago

"ONE CLASSIC MILK TEA AND ONE HONEY OOLONG milk tea with tapioca. Regular sugar, regular ice."

Farrah Lin slid a twenty yuan note across the counter toward the cashier, who smiled in recognition. Four days in Shanghai and Farrah was already a regular at the bubble tea joint by campus. She chose not to dwell on what that meant for her wallet and her waistline.

While the staff prepared her order, Farrah examined the menu. She knew *nai cha* (milk tea) and *xi gua* (watermelon). She recognized a few other Chinese characters but not enough to form a coherent phrase.

"Here you go." The cashier handed Farrah her drinks. "See you tomorrow!"

Farrah blushed. "Thanks."

Note to self: ask Olivia to make tomorrow's run.

Farrah stepped out of the tiny shop and walked back to campus.

The sun began its descent and bathed the city in a warm golden glow. Bicyclists and motorcyclists zipped by, battling with cars for space on the narrow side street. The delicious smells wafting from the restaurants Farrah passed mixed with the far-less-pleasant scents of garbage and construction dust. Street vendors called out to passersby, hawking everything from hats and scarves to books and DVDs.

Farrah made the mistake of making eye contact with one such vendor.

"*Mei nu!*" *Beautiful girl.* It'd be flattering if Farrah didn't know the hard sell that accompanied such a greeting. "Come, come." The elderly vendor beckoned her over. "Where are you from?" she asked in Mandarin.

Farrah hesitated before answering. "America." *Mei guo*. She dragged out the last syllable, unsure whether the admission would hurt or help.

"Ah, America. ABC," the vendor said knowingly. ABC: American-Born Chinese. Farrah had heard that a lot lately. "I have some great books in English." The vendor brandished a copy of *Eat, Pray, Love*. "Only twenty kuai!"

"Thanks, but I'm not interested."

"How about this one?" The woman picked out a Dan Brown novel. "I'll give you a deal. Three books for fifty kuai!"

Farrah didn't need new books, and fifty kuai (around $7 U.S.) seemed pricey for cheap reprints of old novels. But the vendor seemed like a nice old lady, and Farrah didn't have the energy to bargain with her.

She skimmed the English options and went straight for the romance: Jane Austen, Nicholas Sparks, JoJo Moyes.

Okay, Sparks and Moyes write love stories, not romance, but still.

Given the drought in Farrah's dating life, she'd settle for any kind of romantic relationship, even one that ended tragically. Well, maybe not with death, but with a breakup or something. Anything that proved the crazy, head-over-heels love you found in books and movies existed in real life.

After a disappointing freshman year filled with mediocre dates and fumbling stops at third base, Farrah was ready to give up on reality and live in fantasyland full-time.

"I'll take these." She set her drinks on the ground so she could pick up *Pride and Prejudice* (her personal favorite), *The Notebook*, and *Me Before You*. She'd read all of them already, but what the heck, a reread never hurt anybody.

Farrah paid the vendor, who beamed and gushed her thanks before turning her attention to the next passerby.

"*Mei nu!*" The vendor flagged down a young woman in a cobalt dress. "Come, come."

Farrah looped her shopping bag around her wrist and picked up her drinks while the young woman fended off the vendor's aggressive sales pitch. She speed-walked back to campus, taking care not to make eye contact with any more vendors lest she got suckered into buying something else she didn't need.

Farrah stopped at the crosswalk. Instead of crossing when the pedestrian light flashed green, she waited until a group of teenagers stepped off the curb before following them into the jungle that was Shanghai traffic.

Rule #1 of surviving in China: cross when locals cross. There's safety in numbers.

By the time Farrah arrived at Shanghai Foreign Studies University, her study abroad program's host campus, she'd already finished her drink. She tossed the empty container into a nearby trash can and pushed open the door to FEA's lobby.

FEA, a.k.a. Foreign Education Academy, occupied one of the oldest buildings at SFSU. Not only did the four-story building lack an elevator, but the interior design left much to be desired. The lobby had potential—marble floors, tons of natural light streaming in through large windows facing the courtyard—but the furniture was straight out of the '80s (and not in the cool retro kind of way).

A cracked brown leather couch lined the wall beneath the windows alongside mismatched chairs and tables. A spindly magazine stand sagged beneath the weight of dozens of back issues of *Time Out Shanghai*. Faded Chinese landscape paintings hung on the wall, adding to the musty feel.

As usual, Farrah couldn't help mentally redecorating the space. As she took the stairs to the third floor, she swapped out the current furniture for a cushioned wicker set with glass-topped tables, which would visually expand the lobby. Out went the old watercolors and in came the panels of Asian-inspired art—perhaps some up-close representations of the lotus flower or plum blossoms with modern Chinese calligraphy. There could be a wall of bookshelves for—

"Ow!" Farrah had been so absorbed in her design daydream, she slammed into the wall. Her hand shot to her forehead as pain ricocheted through her brain. Fortunately, she couldn't feel a bump.

Olivia's bubble tea also remained intact, thank god. She was scary when she didn't get her sugar fix.

The wall moved. "Are you okay?" it asked.

A walking, talking wall. She must've hit her head harder than she thought.

Farrah peeked out from beneath her hand and found herself staring into a pair of crystal-blue eyes. She recognized those eyes. They'd stared back at her from the cover of *Sports Illustrated* last year, along with the accompanying high cheekbones and cocky grin.

Now, they examined her with a mix of amusement and concern.

"You're not a wall," she blurted.

"No, I'm not." The not-a-wall cocked an eyebrow. A hint of a smile played over his lips. "I've been called a lot of things in my life, but that's a new one."

Farrah fought the flush of embarrassment spreading across her face. Of all the people she could've run into, she had to run into Blake Ryan.

Even though she wasn't a sports fan, she knew who he was. Everyone did. A hotshot football player from Texas who caused a national uproar when he quit the team at the beginning of the year. Besides the *Sports Illustrated* cover, Farrah remembered Blake from an ESPN documentary about the most talented college athletes in the country. Farrah's roommate last year forced her to watch it because she was obsessed with the point guard on CCU's basketball team, and she needed someone she could gush to.

It'd been the most boring seventy-five minutes of Farrah's life, but at least there'd been plenty of eye candy, none of whom were dishier than the Texan standing in front of her.

Six feet two inches of tanned skin and chiseled muscle, topped with golden hair, glacial-blue eyes, and cheekbones that could cut ice. He wasn't Farrah's type, but she had to admit the boy was fire. Blake looked the way she'd pictured Apollo looking when she learned about Greek mythology in seventh grade.

"Well, you're really hard." The words slipped out before Farrah could catch them.

I did not just say that out loud.

The flush traveled from her face to the rest of her body. No matter how hard she prayed, the floor didn't open up and swallow her whole, that bastard.

Blake's other eyebrow shot up. "I mean, your *chest* is really hard. Nothing else. Although I'm sure it could be hard if it wanted to be."

Kill me.

The hint of amusement blossomed into a full-fledged grin, revealing twin dimples that should have been classified as lethal weapons.

"It sure can," Blake drawled. "Especially when I'm around someone as beautiful as you."

Farrah's mortification screeched to a halt. "Oh, *please.* Do they actually work for you?"

"Excuse me?"

"Your cheesy pickup lines. Do they actually work for you?"

"I've never had any complaints. Besides, look at me." Blake gestured at himself. "I don't need pickup lines."

"Wow." Farrah shook her head. *Typical jock.* "It must be difficult walking around with such a big head."

"Babe, that's not the only part of me that's big."

Farrah couldn't help it; her eyes dropped to the region below Blake's belt. An image of what hid behind the denim flashed through her mind's eye. Her mouth went dry.

"I'm talking about my chest, of course." Blake shook with laughter.

Farrah's gaze snapped up to his face. "I knew that." The mortification crept back up her neck.

"Sure. Since you've already undressed me with your eyes, we should—"

"I did *not* undress you—"

"Properly introduce ourselves." He held out his hand. "I'm Blake."

She knew who he was, and they both knew it. Farrah played along because (1) her mother raised her to be a polite human being, and (2) while she knew his name, there was every chance he didn't know hers. They'd met briefly at orientation dinner the first night, but there were seventy students in FEA. Farrah herself couldn't remember the names of half the people she'd met. "I'm Farrah."

Acknowledgments

One of my beta readers said *King of Sloth* felt like a love letter to rom-coms, and you know what? It was.

Here's to "unrealistic" happily ever afters, kisses on top of the Empire State Building, and the idea that love always prevails, even when it's between the unlikeliest of partners.

Xavier and Sloane have my heart, and I adored every minute I spent with them. However, their story wouldn't have been possible without some help along the way, so I'm taking this moment to say thank you.

To Becca—What can I say that I haven't already said? Thank you for being my sounding board and biggest cheerleader. Whether I'm stuck on a plot point or just need someone to talk to, you're always there, and I'm so grateful to call you my friend.

To my alpha readers Brittney, Rebecca, and Salma—Your reactions and emojis never fail to make me smile, and your feedback helps make my stories shine. Thank you for being my ride or dies!

To Ana and Aliah—Thank you so much for your detailed notes, insights into Colombian culture, and Spanish translation wizardry. I couldn't have done this without you.

To my beta readers Tori, Theresa, Malia, and Jessica—You each brought something unique to the table that made me see different parts of the story in different lights. Thank you so much for sharing your time and suggestions with me; you helped bring this book to the next level.

To Amy—Thank you for editing this book. Your eye for detail is always appreciated!

To Mary Catherine Gebhard—Thank you for sharing your notes and feedback regarding the Chronic Fatigue Syndrome representation. I deeply appreciate you sharing your time and expertise.

To Cat—We have another cover in the books! (No pun intended.) Working with you is always a delight. Thank you for being not only an amazing designer but also an amazing human being.

To the incredible teams at Bloom and Piatkus—Thank you for your endless support. We've hit so many milestones together, and I'm excited to see what else the future brings!

To my agent Kimberly and the Brower Literary team—I am so grateful to have you in my corner. You're all rock stars!

To Nina, Kim, and everyone at Valentine PR—Thank you for making my releases so smooth behind the scenes. I don't know what I'd do without you.

Finally, to my readers—Thank you for being the best part of my author journey. I never take your time, love, or support for granted, and I hope you loved reading *King of Sloth* as much as I loved writing it.

Much love,
Ana

Keep in Touch with Ana Huang

Reader Group: facebook.com/groups/anastwistedsquad
Website: anahuang.com
BookBub: bookbub.com/profile/ana-huang
Instagram: instagram.com/authoranahuang
TikTok: tiktok.com/@authoranahuang
Goodreads: goodreads.com/anahuang

About the Author

Ana Huang is a #1 *New York Times, Sunday Times, Wall Street Journal, USA Today*, and #1 Amazon bestselling author. Best known for her Twisted series, she writes New Adult and contemporary romance with deliciously alpha heroes, strong heroines, and plenty of steam, angst, and swoon.

Her books have been translated in over two dozen languages and featured in outlets such as NPR, *Cosmopolitan, Financial Times*, and *Glamour UK*.

A self-professed travel enthusiast, she loves incorporating beautiful destinations into her stories and will never say no to a good chai latte.

Also by Ana Huang

KINGS OF SIN SERIES

A series of interconnected standalones

King of Wrath

King of Pride

King of Greed

King of Sloth

TWISTED SERIES

A series of interconnected standalones

Twisted Love

Twisted Games

Twisted Hate

Twisted Lies

IF LOVE SERIES

If We Ever Meet Again (Duet Book 1)

If the Sun Never Sets (Duet Book 2)

If Love Had a Price (Standalone)

If We Were Perfect (Standalone)